Ao Haru Ride

The scent of air after rain...
In the light around us, I felt your heartbeat.

4

IO SAKISAKA

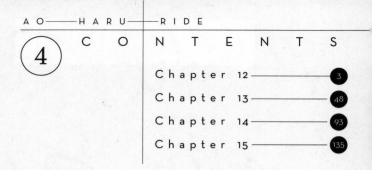

4 C O N T E N T S

Chapter 12 —————— 3

Chapter 13 —————— 48

Chapter 14 —————— 93

Chapter 15 —————— 135

S T O R Y T H U S F A R

In junior high, Futaba Yoshioka was quiet and disliked all boys—except for Tanaka, her first love. Their romance was cut short when he suddenly transferred schools, leaving behind an unresolved misunderstanding. As a tomboy in high school, Futaba is reunited with a completely changed Tanaka, who goes by the name of Kou Mabuchi.

In her second year of high school, Futaba commits to being true to herself and her friends. When she finds out that her friend Yuri likes Kou, she realizes she still has feelings for him too and tells Yuri.

After Kou scores poorly on midterms, the gang invites themselves over for a study group. Kou and Yuri are alone in the kitchen together, and it seems something may have happened between them...

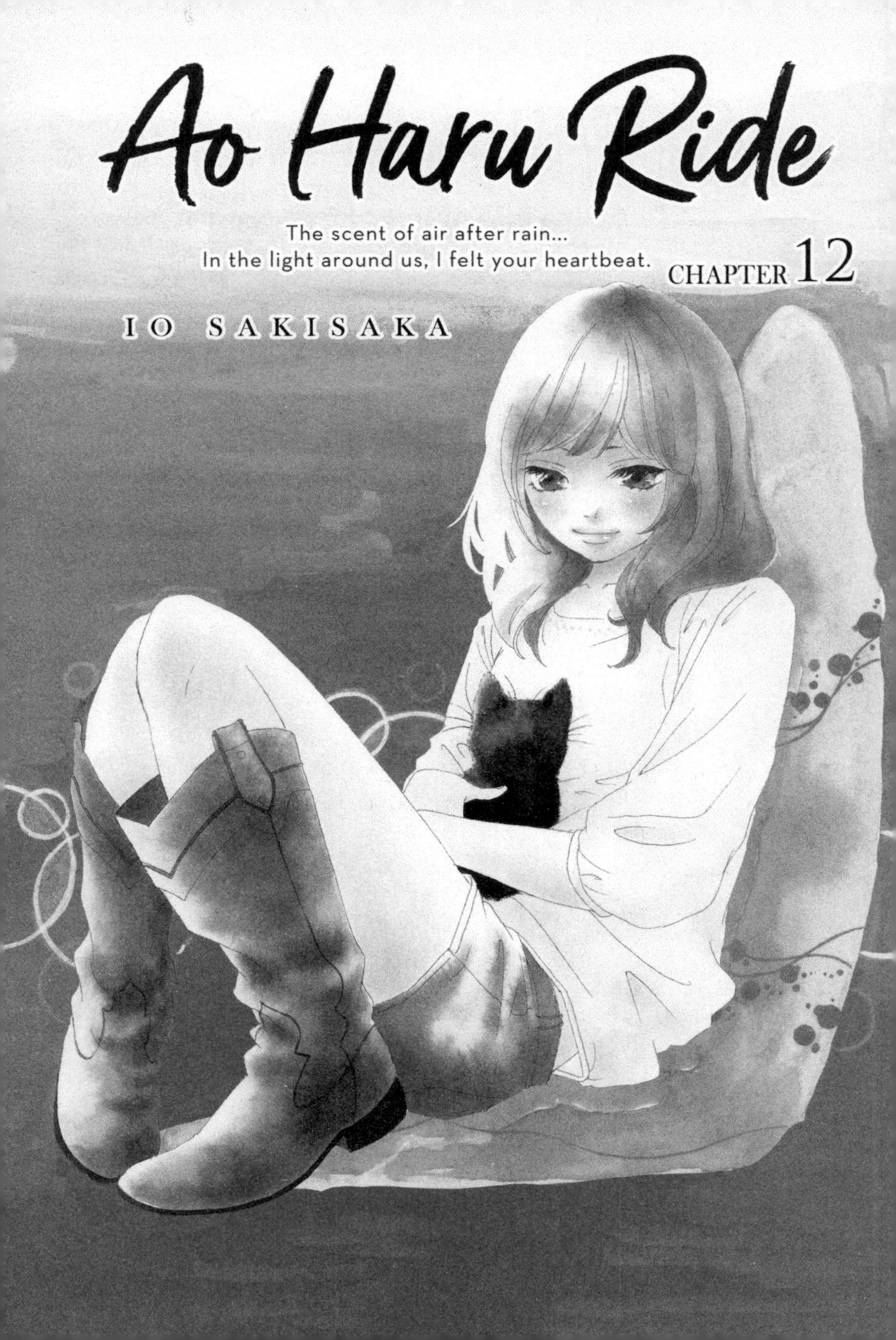
Ao Haru Ride
The scent of air after rain...
In the light around us, I felt your heartbeat.
CHAPTER 12
IO SAKISAKA

GREETINGS

Hi! ☆ I'm Io Sakisaka. Thank you for picking up a copy of *Ao Haru Ride* volume 4.

I really enjoy drawing girls in love. I find it endearing how they make mistakes but still try their best. The truth is that I'm sometimes jealous of them! They're radiant... They do things I could never do. That makes me take extra care when illustrating the details of their lives, which often results in the stories getting sidetracked. (*laugh*)

I hope this book can fill some gaps in our lives... and that it makes your hearts flutter just a little!

I hope you'll read this volume through to the end!

 Io Sakisaka

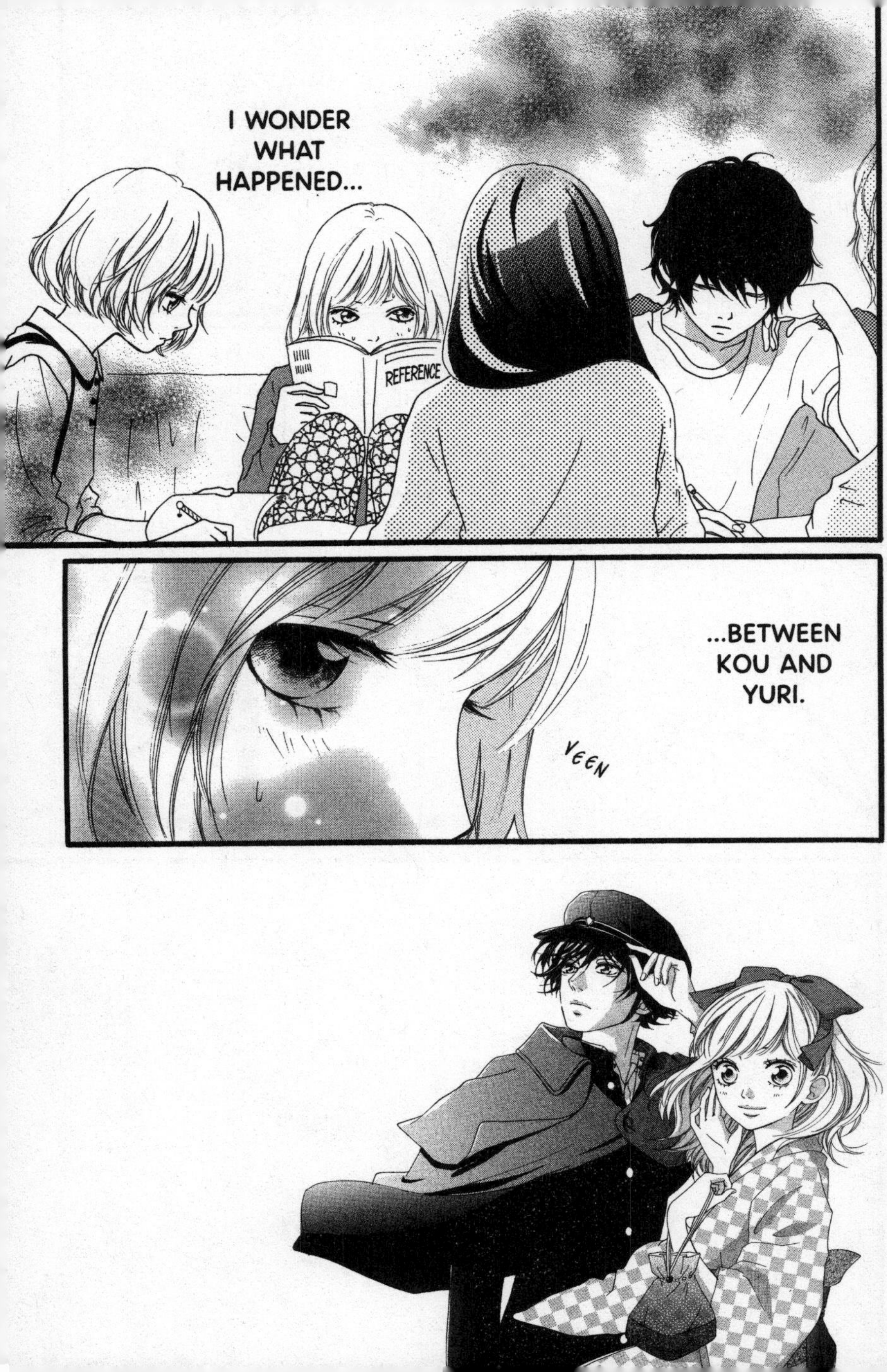
I WONDER WHAT HAPPENED...
REFERENCE
...BETWEEN KOU AND YURI.
VEEN

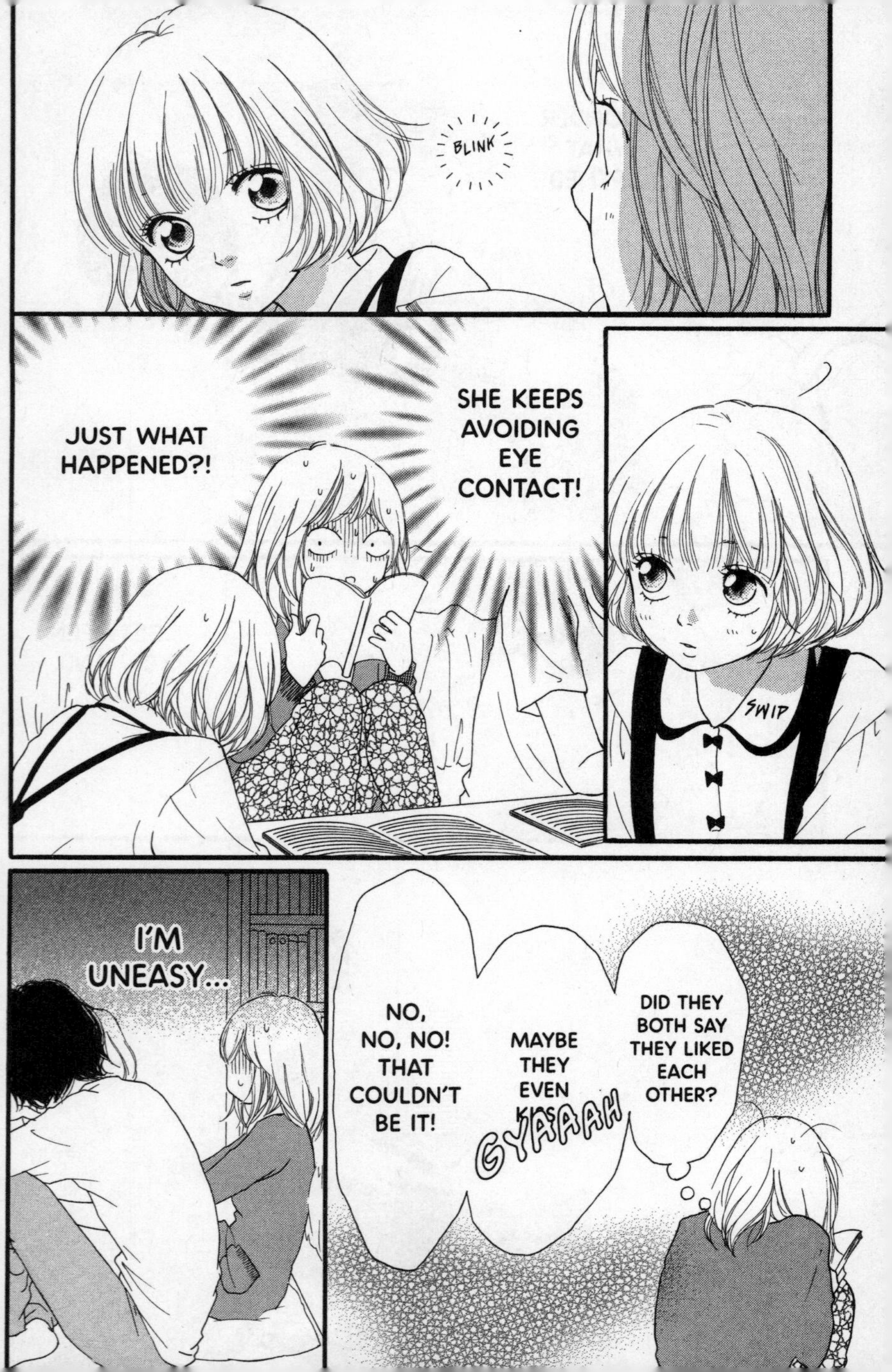
BLINK
SWIP
SHE KEEPS AVOIDING EYE CONTACT!
JUST WHAT HAPPENED?!
DID THEY BOTH SAY THEY LIKED EACH OTHER?
MAYBE THEY EVEN
GYAAAH
NO, NO, NO! THAT COULDN'T BE IT!
I'M UNEASY...

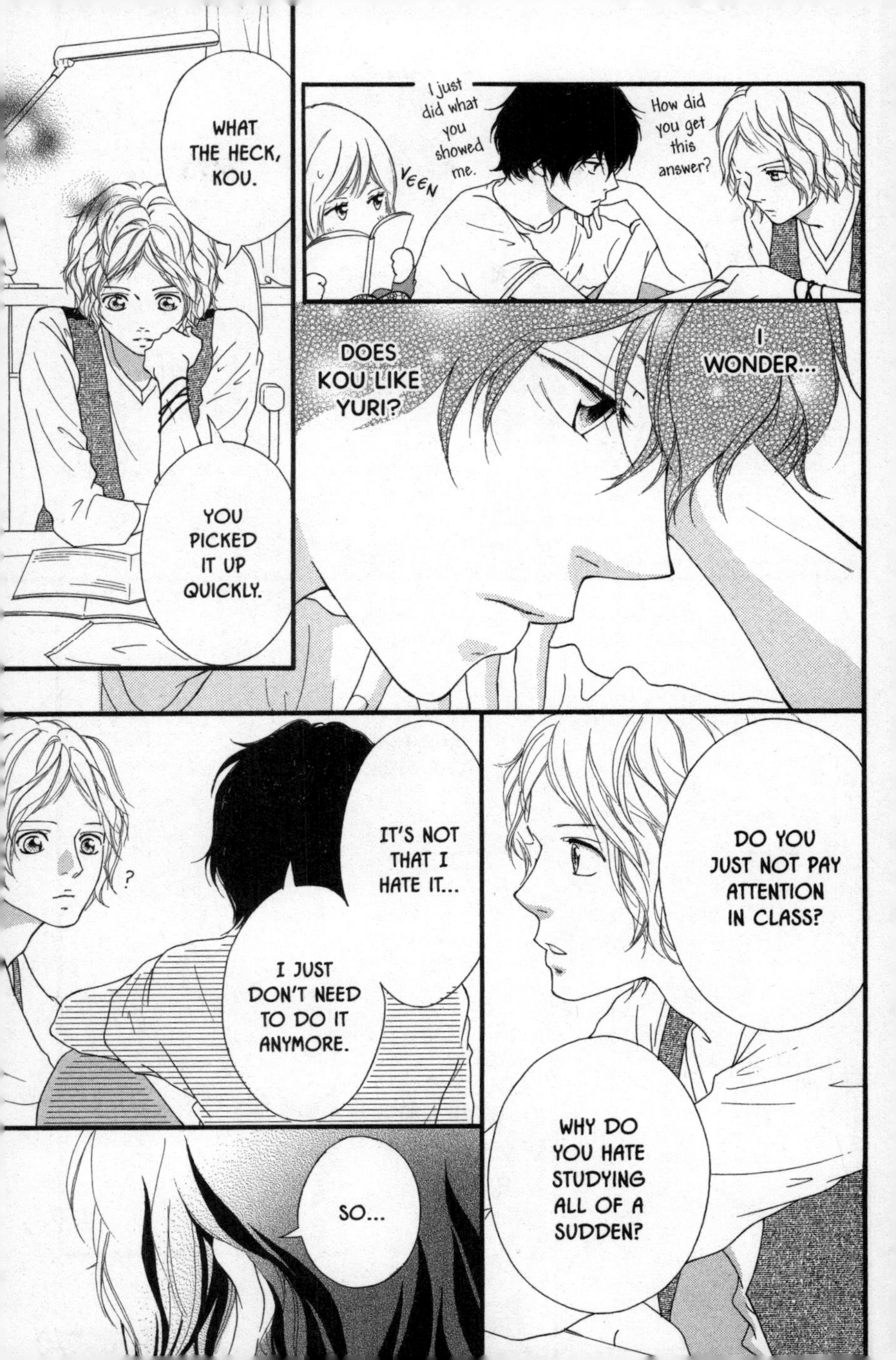
How did you get this answer?
I just did what you showed me.
VEEN
I WONDER...
DOES KOU LIKE YURI?
WHAT THE HECK, KOU.
YOU PICKED IT UP QUICKLY.
DO YOU JUST NOT PAY ATTENTION IN CLASS?
WHY DO YOU HATE STUDYING ALL OF A SUDDEN?
IT'S NOT THAT I HATE IT...
I JUST DON'T NEED TO DO IT ANYMORE.
?
SO...

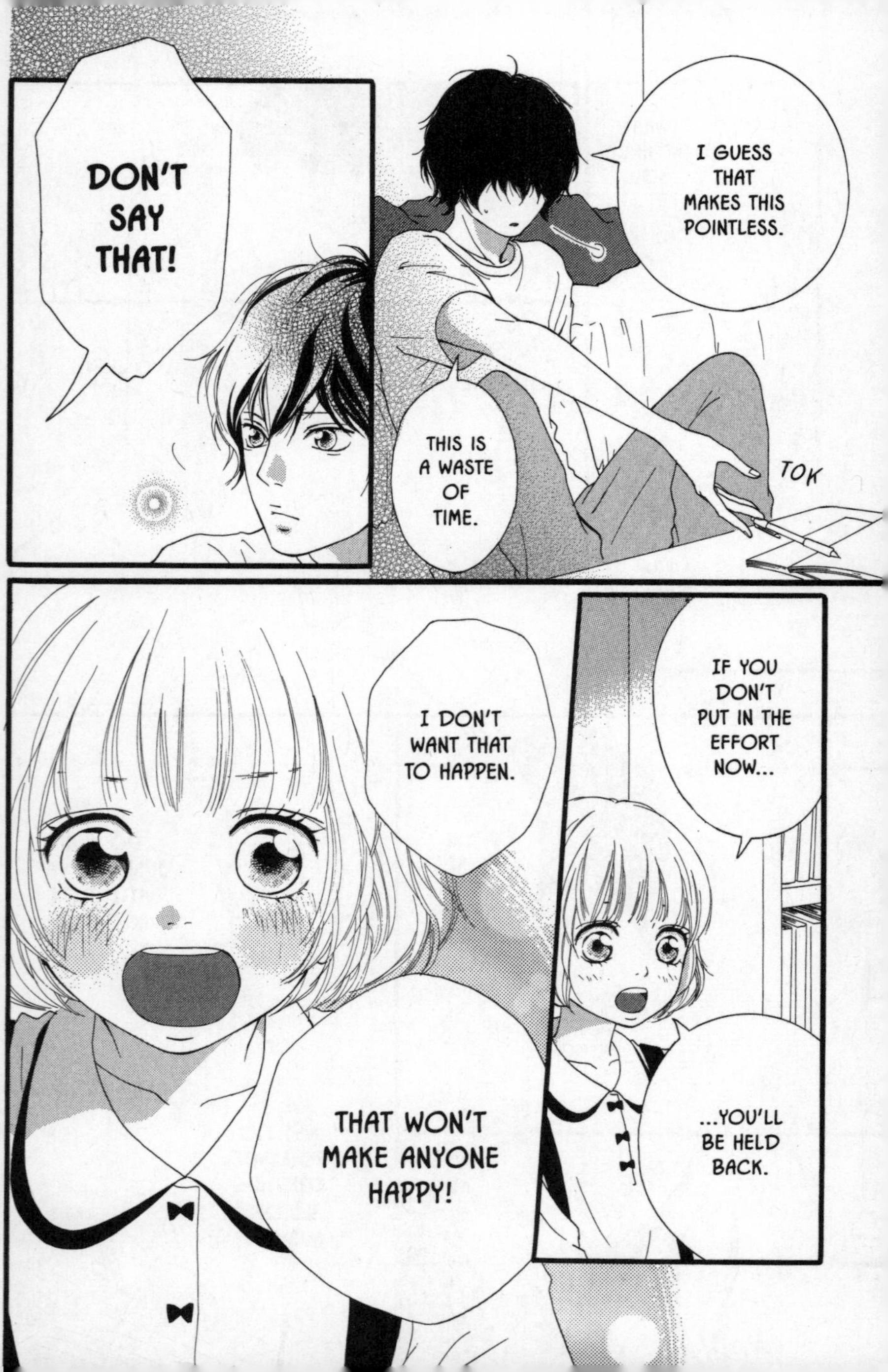
I GUESS THAT MAKES THIS POINTLESS.
THIS IS A WASTE OF TIME.
TOK
DON'T SAY THAT!
IF YOU DON'T PUT IN THE EFFORT NOW...
...YOU'LL BE HELD BACK.
I DON'T WANT THAT TO HAPPEN.
THAT WON'T MAKE ANYONE HAPPY!

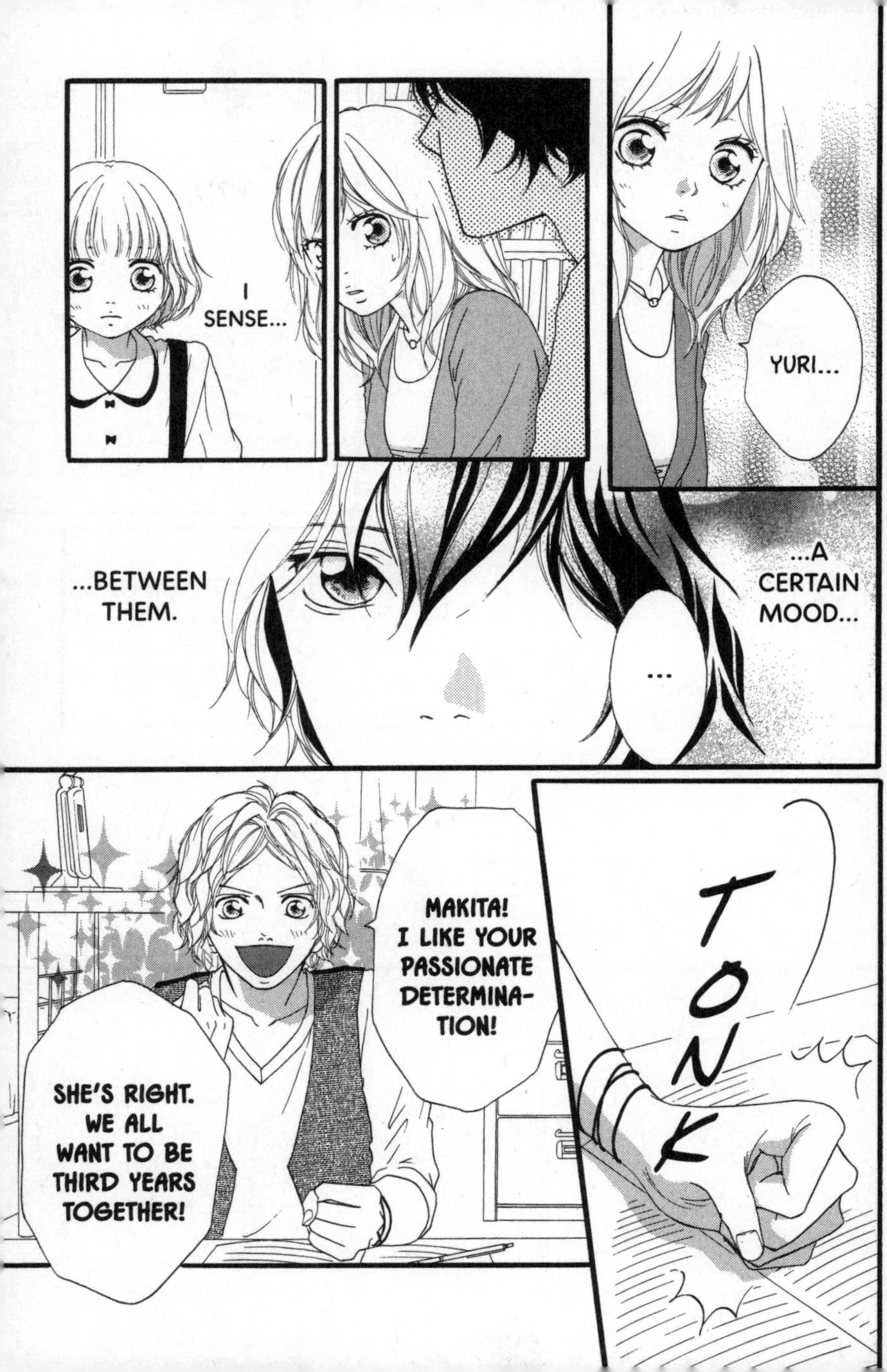
YURI...
I SENSE...
...A CERTAIN MOOD...
...
...BETWEEN THEM.
TONK
MAKITA! I LIKE YOUR PASSIONATE DETERMINATION!
SHE'S RIGHT. WE ALL WANT TO BE THIRD YEARS TOGETHER!

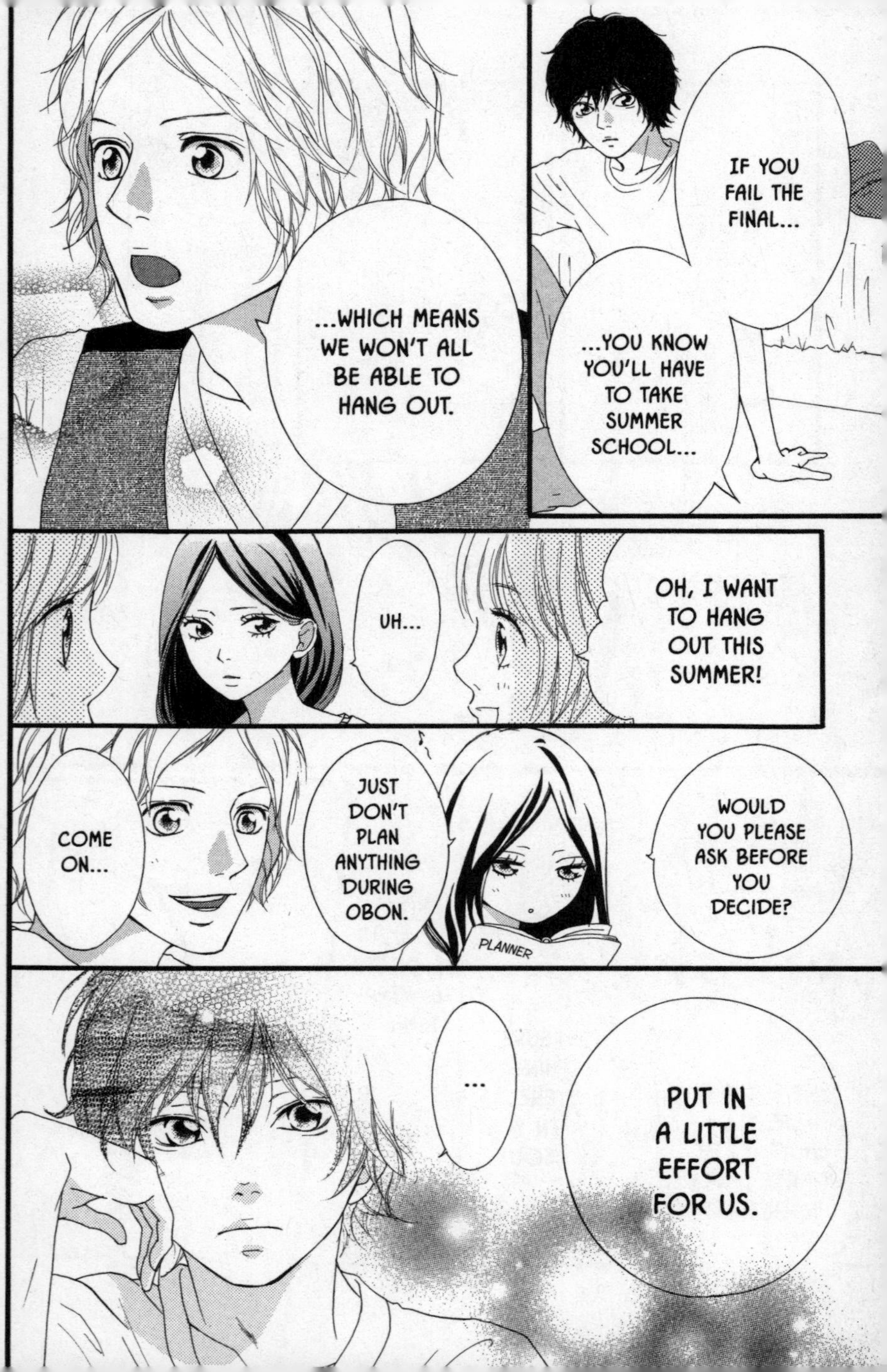
IF YOU FAIL THE FINAL...
...YOU KNOW YOU'LL HAVE TO TAKE SUMMER SCHOOL...
...WHICH MEANS WE WON'T ALL BE ABLE TO HANG OUT.
OH, I WANT TO HANG OUT THIS SUMMER!
UH...
WOULD YOU PLEASE ASK BEFORE YOU DECIDE?
PLANNER
JUST DON'T PLAN ANYTHING DURING OBON.
COME ON...
PUT IN A LITTLE EFFORT FOR US.
...

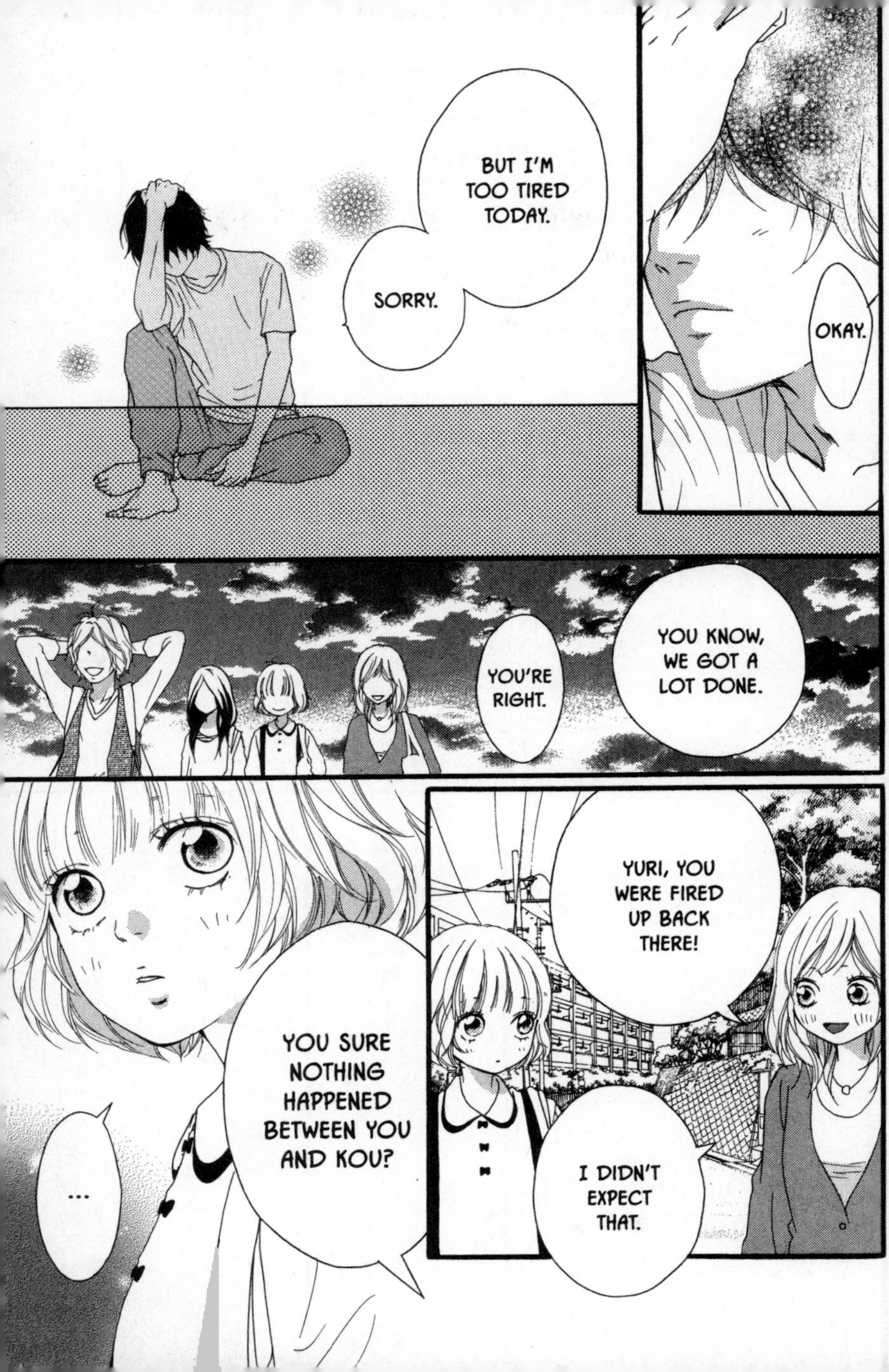
OKAY.
BUT I'M TOO TIRED TODAY.
SORRY.
YOU KNOW, WE GOT A LOT DONE.
YOU'RE RIGHT.
YURI, YOU WERE FIRED UP BACK THERE!
I DIDN'T EXPECT THAT.
YOU SURE NOTHING HAPPENED BETWEEN YOU AND KOU?
...

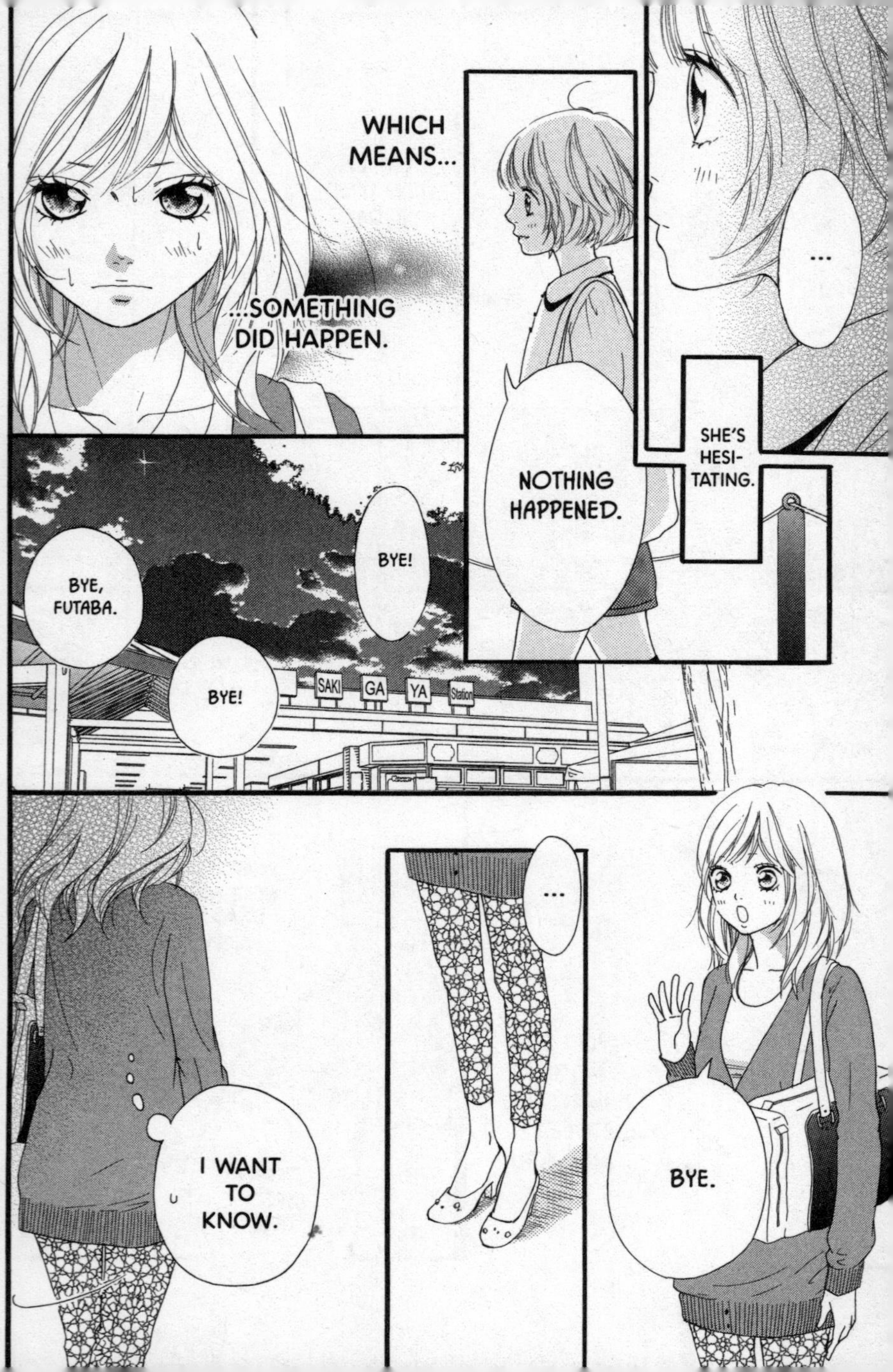
...
SHE'S HESI-TATING.
NOTHING HAPPENED.
WHICH MEANS...
...SOMETHING DID HAPPEN.
BYE!
BYE, FUTABA.
BYE!
SAKI GA YA Station
BYE.
...
I WANT TO KNOW.

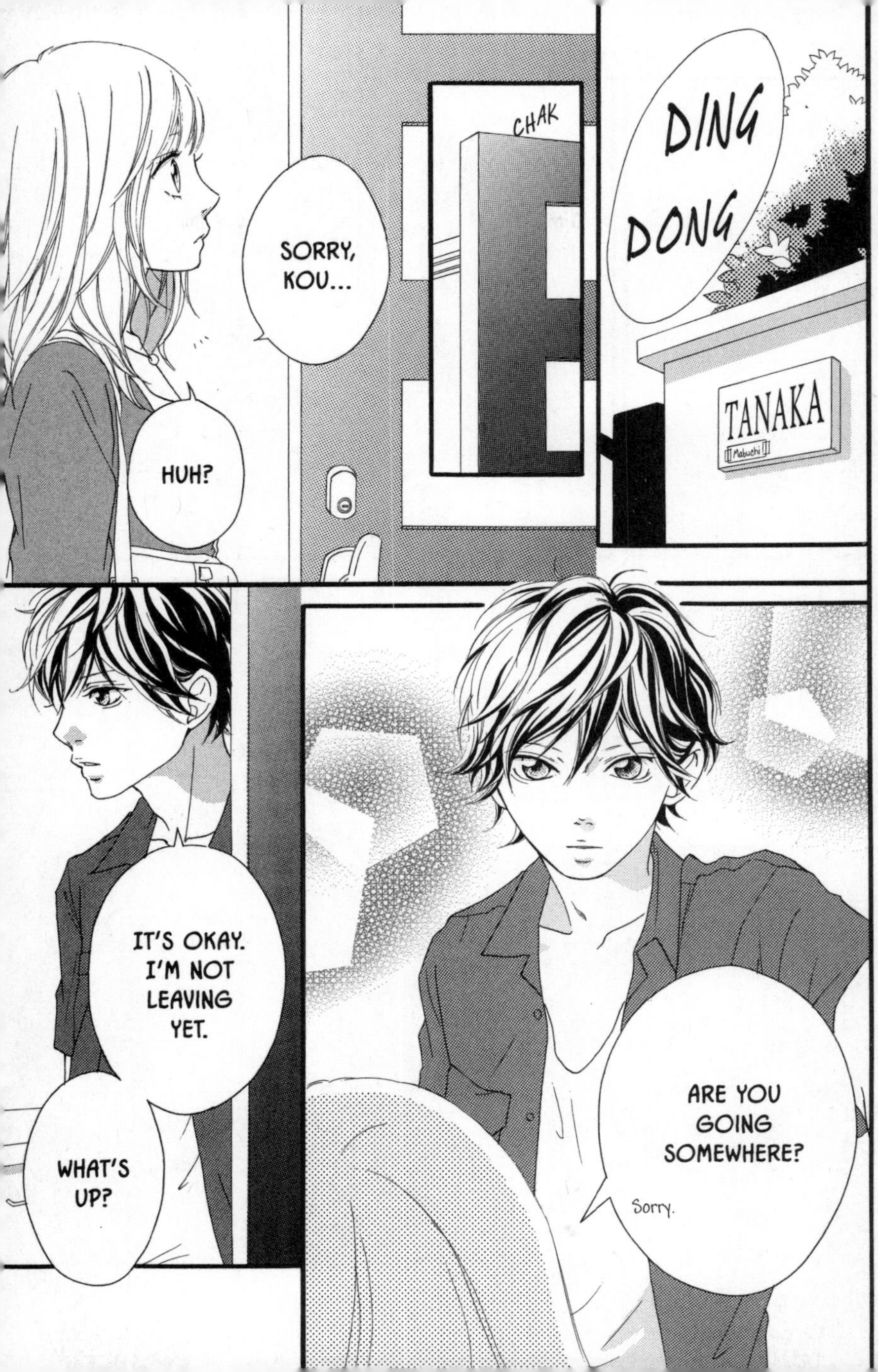
DING DONG
TANAKA
Mabuchi
CHAK
SORRY, KOU...
HUH?
ARE YOU GOING SOMEWHERE?
Sorry.
IT'S OKAY. I'M NOT LEAVING YET.
WHAT'S UP?

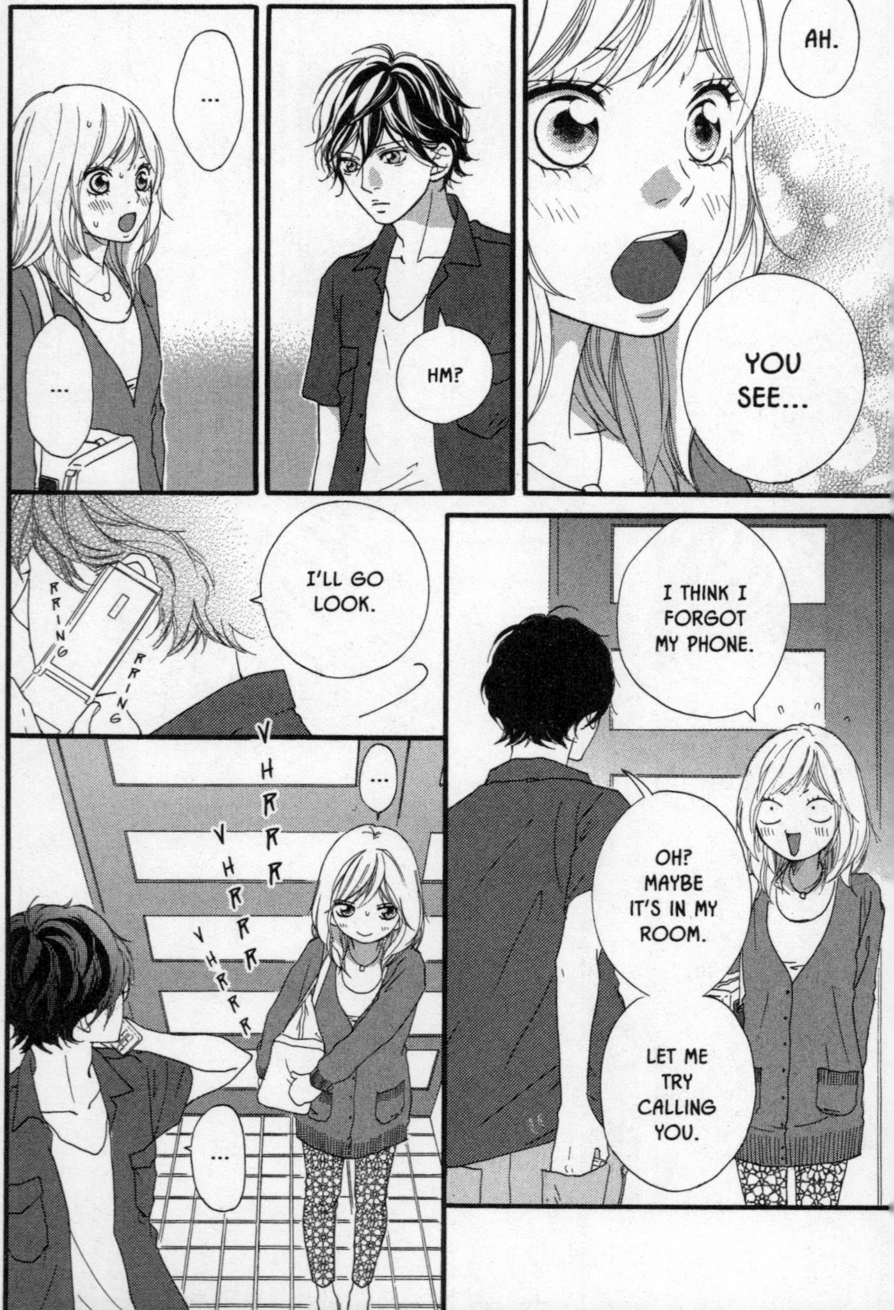
AH.
YOU SEE...
HM?
...
...
I THINK I FORGOT MY PHONE.
OH? MAYBE IT'S IN MY ROOM.
LET ME TRY CALLING YOU.
I'LL GO LOOK.
RRING
RRING
...
VHRRR
VHRRR
VHRRRR
...

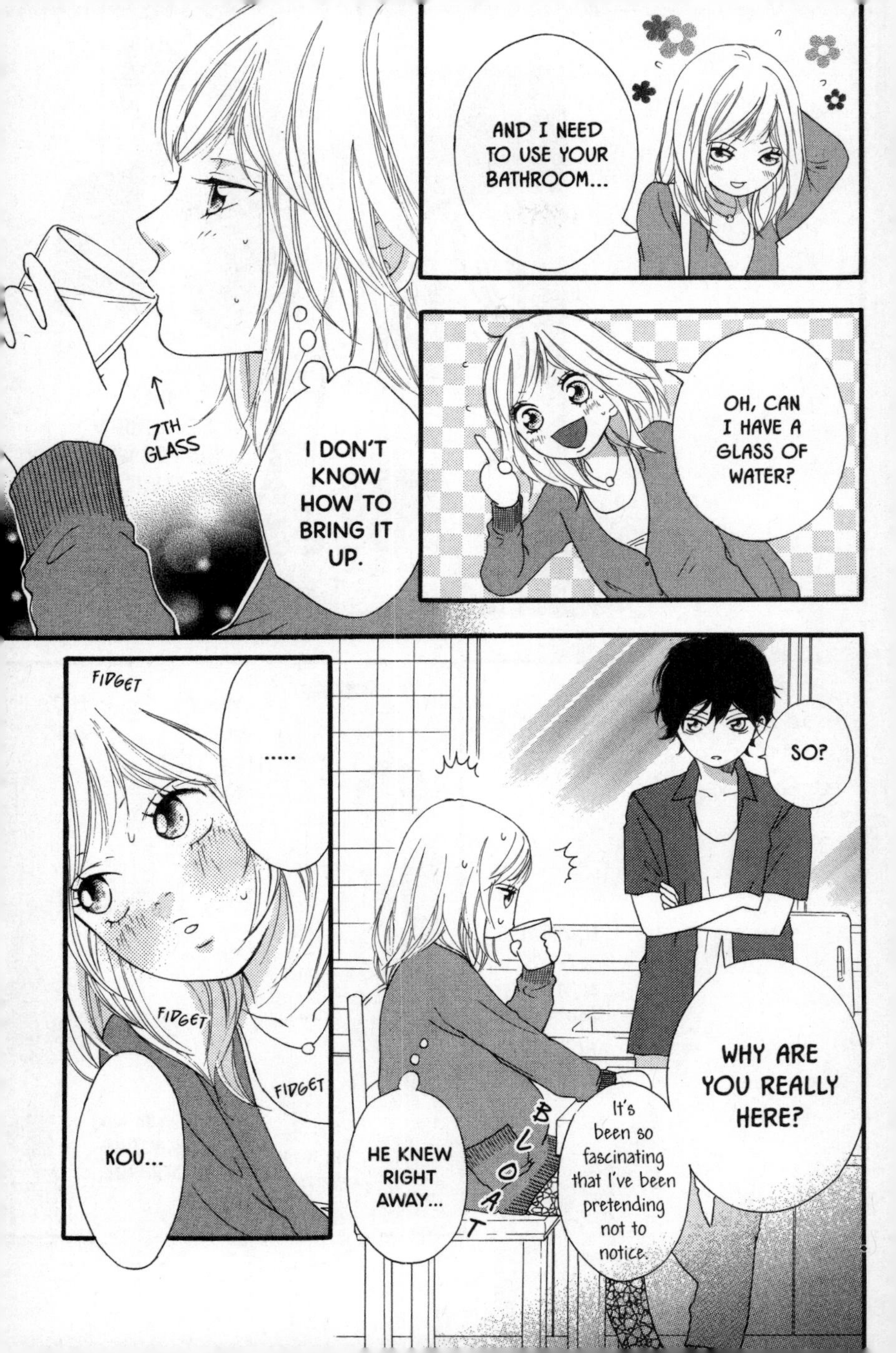
AND I NEED TO USE YOUR BATHROOM...
OH, CAN I HAVE A GLASS OF WATER?
7TH GLASS
I DON'T KNOW HOW TO BRING IT UP.
SO?
WHY ARE YOU REALLY HERE?
It's been so fascinating that I've been pretending not to notice.
HE KNEW RIGHT AWAY...
BLOAT
FIDGET
.....
FIDGET
FIDGET
KOU...

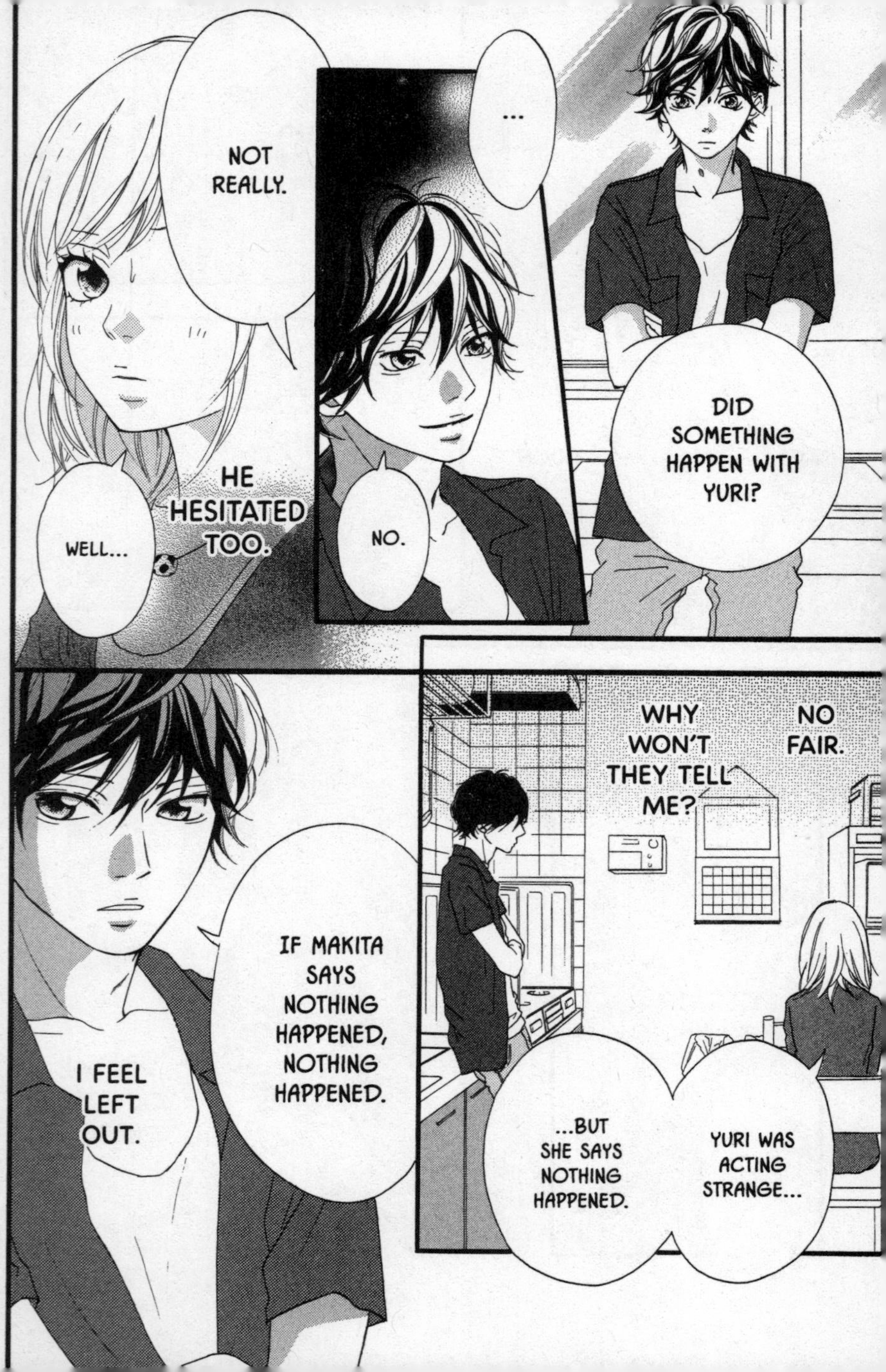
DID SOMETHING HAPPEN WITH YURI?
...
NO.
NOT REALLY.
HE HESITATED TOO.
WELL...
NO FAIR.
WHY WON'T THEY TELL ME?
YURI WAS ACTING STRANGE...
...BUT SHE SAYS NOTHING HAPPENED.
IF MAKITA SAYS NOTHING HAPPENED, NOTHING HAPPENED.
I FEEL LEFT OUT.

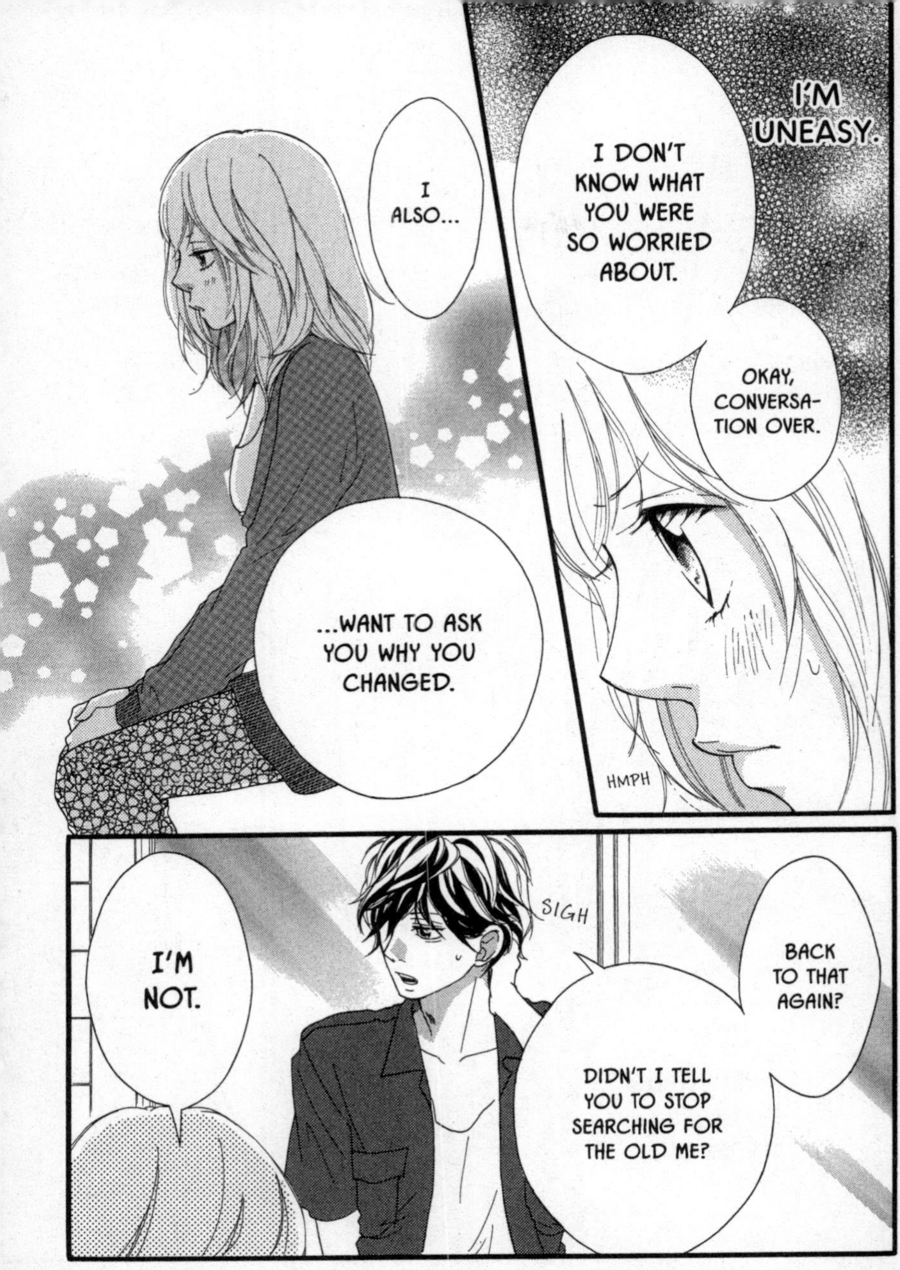
I'M UNEASY.
I DON'T KNOW WHAT YOU WERE SO WORRIED ABOUT.
OKAY, CONVERSATION OVER.
HMPH
I ALSO...
...WANT TO ASK YOU WHY YOU CHANGED.
BACK TO THAT AGAIN?
DIDN'T I TELL YOU TO STOP SEARCHING FOR THE OLD ME?
SIGH
I'M NOT.

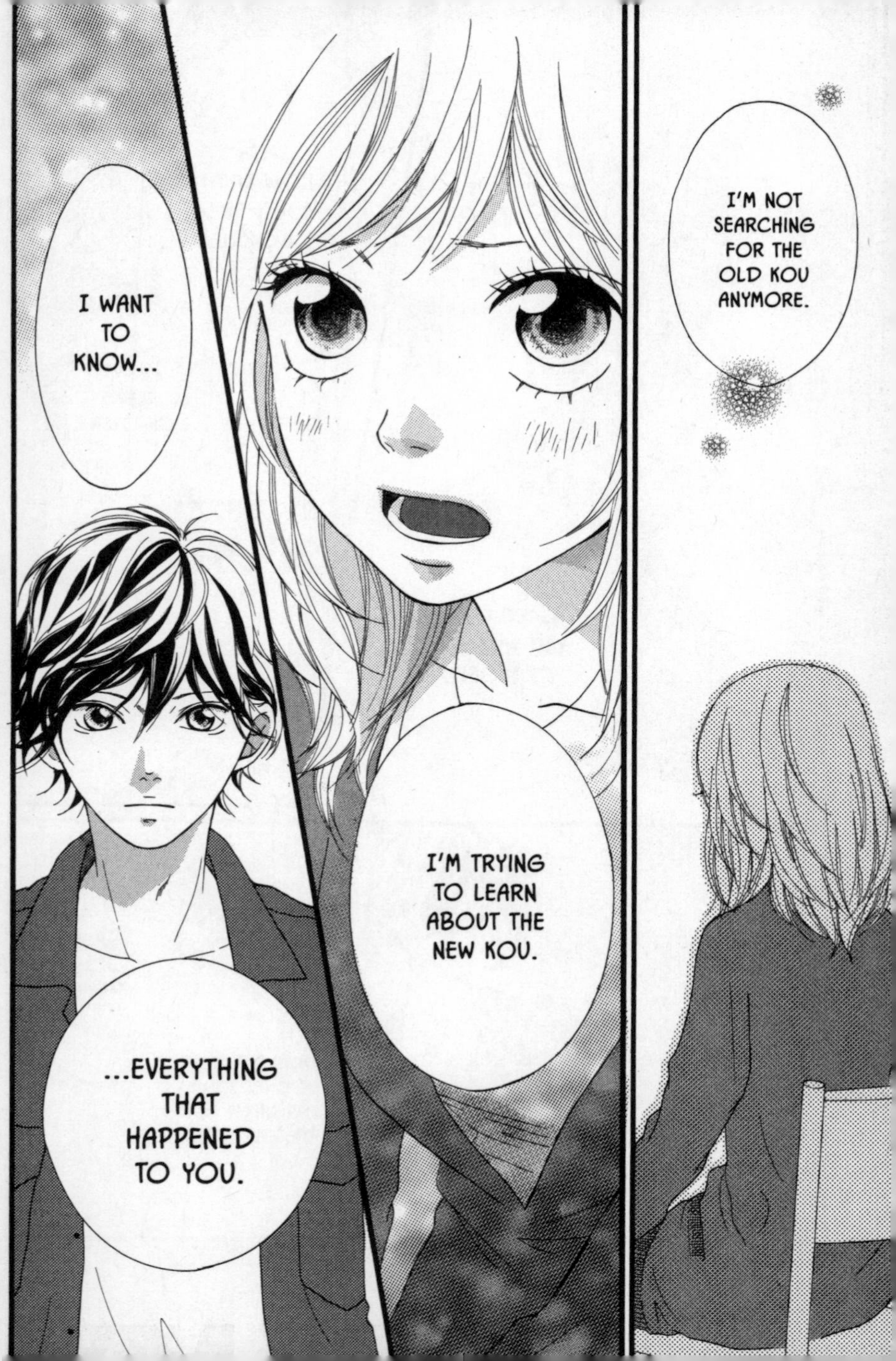
I'M NOT SEARCHING FOR THE OLD KOU ANYMORE.
I'M TRYING TO LEARN ABOUT THE NEW KOU.
I WANT TO KNOW...
...EVERYTHING THAT HAPPENED TO YOU.

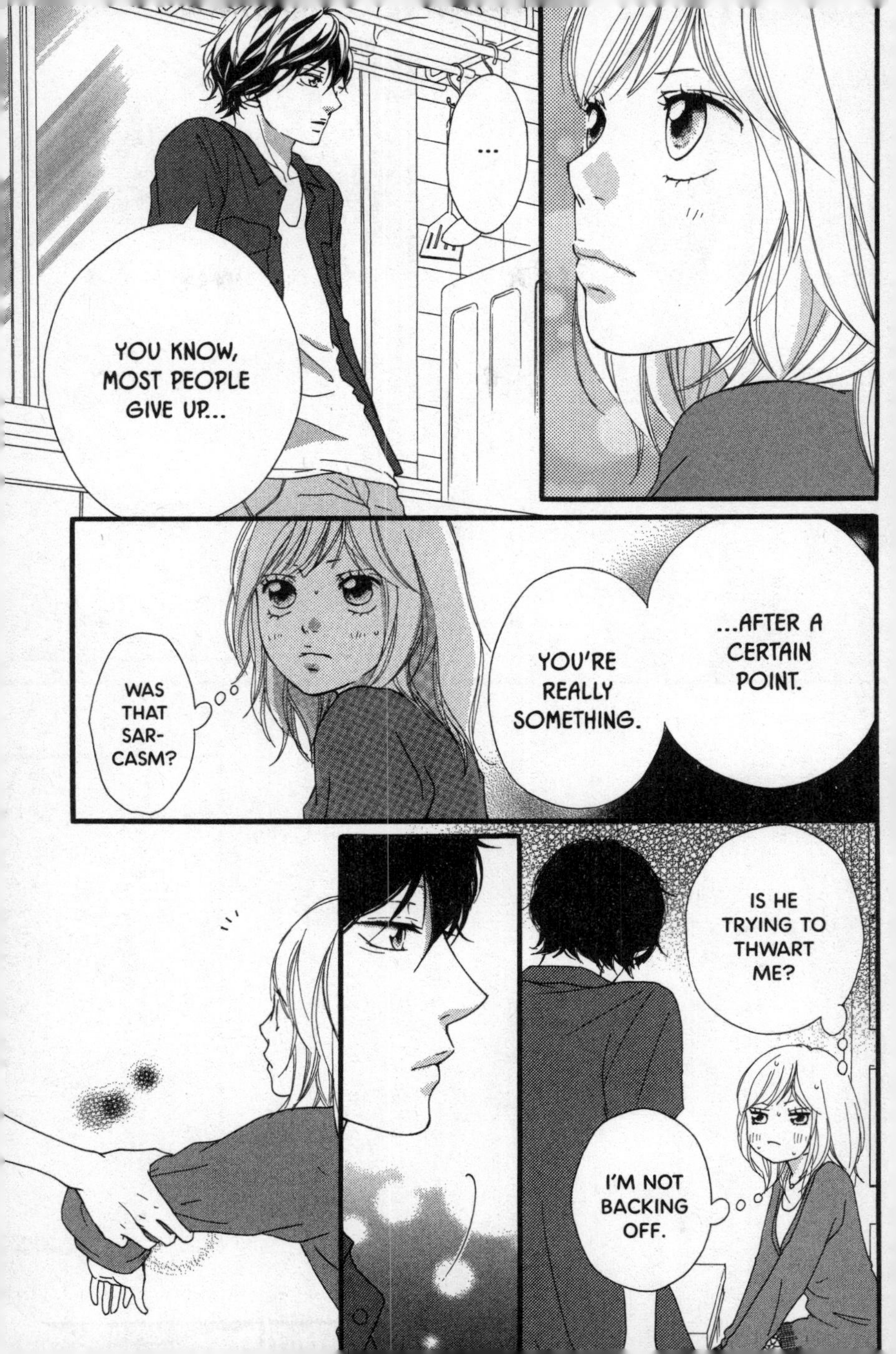
...
YOU KNOW, MOST PEOPLE GIVE UP...
...AFTER A CERTAIN POINT.
YOU'RE REALLY SOMETHING.
WAS THAT SAR-CASM?
IS HE TRYING TO THWART ME?
I'M NOT BACKING OFF.

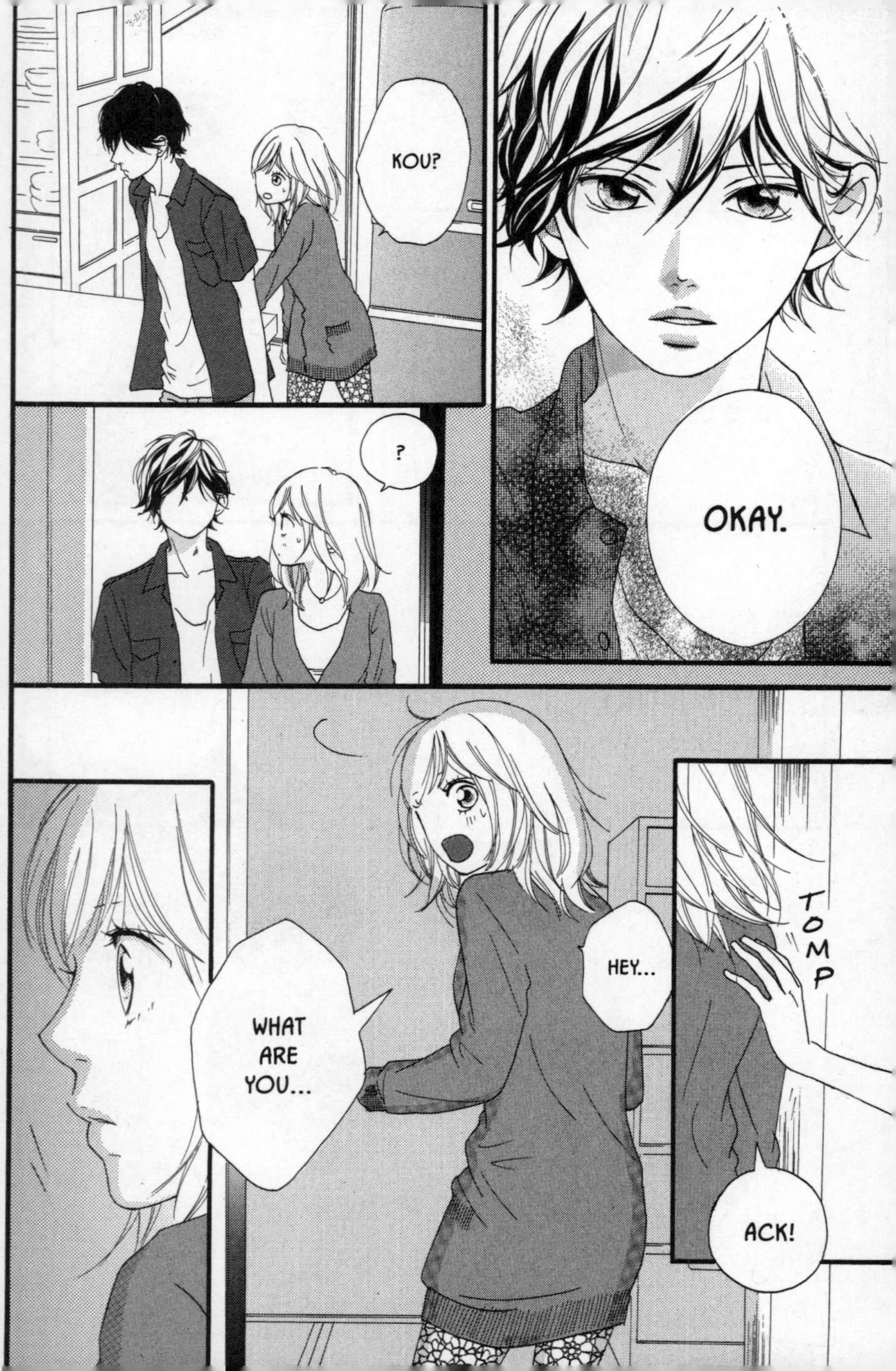
OKAY.
KOU?
?
TOMP
ACK!
HEY...
WHAT ARE YOU...

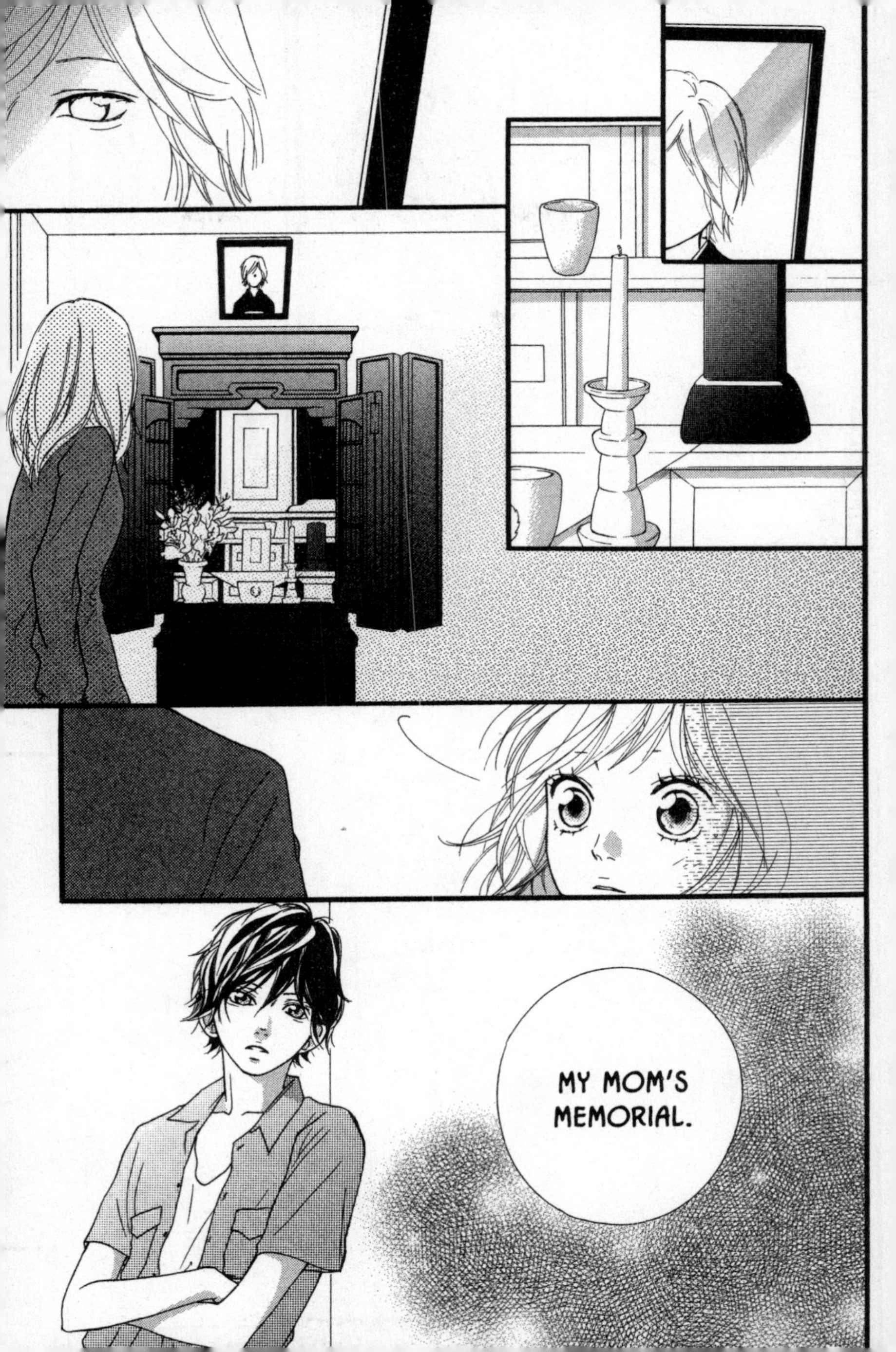
MY MOM'S MEMORIAL.

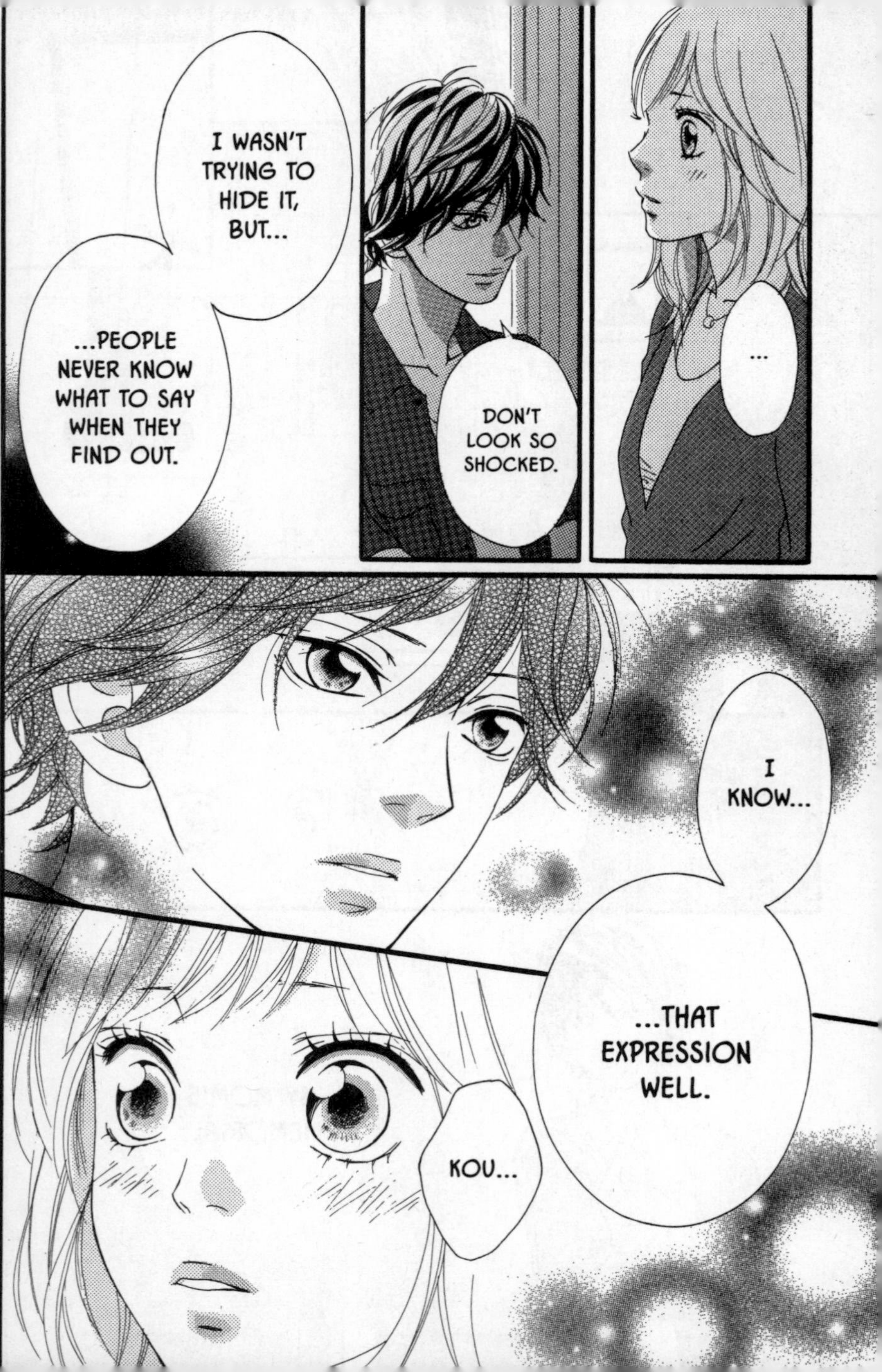
...
DON'T LOOK SO SHOCKED.
I WASN'T TRYING TO HIDE IT, BUT...
...PEOPLE NEVER KNOW WHAT TO SAY WHEN THEY FIND OUT.
I KNOW...
...THAT EXPRESSION WELL.
KOU...

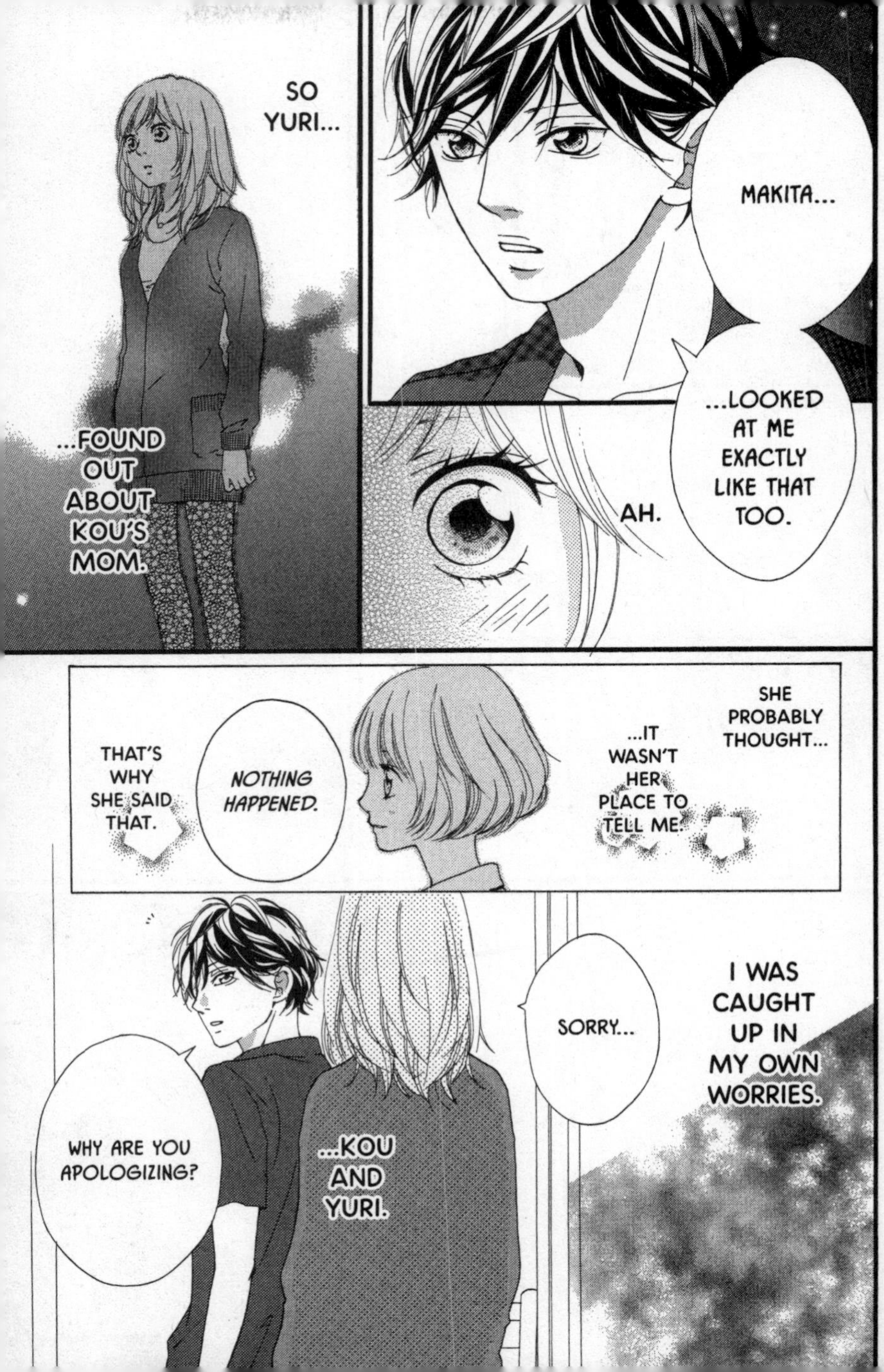
MAKITA...
...LOOKED AT ME EXACTLY LIKE THAT TOO.
AH.
SO YURI...
...FOUND OUT ABOUT KOU'S MOM.
SHE PROBABLY THOUGHT...
...IT WASN'T HER PLACE TO TELL ME.
NOTHING HAPPENED.
THAT'S WHY SHE SAID THAT.
I WAS CAUGHT UP IN MY OWN WORRIES.
SORRY...
...KOU AND YURI.
WHY ARE YOU APOLOGIZING?

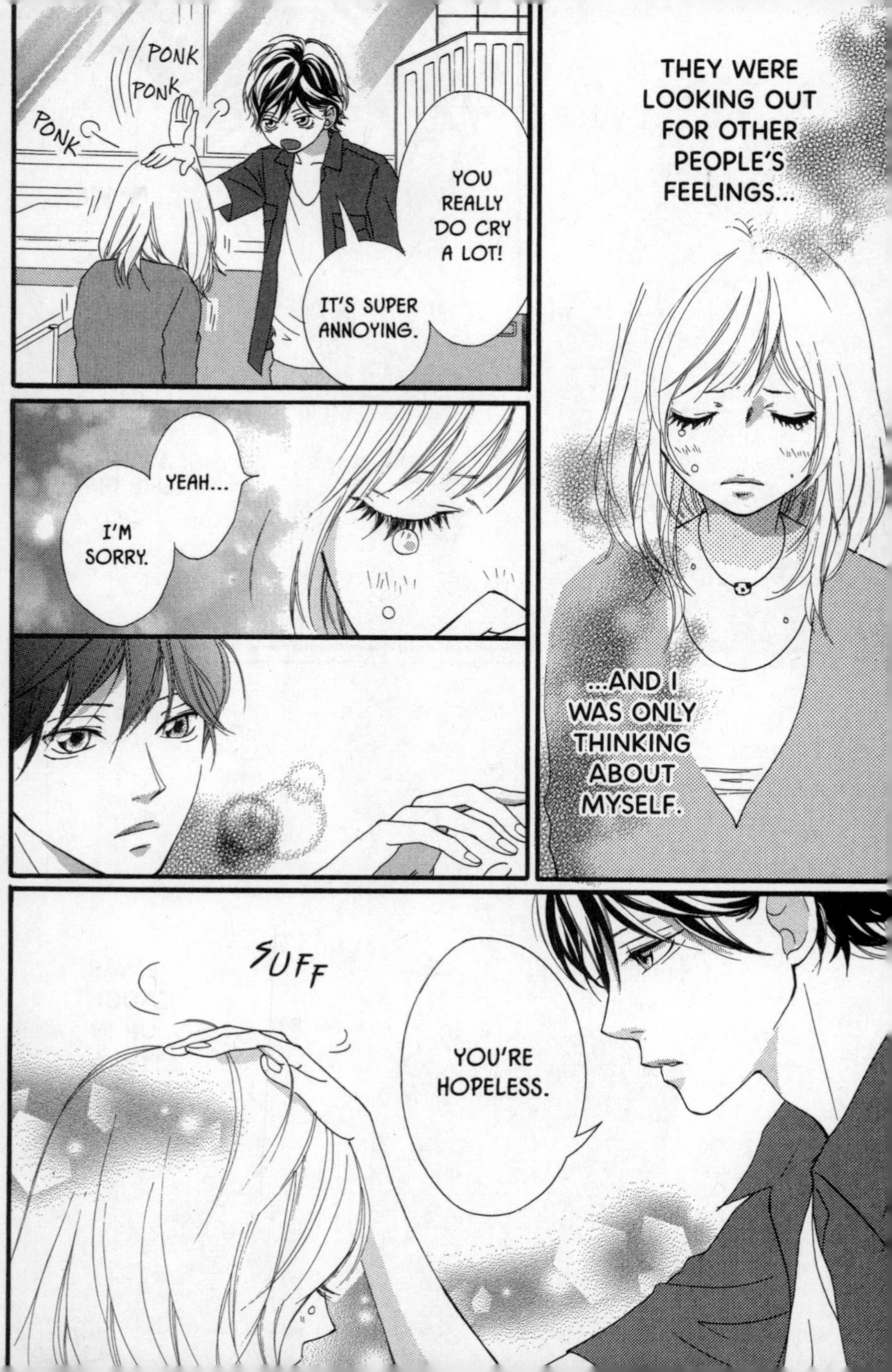
THEY WERE LOOKING OUT FOR OTHER PEOPLE'S FEELINGS...
...AND I WAS ONLY THINKING ABOUT MYSELF.
PONK
PONK
PONK
YOU REALLY DO CRY A LOT!
IT'S SUPER ANNOYING.
YEAH...
I'M SORRY.
YOU'RE HOPELESS.
SUFF

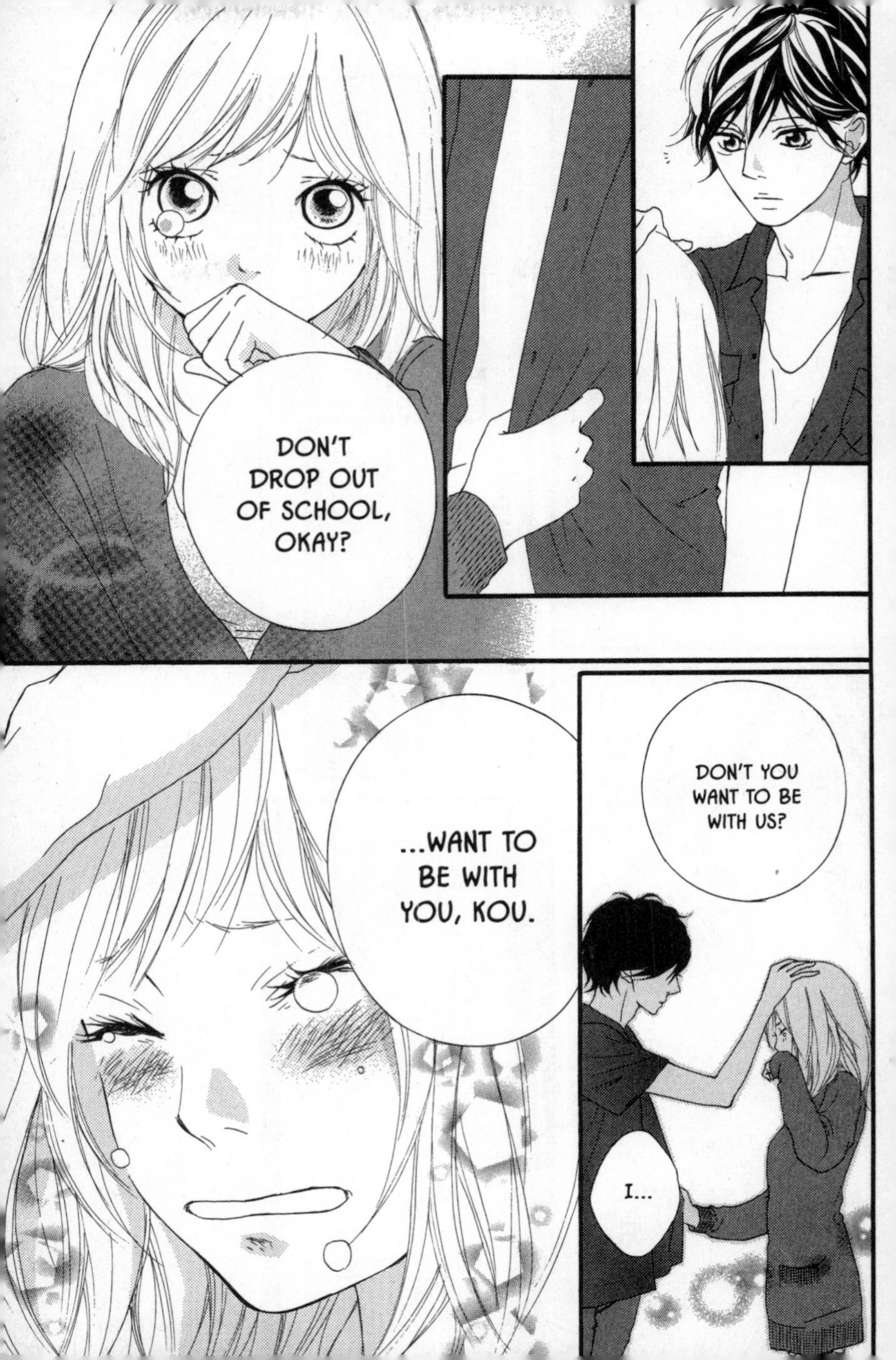
DON'T DROP OUT OF SCHOOL, OKAY?
DON'T YOU WANT TO BE WITH US?
I...
...WANT TO BE WITH YOU, KOU.

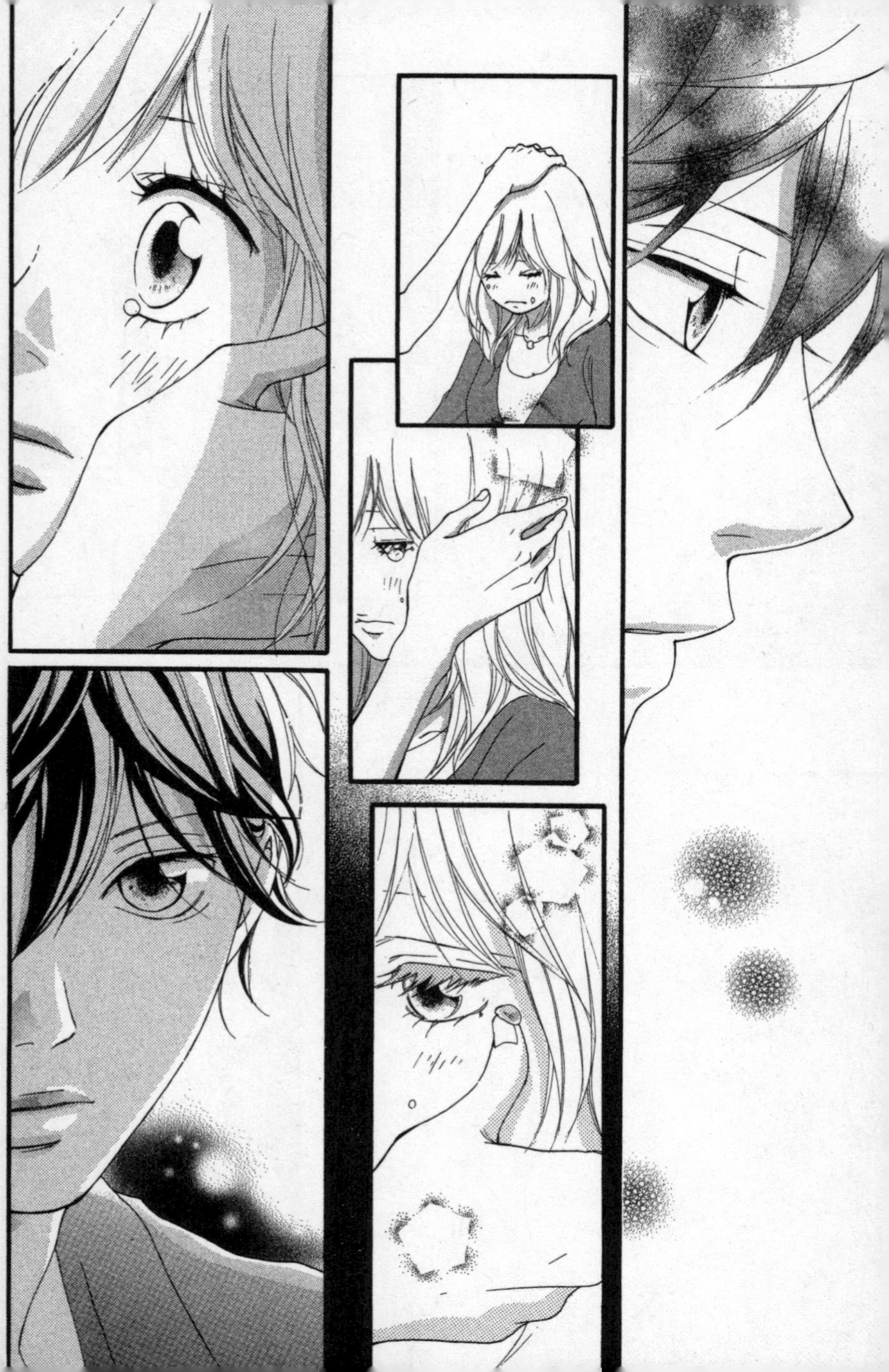

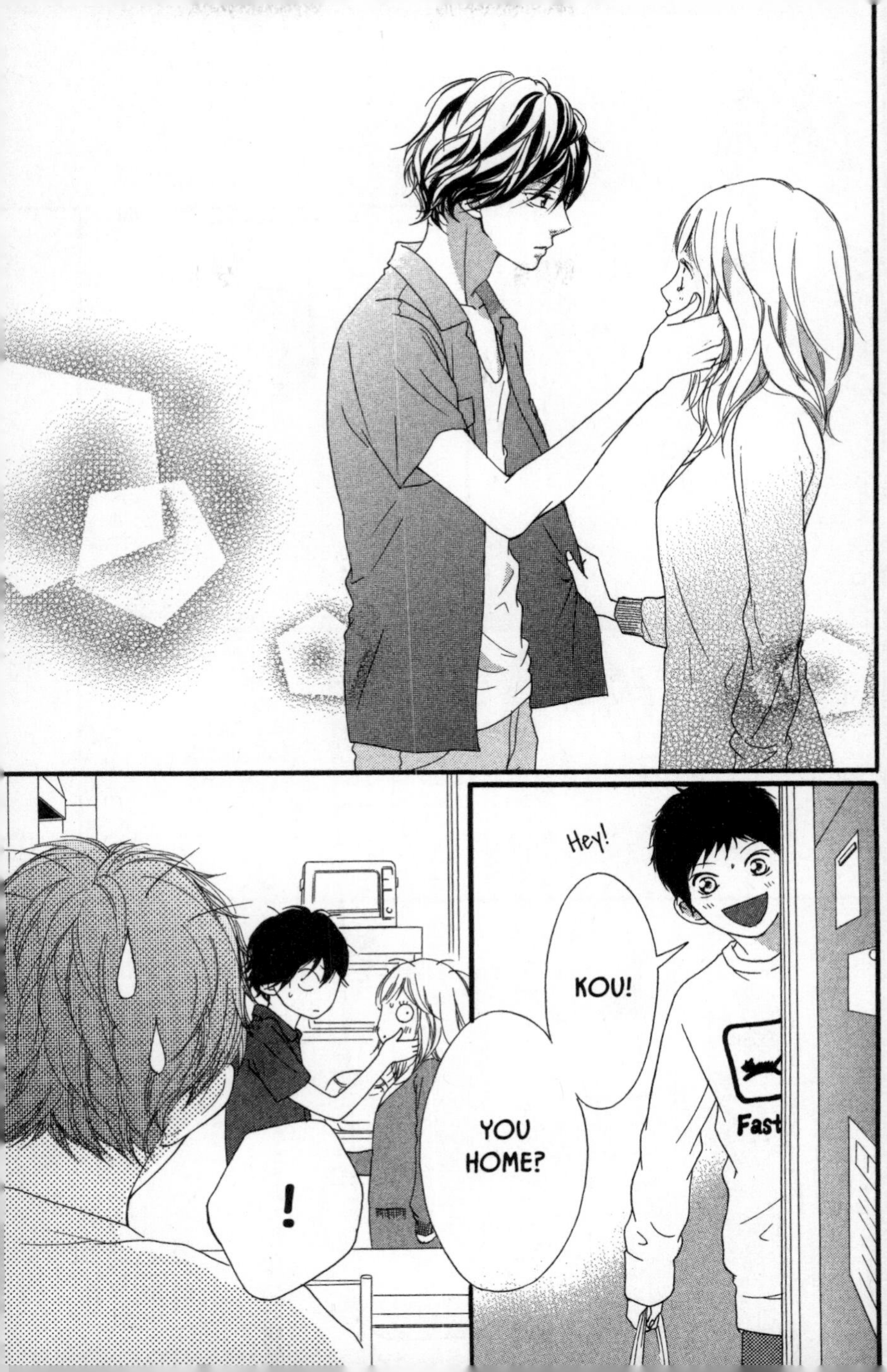
Hey!
KOU!
YOU HOME?
Fast
!

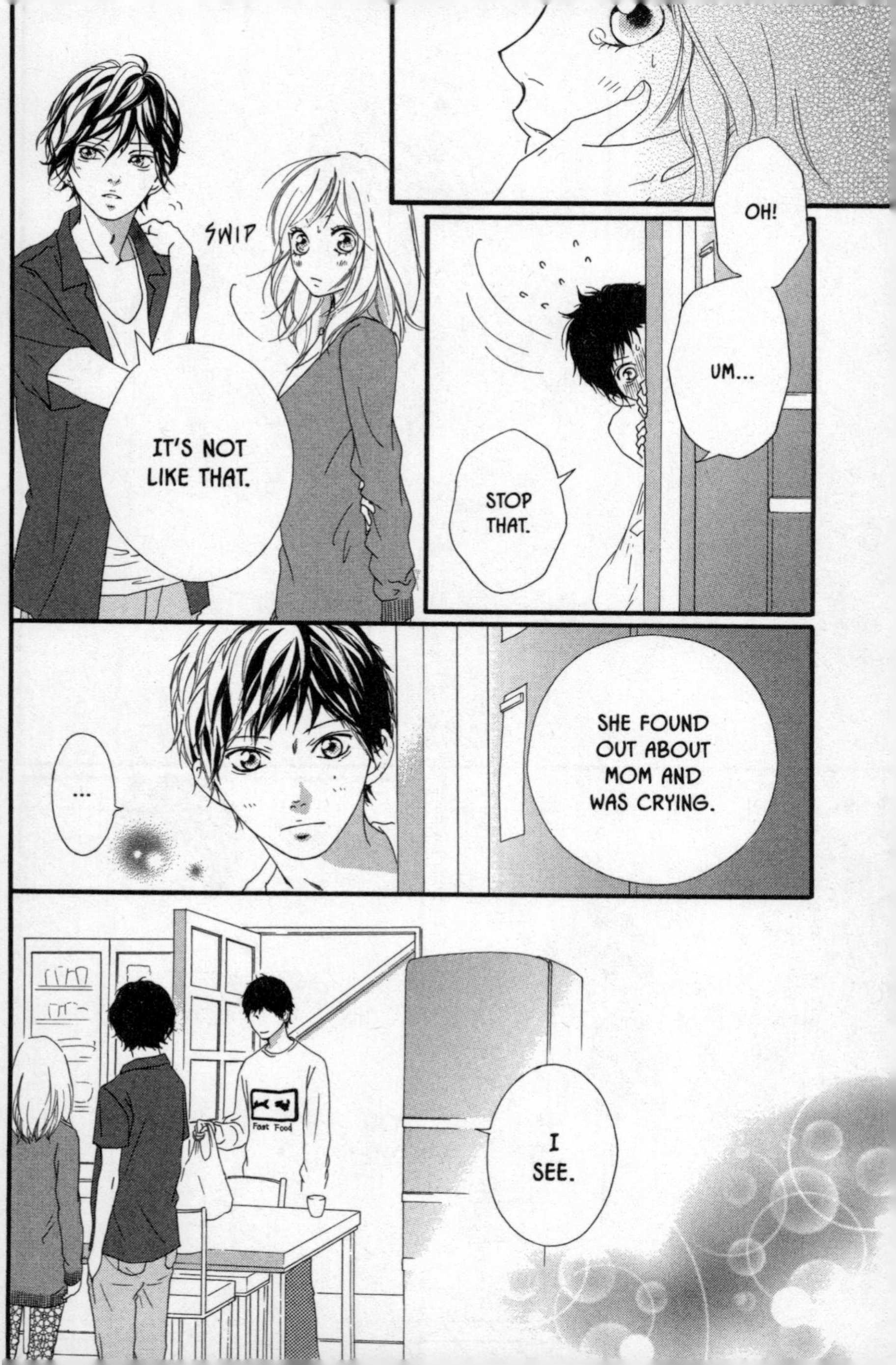
OH!
UM...
STOP THAT.
SWIP
IT'S NOT LIKE THAT.
SHE FOUND OUT ABOUT MOM AND WAS CRYING.
...
Fast Food
I SEE.

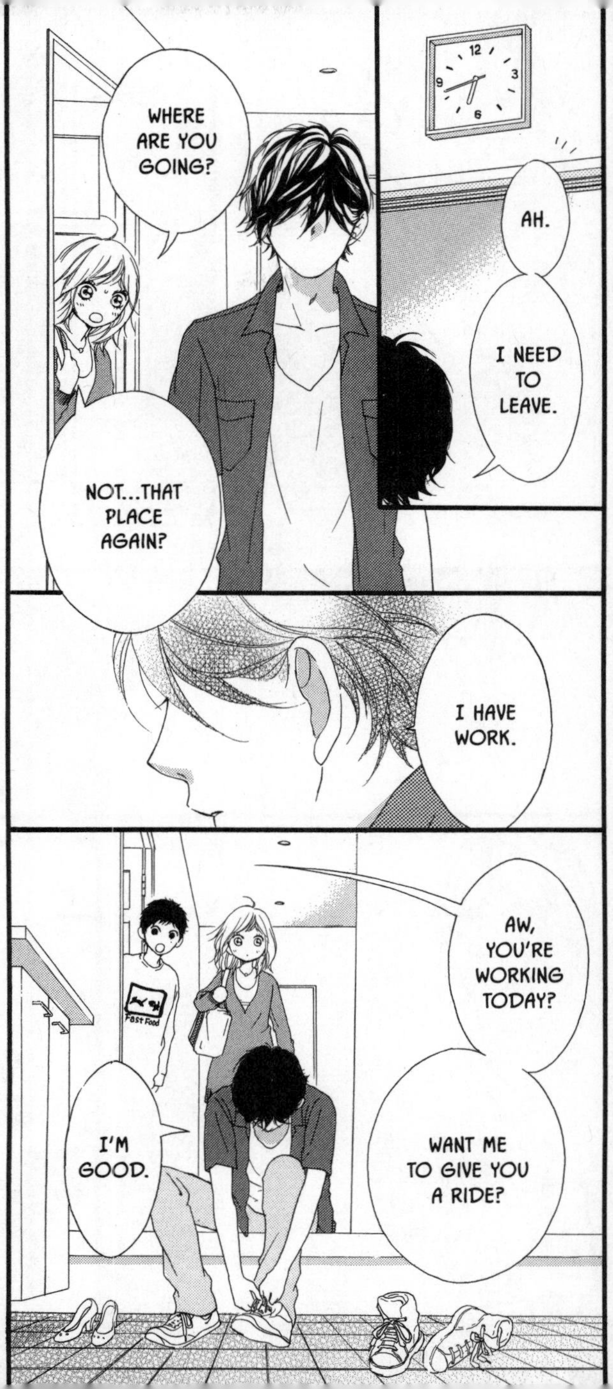
AH.
I NEED TO LEAVE.
WHERE ARE YOU GOING?
NOT...THAT PLACE AGAIN?
I HAVE WORK.
AW, YOU'RE WORKING TODAY?
WANT ME TO GIVE YOU A RIDE?
I'M GOOD.

Towelket Club Diaries

The Towelket Club is for people who love soft-to-the-touch stuff and fluff. I still receive letters from many people requesting to join. Of course everyone is very welcome. ♡ But it's not like we're going to get together and do activities. (*laugh*) I use towelkets when I sleep, but I also always have one at hand when I watch my favorite TV shows and movies. When I'm down, I wrap one around my neck like a shawl. And when I wash them, I use plenty of fabric softener and fluff them in the dryer. Almost ritualistically I bury my face in their fluff and frolic about. Such are my activities lately.

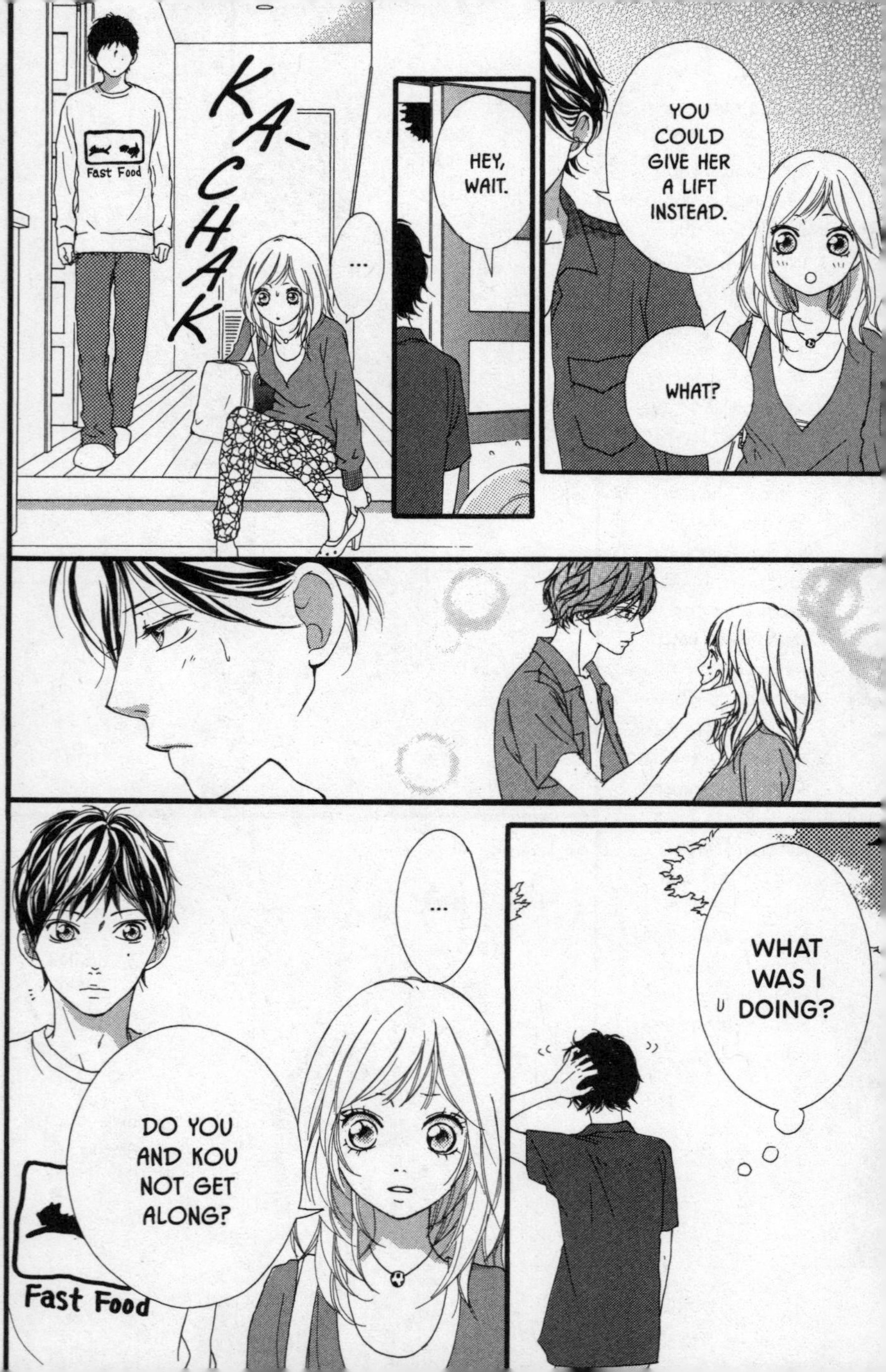
YOU COULD GIVE HER A LIFT INSTEAD.
WHAT?
HEY, WAIT.
...
KA-CHAK
Fast Food
WHAT WAS I DOING?
...
DO YOU AND KOU NOT GET ALONG?
Fast Food

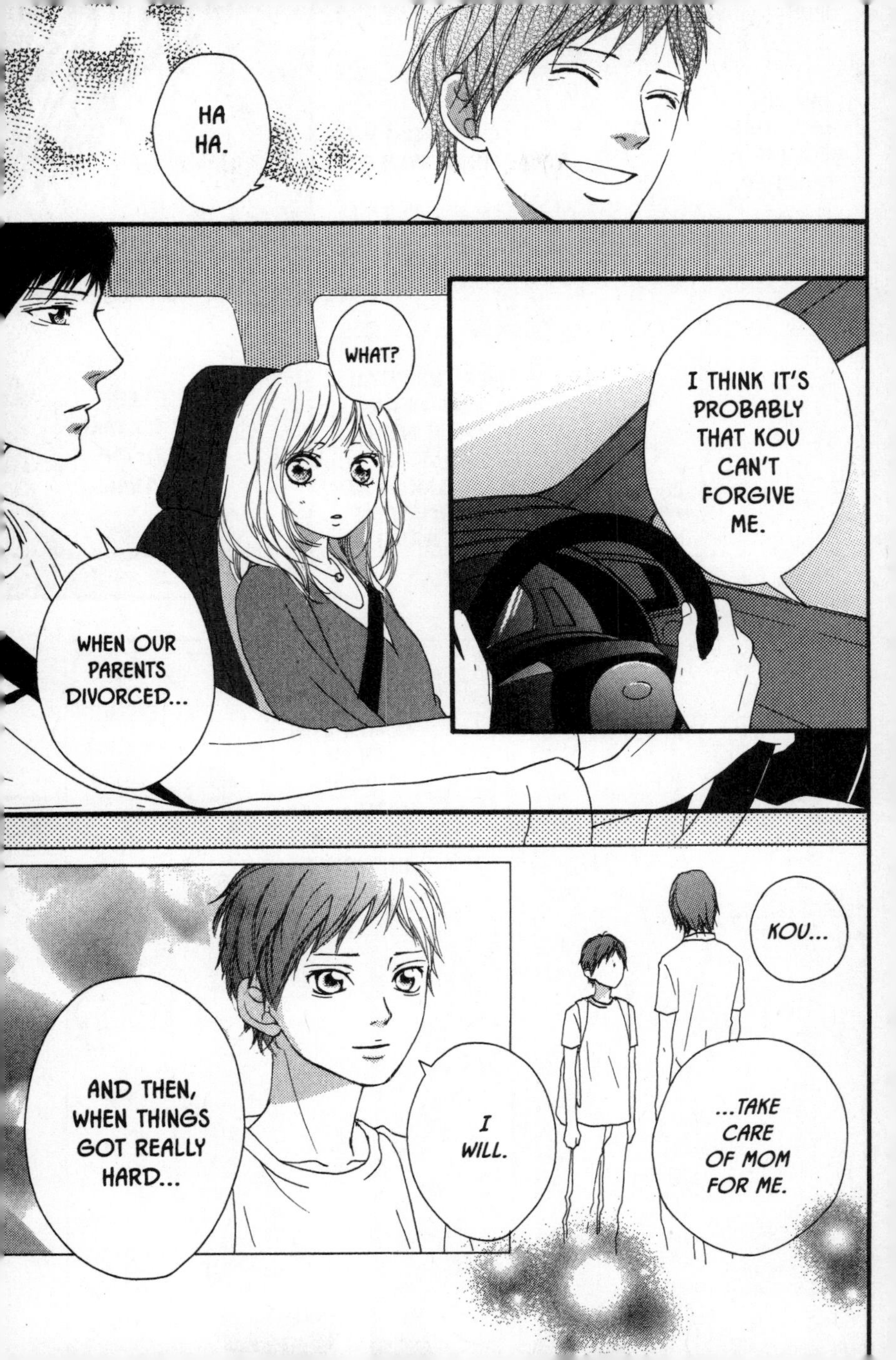
HA HA.
I THINK IT'S PROBABLY THAT KOU CAN'T FORGIVE ME.
WHAT?
WHEN OUR PARENTS DIVORCED...
KOU...
...TAKE CARE OF MOM FOR ME.
I WILL.
AND THEN, WHEN THINGS GOT REALLY HARD...

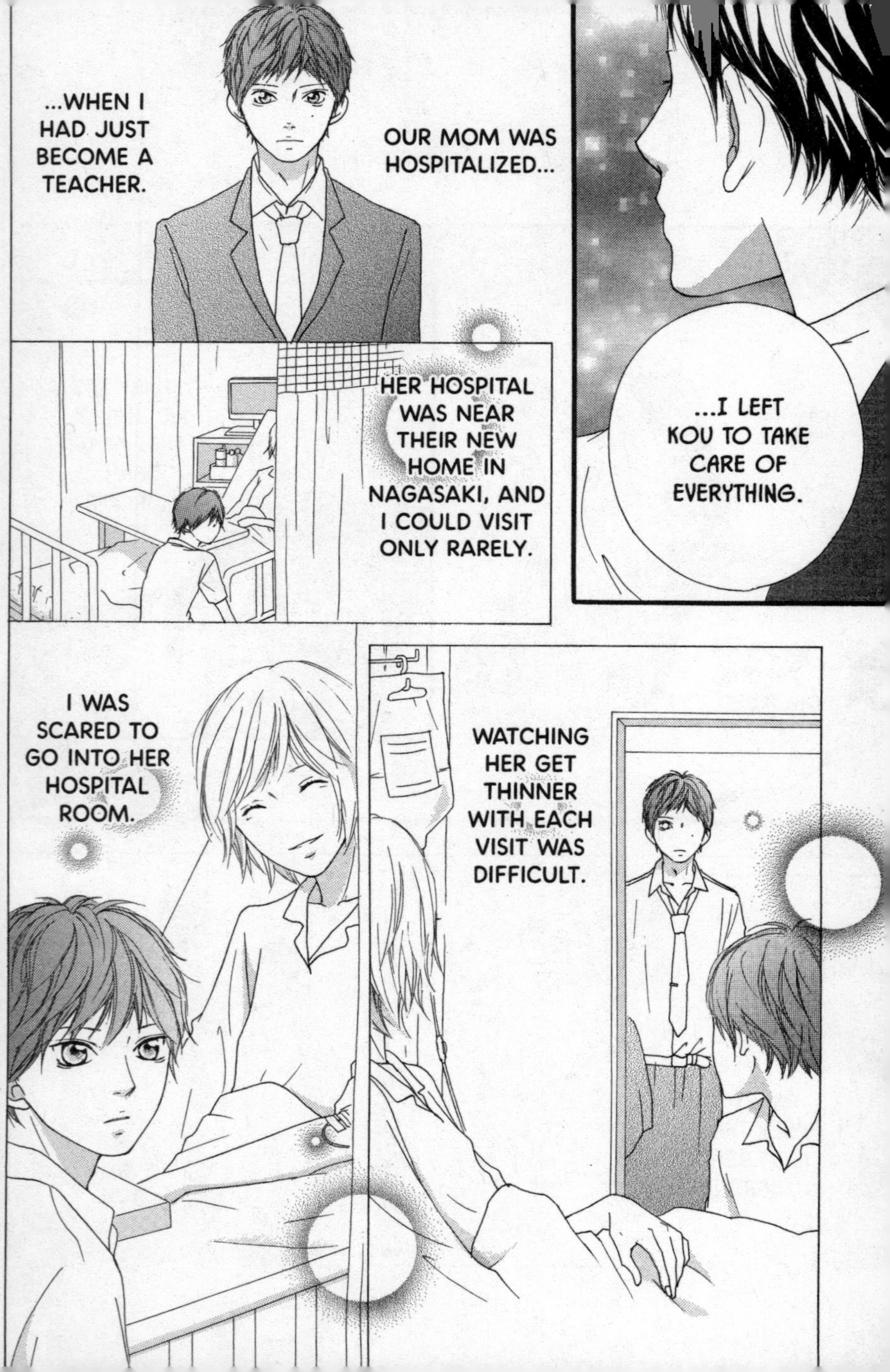
...I LEFT KOU TO TAKE CARE OF EVERYTHING.
OUR MOM WAS HOSPITALIZED...
...WHEN I HAD JUST BECOME A TEACHER.
HER HOSPITAL WAS NEAR THEIR NEW HOME IN NAGASAKI, AND I COULD VISIT ONLY RARELY.
WATCHING HER GET THINNER WITH EACH VISIT WAS DIFFICULT.
I WAS SCARED TO GO INTO HER HOSPITAL ROOM.

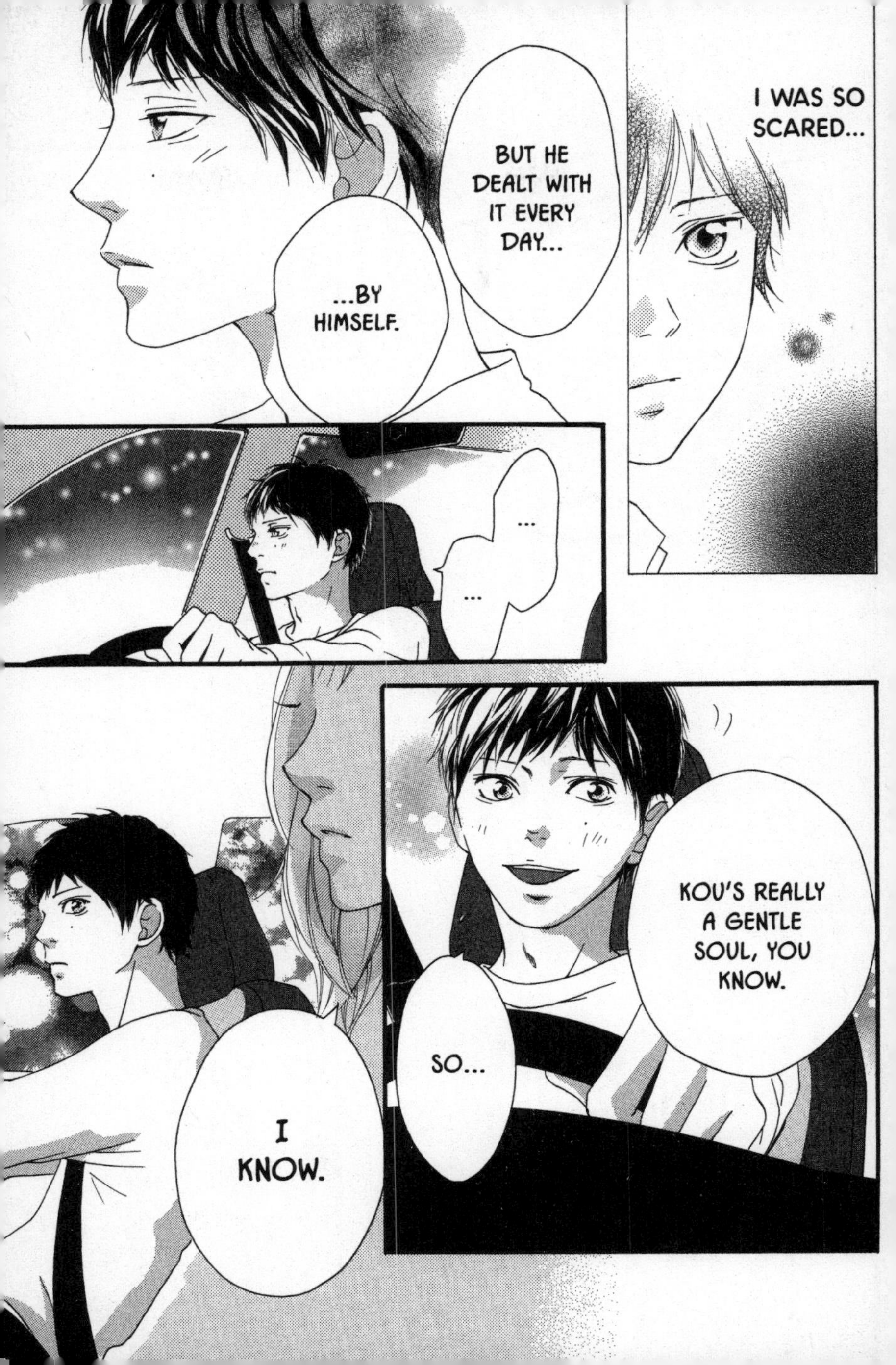
I WAS SO SCARED...
BUT HE DEALT WITH IT EVERY DAY...
...BY HIMSELF.
...
...
KOU'S REALLY A GENTLE SOUL, YOU KNOW.
SO...
I KNOW.

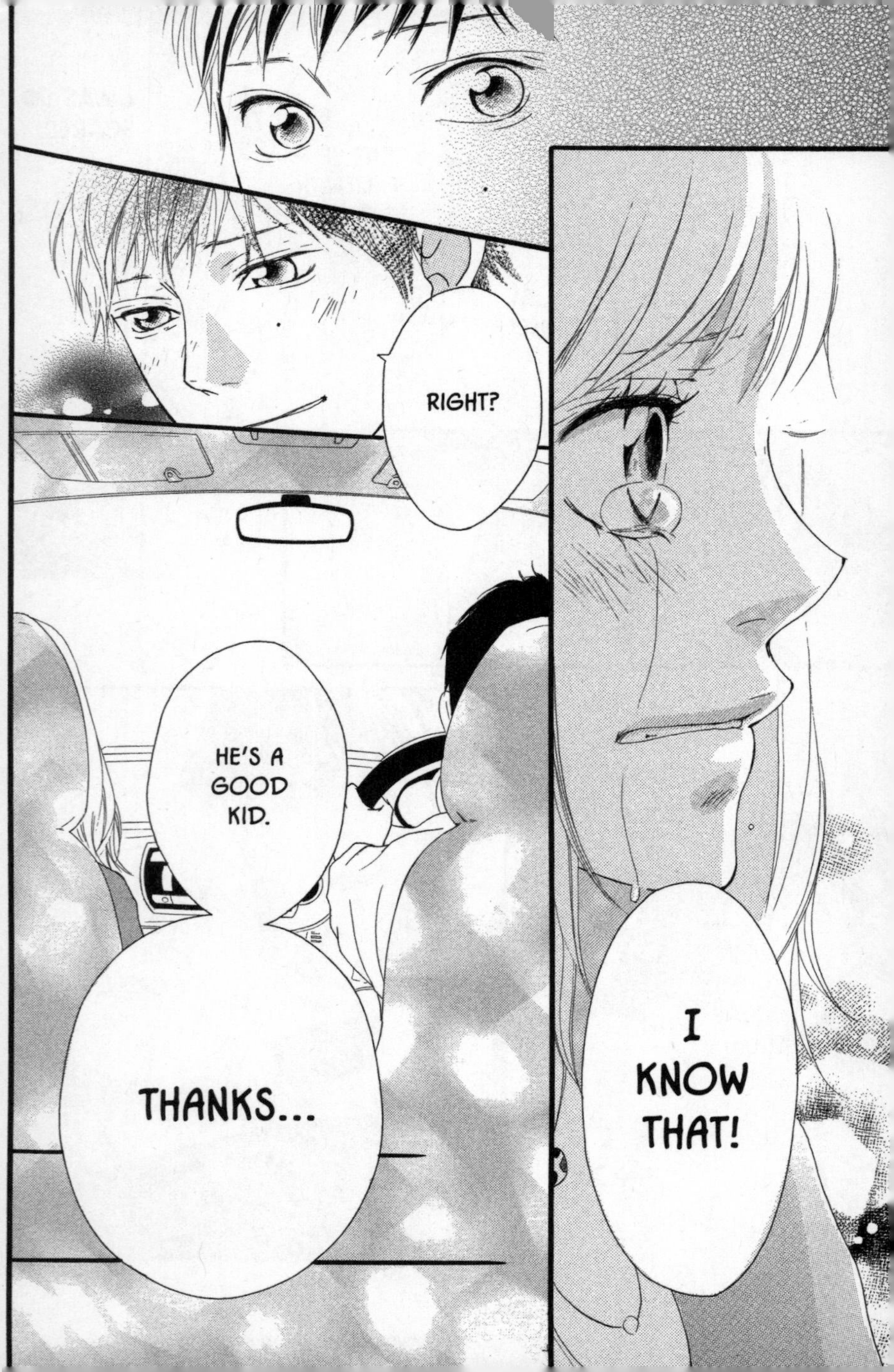
RIGHT?
I KNOW THAT!
HE'S A GOOD KID.
THANKS...

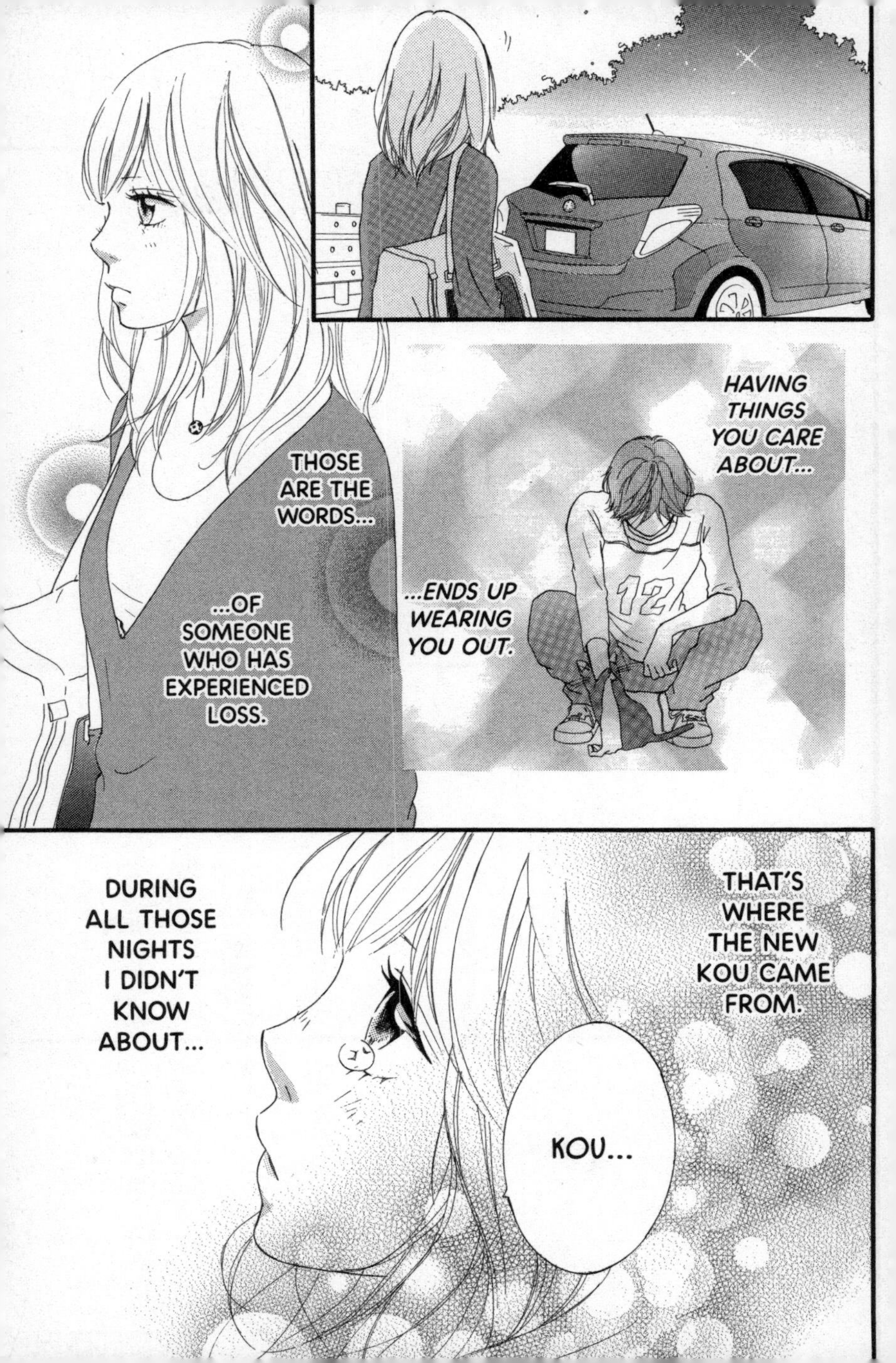
HAVING THINGS YOU CARE ABOUT...
...ENDS UP WEARING YOU OUT.
THOSE ARE THE WORDS...
...OF SOMEONE WHO HAS EXPERIENCED LOSS.
THAT'S WHERE THE NEW KOU CAME FROM.
KOU...
DURING ALL THOSE NIGHTS I DIDN'T KNOW ABOUT...

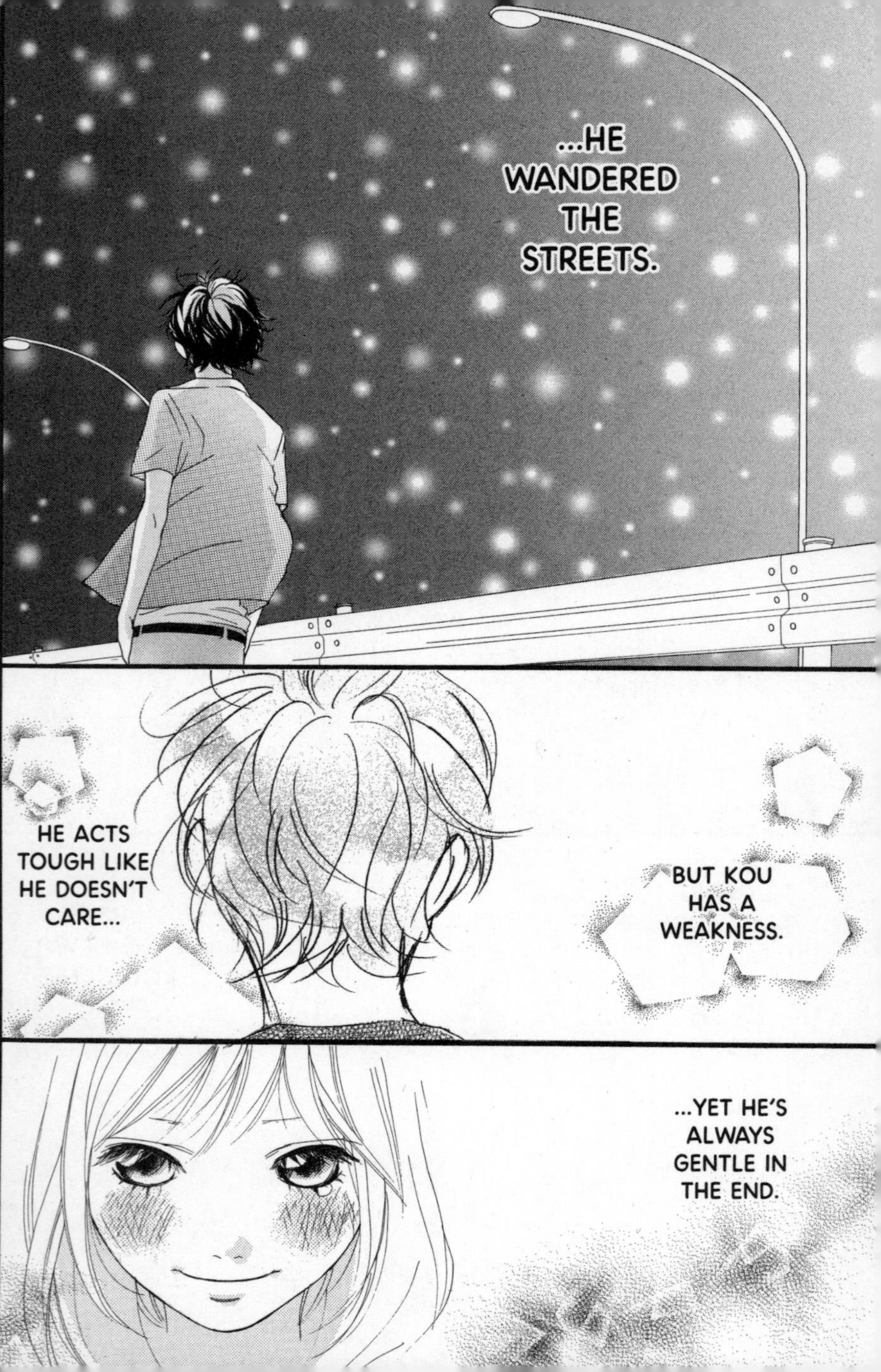
...HE WANDERED THE STREETS.
HE ACTS TOUGH LIKE HE DOESN'T CARE...
BUT KOU HAS A WEAKNESS.
...YET HE'S ALWAYS GENTLE IN THE END.

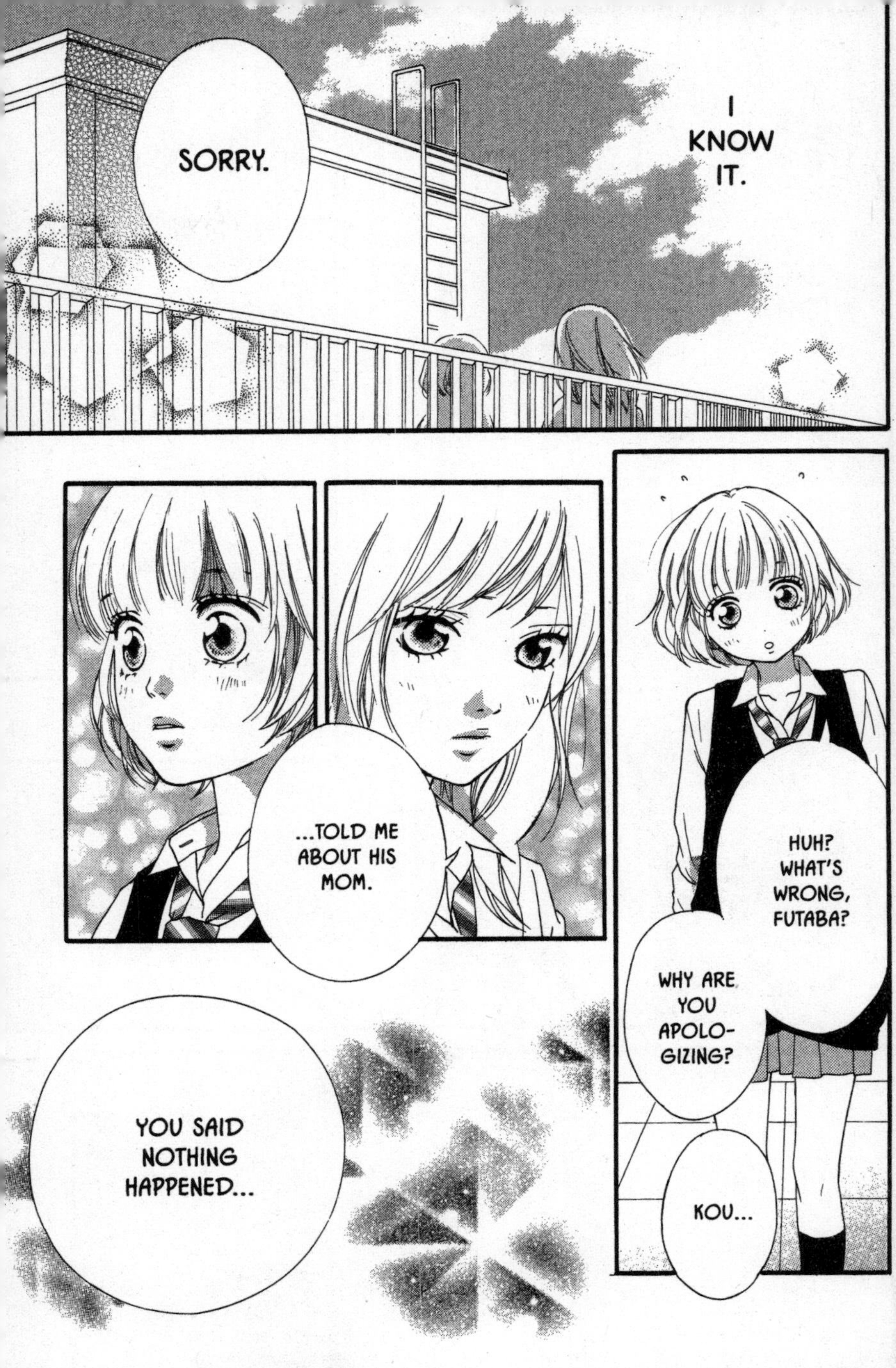
I KNOW IT.
SORRY.
HUH? WHAT'S WRONG, FUTABA?
WHY ARE YOU APOLO-GIZING?
KOU...
...TOLD ME ABOUT HIS MOM.
YOU SAID NOTHING HAPPENED...

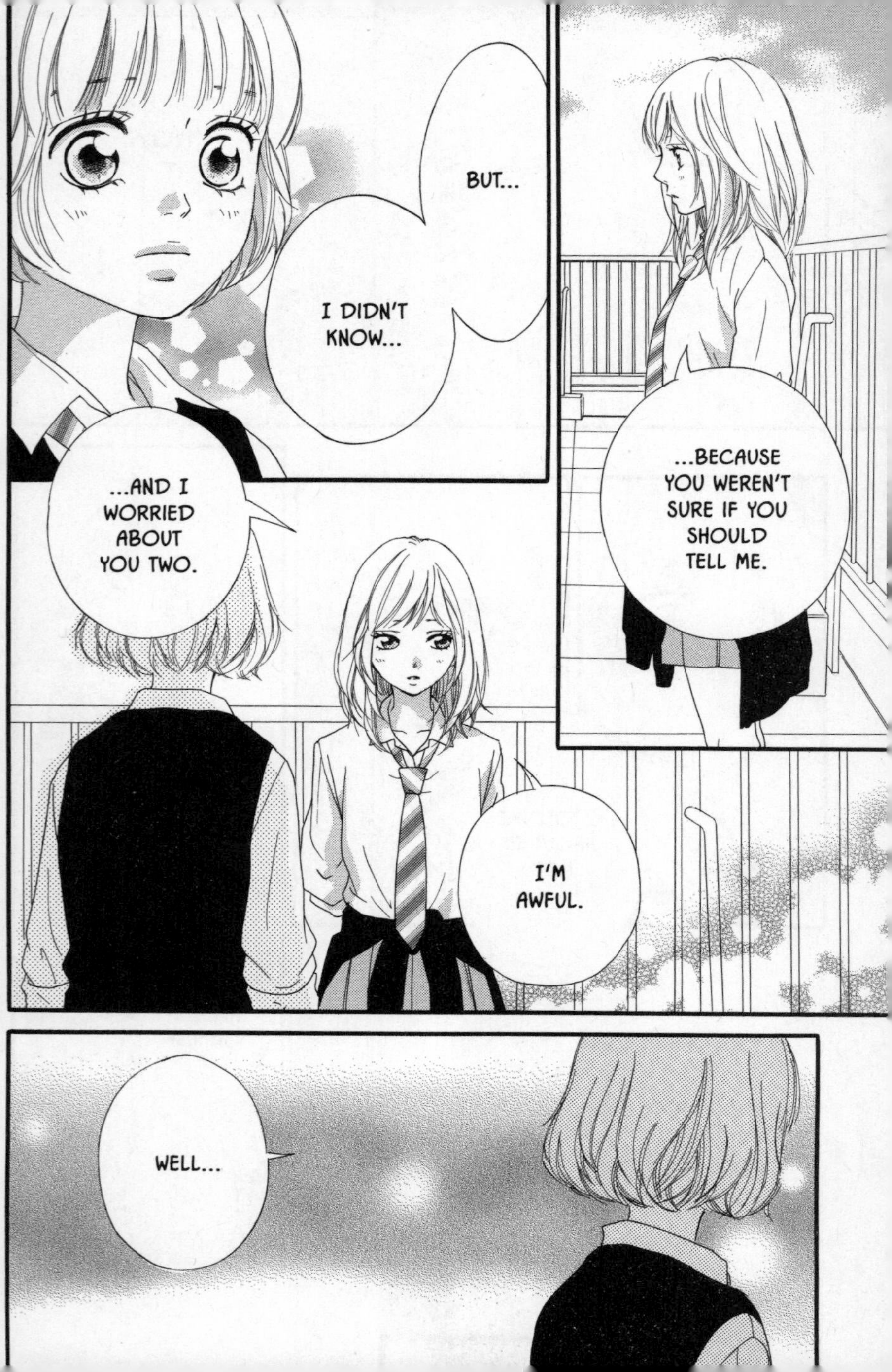
...BECAUSE YOU WEREN'T SURE IF YOU SHOULD TELL ME.
BUT...
I DIDN'T KNOW...
...AND I WORRIED ABOUT YOU TWO.
I'M AWFUL.
WELL...

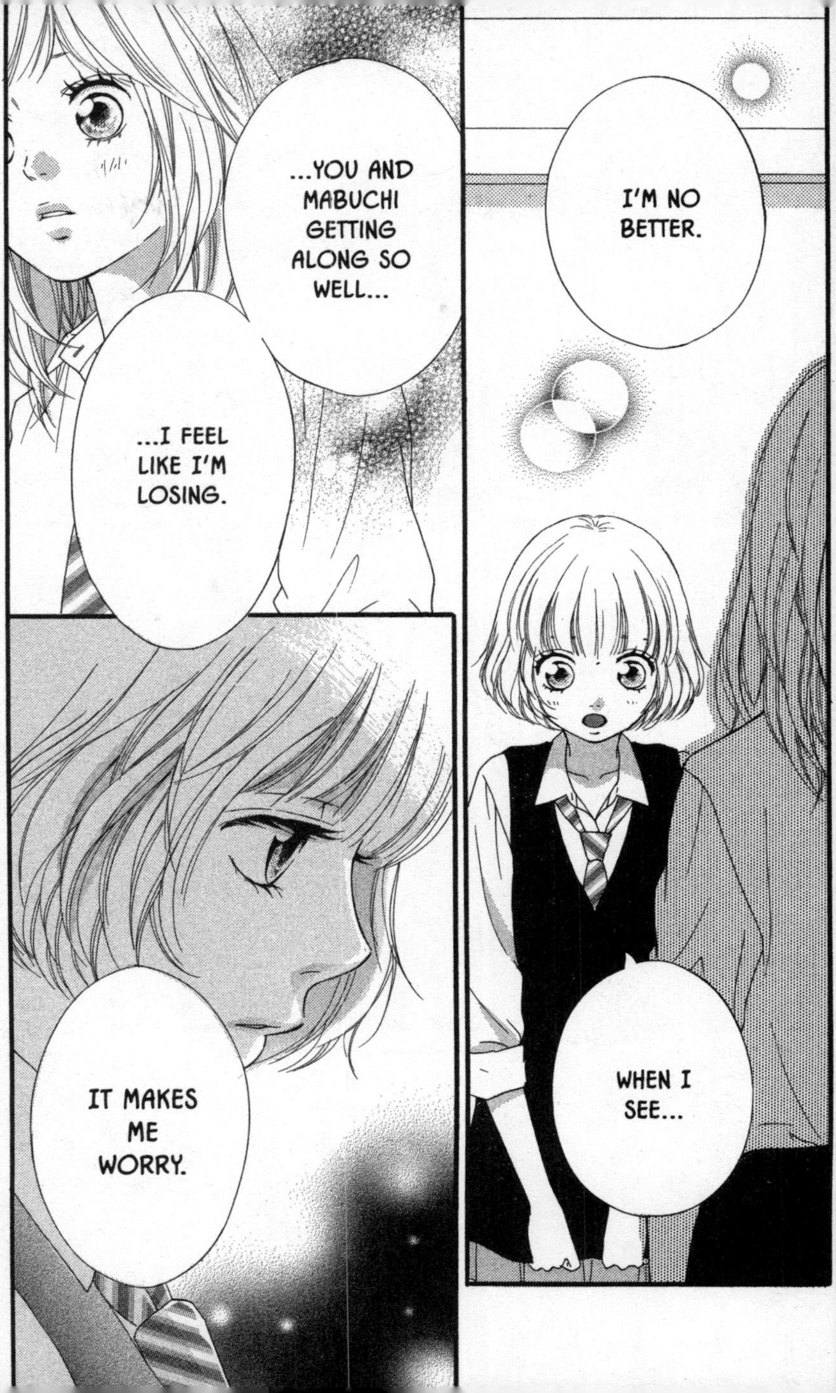
I'M NO BETTER.
WHEN I SEE...
...YOU AND MABUCHI GETTING ALONG SO WELL...
...I FEEL LIKE I'M LOSING.
IT MAKES ME WORRY.

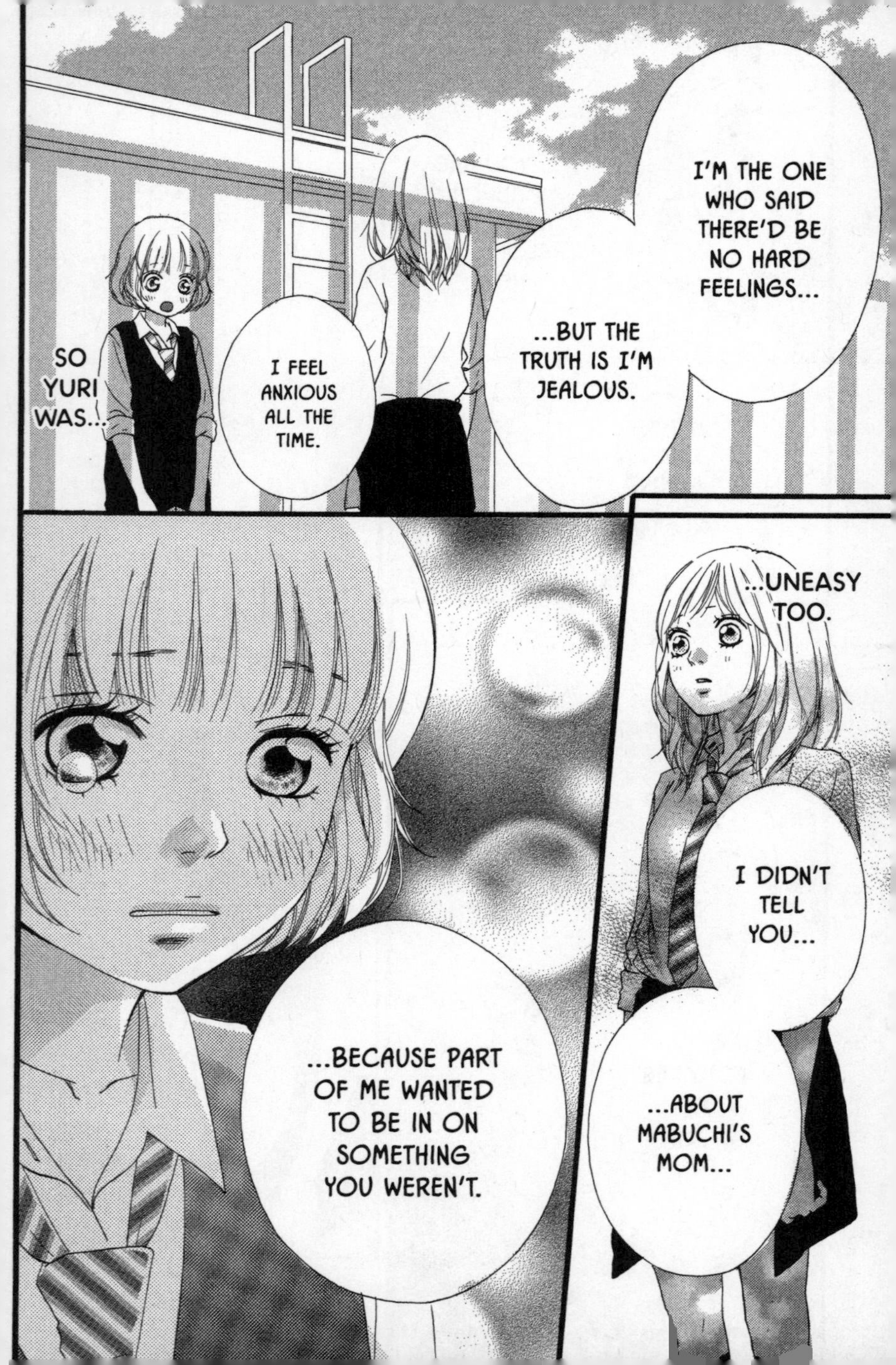
I'M THE ONE WHO SAID THERE'D BE NO HARD FEELINGS...
...BUT THE TRUTH IS I'M JEALOUS.
I FEEL ANXIOUS ALL THE TIME.
SO YURI WAS...
...UNEASY TOO.
I DIDN'T TELL YOU...
...ABOUT MABUCHI'S MOM...
...BECAUSE PART OF ME WANTED TO BE IN ON SOMETHING YOU WEREN'T.

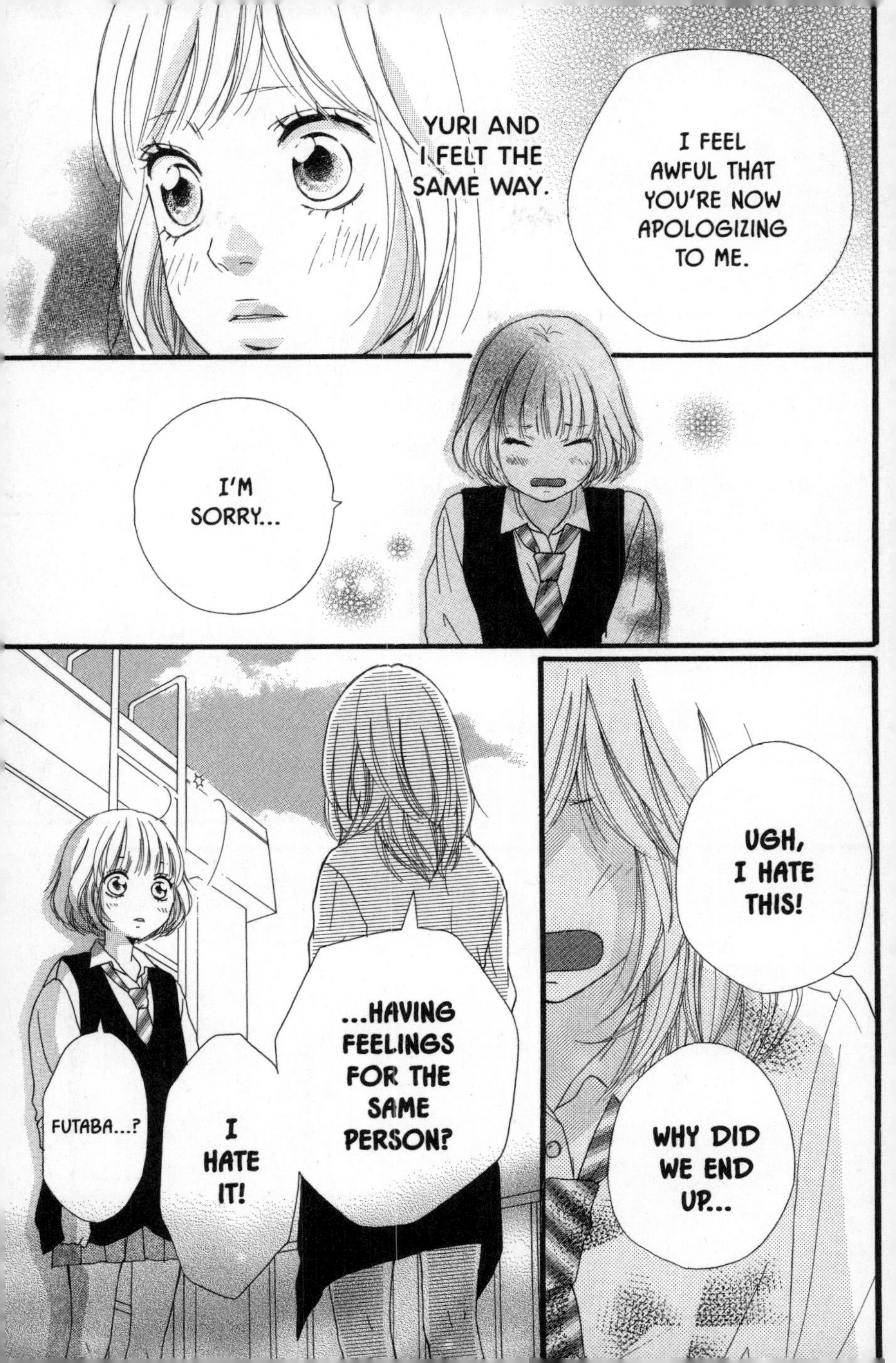
I FEEL AWFUL THAT YOU'RE NOW APOLOGIZING TO ME.
YURI AND I FELT THE SAME WAY.
I'M SORRY...
UGH, I HATE THIS!
WHY DID WE END UP...
...HAVING FEELINGS FOR THE SAME PERSON?
I HATE IT!
FUTABA...?

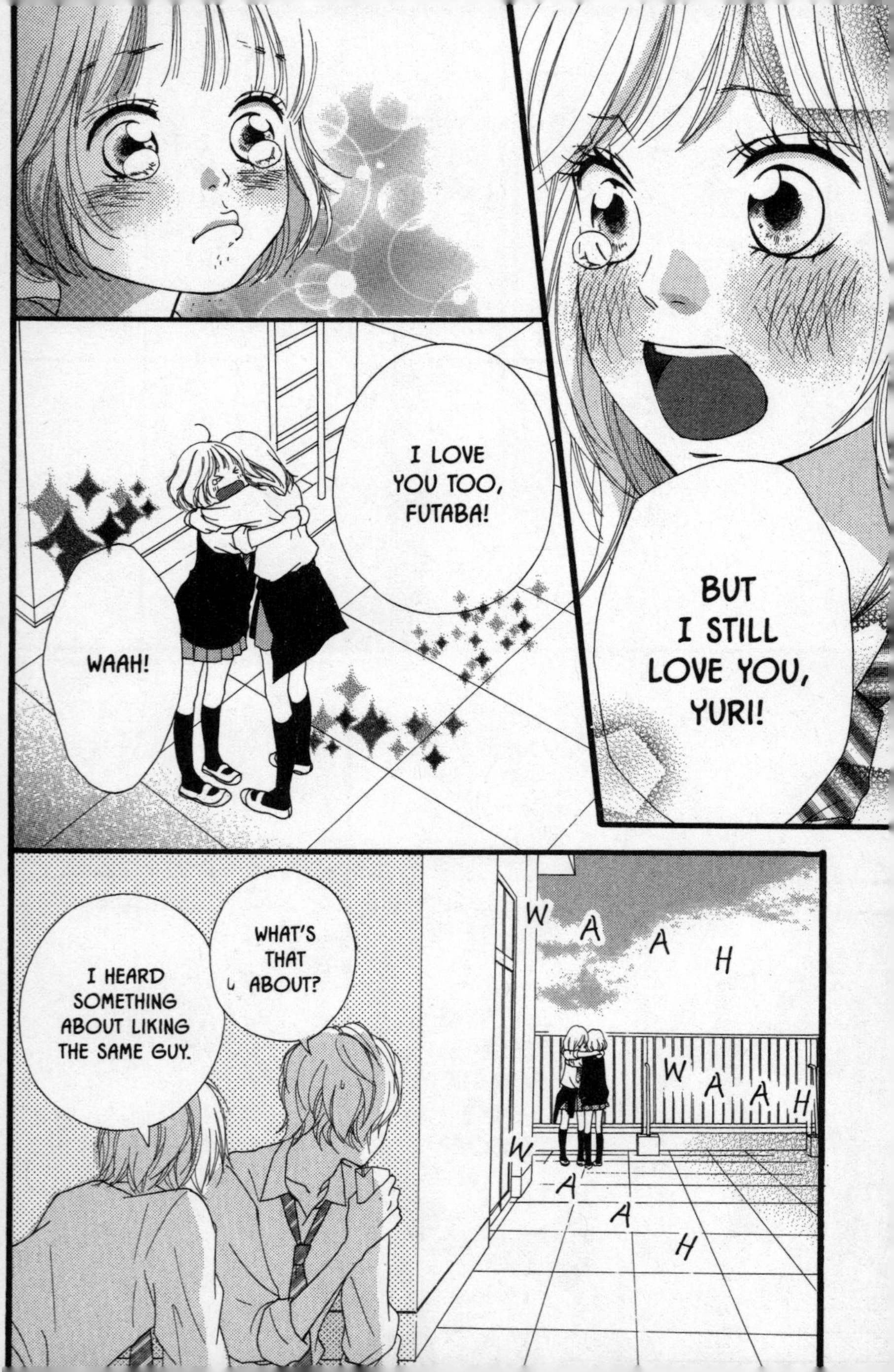
BUT I STILL LOVE YOU, YURI!
I LOVE YOU TOO, FUTABA!
WAAH!
WAAH
WAAAH
WAAAH
WHAT'S THAT ABOUT?
I HEARD SOMETHING ABOUT LIKING THE SAME GUY.

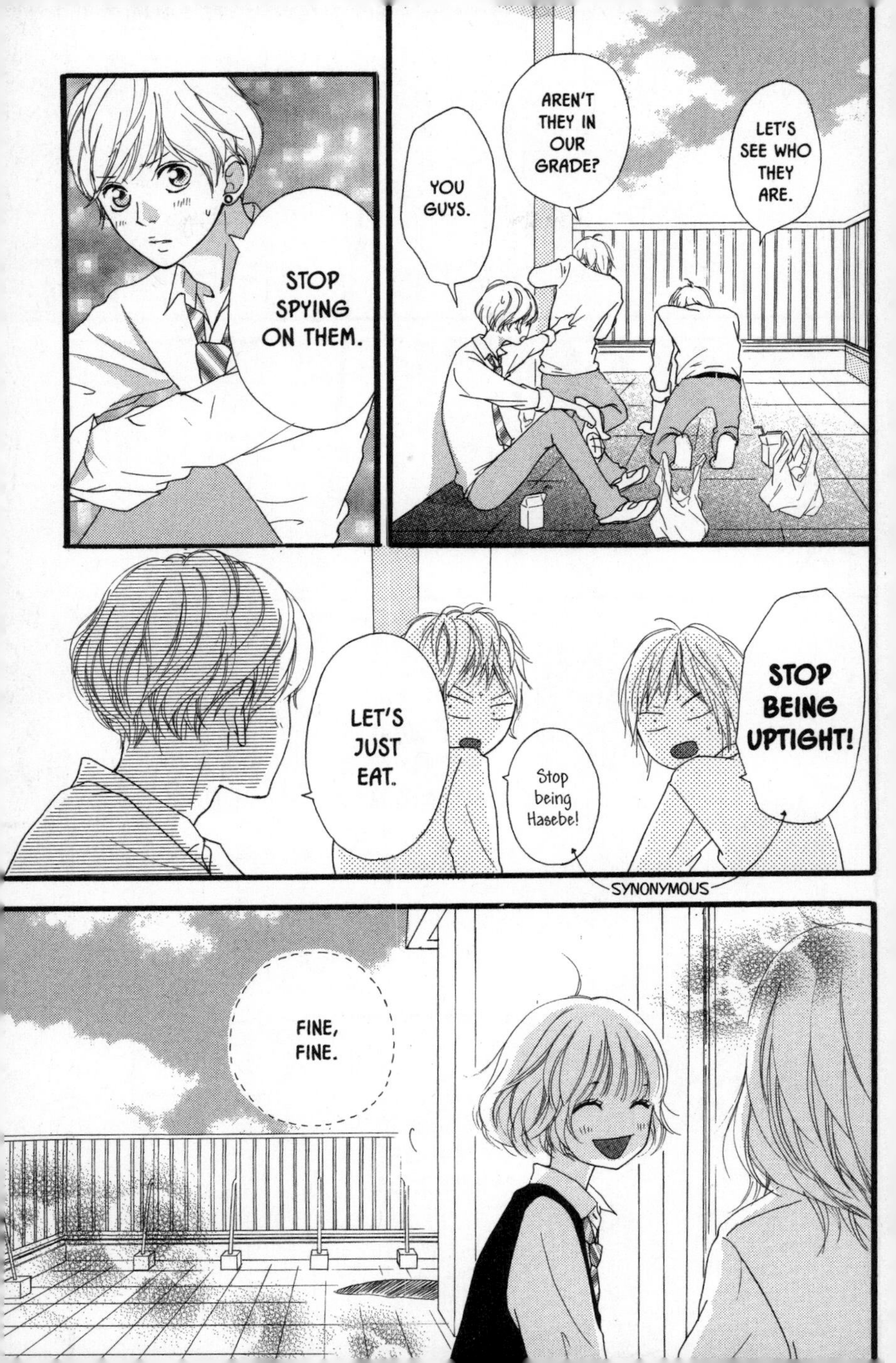
LET'S SEE WHO THEY ARE.
AREN'T THEY IN OUR GRADE?
YOU GUYS.
STOP SPYING ON THEM.
STOP BEING UPTIGHT!
Stop being Hasebe!
LET'S JUST EAT.
SYNONYMOUS
FINE, FINE.

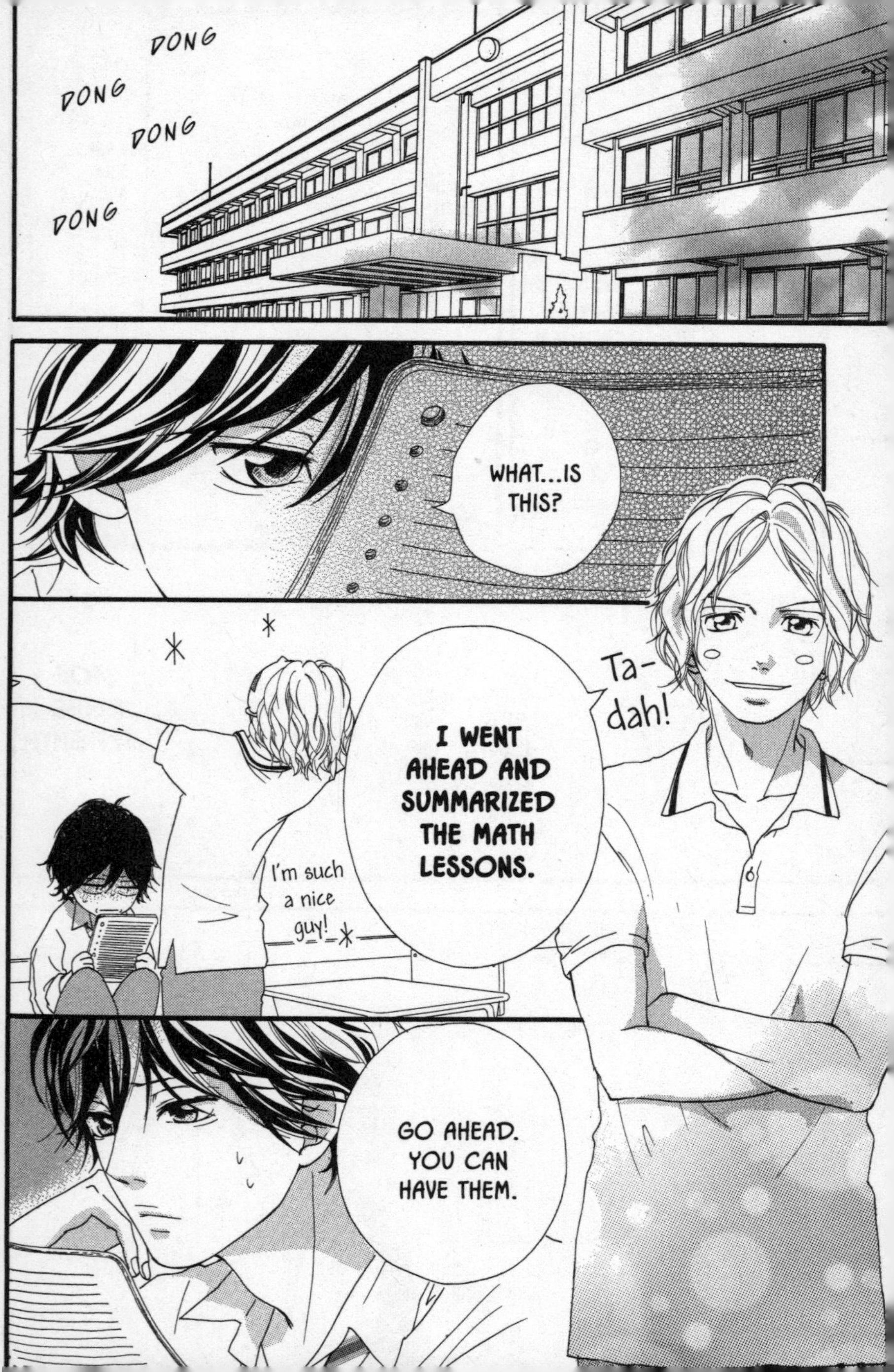
DONG
DONG
DONG
DONG
WHAT...IS THIS?
Ta-dah!
I WENT AHEAD AND SUMMARIZED THE MATH LESSONS.
I'm such a nice guy!
GO AHEAD. YOU CAN HAVE THEM.

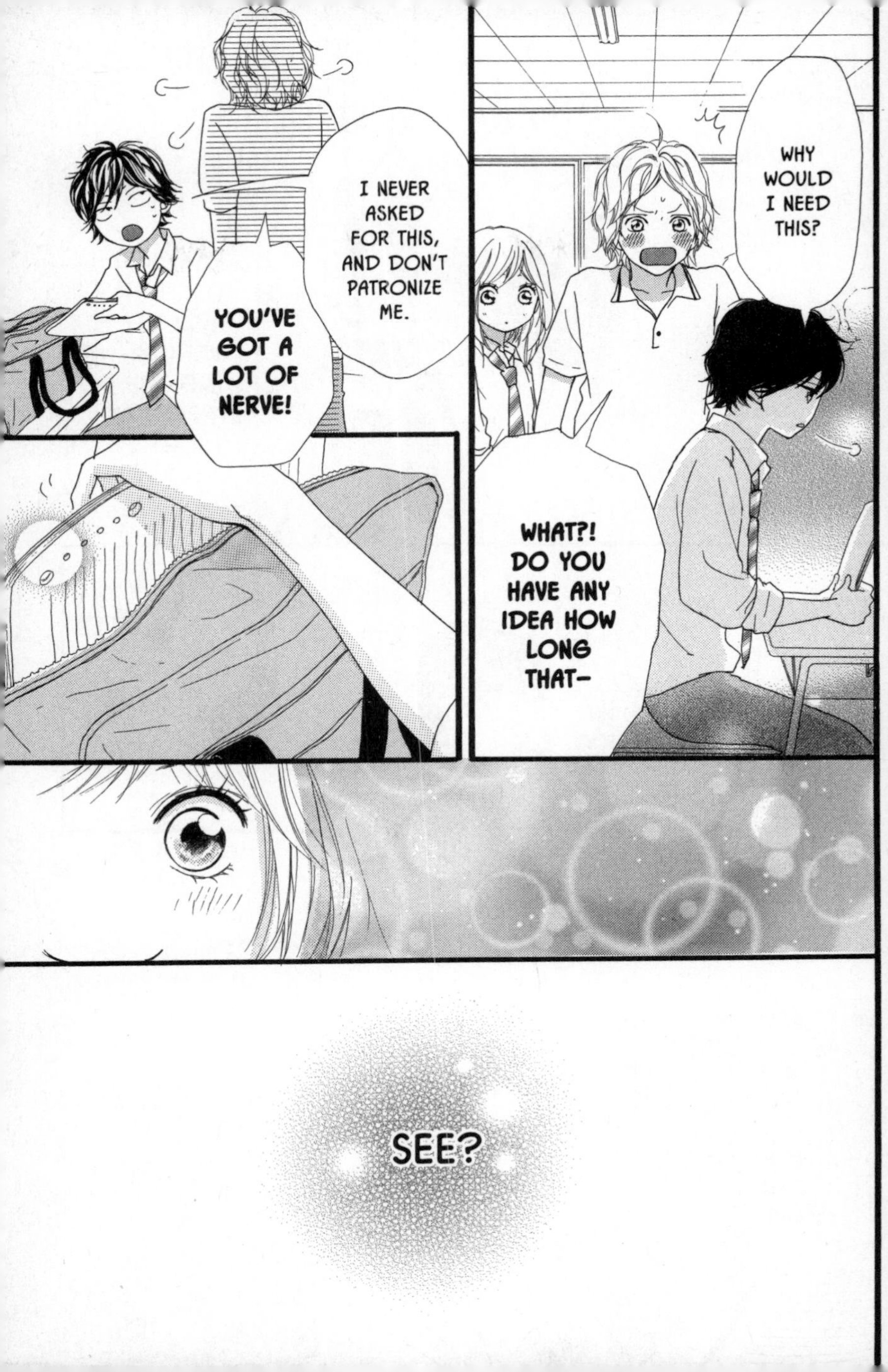
WHY WOULD I NEED THIS?
WHAT?! DO YOU HAVE ANY IDEA HOW LONG THAT-
I NEVER ASKED FOR THIS, AND DON'T PATRONIZE ME.
YOU'VE GOT A LOT OF NERVE!
SEE?

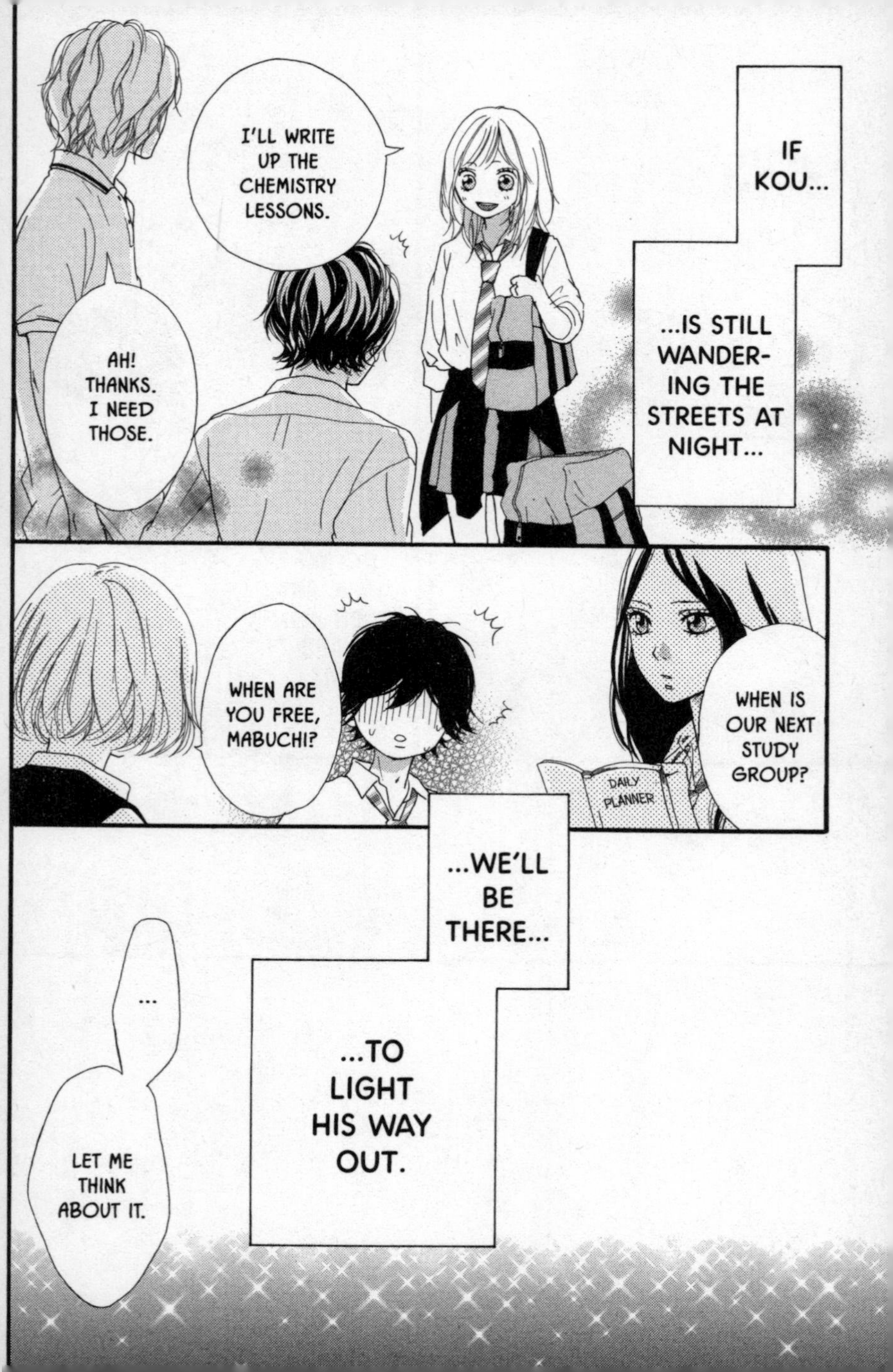
IF KOU...
...IS STILL WANDER-ING THE STREETS AT NIGHT...
I'LL WRITE UP THE CHEMISTRY LESSONS.
AH! THANKS. I NEED THOSE.
WHEN IS OUR NEXT STUDY GROUP?
DAILY PLANNER
WHEN ARE YOU FREE, MABUCHI?
...WE'LL BE THERE...
...TO LIGHT HIS WAY OUT.
...
LET ME THINK ABOUT IT.

AO HARU RIDE CHARACTERS ⑤

Shuko Murao

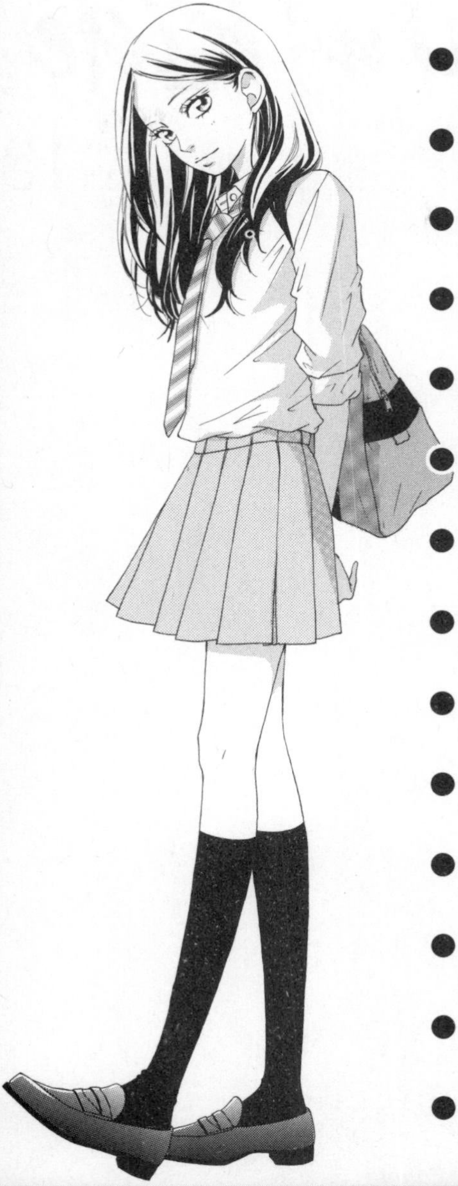

Birthday:
November 20th

Astrological Sign, Blood Type:
Scorpio, type A

Height, Weight:
5'6", 108 lbs.

Favorite Subject:
English

Least Favorite Subject:
Science

Favorite Food:
Avocado sandwich

Least Favorite Food:
Eel

Favorite Music:
Sakanaction

Siblings:
Older sister

Age When First Crush Happened:
Third grade

Fun Fact:
I like watching comedy shows.

Favorite Snack:
Jagabee potato snacks

Favorite Drink:
Hot chocolate

Favorite Color:
Black

Ao Haru Ride

The scent of air after rain...
In the light around us, I felt your heartbeat.

CHAPTER 13

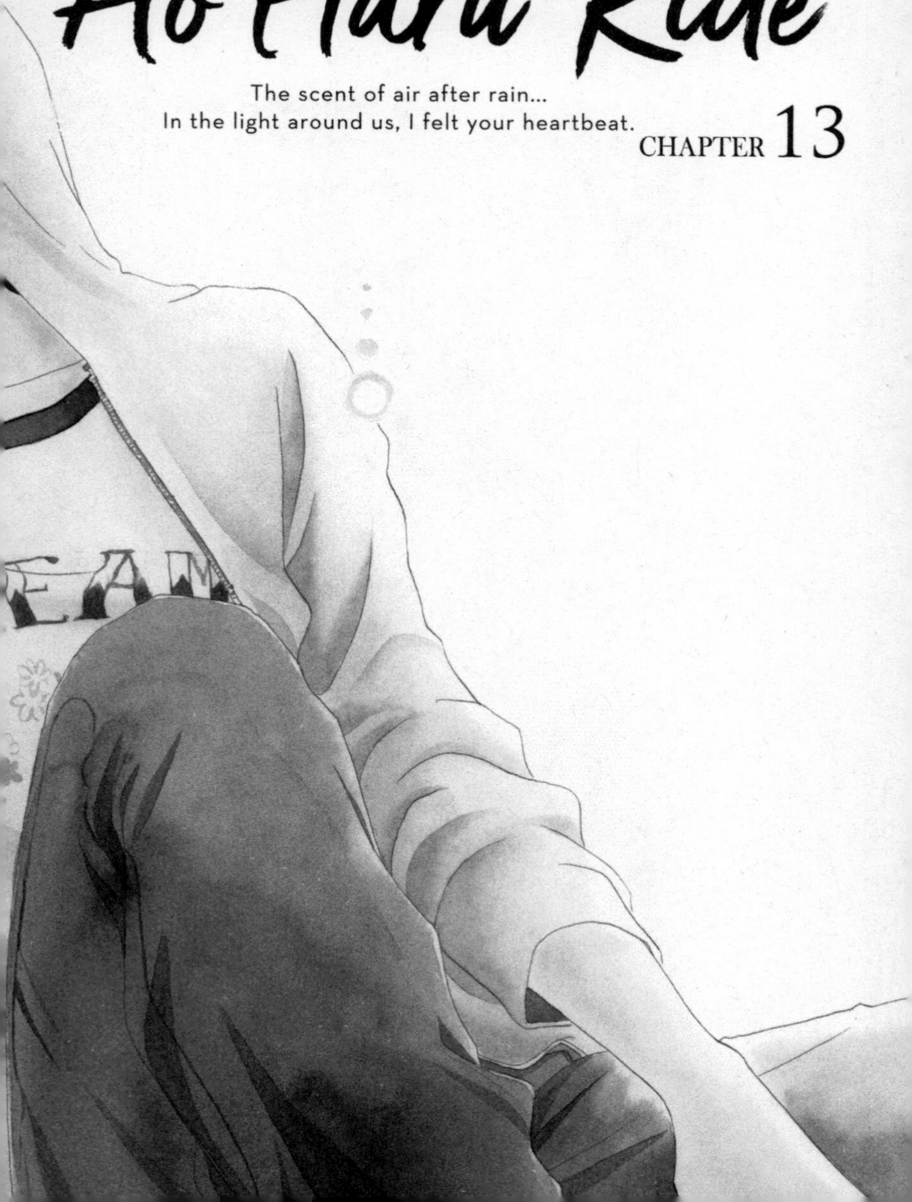

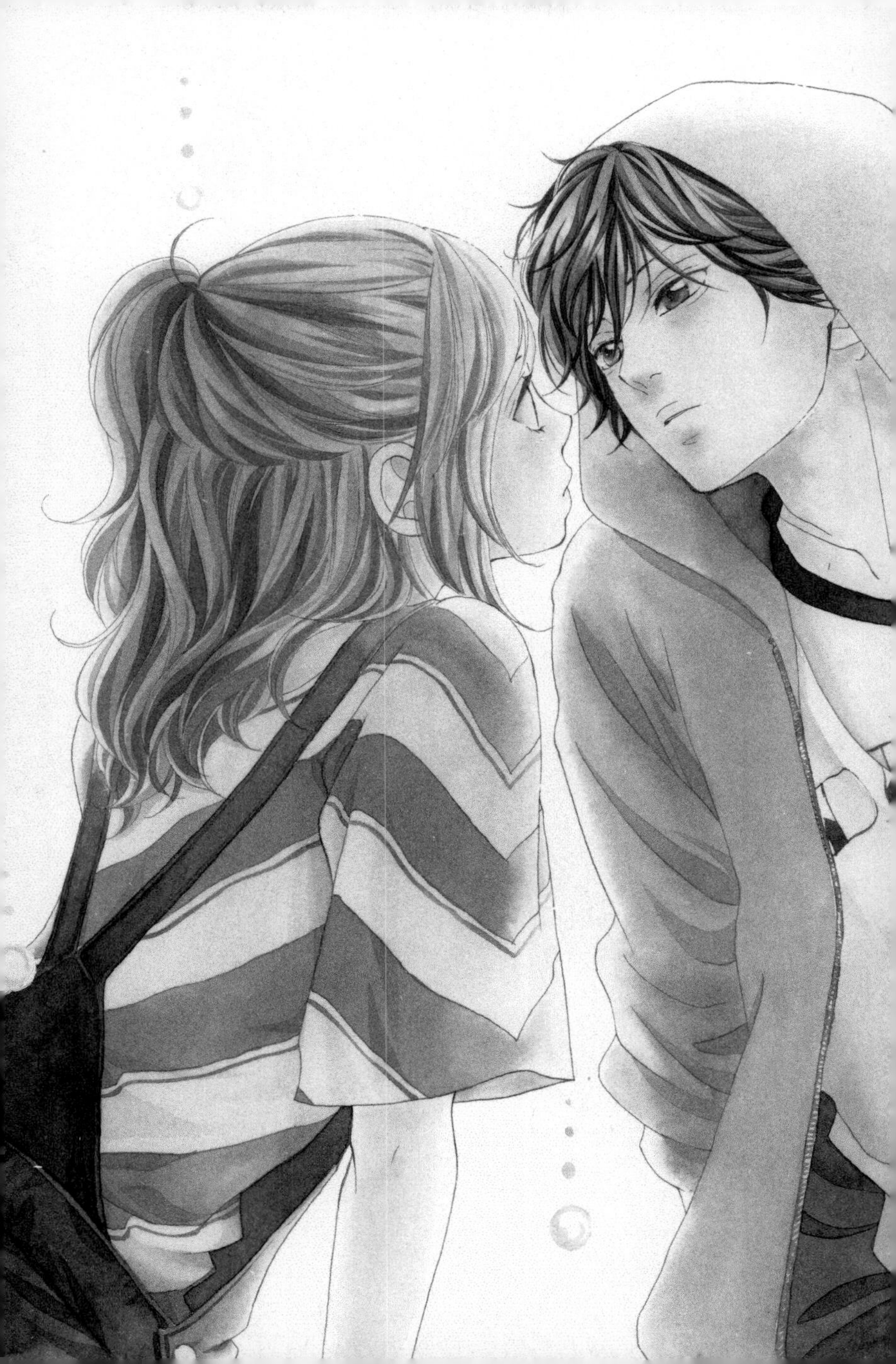

AO HARU RIDE CHARACTERS 6

Yoichi Tanaka

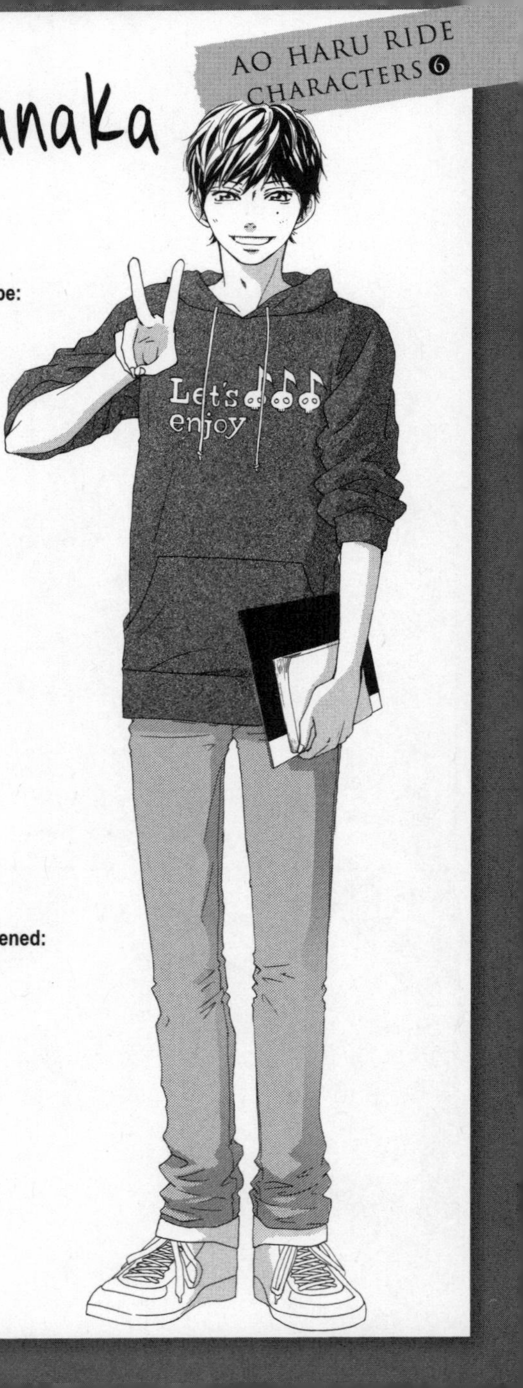
Let's
enjoy

- **Birthday:**
  April 30th
- **Astrological Sign, Blood Type:**
  Taurus, type O
- **Height, Weight:**
  5'11", 146 lbs.
- **Favorite Subject:**
  English
- **Least Favorite Subject:**
  Art
- **Favorite Food:**
  Curry
- **Least Favorite Food:**
  Liver
- **Favorite Music:**
  Janis Joplin
- **Siblings:**
  Younger brother
- **Age When First Crush Happened:**
  Second year of junior high
- **Fun Fact:**
  I can't wink.
- **Favorite Snack:**
  Crunchy pickled plums
- **Favorite Drink:**
  Cola
- **Favorite Color:**
  Emerald green

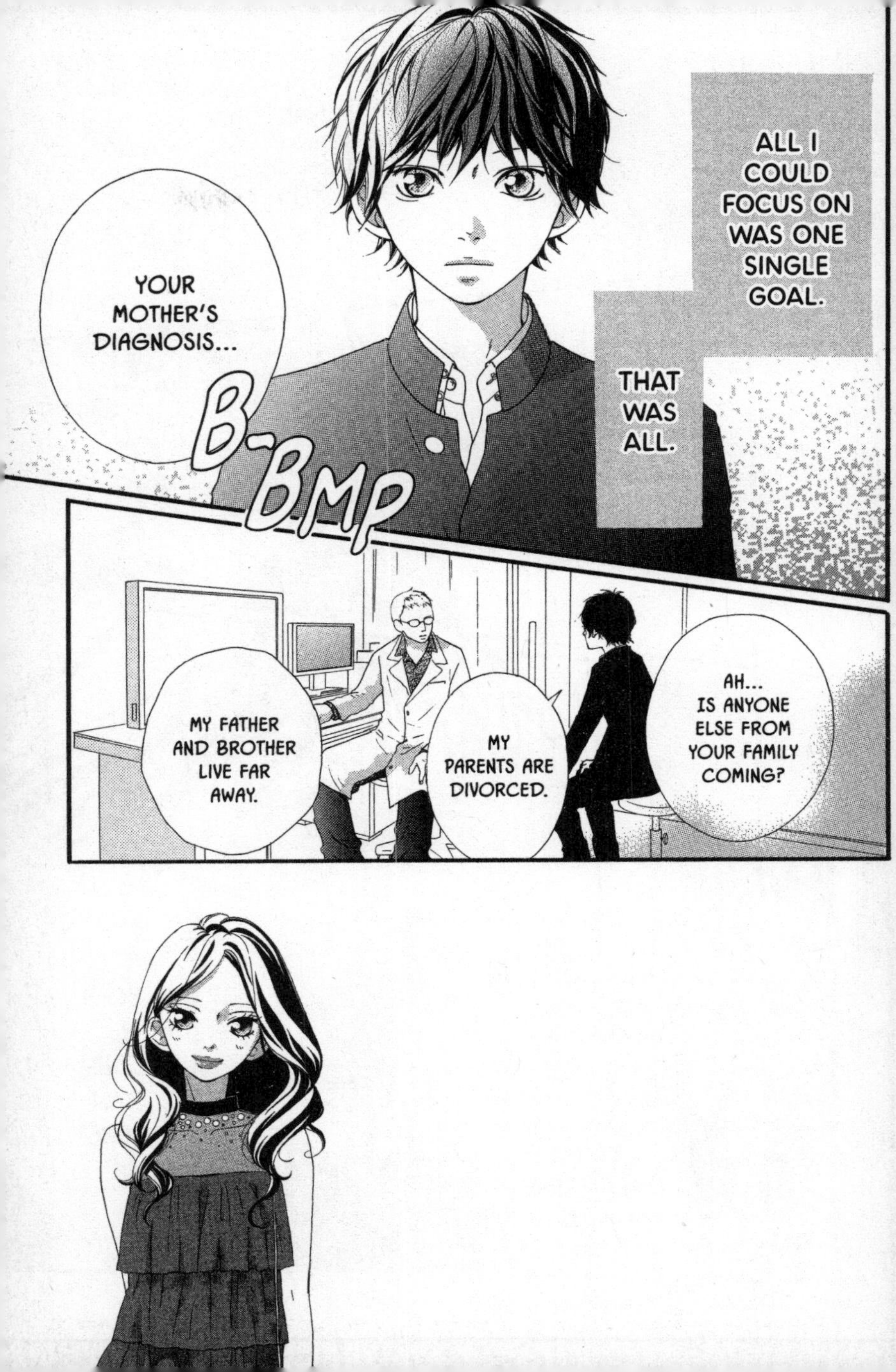
ALL I COULD FOCUS ON WAS ONE SINGLE GOAL.
THAT WAS ALL.
YOUR MOTHER'S DIAGNOSIS...
B-BMP
AH... IS ANYONE ELSE FROM YOUR FAMILY COMING?
MY PARENTS ARE DIVORCED.
MY FATHER AND BROTHER LIVE FAR AWAY.

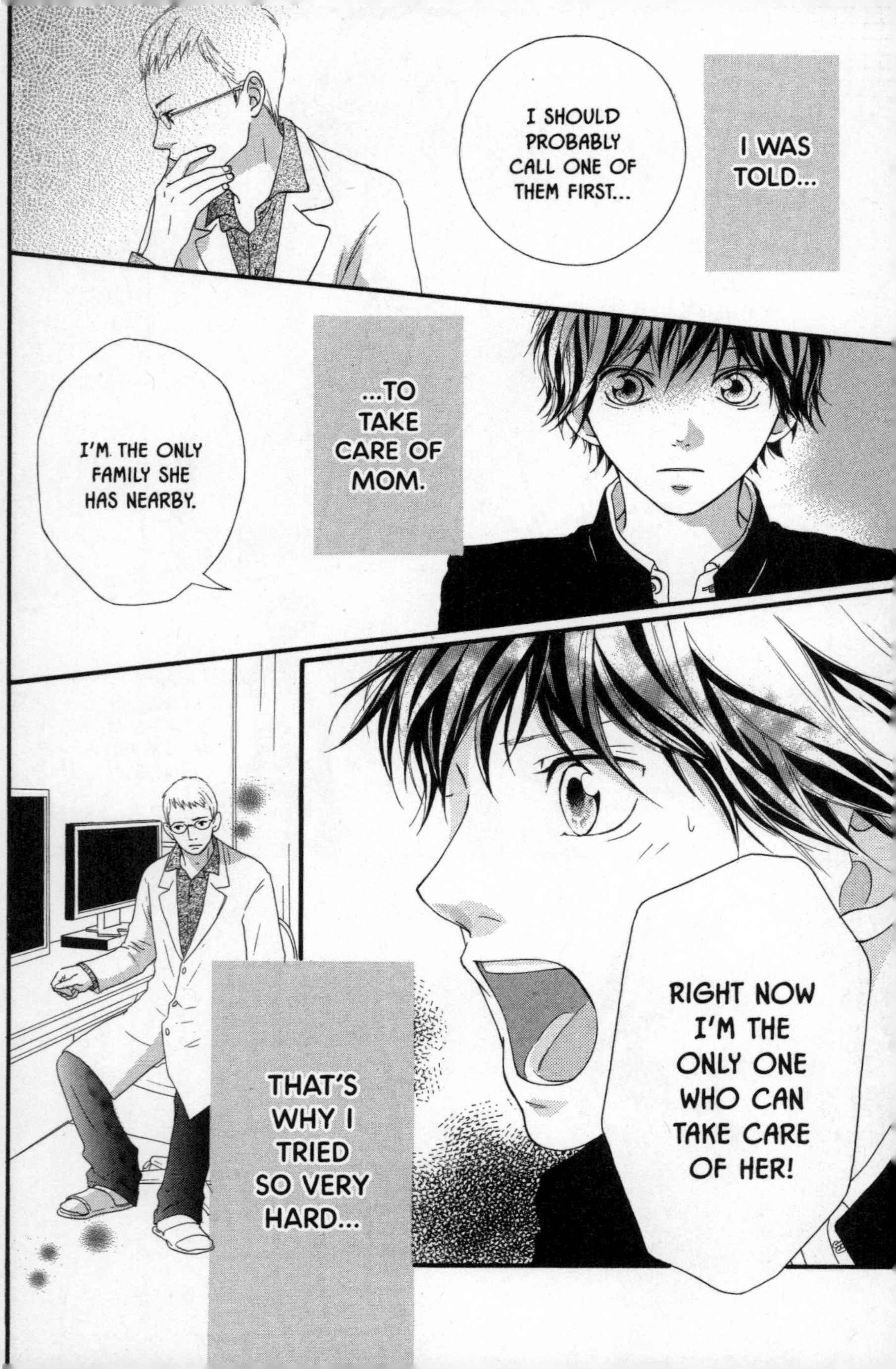
I WAS TOLD...
I SHOULD PROBABLY CALL ONE OF THEM FIRST...
...TO TAKE CARE OF MOM.
I'M THE ONLY FAMILY SHE HAS NEARBY.
RIGHT NOW I'M THE ONLY ONE WHO CAN TAKE CARE OF HER!
THAT'S WHY I TRIED SO VERY HARD...

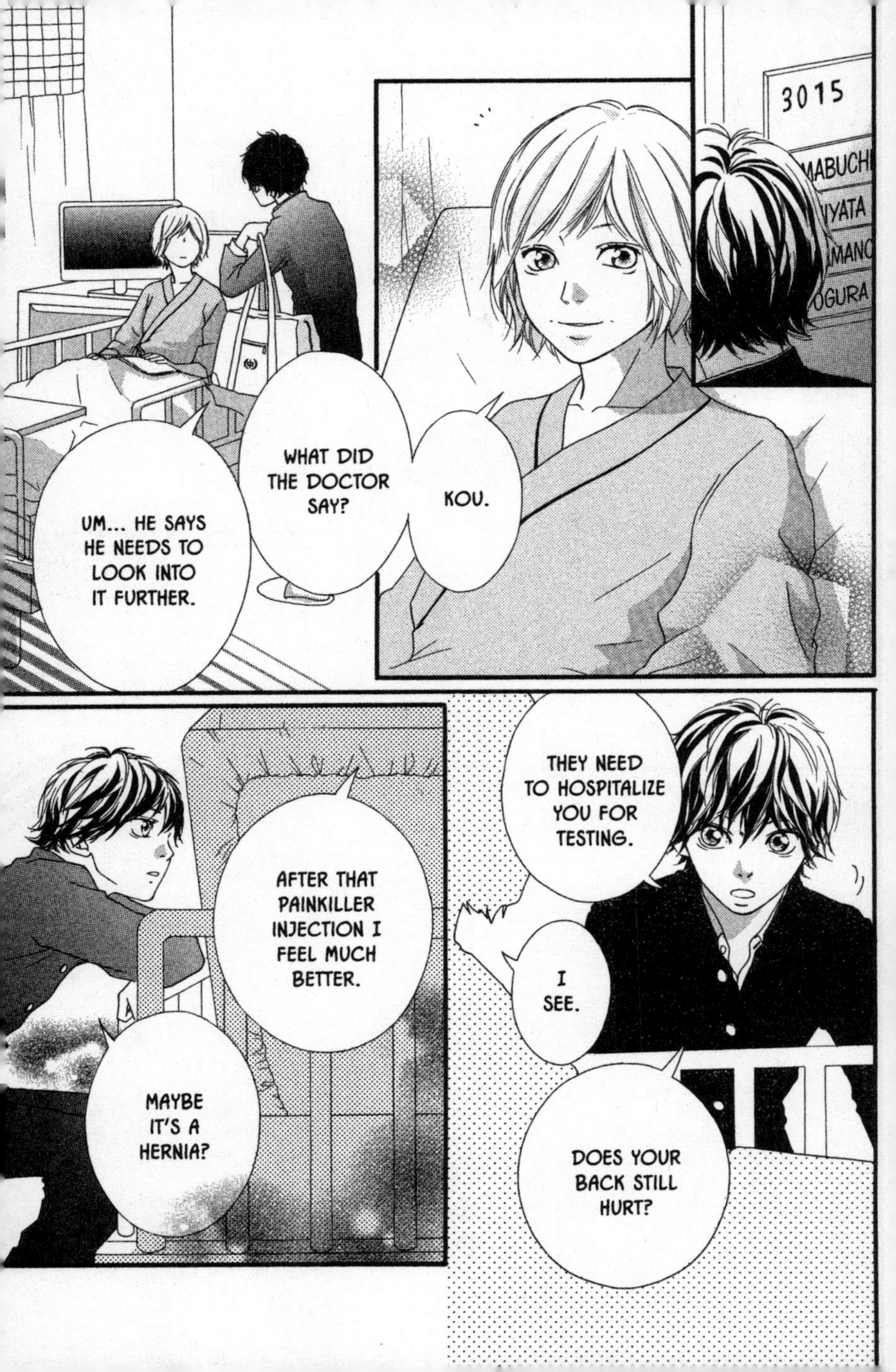
3015
KOU.
WHAT DID THE DOCTOR SAY?
UM... HE SAYS HE NEEDS TO LOOK INTO IT FURTHER.
THEY NEED TO HOSPITALIZE YOU FOR TESTING.
I SEE.
DOES YOUR BACK STILL HURT?
AFTER THAT PAINKILLER INJECTION I FEEL MUCH BETTER.
MAYBE IT'S A HERNIA?

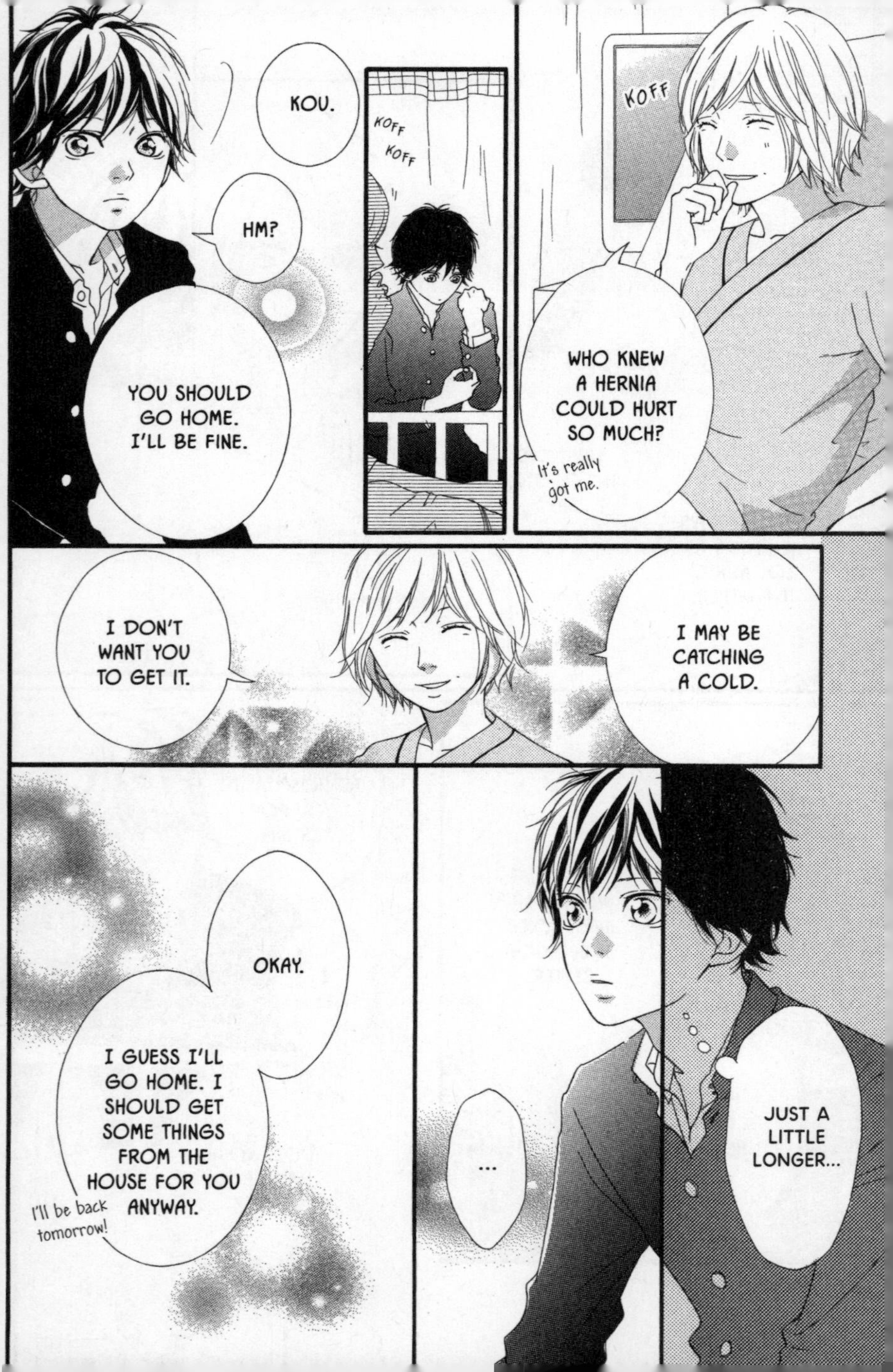
KOFF
WHO KNEW A HERNIA COULD HURT SO MUCH?
It's really got me.
KOFF
KOFF
KOU.
HM?
YOU SHOULD GO HOME. I'LL BE FINE.
I MAY BE CATCHING A COLD.
I DON'T WANT YOU TO GET IT.
JUST A LITTLE LONGER...
...
OKAY.
I GUESS I'LL GO HOME. I SHOULD GET SOME THINGS FROM THE HOUSE FOR YOU ANYWAY.
I'll be back tomorrow!

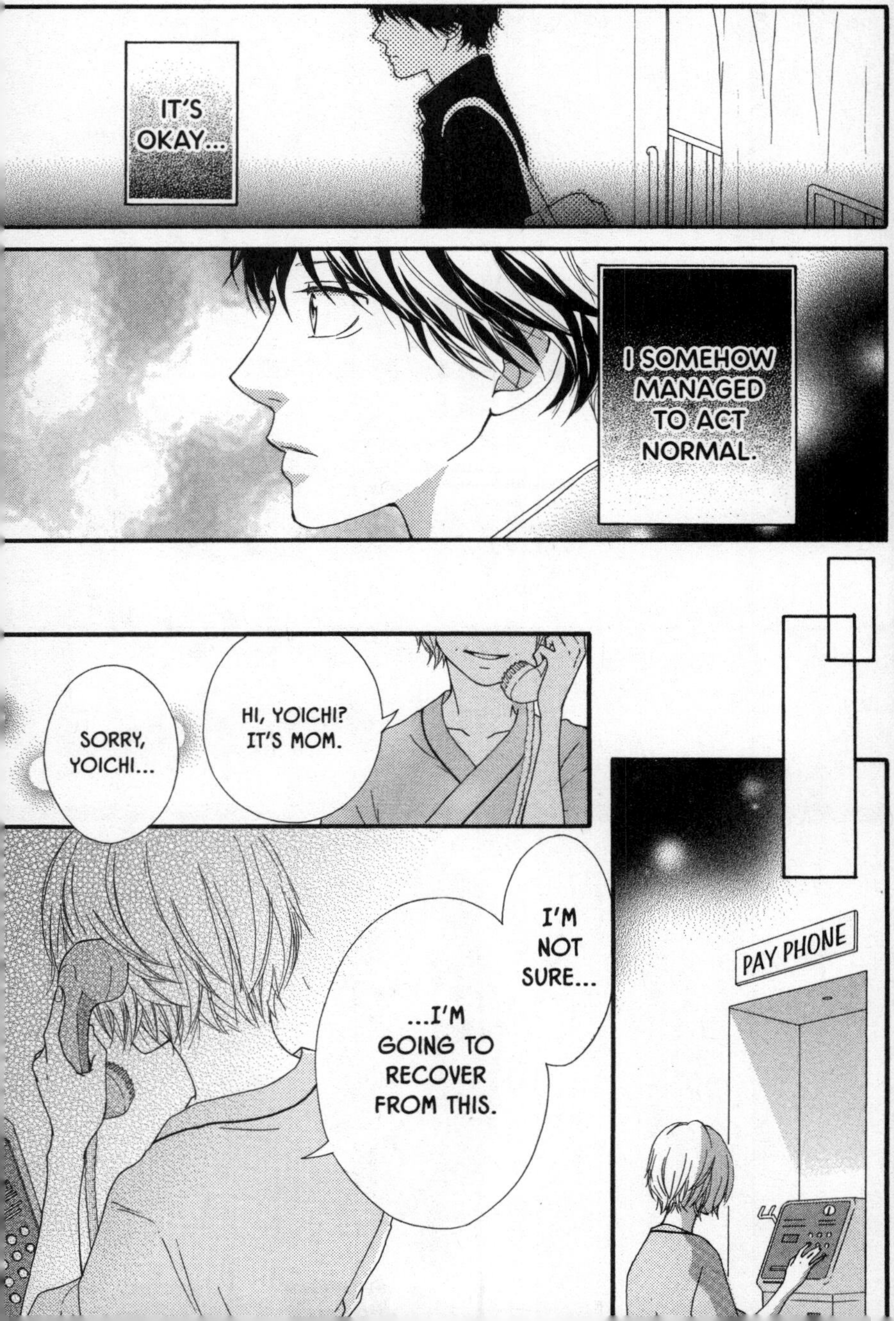
IT'S OKAY...
I SOMEHOW MANAGED TO ACT NORMAL.
PAY PHONE
HI, YOICHI? IT'S MOM.
SORRY, YOICHI...
I'M NOT SURE...
...I'M GOING TO RECOVER FROM THIS.

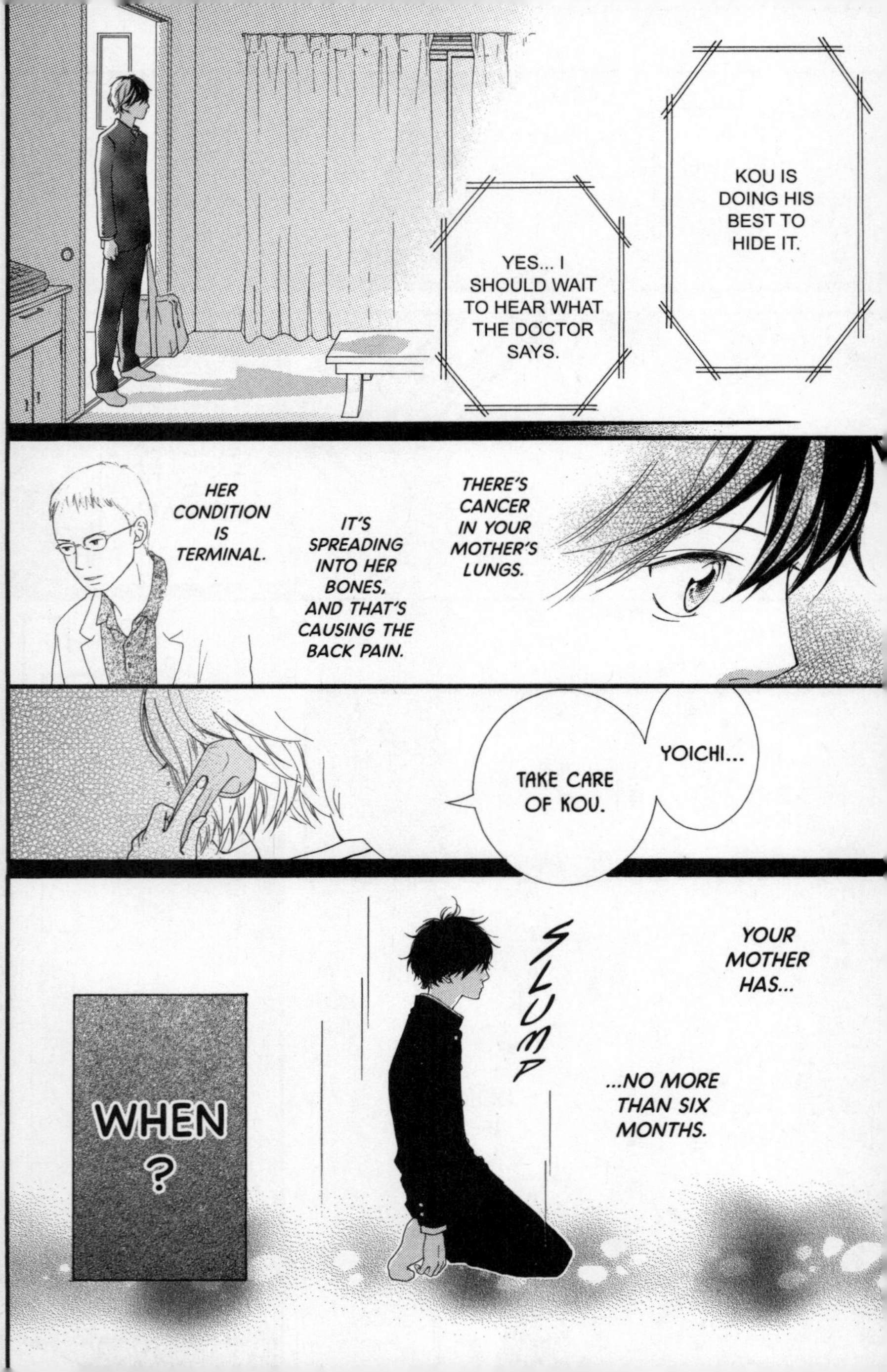
KOU IS DOING HIS BEST TO HIDE IT.
YES... I SHOULD WAIT TO HEAR WHAT THE DOCTOR SAYS.
THERE'S CANCER IN YOUR MOTHER'S LUNGS.
IT'S SPREADING INTO HER BONES, AND THAT'S CAUSING THE BACK PAIN.
HER CONDITION IS TERMINAL.
YOICHI...
TAKE CARE OF KOU.
YOUR MOTHER HAS...
...NO MORE THAN SIX MONTHS.
SLUMP
WHEN?

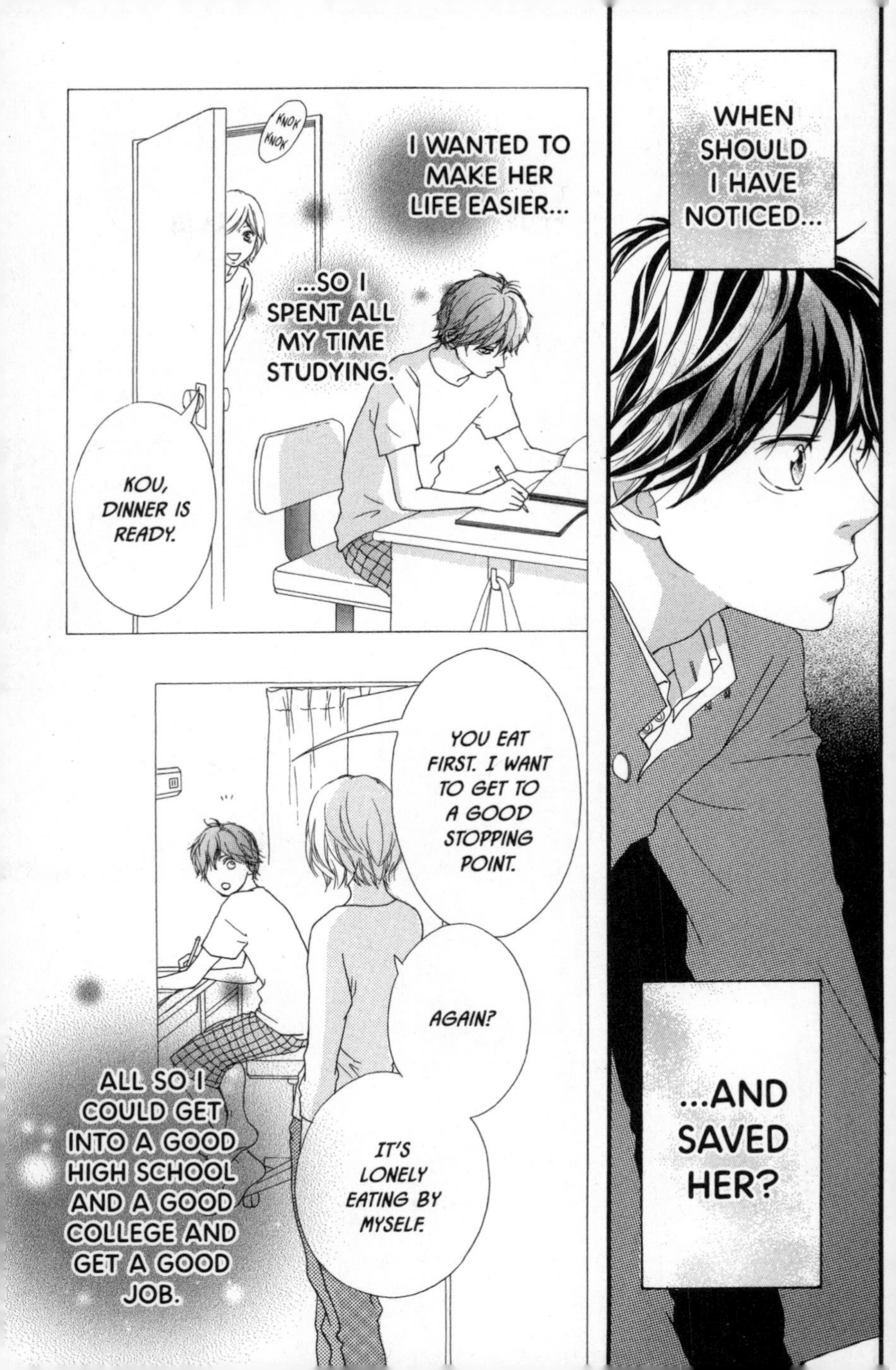
WHEN SHOULD I HAVE NOTICED...
...AND SAVED HER?
I WANTED TO MAKE HER LIFE EASIER...
KNOK KNOK
...SO I SPENT ALL MY TIME STUDYING.
KOU, DINNER IS READY.
YOU EAT FIRST. I WANT TO GET TO A GOOD STOPPING POINT.
AGAIN?
IT'S LONELY EATING BY MYSELF.
ALL SO I COULD GET INTO A GOOD HIGH SCHOOL AND A GOOD COLLEGE AND GET A GOOD JOB.

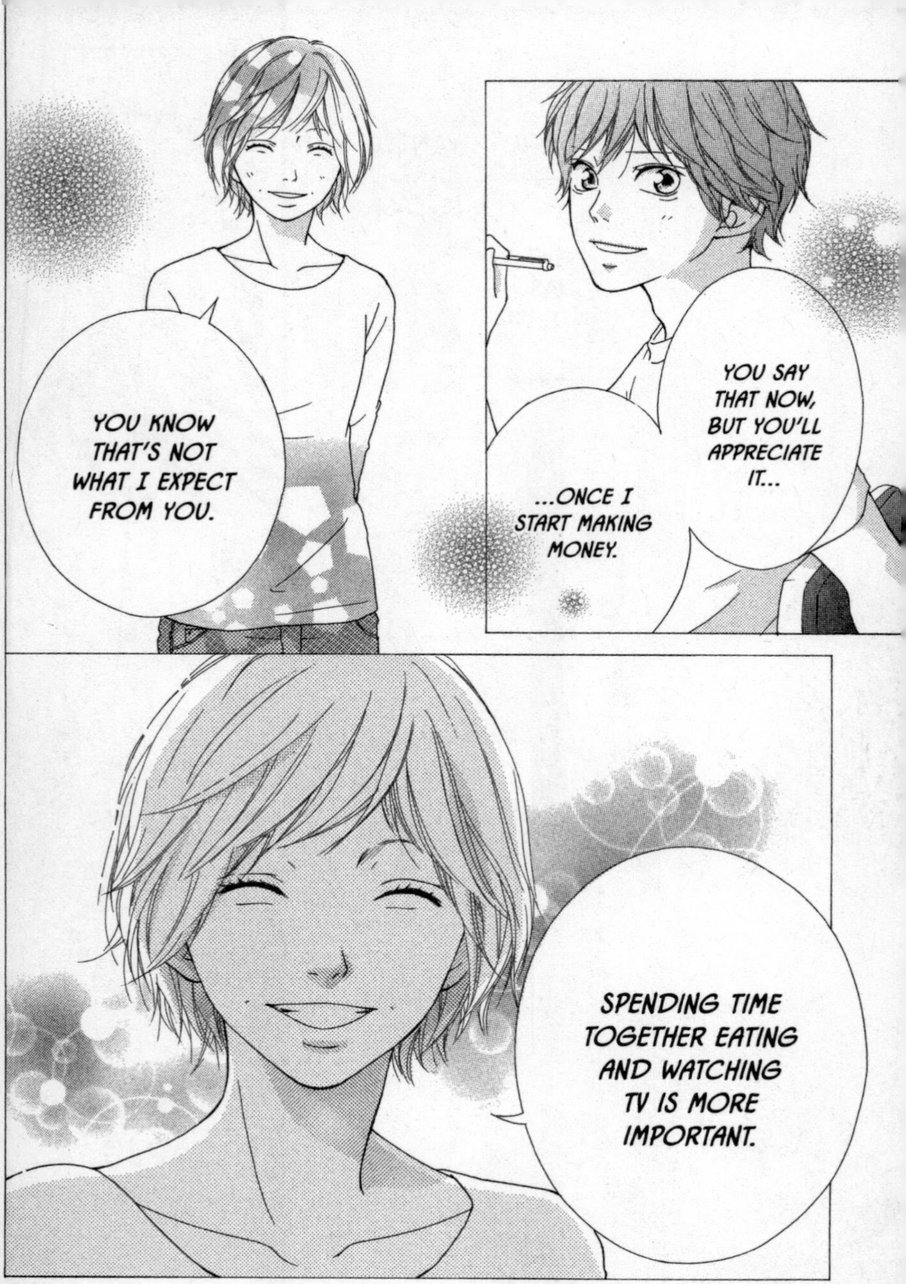
YOU SAY THAT NOW, BUT YOU'LL APPRECIATE IT...
...ONCE I START MAKING MONEY.
YOU KNOW THAT'S NOT WHAT I EXPECT FROM YOU.
SPENDING TIME TOGETHER EATING AND WATCHING TV IS MORE IMPORTANT.

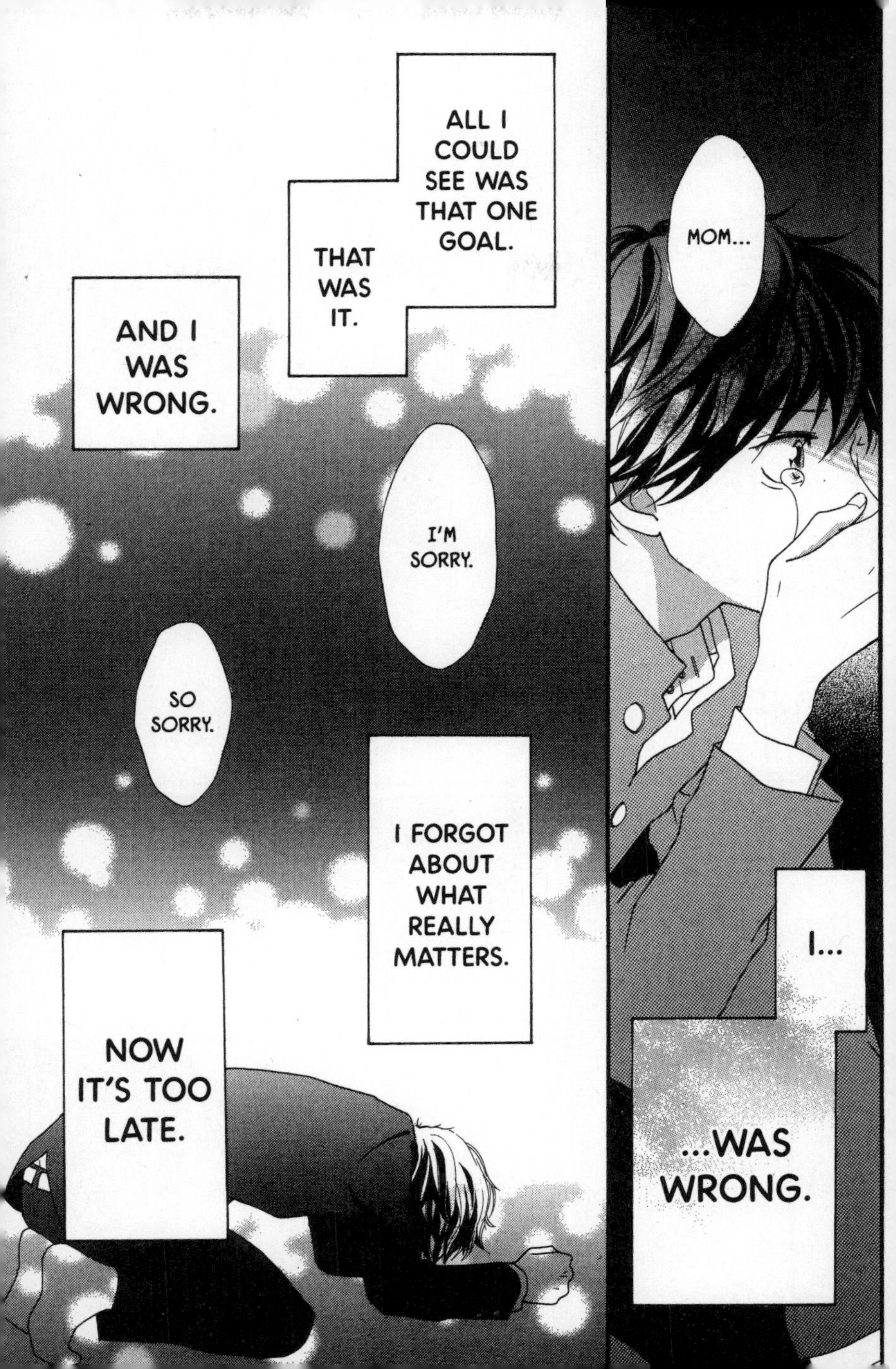
MOM...
I...
...WAS WRONG.
ALL I COULD SEE WAS THAT ONE GOAL.
THAT WAS IT.
AND I WAS WRONG.
I'M SORRY.
SO SORRY.
I FORGOT ABOUT WHAT REALLY MATTERS.
NOW IT'S TOO LATE.

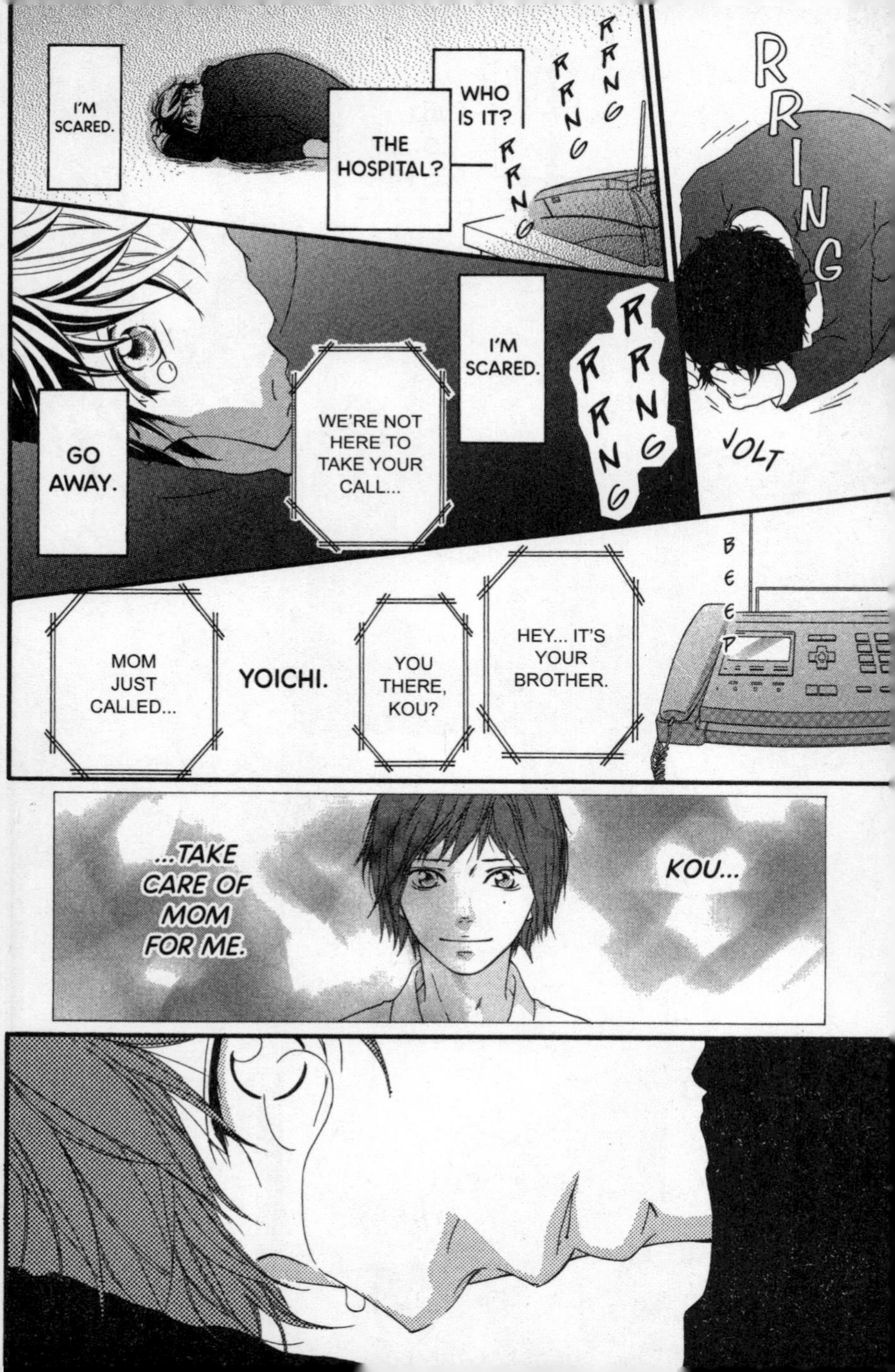
RRING
JOLT
RRNG
RRNG
RRNG
WHO IS IT?
THE HOSPITAL?
I'M SCARED.
RRNG
RRNG
I'M SCARED.
WE'RE NOT HERE TO TAKE YOUR CALL...
GO AWAY.
BEEP
HEY... IT'S YOUR BROTHER.
YOU THERE, KOU?
YOICHI.
MOM JUST CALLED...
KOU...
...TAKE CARE OF MOM FOR ME.

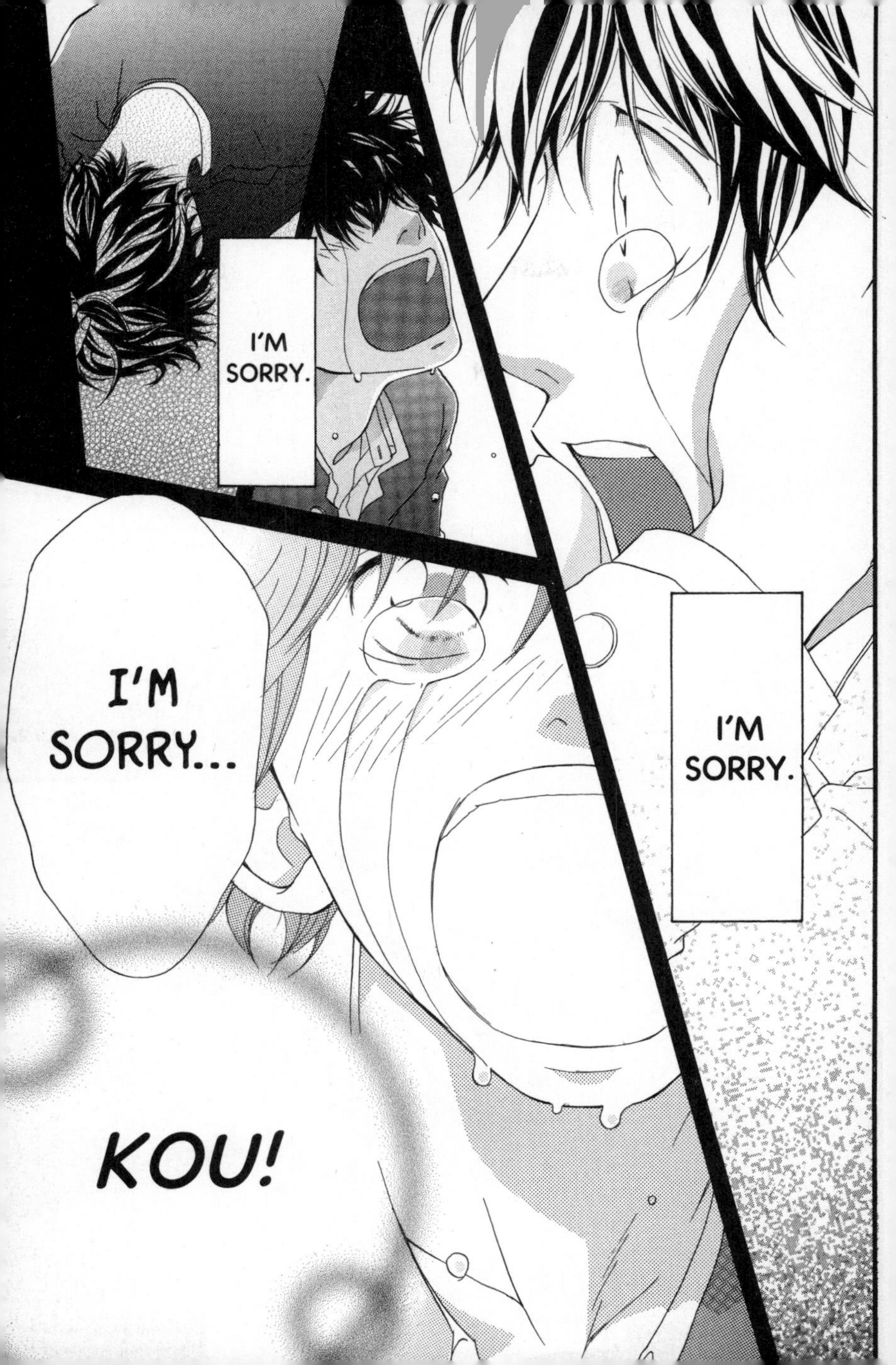
I'M SORRY.
I'M SORRY.
I'M SORRY...
KOU!

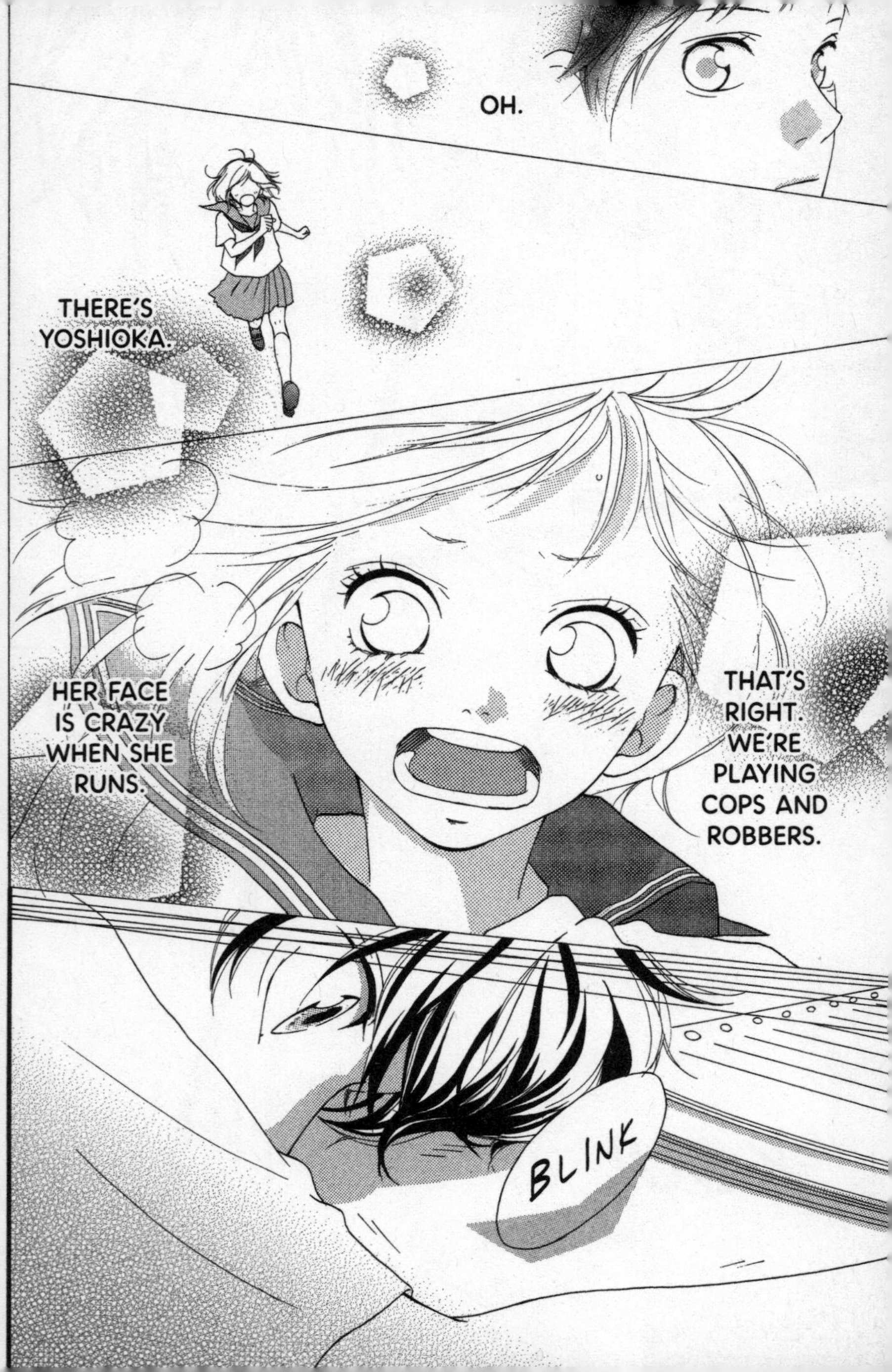
OH.
THERE'S YOSHIOKA.
THAT'S RIGHT. WE'RE PLAYING COPS AND ROBBERS.
HER FACE IS CRAZY WHEN SHE RUNS.
BLINK

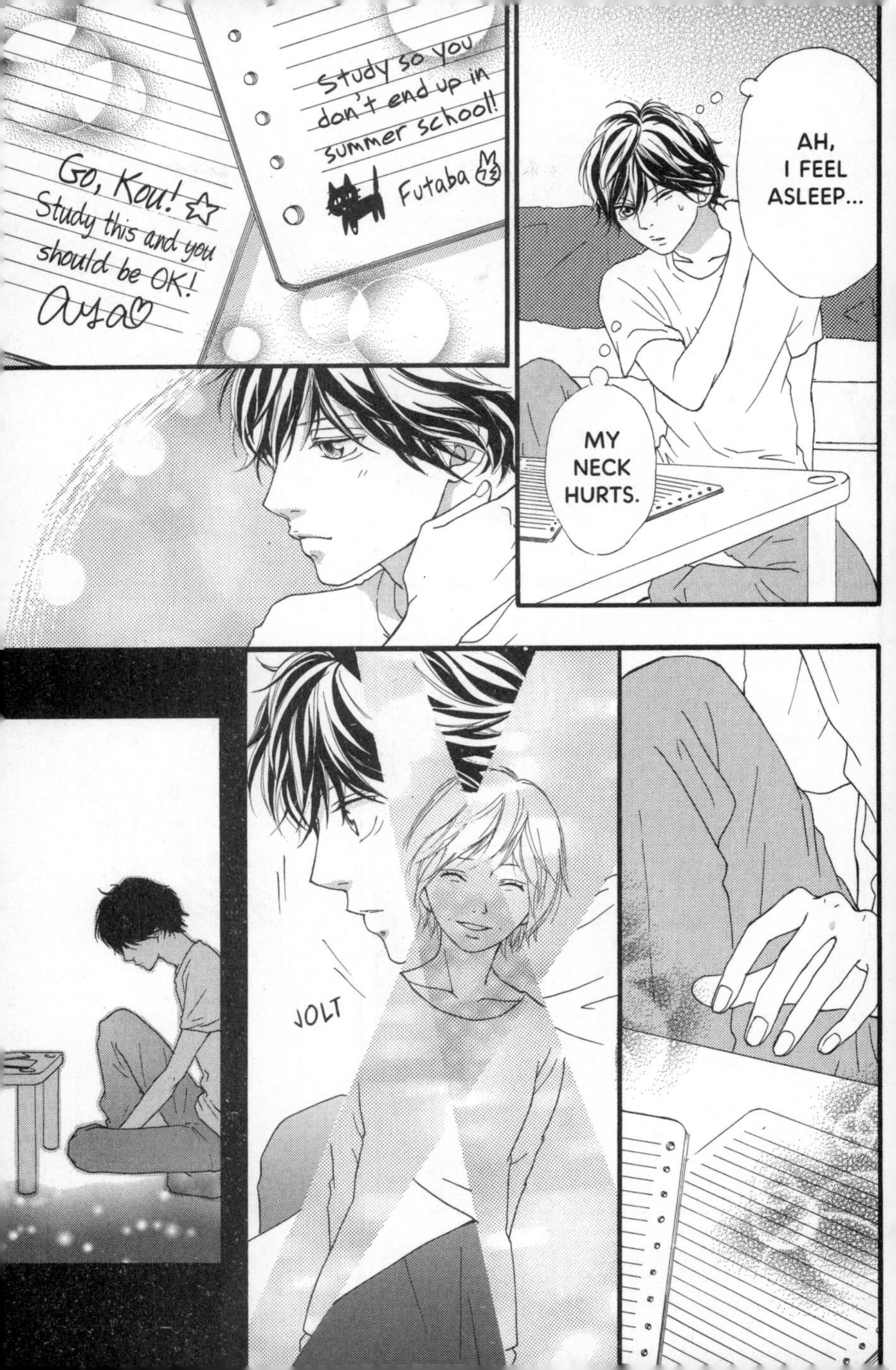
AH, I FEEL ASLEEP...
MY NECK HURTS.
Study so you don't end up in summer school!!
Futaba
Go, Kou! ☆
Study this and you should be OK!
Aya♡
JOLT

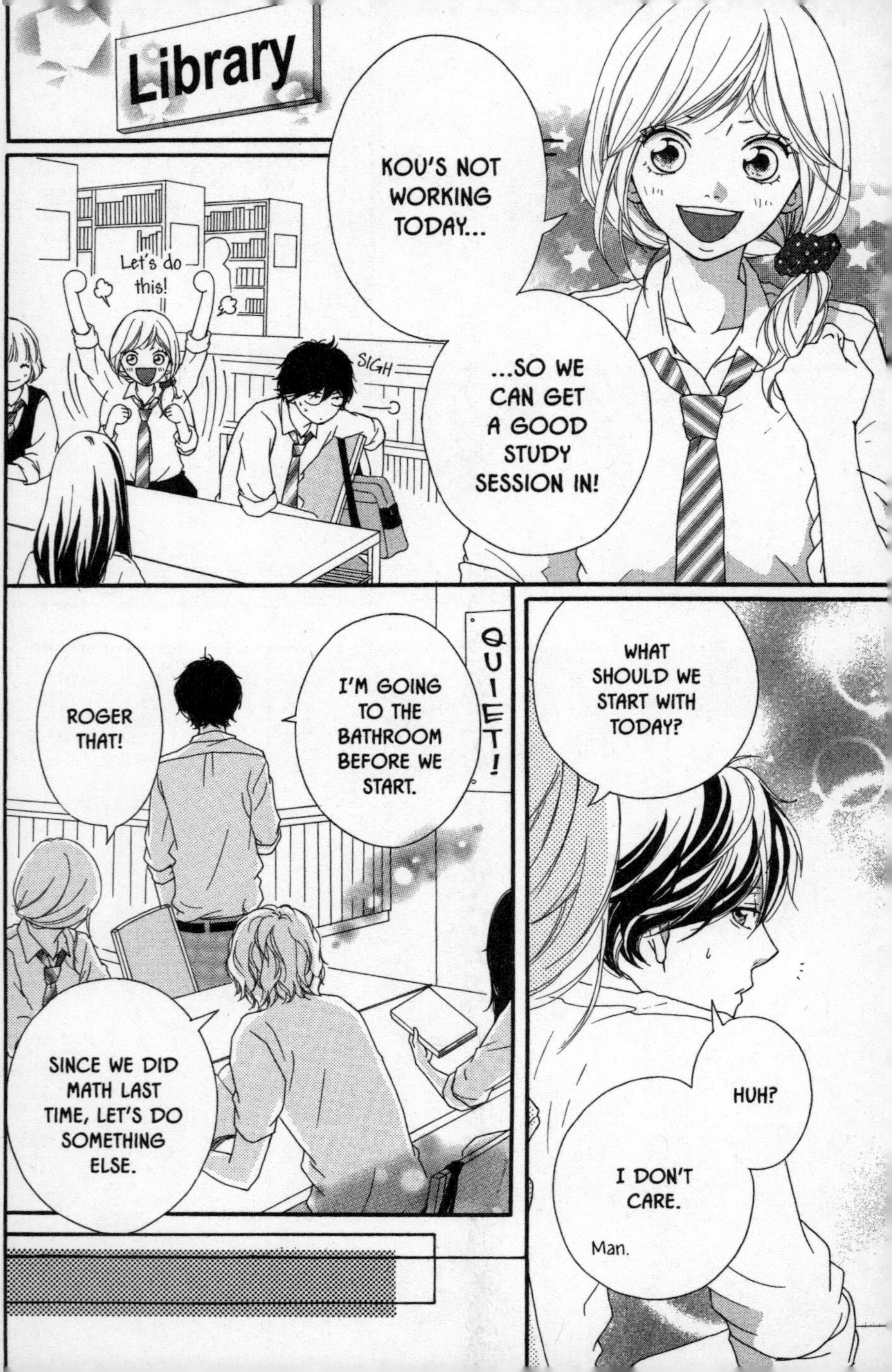
KOU'S NOT WORKING TODAY...
...SO WE CAN GET A GOOD STUDY SESSION IN!
Library
Let's do this!
SIGH
WHAT SHOULD WE START WITH TODAY?
HUH?
I DON'T CARE.
Man.
QUIET!
I'M GOING TO THE BATHROOM BEFORE WE START.
ROGER THAT!
SINCE WE DID MATH LAST TIME, LET'S DO SOMETHING ELSE.

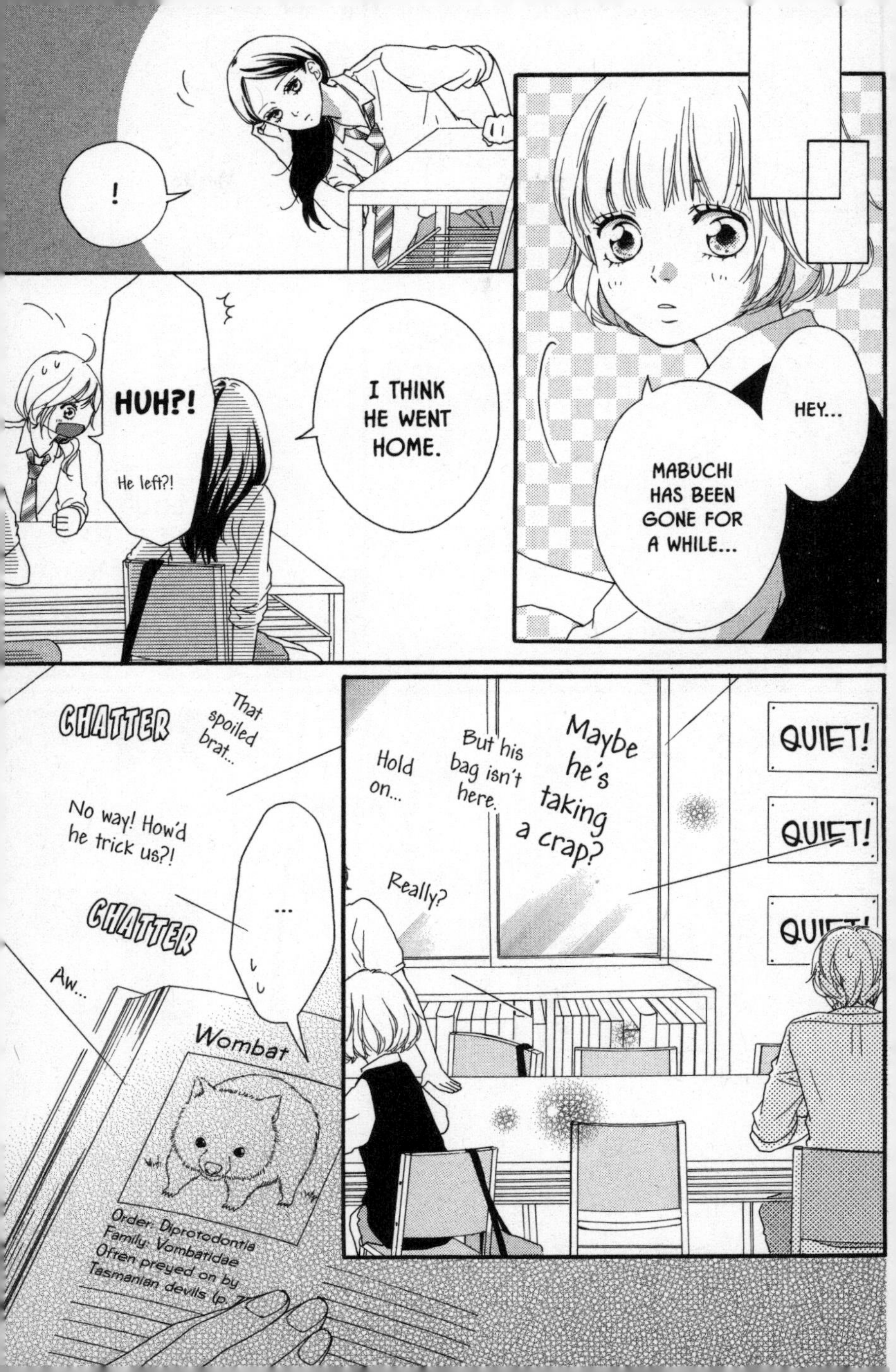
HEY...
MABUCHI HAS BEEN GONE FOR A WHILE...
!
I THINK HE WENT HOME.
HUH?!
He left?!
QUIET!
QUIET!
Maybe he's taking a crap?
But his bag isn't here.
Hold on...
Really?
That spoiled brat...
CHATTER
No way! How'd he trick us?!
...
CHATTER
Aw...
Wombat
Order: Diprotodontia
Family: Vombatidae
Often preyed on by
Tasmanian devils (p.

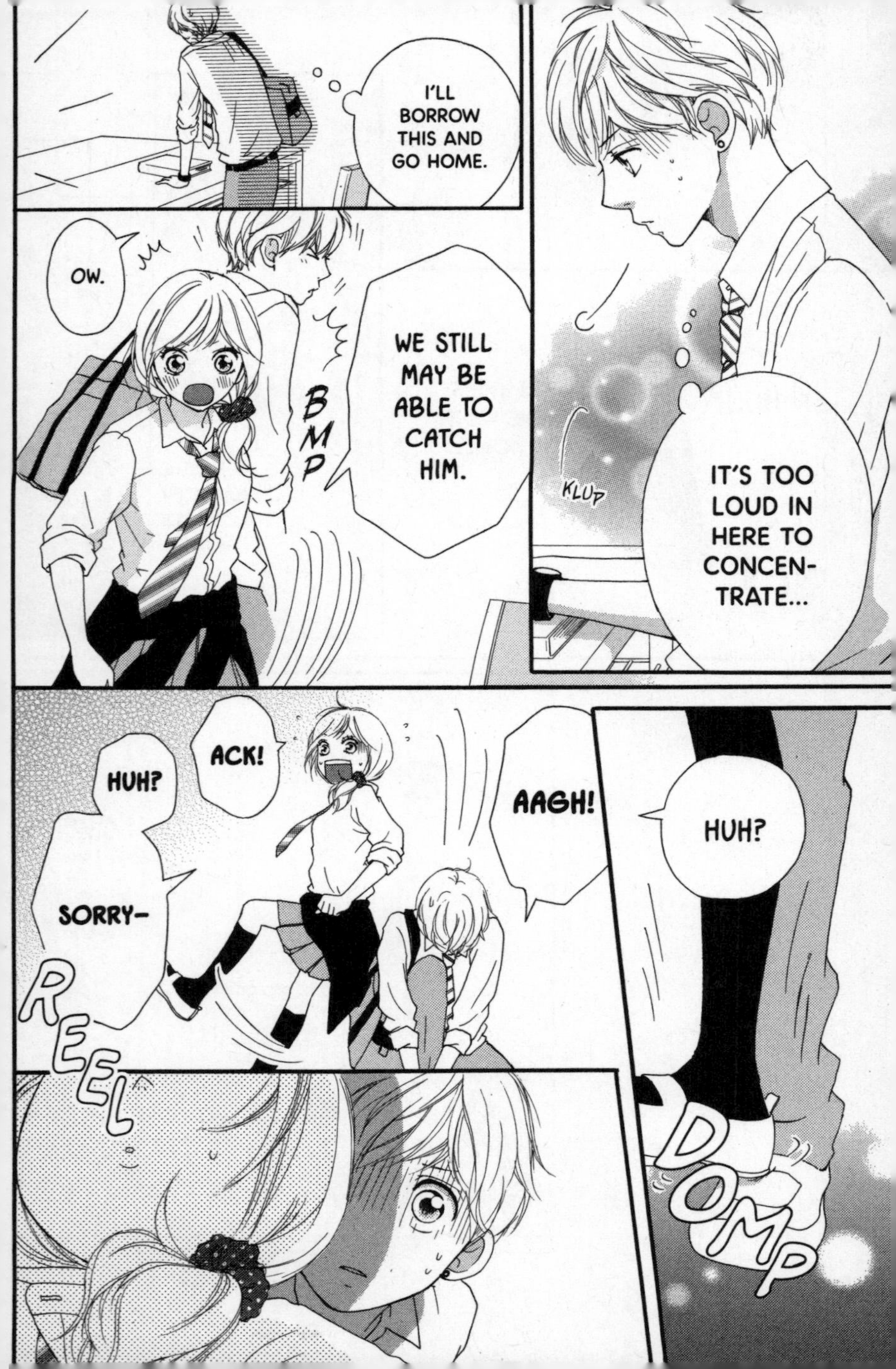
IT'S TOO LOUD IN HERE TO CONCENTRATE...
KLUP
I'LL BORROW THIS AND GO HOME.
WE STILL MAY BE ABLE TO CATCH HIM.
BMP
OW.
HUH?
DOMP
AAGH!
ACK!
HUH?
SORRY-
REEL

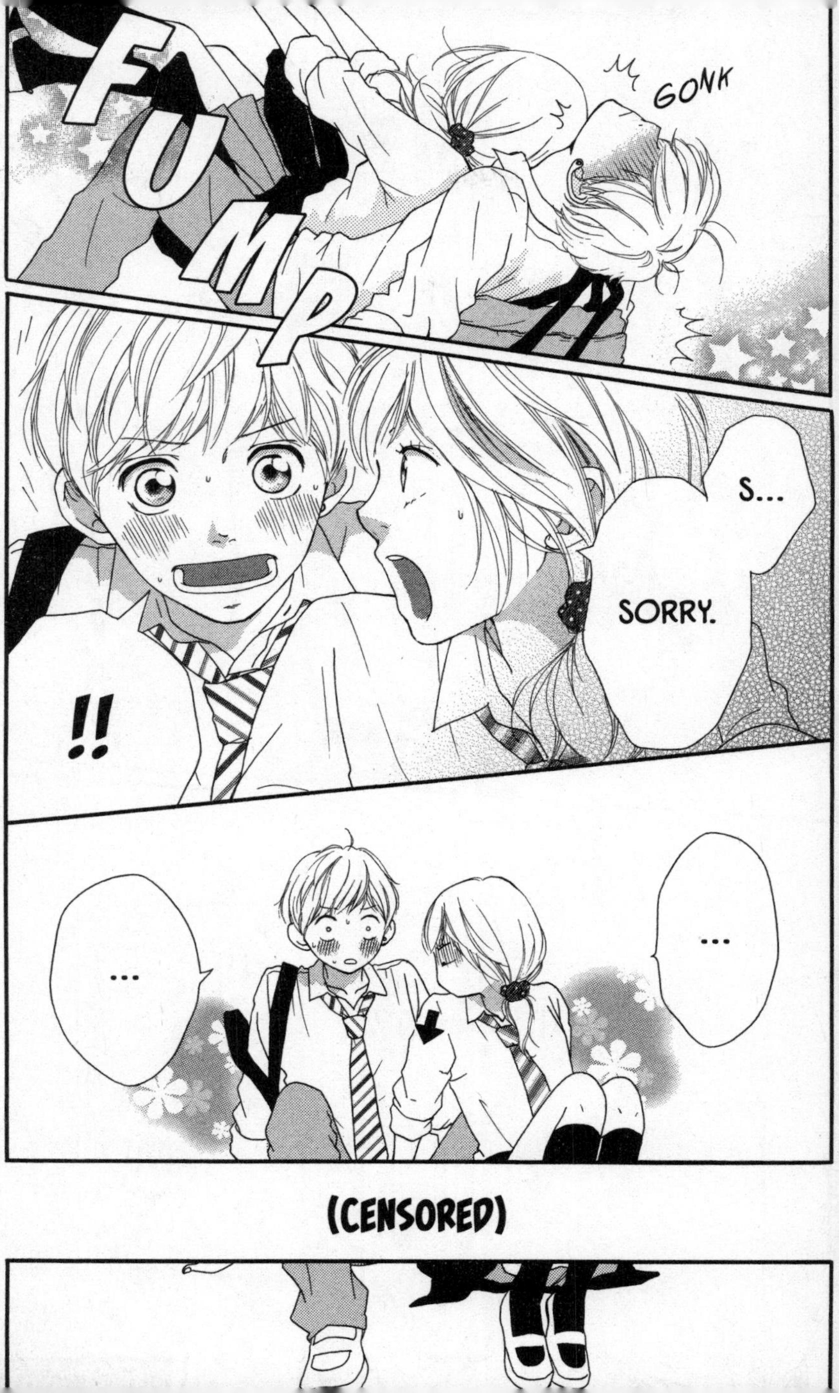
GONK
FUMP
S...
SORRY.
!!
...
...
(CENSORED)

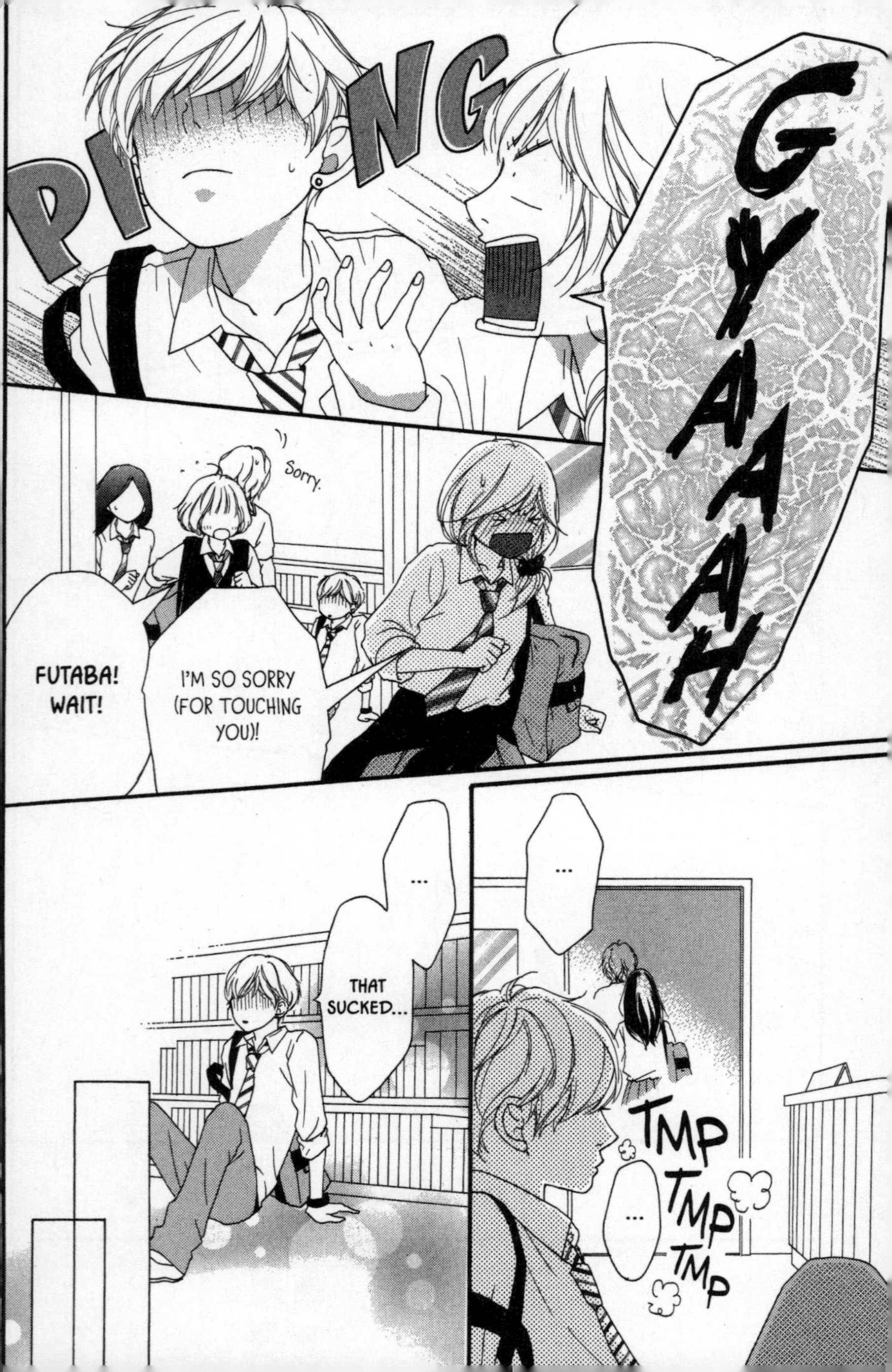
GYAAAH
PING
Sorry.
I'M SO SORRY (FOR TOUCHING YOU)!
FUTABA! WAIT!
...
TMP TMP TMP TMP
...
...
THAT SUCKED...

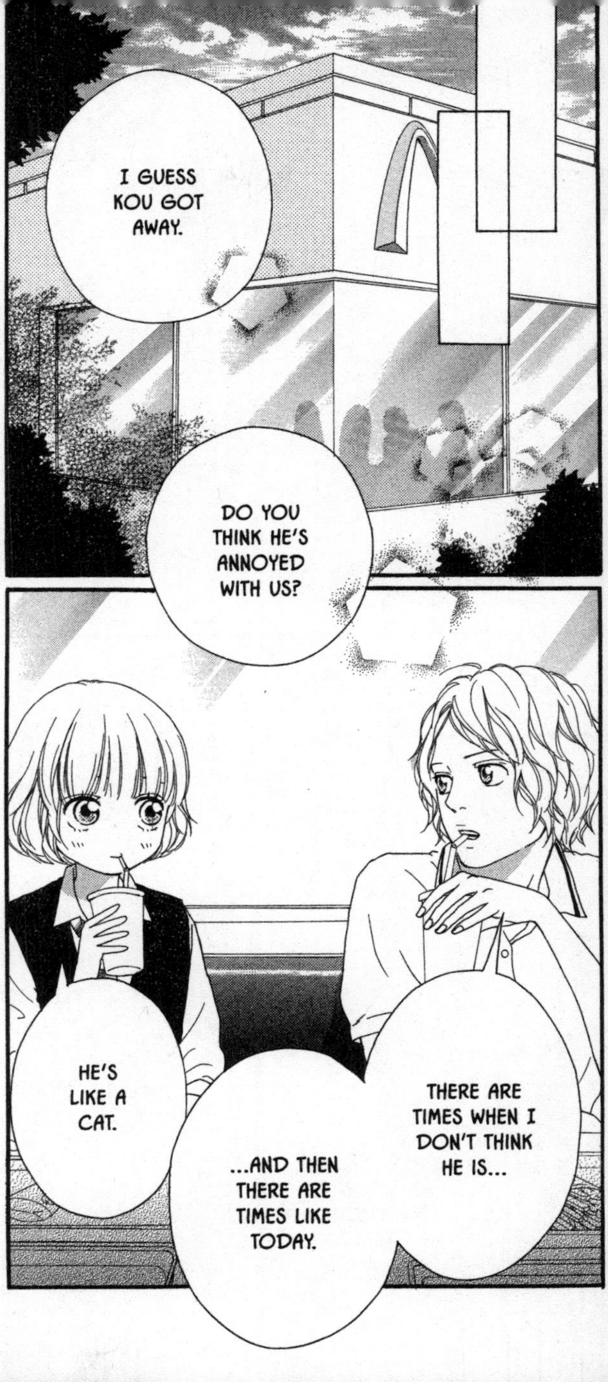
I GUESS KOU GOT AWAY.
DO YOU THINK HE'S ANNOYED WITH US?
THERE ARE TIMES WHEN I DON'T THINK HE IS...
...AND THEN THERE ARE TIMES LIKE TODAY.
HE'S LIKE A CAT.

Diet

My weight has been creeping up on me. Until a few years ago, I could simply watch what I ate and drop pounds easily, but as I age, I find that it really does not come off! I hate it, and the flab just keeps piling on... By the time I notice, my jeans are too tight. If I keep going like this, he's not going to like me! He likes girls with lithe and smooth body lines. That's the song he sang! ← A certain game character. (*laugh*) Anyway, I'm half joking (and half serious). I do want to try to lose some weight. If you don't see me write about this topic again in the next volume, it will mean that I completely failed in my mission...

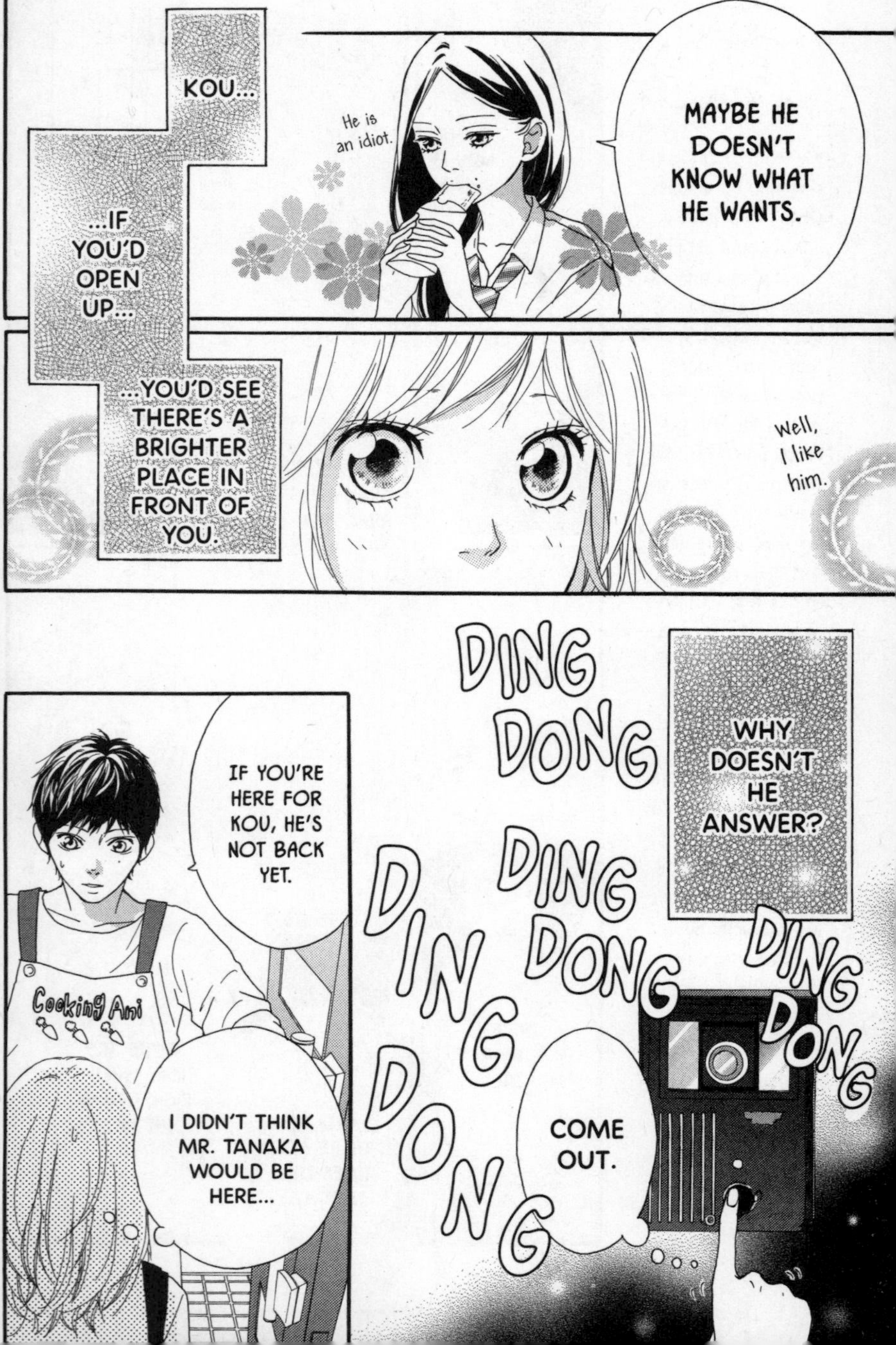
MAYBE HE DOESN'T KNOW WHAT HE WANTS.
He is an idiot.
KOU...
...IF YOU'D OPEN UP...
Well, I like him.
...YOU'D SEE THERE'S A BRIGHTER PLACE IN FRONT OF YOU.
WHY DOESN'T HE ANSWER?
DING DONG
DING DONG
DING DONG
COME OUT.
DING DONG
IF YOU'RE HERE FOR KOU, HE'S NOT BACK YET.
Cooking Ani
I DIDN'T THINK MR. TANAKA WOULD BE HERE...

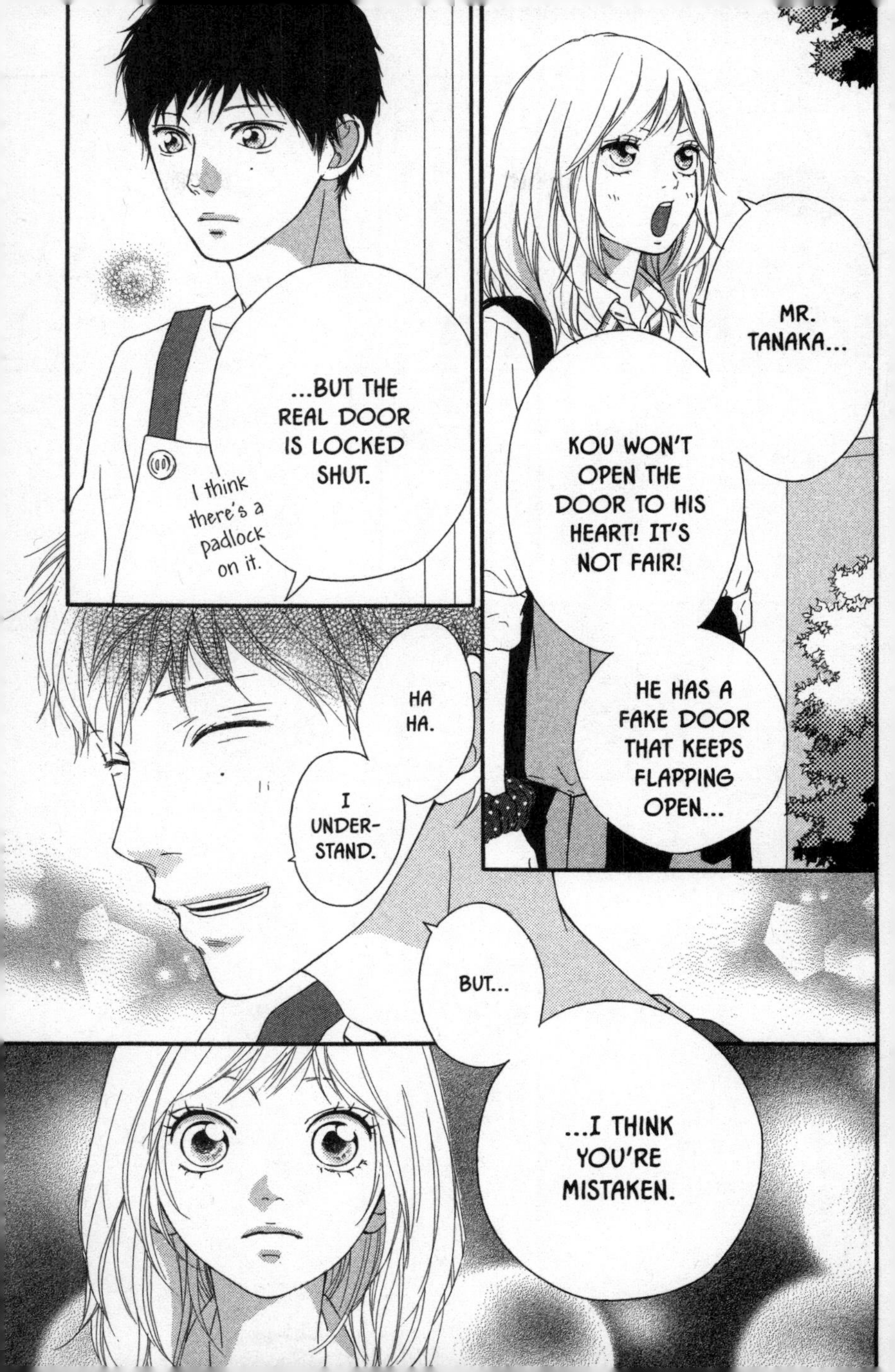
MR. TANAKA...
KOU WON'T OPEN THE DOOR TO HIS HEART! IT'S NOT FAIR!
HE HAS A FAKE DOOR THAT KEEPS FLAPPING OPEN...
...BUT THE REAL DOOR IS LOCKED SHUT.
I think there's a padlock on it.
HA HA.
I UNDERSTAND.
BUT...
...I THINK YOU'RE MISTAKEN.

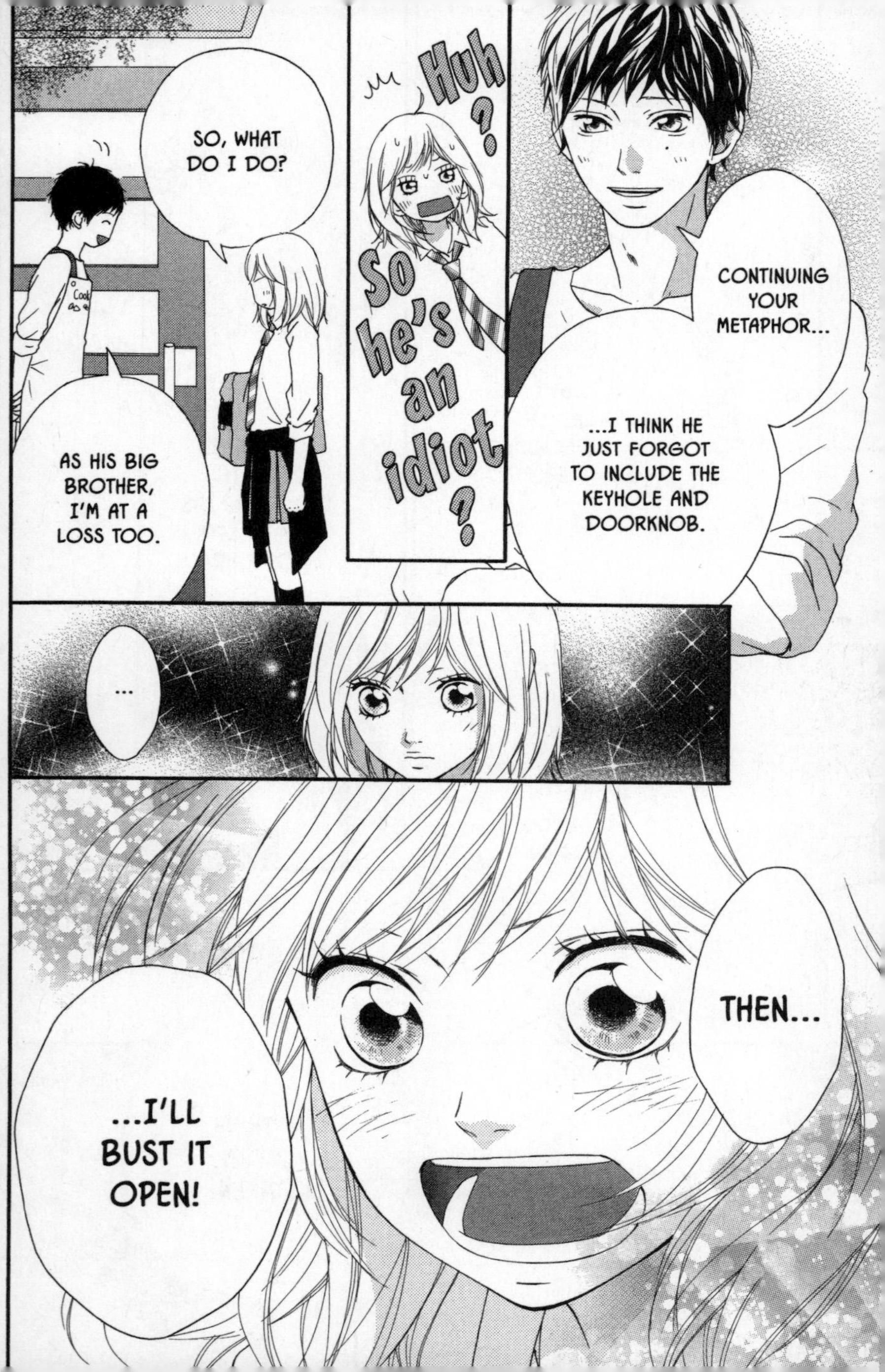
CONTINUING YOUR METAPHOR...
...I THINK HE JUST FORGOT TO INCLUDE THE KEYHOLE AND DOORKNOB.
Huh?
So he's an idiot?
SO, WHAT DO I DO?
AS HIS BIG BROTHER, I'M AT A LOSS TOO.
...
THEN...
...I'LL BUST IT OPEN!

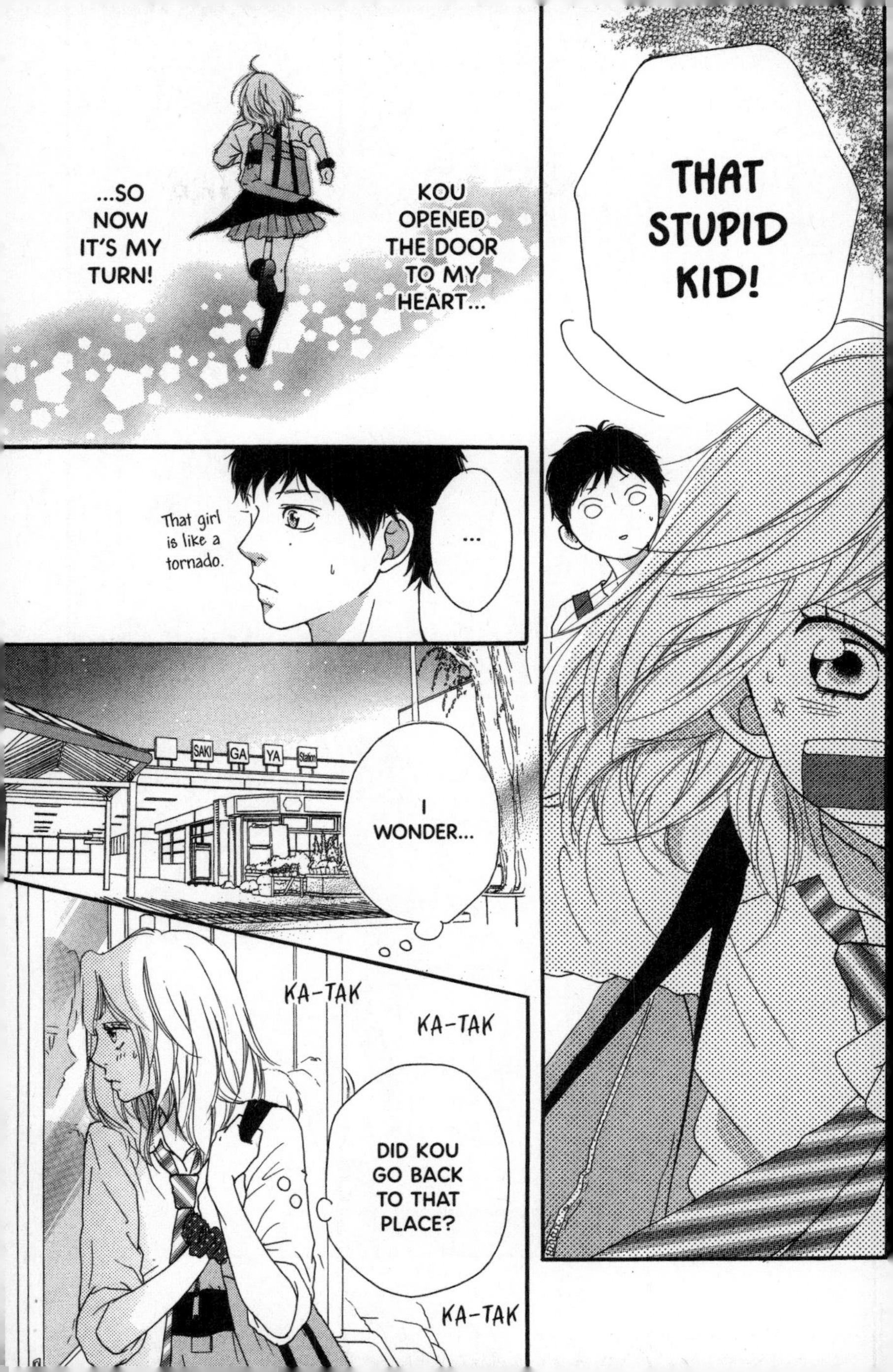
THAT STUPID KID!
KOU OPENED THE DOOR TO MY HEART...
...SO NOW IT'S MY TURN!
...
That girl is like a tornado.
SAKI GA YA Station
I WONDER...
KA-TAK
KA-TAK
DID KOU GO BACK TO THAT PLACE?
KA-TAK

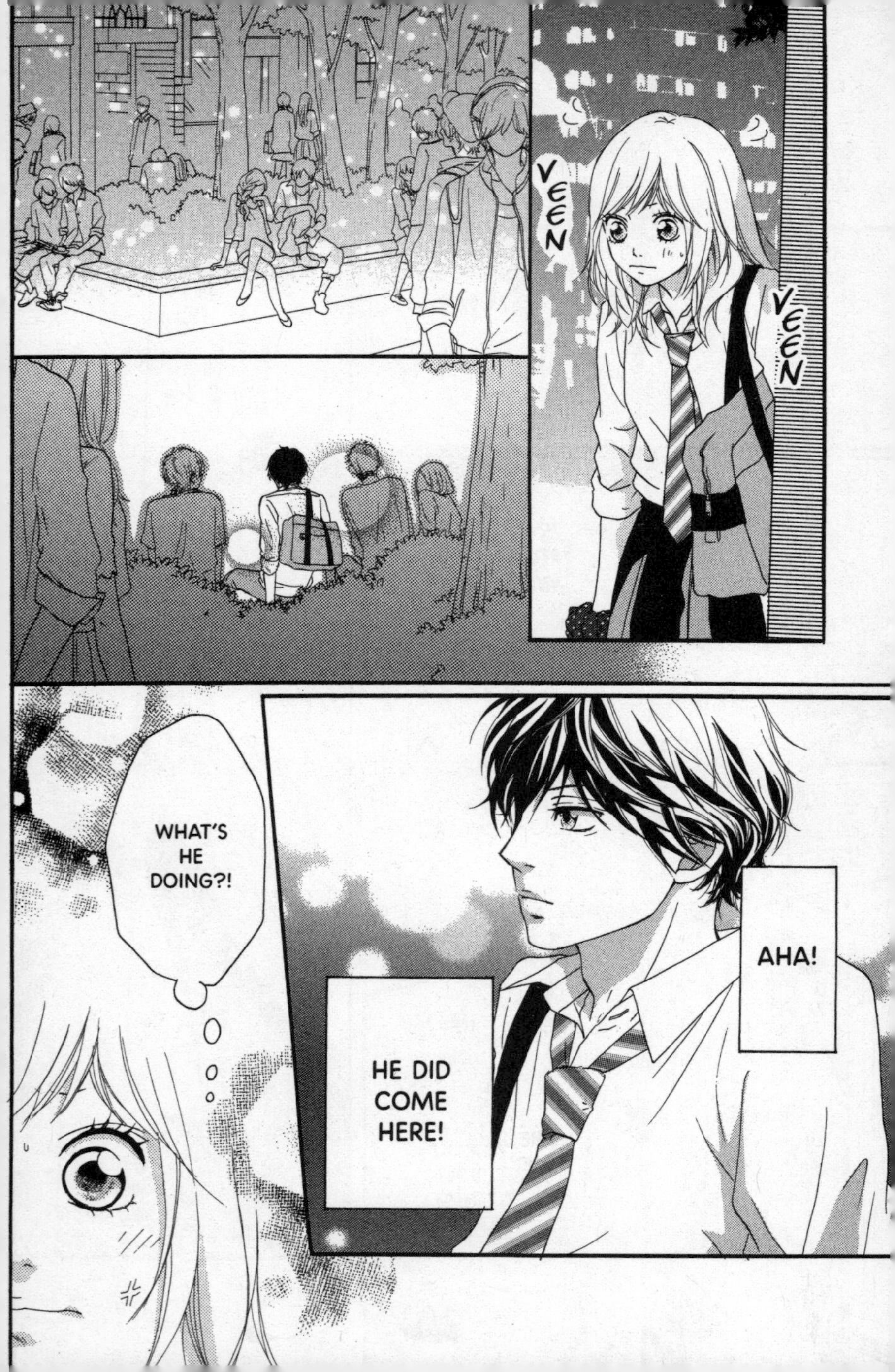
VEEN
VEEN
AHA!
HE DID COME HERE!
WHAT'S HE DOING?!

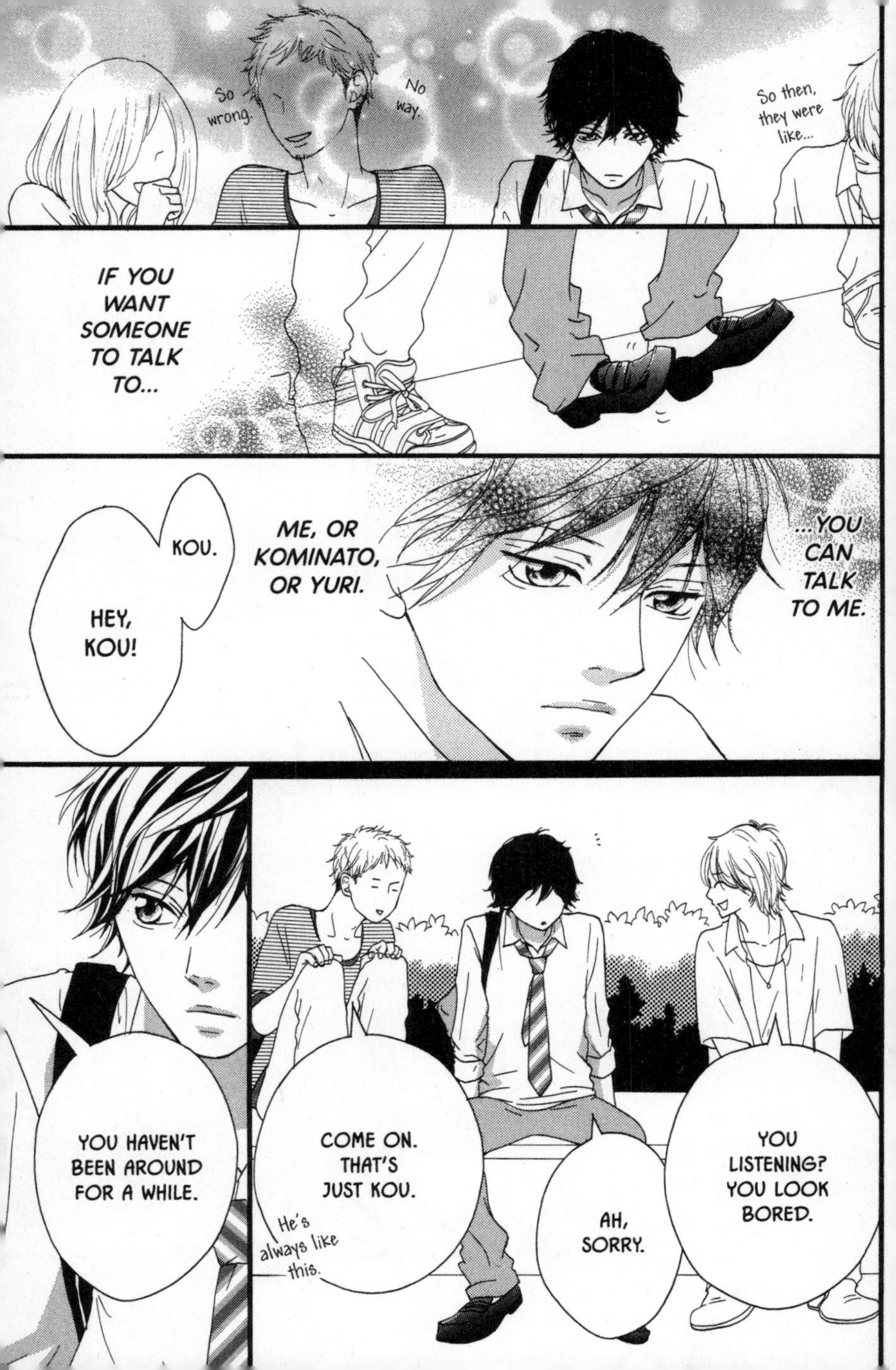
So then, they were like...
No way.
So wrong.
IF YOU WANT SOMEONE TO TALK TO...
...YOU CAN TALK TO ME.
ME, OR KOMINATO, OR YURI.
KOU.
HEY, KOU!
YOU LISTENING? YOU LOOK BORED.
AH, SORRY.
COME ON. THAT'S JUST KOU.
He's always like this.
YOU HAVEN'T BEEN AROUND FOR A WHILE.

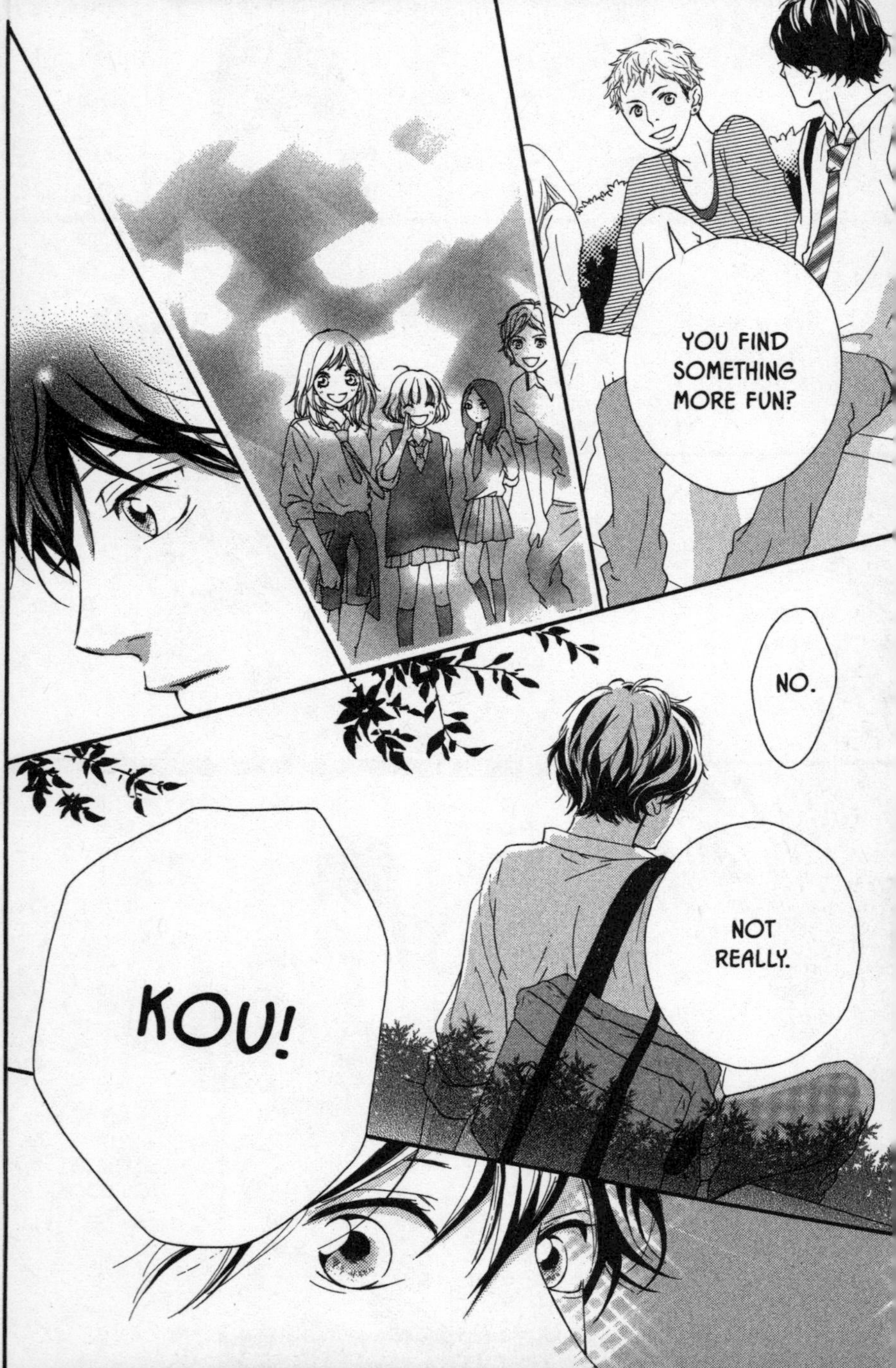
YOU FIND SOMETHING MORE FUN?
NO.
NOT REALLY.
KOU!

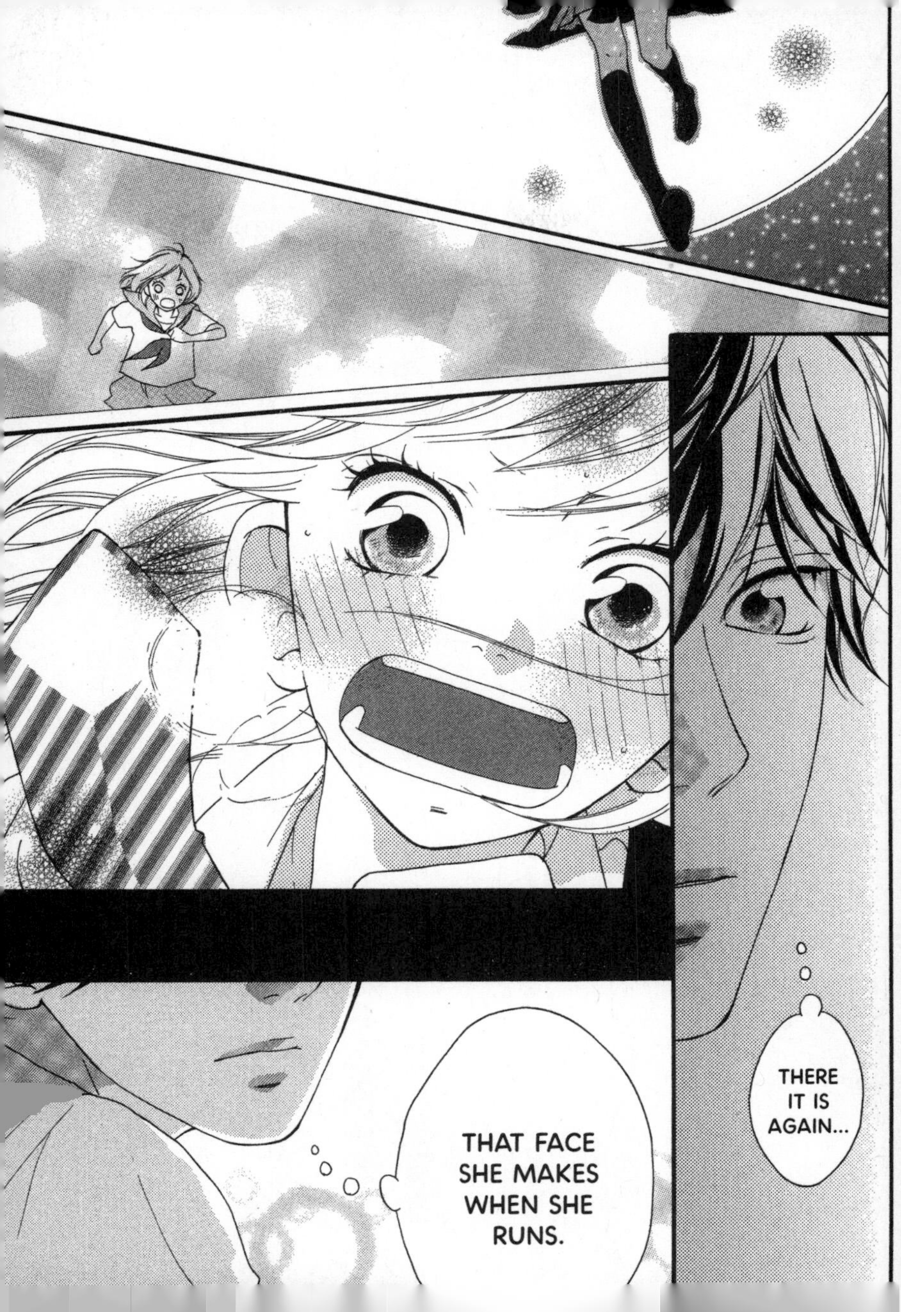
THERE IT IS AGAIN...
THAT FACE SHE MAKES WHEN SHE RUNS.

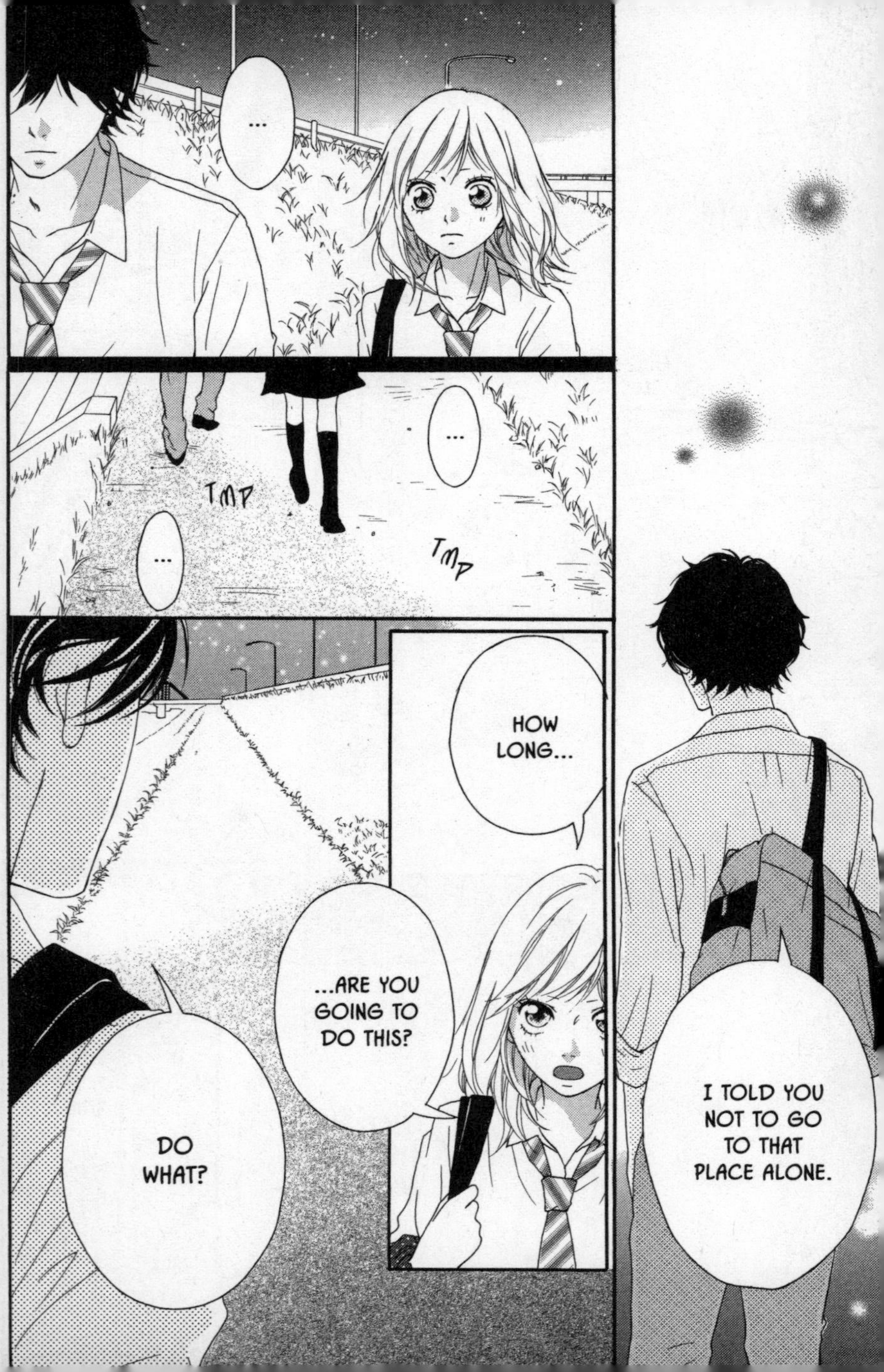
...
...
TMP
...
TMP
I TOLD YOU NOT TO GO TO THAT PLACE ALONE.
HOW LONG...
...ARE YOU GOING TO DO THIS?
DO WHAT?

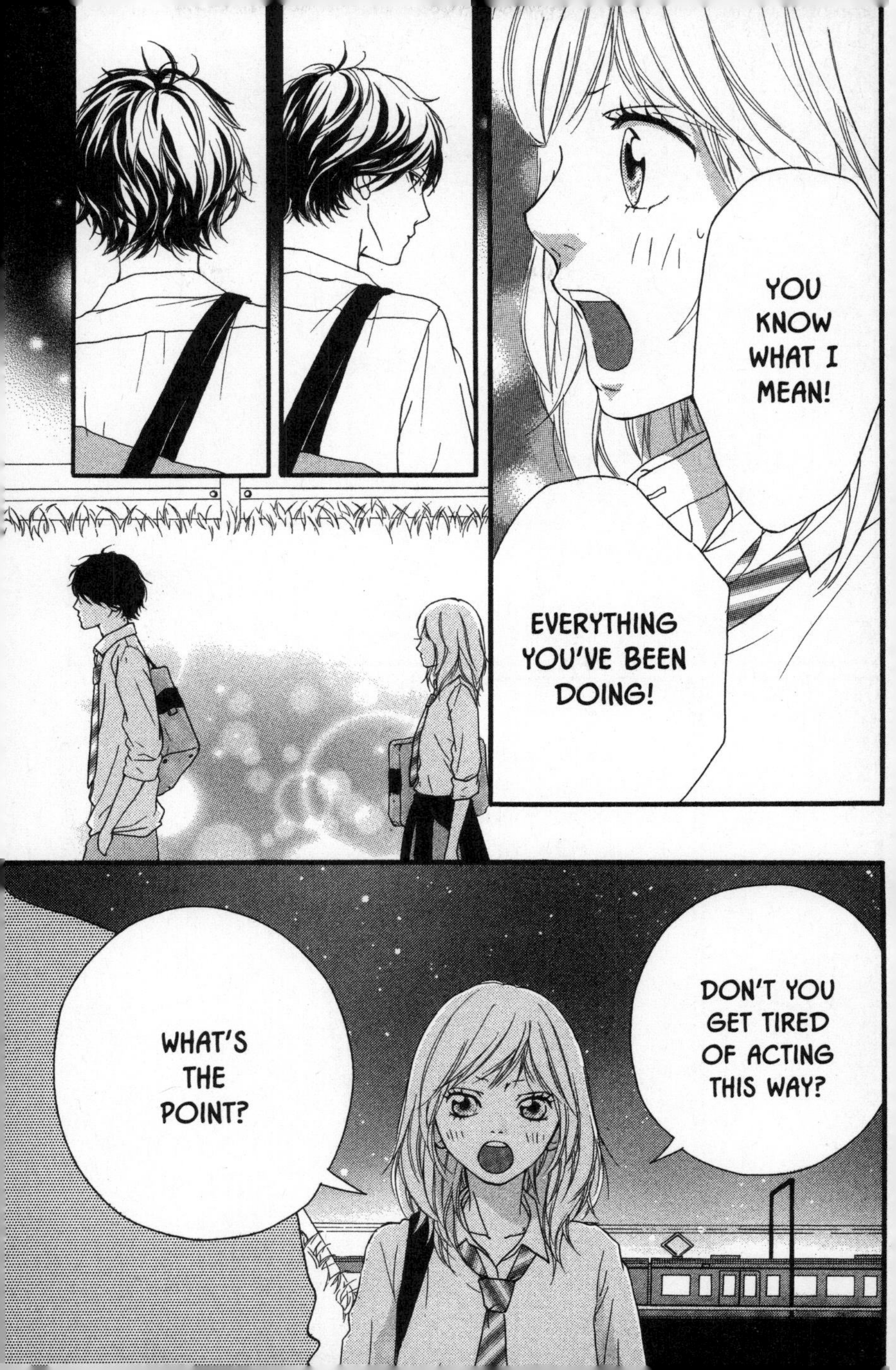
YOU KNOW WHAT I MEAN!
EVERYTHING YOU'VE BEEN DOING!
DON'T YOU GET TIRED OF ACTING THIS WAY?
WHAT'S THE POINT?

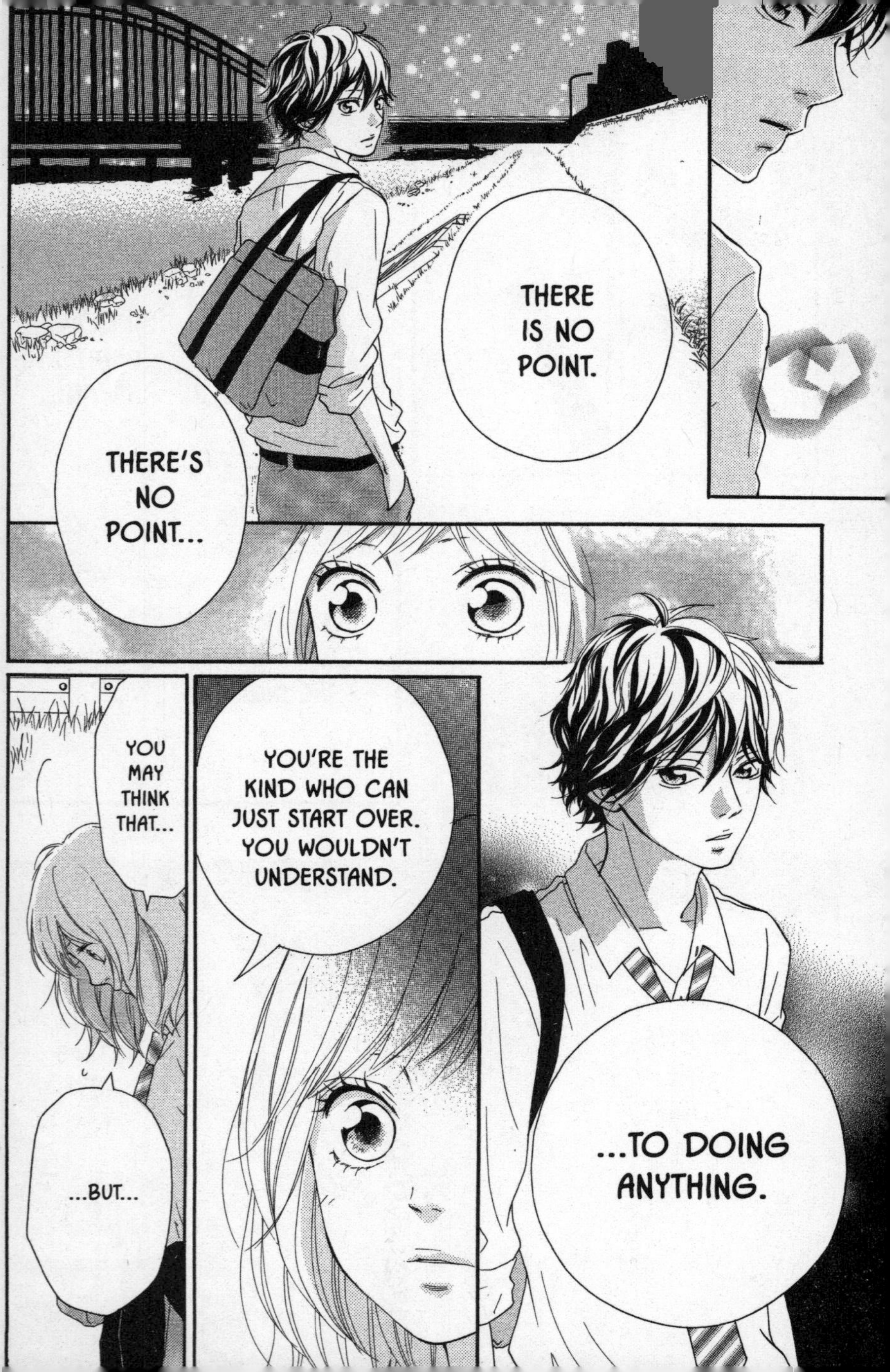
THERE IS NO POINT.
THERE'S NO POINT...
...TO DOING ANYTHING.
YOU'RE THE KIND WHO CAN JUST START OVER. YOU WOULDN'T UNDERSTAND.
YOU MAY THINK THAT...
...BUT...

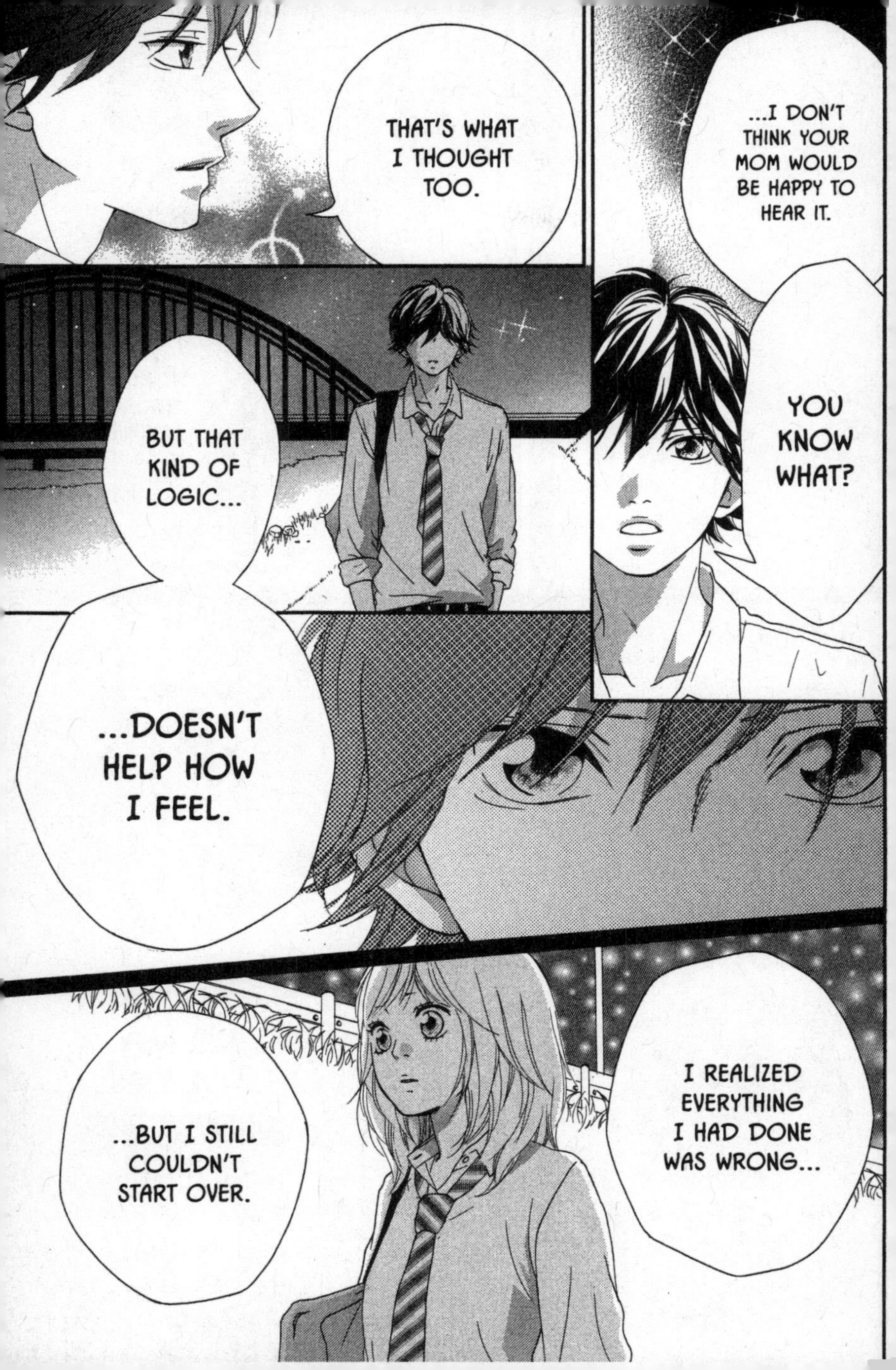
...I DON'T THINK YOUR MOM WOULD BE HAPPY TO HEAR IT.
THAT'S WHAT I THOUGHT TOO.
YOU KNOW WHAT?
BUT THAT KIND OF LOGIC...
...DOESN'T HELP HOW I FEEL.
I REALIZED EVERYTHING I HAD DONE WAS WRONG...
...BUT I STILL COULDN'T START OVER.

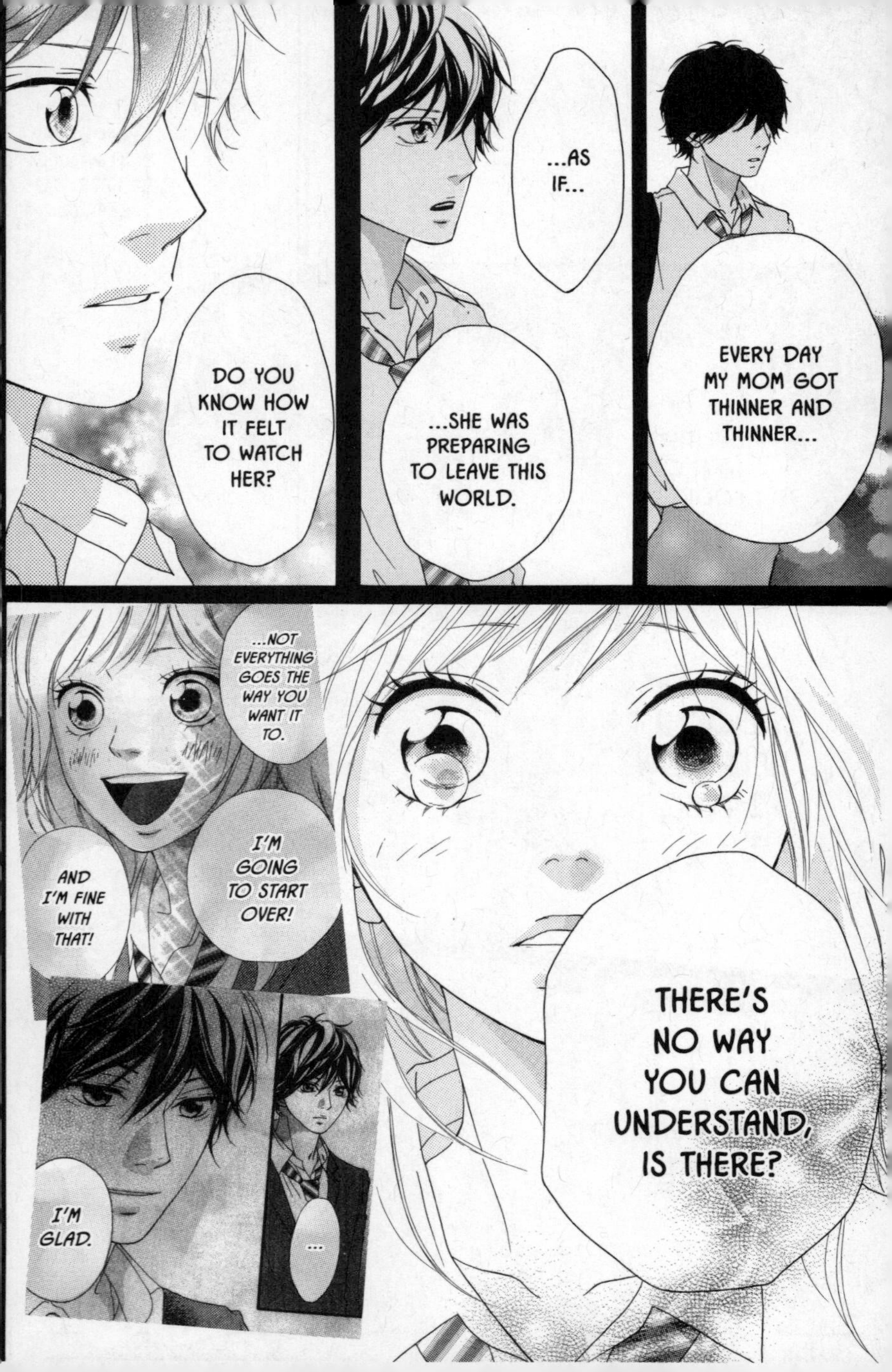
EVERY DAY MY MOM GOT THINNER AND THINNER...
...AS IF...
...SHE WAS PREPARING TO LEAVE THIS WORLD.
DO YOU KNOW HOW IT FELT TO WATCH HER?
THERE'S NO WAY YOU CAN UNDERSTAND, IS THERE?
...NOT EVERYTHING GOES THE WAY YOU WANT IT TO.
I'M GOING TO START OVER!
AND I'M FINE WITH THAT!
...
I'M GLAD.

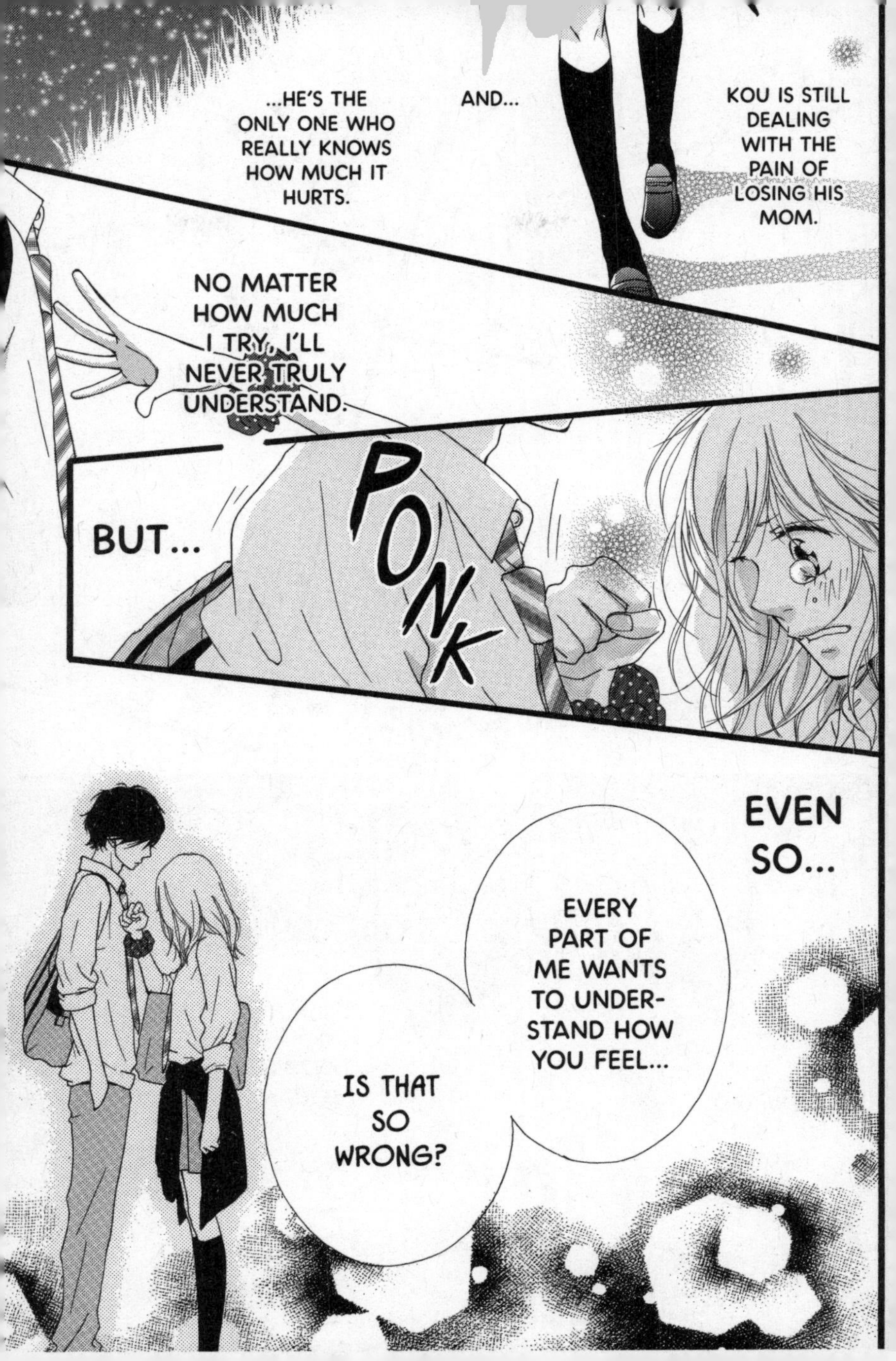
KOU IS STILL DEALING WITH THE PAIN OF LOSING HIS MOM.
AND...
...HE'S THE ONLY ONE WHO REALLY KNOWS HOW MUCH IT HURTS.
NO MATTER HOW MUCH I TRY, I'LL NEVER TRULY UNDERSTAND.
PONK
BUT...
EVEN SO...
EVERY PART OF ME WANTS TO UNDER-STAND HOW YOU FEEL...
IS THAT SO WRONG?

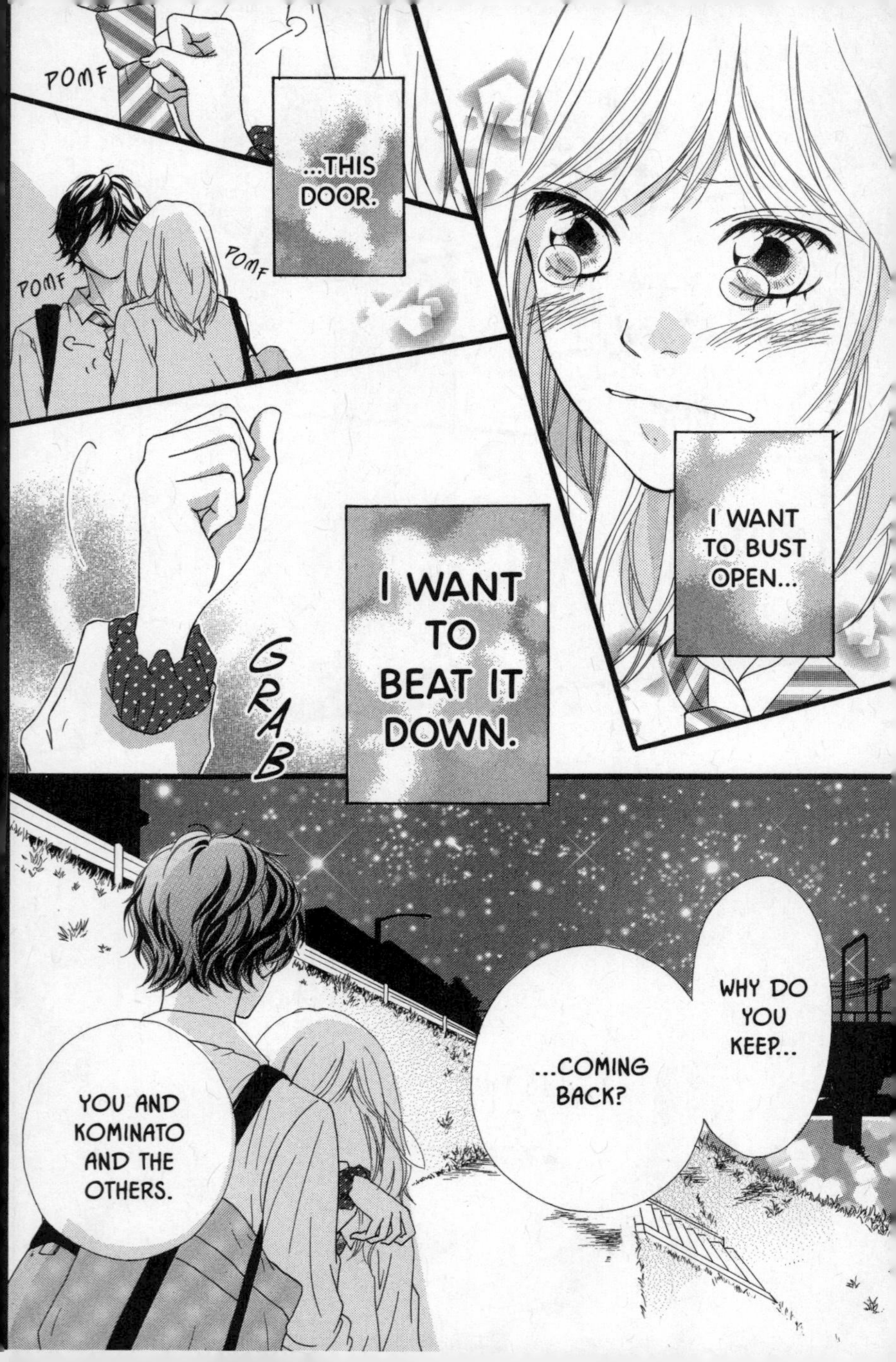
I WANT TO BUST OPEN...
POMF
...THIS DOOR.
POMF
POMF
I WANT TO BEAT IT DOWN.
GRAB
WHY DO YOU KEEP...
...COMING BACK?
YOU AND KOMINATO AND THE OTHERS.

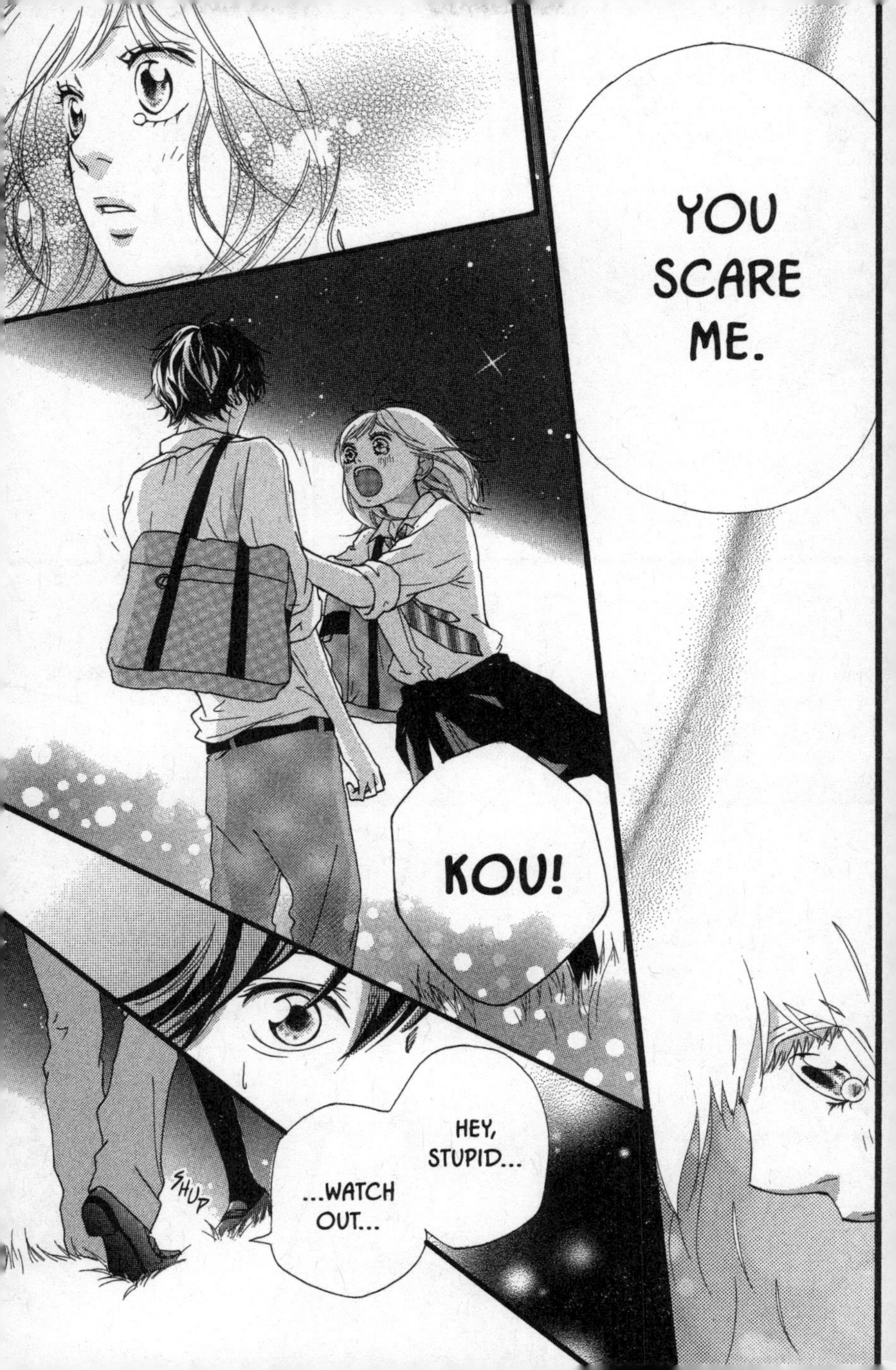
YOU SCARE ME.
KOU!
HEY, STUPID...
...WATCH OUT...
SHUP

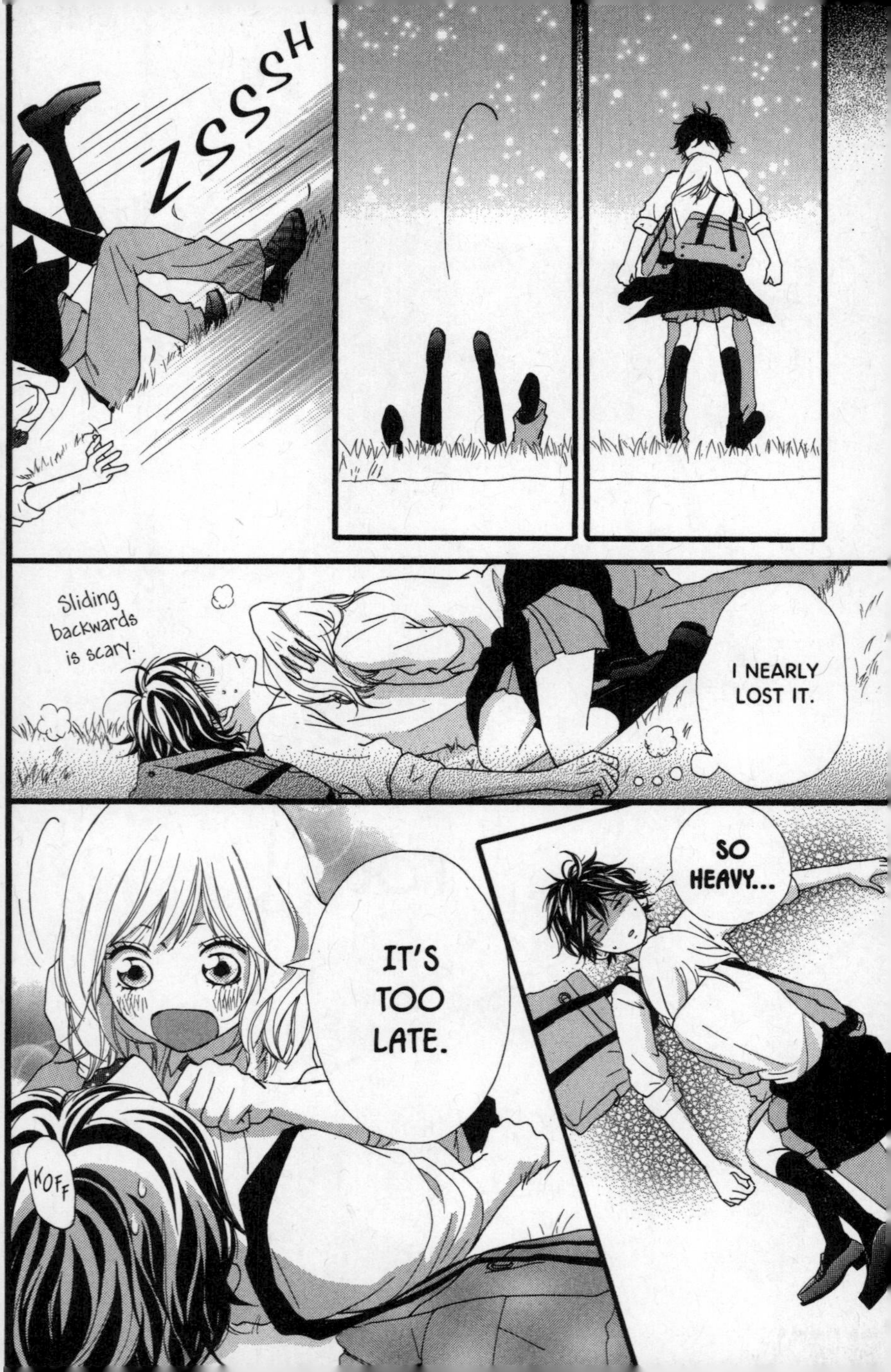
ZSSSH
Sliding backwards is scary.
I NEARLY LOST IT.
SO HEAVY...
IT'S TOO LATE.
KOFF

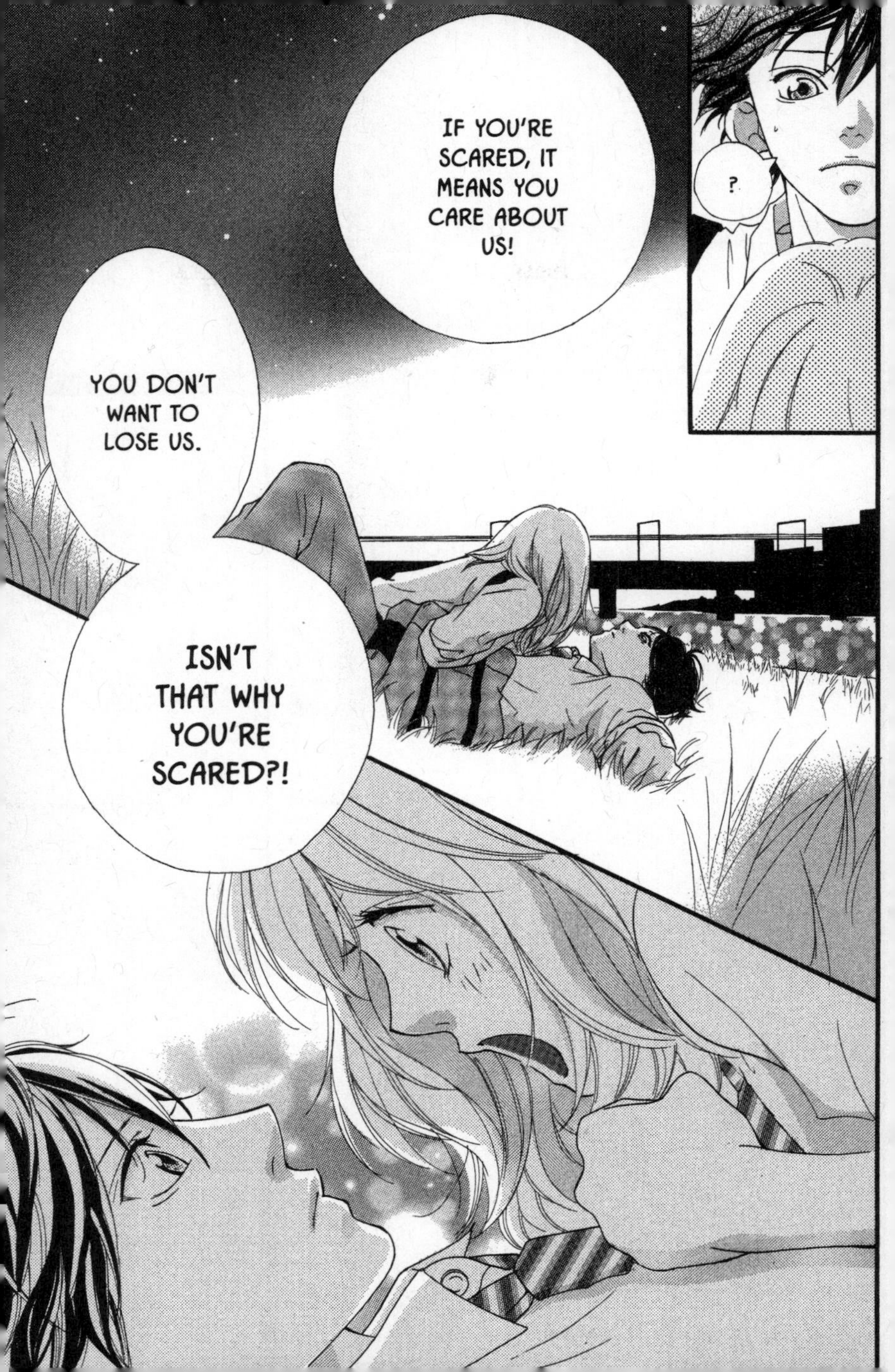
?
IF YOU'RE SCARED, IT MEANS YOU CARE ABOUT US!
YOU DON'T WANT TO LOSE US.
ISN'T THAT WHY YOU'RE SCARED?!

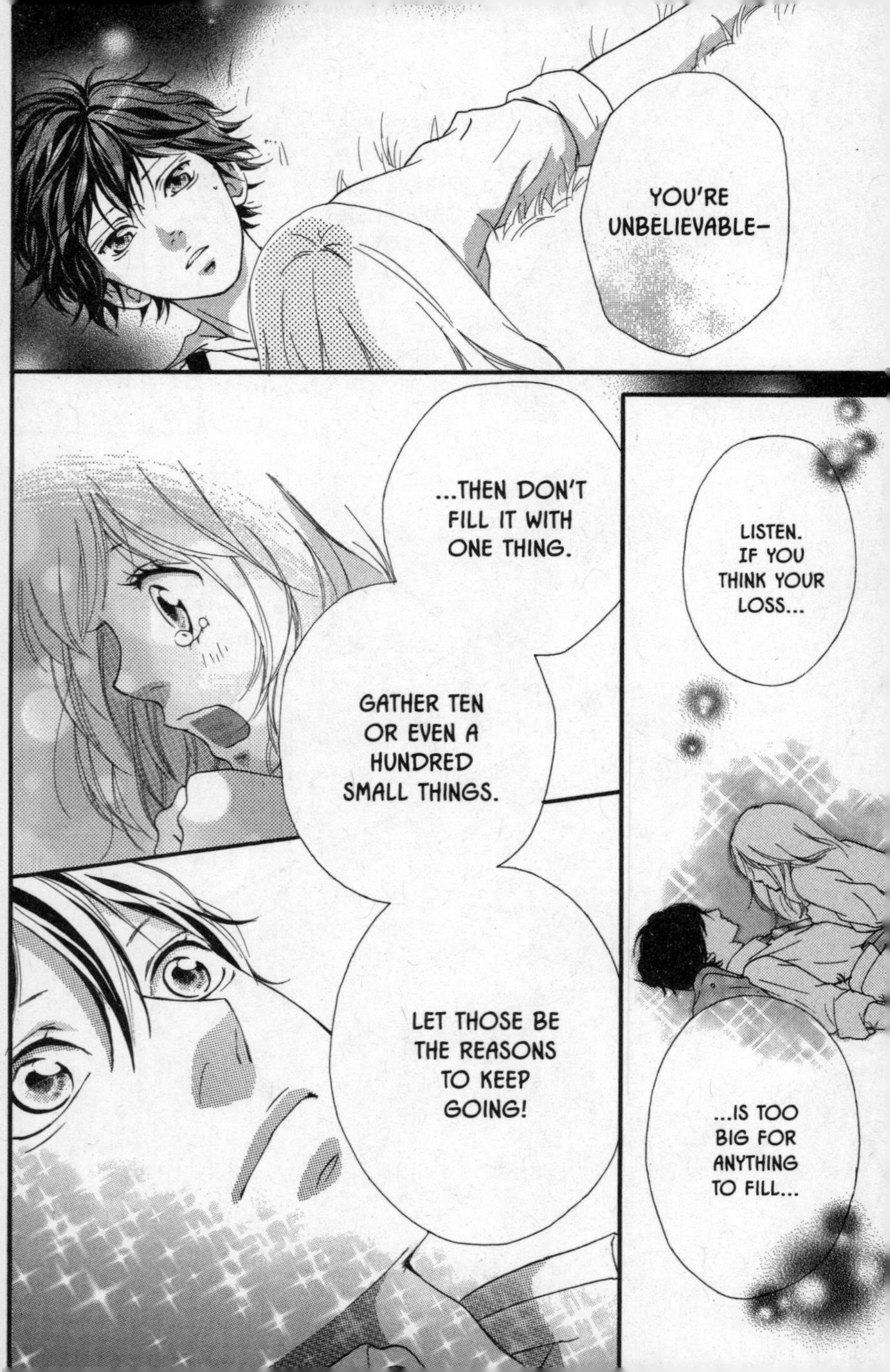
YOU'RE UNBELIEVABLE–
LISTEN. IF YOU THINK YOUR LOSS...
...IS TOO BIG FOR ANYTHING TO FILL...
...THEN DON'T FILL IT WITH ONE THING.
GATHER TEN OR EVEN A HUNDRED SMALL THINGS.
LET THOSE BE THE REASONS TO KEEP GOING!

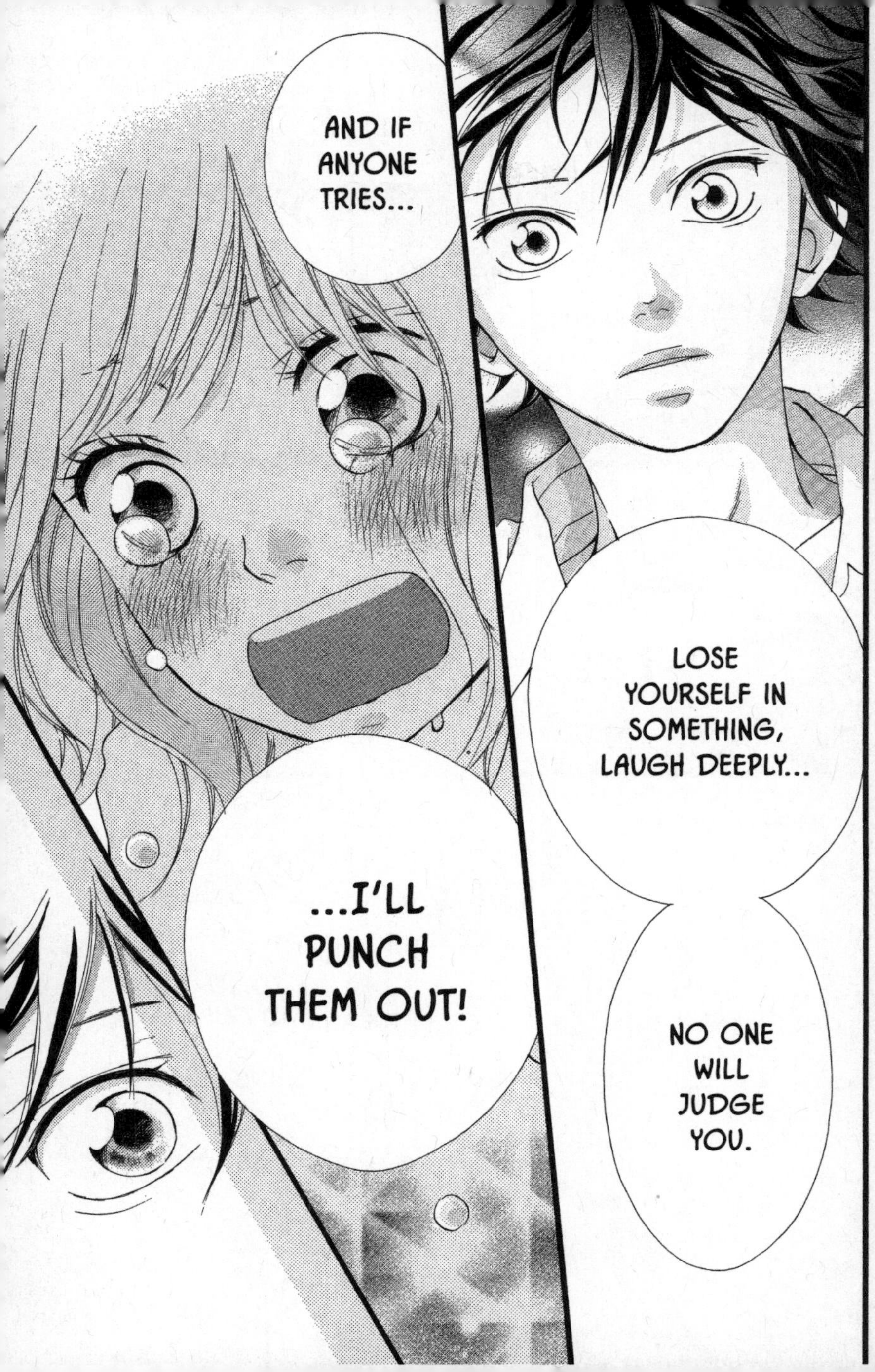
LOSE YOURSELF IN SOMETHING, LAUGH DEEPLY...
NO ONE WILL JUDGE YOU.
AND IF ANYONE TRIES...
...I'LL PUNCH THEM OUT!

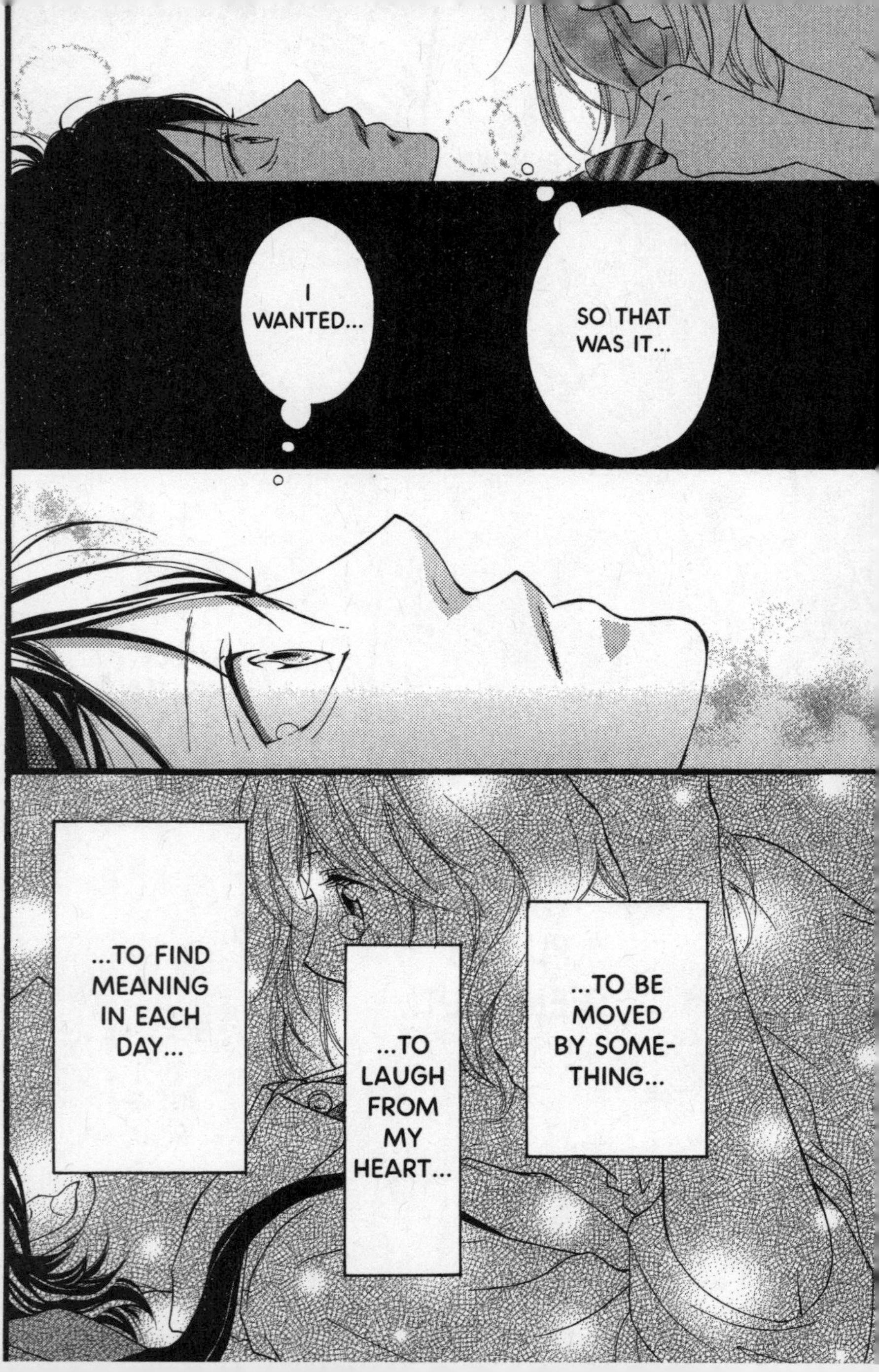
SO THAT WAS IT...
I WANTED...
...TO BE MOVED BY SOME-THING...
...TO LAUGH FROM MY HEART...
...TO FIND MEANING IN EACH DAY...

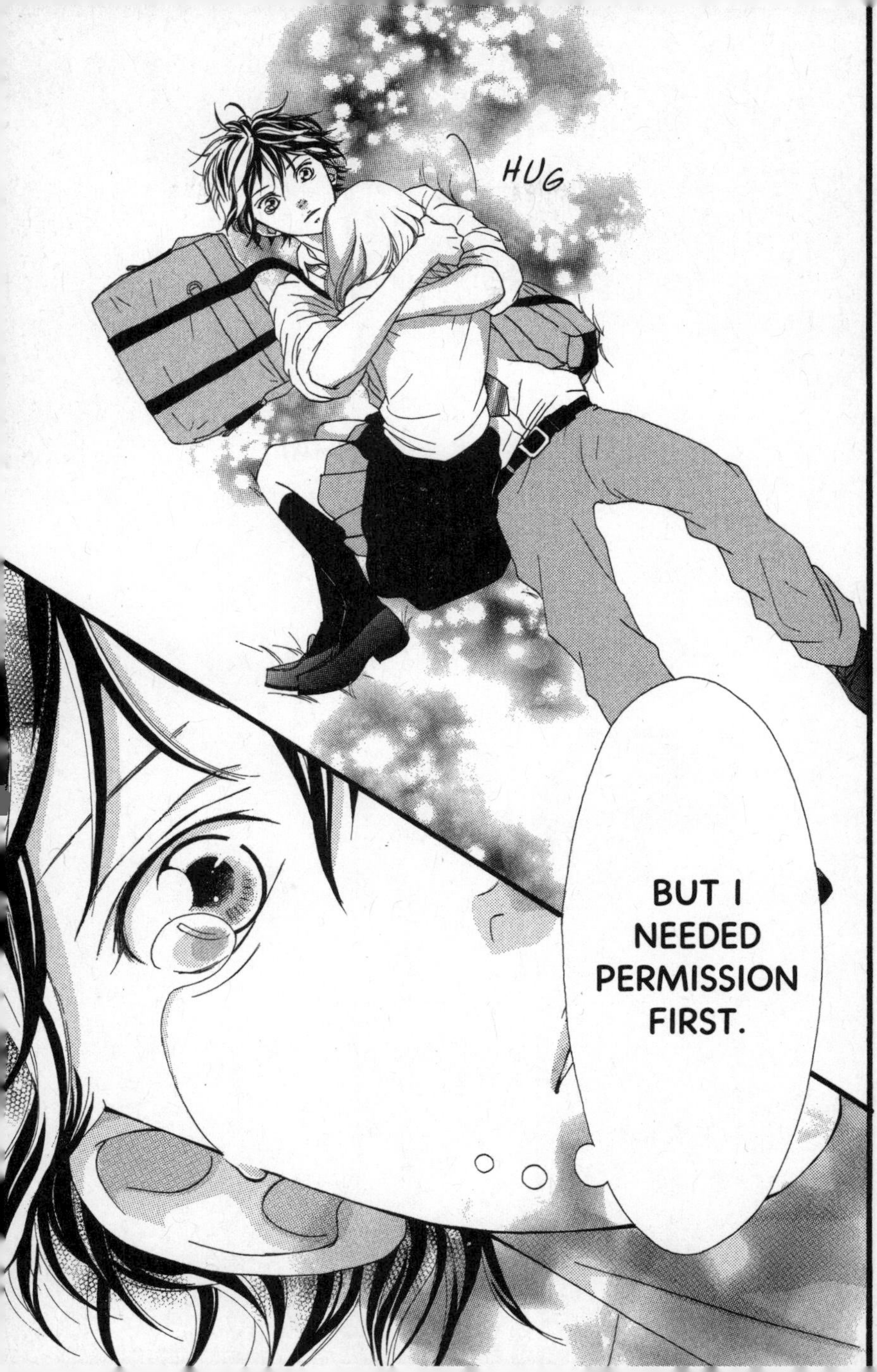
HUG
BUT I NEEDED PERMISSION FIRST.

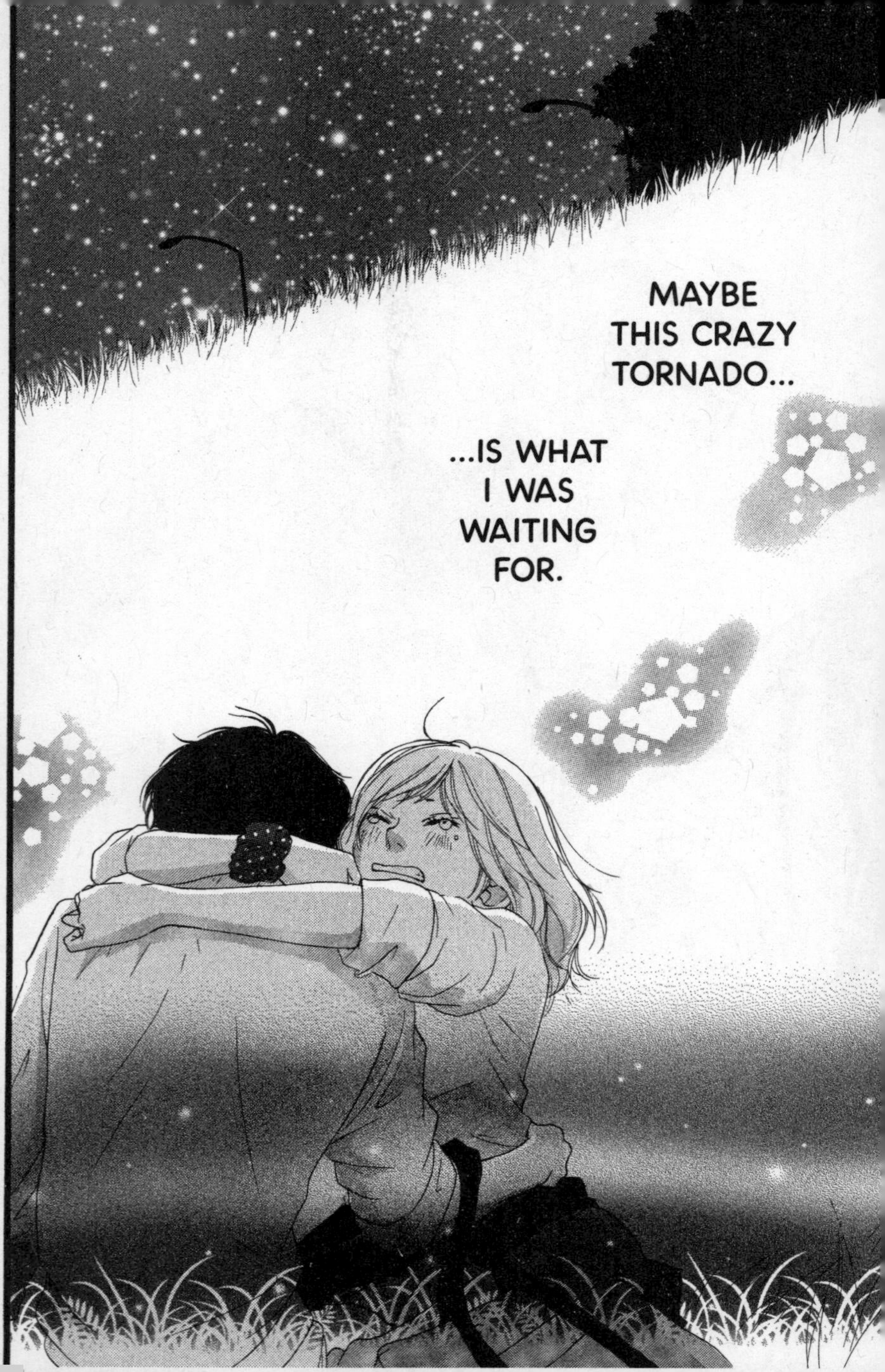
MAYBE THIS CRAZY TORNADO...
...IS WHAT I WAS WAITING FOR.

Ao Haru Ride

The scent of air after rain...
In the light around us, I felt your heartbeat.

CHAPTER 14

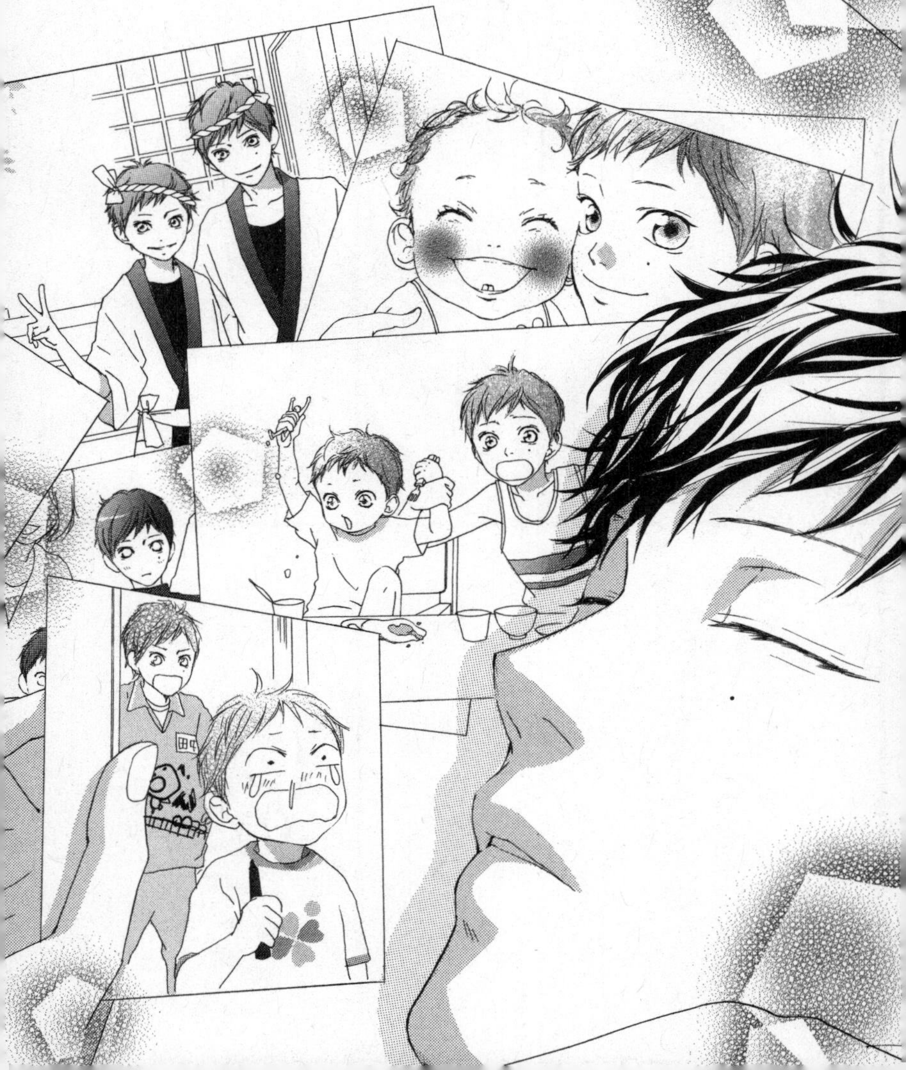
田中

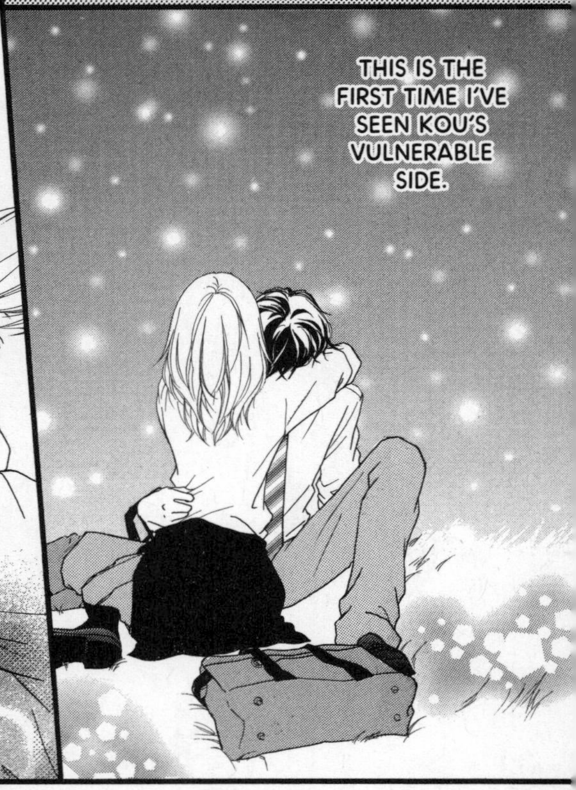
THIS IS THE FIRST TIME I'VE SEEN KOU'S VULNERABLE SIDE.
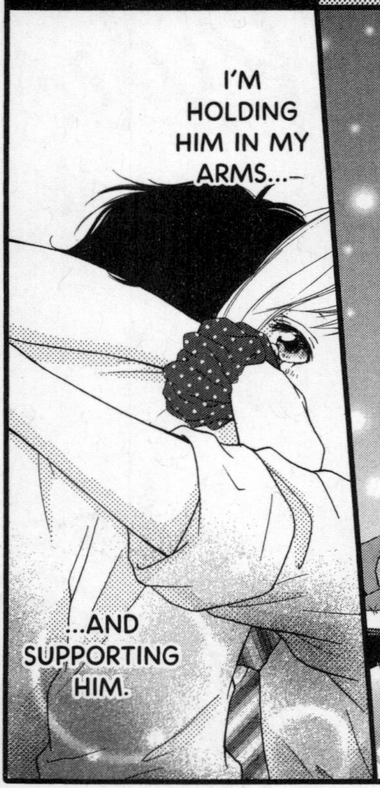
I'M HOLDING HIM IN MY ARMS...
...AND SUPPORTING HIM.
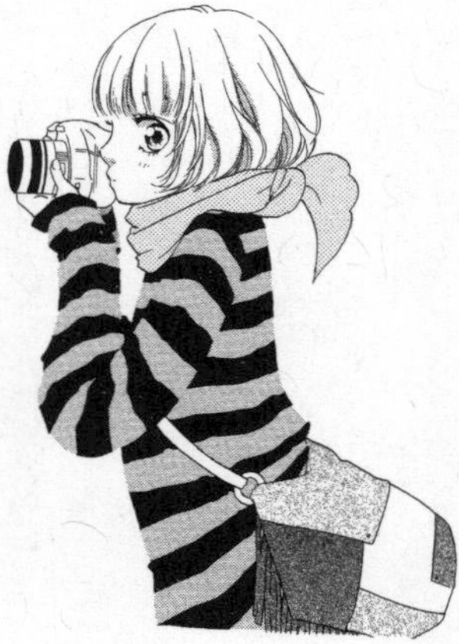

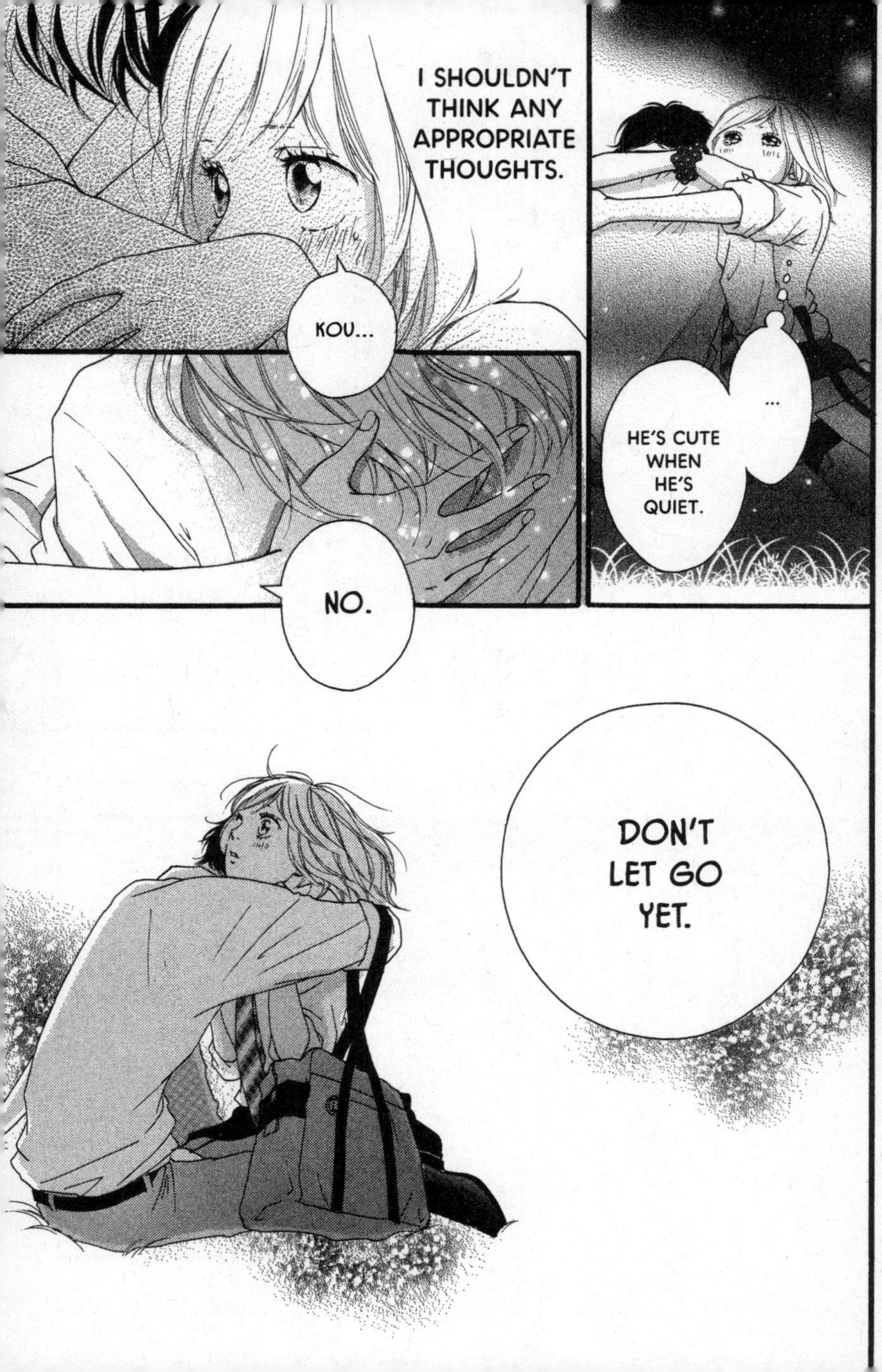
...
HE'S CUTE WHEN HE'S QUIET.
I SHOULDN'T THINK ANY APPROPRIATE THOUGHTS.
KOU...
NO.
DON'T LET GO YET.

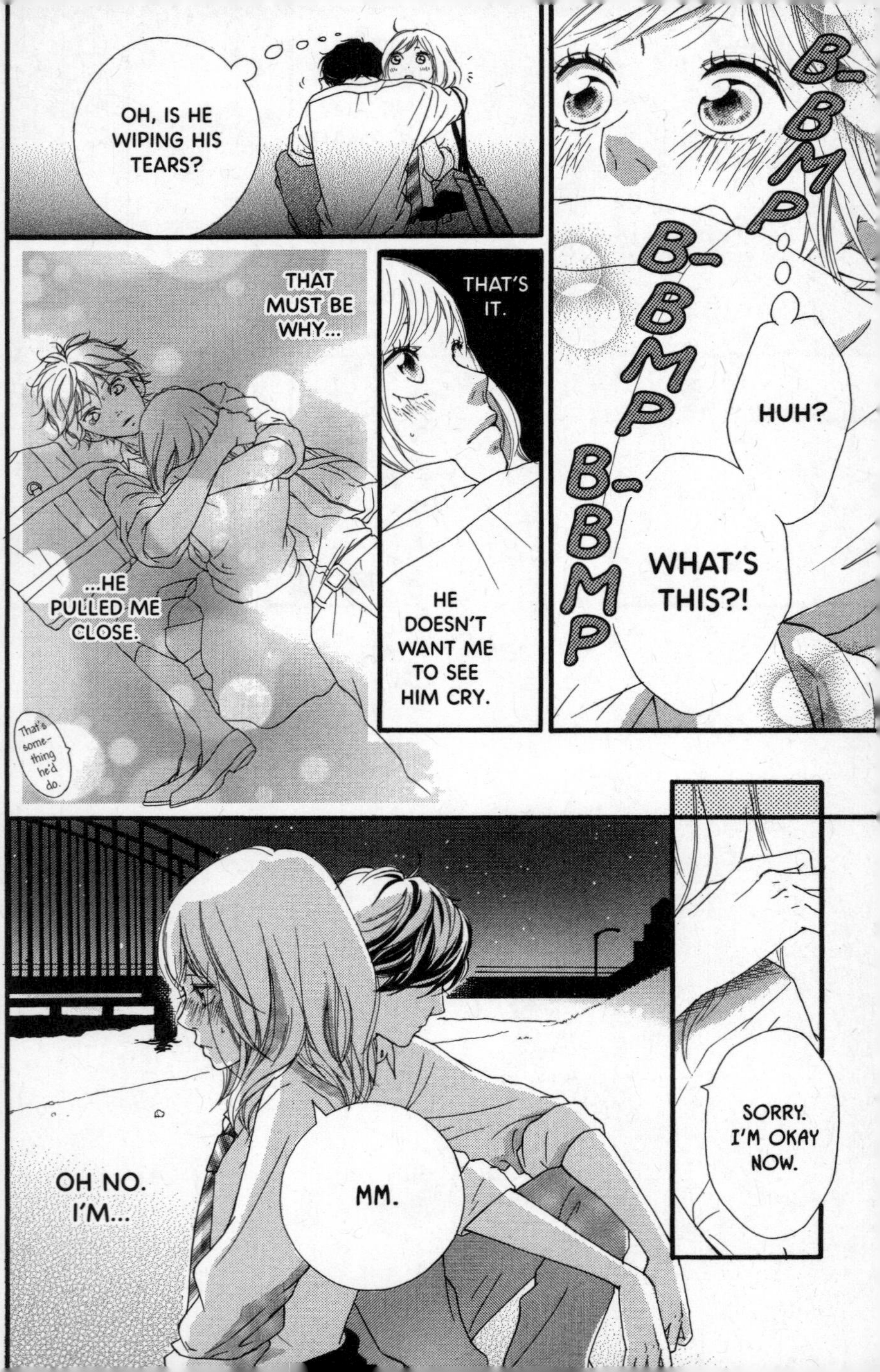
B-BMP
B-BMP
B-BMP
HUH?
WHAT'S THIS?!
OH, IS HE WIPING HIS TEARS?
THAT'S IT.
HE DOESN'T WANT ME TO SEE HIM CRY.
THAT MUST BE WHY...
...HE PULLED ME CLOSE.
That's something he'd do.
SORRY. I'M OKAY NOW.
MM.
OH NO. I'M...

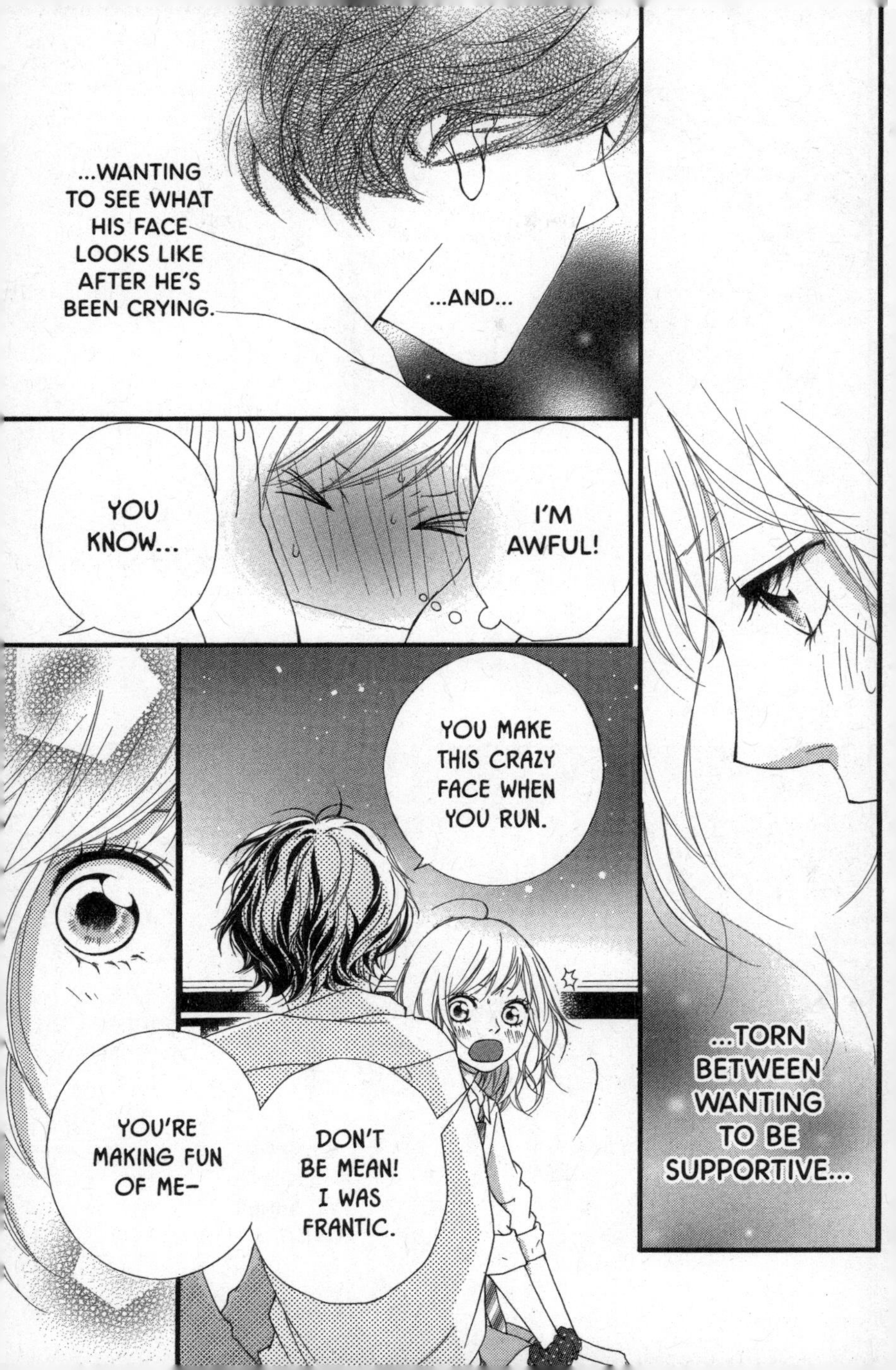
...TORN BETWEEN WANTING TO BE SUPPORTIVE...
...AND...
...WANTING TO SEE WHAT HIS FACE LOOKS LIKE AFTER HE'S BEEN CRYING.
I'M AWFUL!
YOU KNOW...
YOU MAKE THIS CRAZY FACE WHEN YOU RUN.
DON'T BE MEAN! I WAS FRANTIC.
YOU'RE MAKING FUN OF ME–

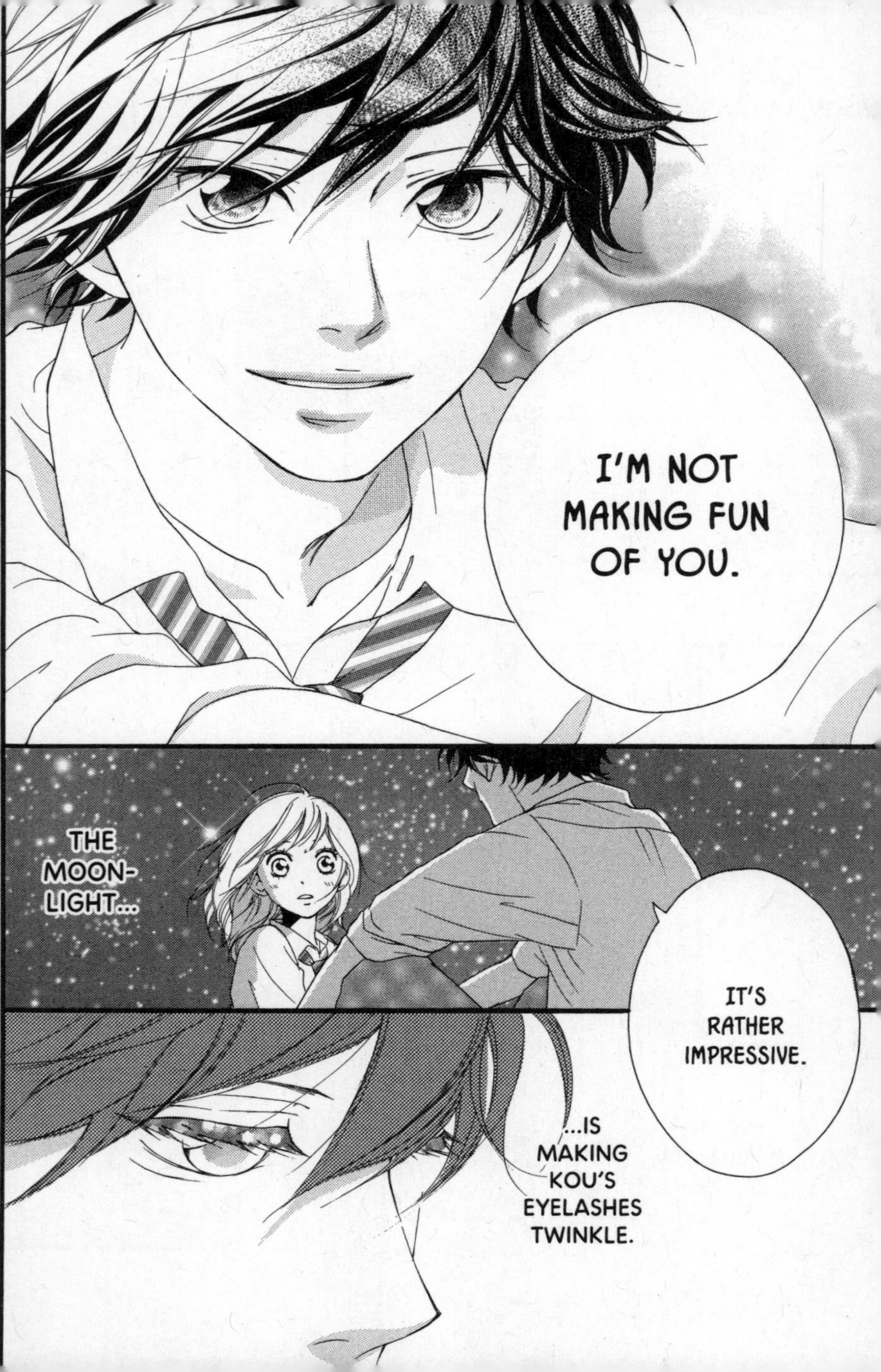
I'M NOT MAKING FUN OF YOU.
IT'S RATHER IMPRESSIVE.
THE MOON-LIGHT...
...IS MAKING KOU'S EYELASHES TWINKLE.

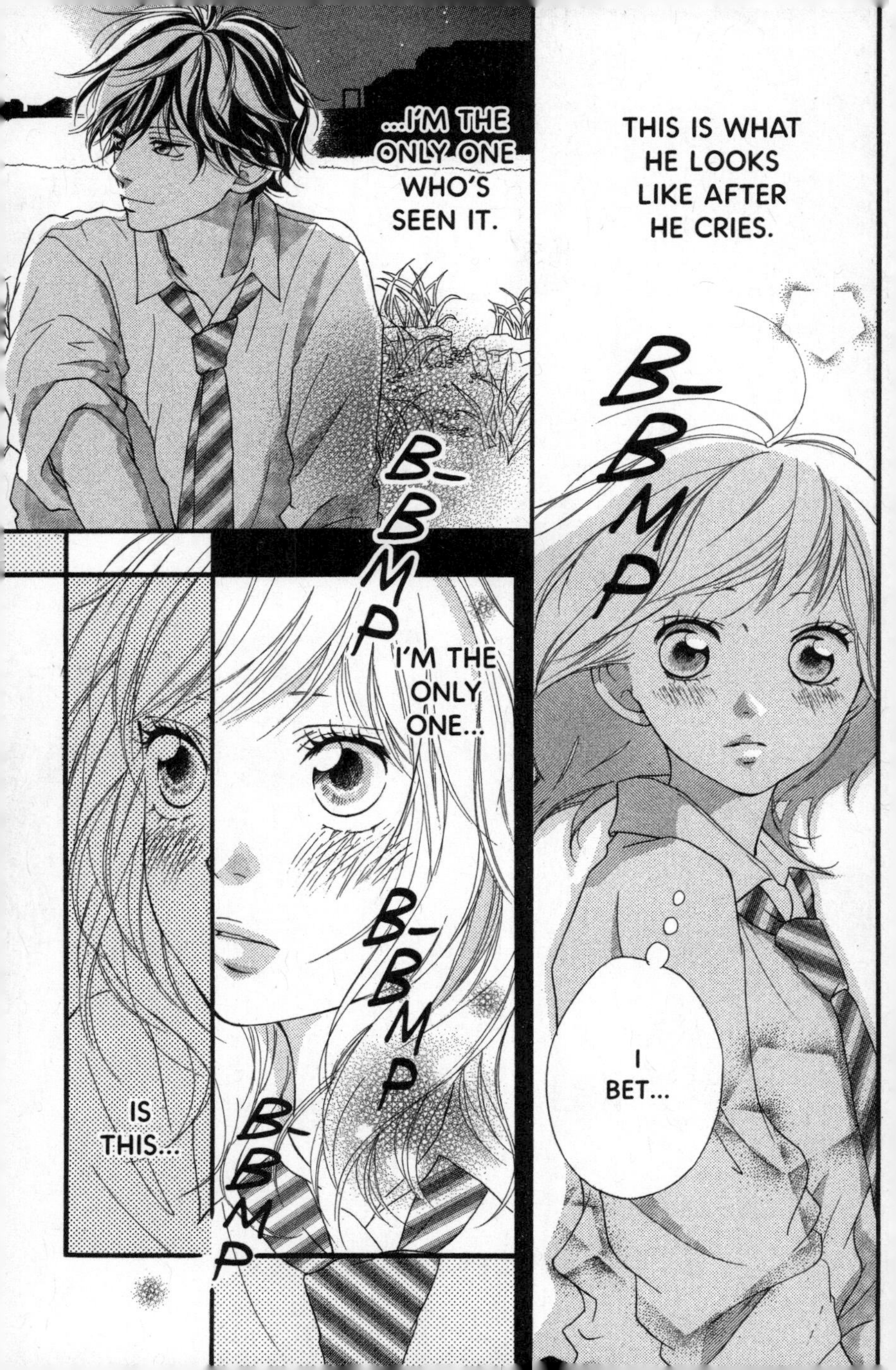
THIS IS WHAT HE LOOKS LIKE AFTER HE CRIES.
B-BMP
I BET...
...I'M THE ONLY ONE WHO'S SEEN IT.
B-BMP
I'M THE ONLY ONE...
B-BMP
B-BMP
IS THIS...

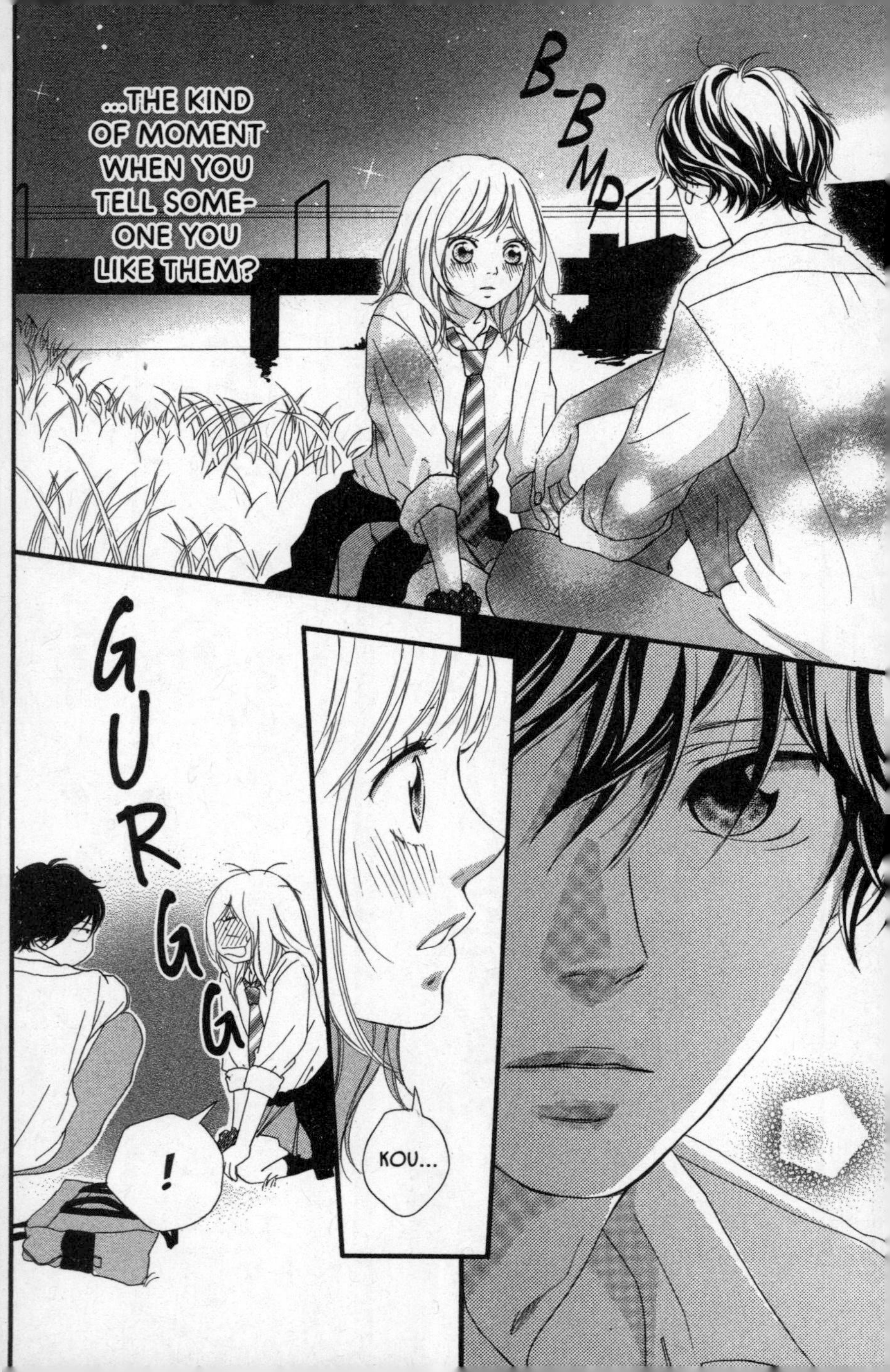
B-BMP
...THE KIND OF MOMENT WHEN YOU TELL SOME-ONE YOU LIKE THEM?
KOU...
GURGG
!

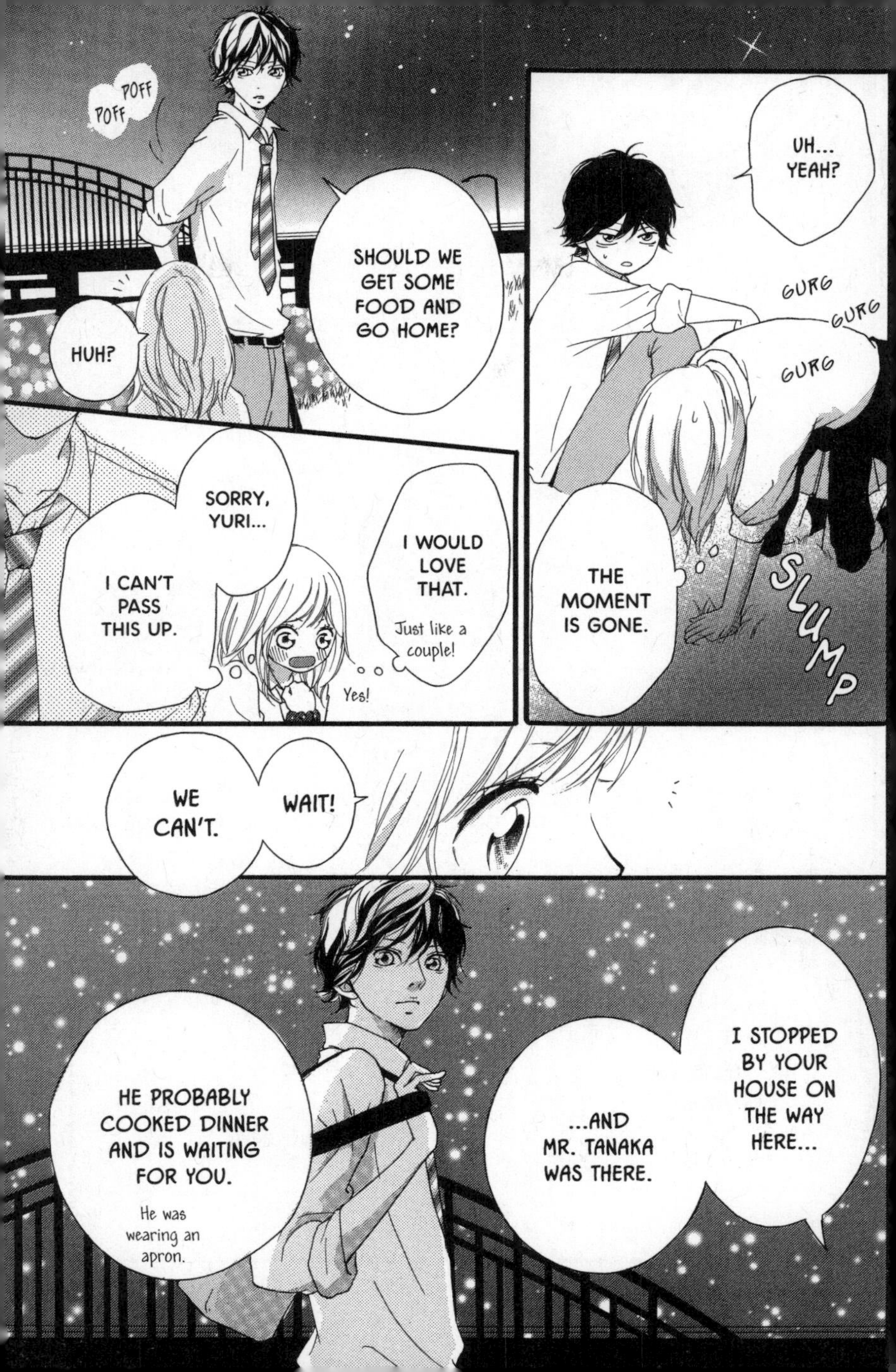
POFF
POFF
SHOULD WE GET SOME FOOD AND GO HOME?
HUH?
I WOULD LOVE THAT.
Just like a couple!
Yes!
SORRY, YURI...
I CAN'T PASS THIS UP.
UH... YEAH?
GURG
GURG
GURG
THE MOMENT IS GONE.
SLUMP
WAIT!
WE CAN'T.
I STOPPED BY YOUR HOUSE ON THE WAY HERE...
...AND MR. TANAKA WAS THERE.
HE PROBABLY COOKED DINNER AND IS WAITING FOR YOU.
He was wearing an apron.

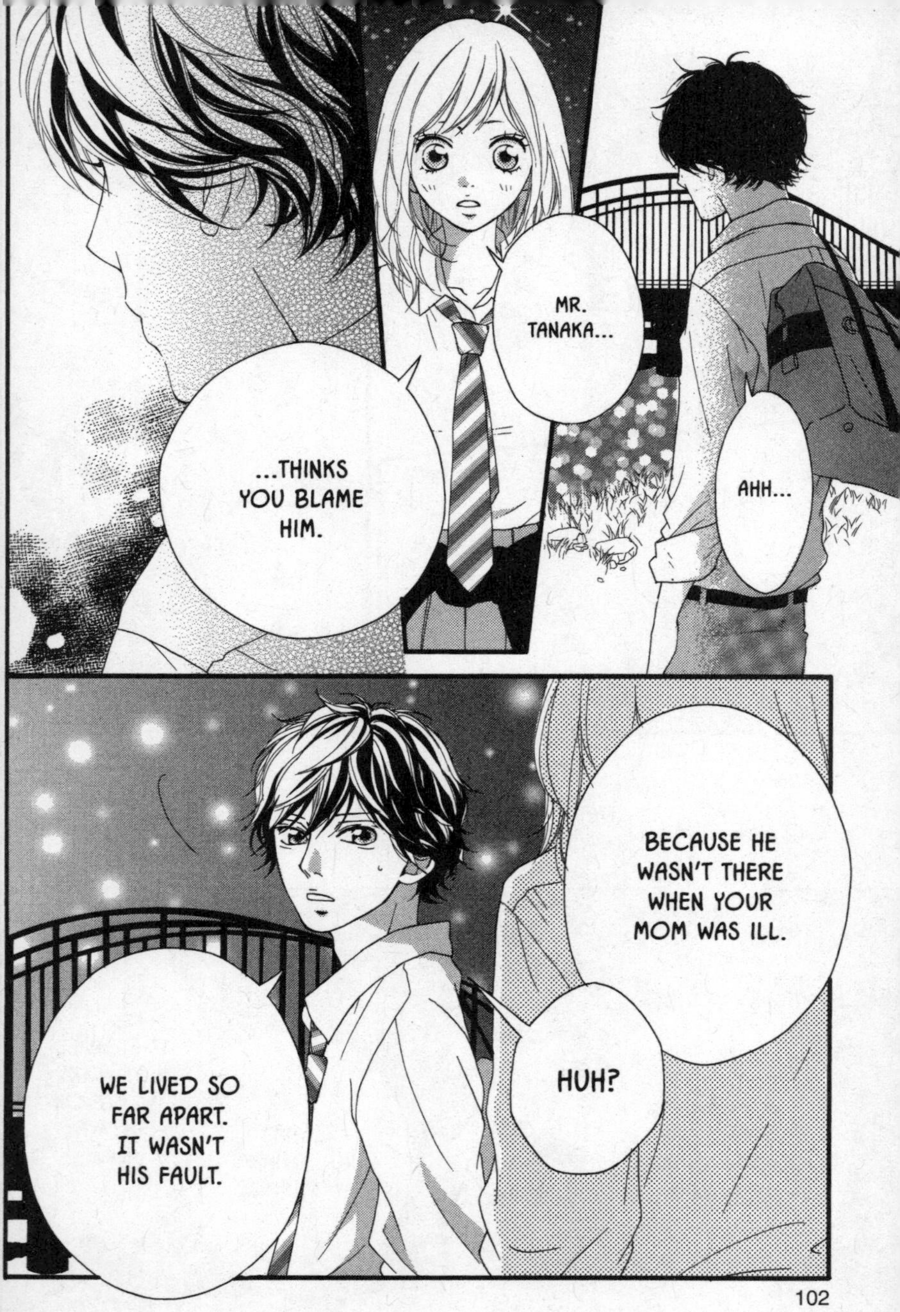
AHH...
MR. TANAKA...
...THINKS YOU BLAME HIM.
BECAUSE HE WASN'T THERE WHEN YOUR MOM WAS ILL.
HUH?
WE LIVED SO FAR APART. IT WASN'T HIS FAULT.

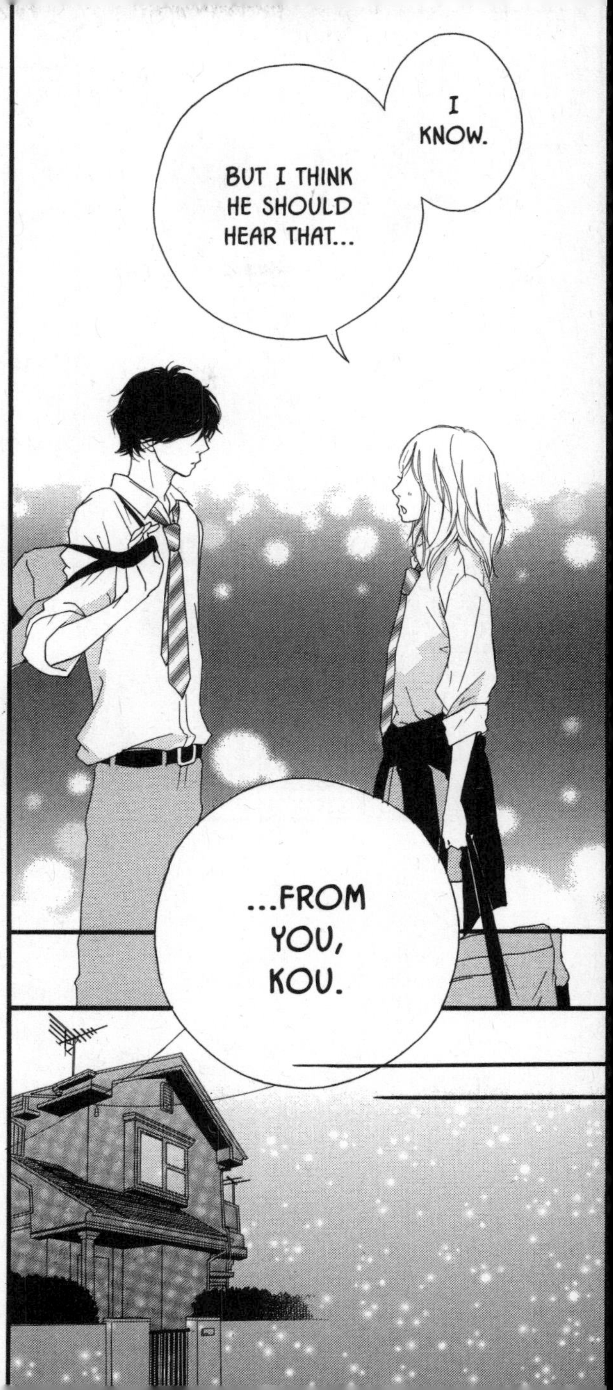
I KNOW.
BUT I THINK HE SHOULD HEAR THAT...
...FROM YOU, KOU.

MUSIC

The cover illustration for volume 4 was done while listening exclusively to songs by Capsule. In particular, I listened to "Love or Lies" on repeat for an entire day. After I finished the cover, whenever I heard that song I thought of Kou's face. That's how much I relied on it. (*laugh*) It's really a good song. I hope you'll listen to it too.☆ I usually listen to music when I draw, and I would love any recommendations from you. ♡ Oh, but not calming music, really. While I draw I like to listen to upbeat songs—the kind that make your heart pound! I'd love your recs on any music like that!

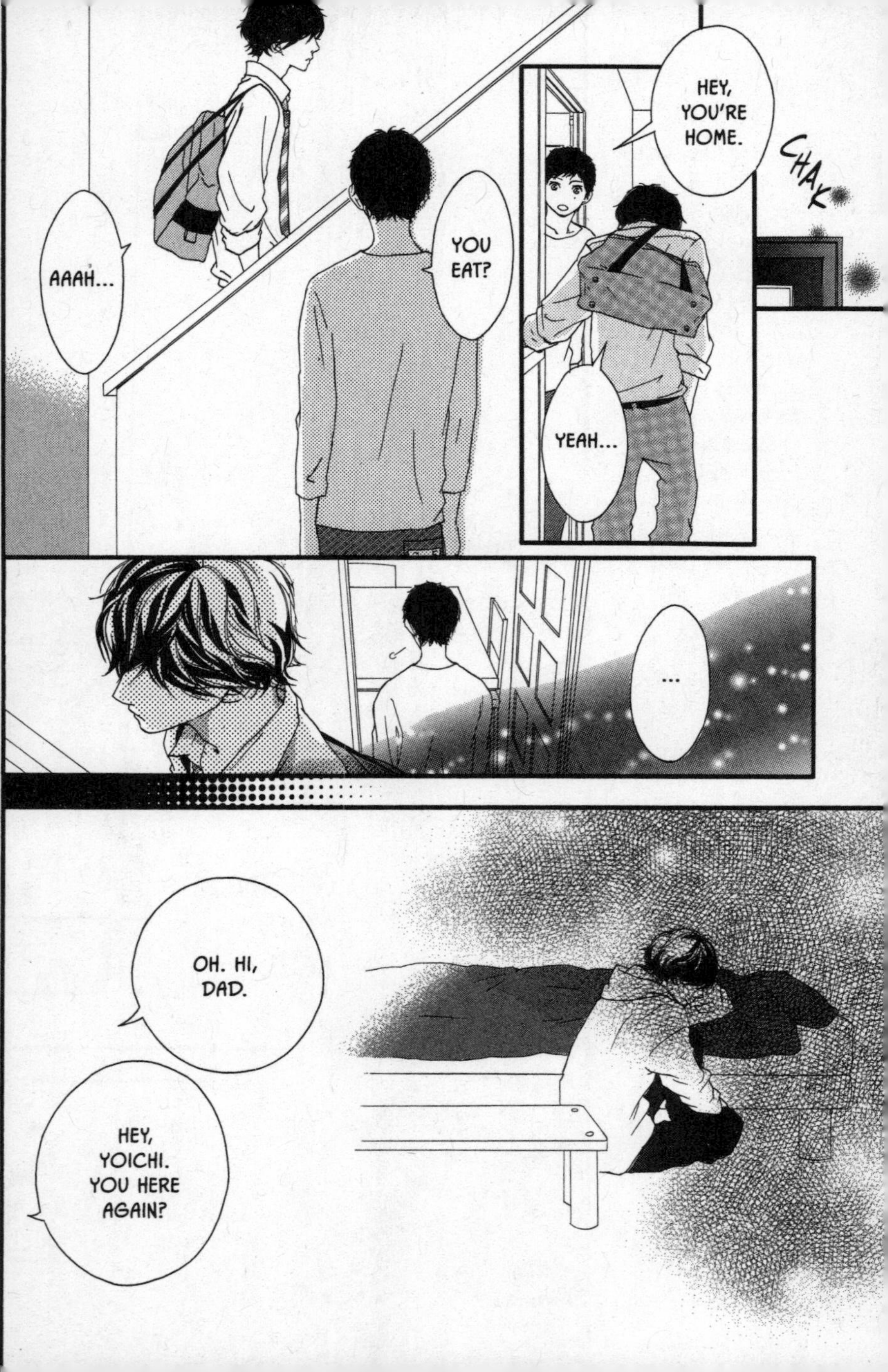
CHAK
HEY, YOU'RE HOME.
YEAH...
YOU EAT?
AAAH...
...
OH. HI, DAD.
HEY, YOICHI. YOU HERE AGAIN?

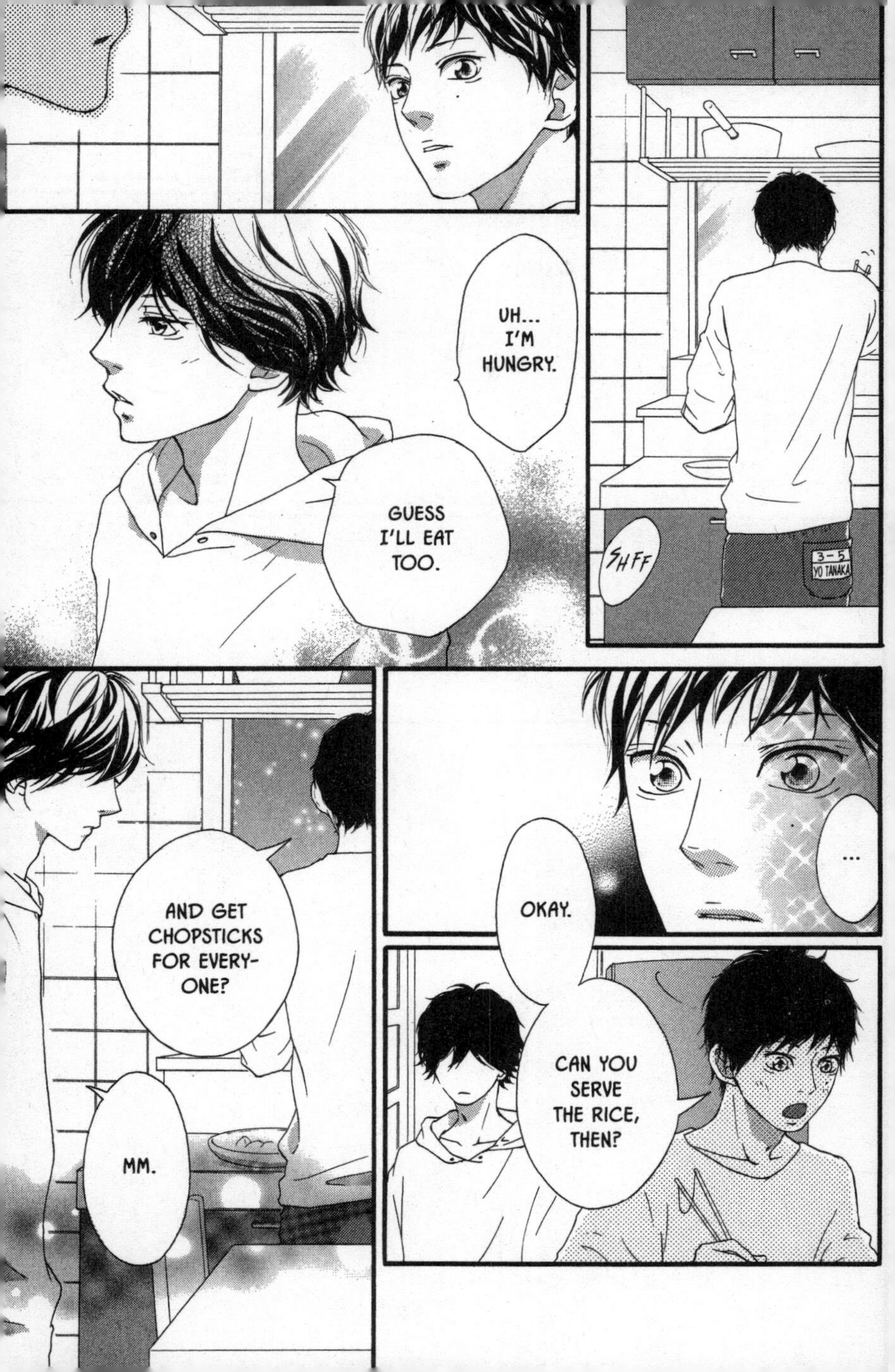
SHFF
3-5
YO TANAKA
UH... I'M HUNGRY.
GUESS I'LL EAT TOO.
...
OKAY.
CAN YOU SERVE THE RICE, THEN?
AND GET CHOPSTICKS FOR EVERY-ONE?
MM.

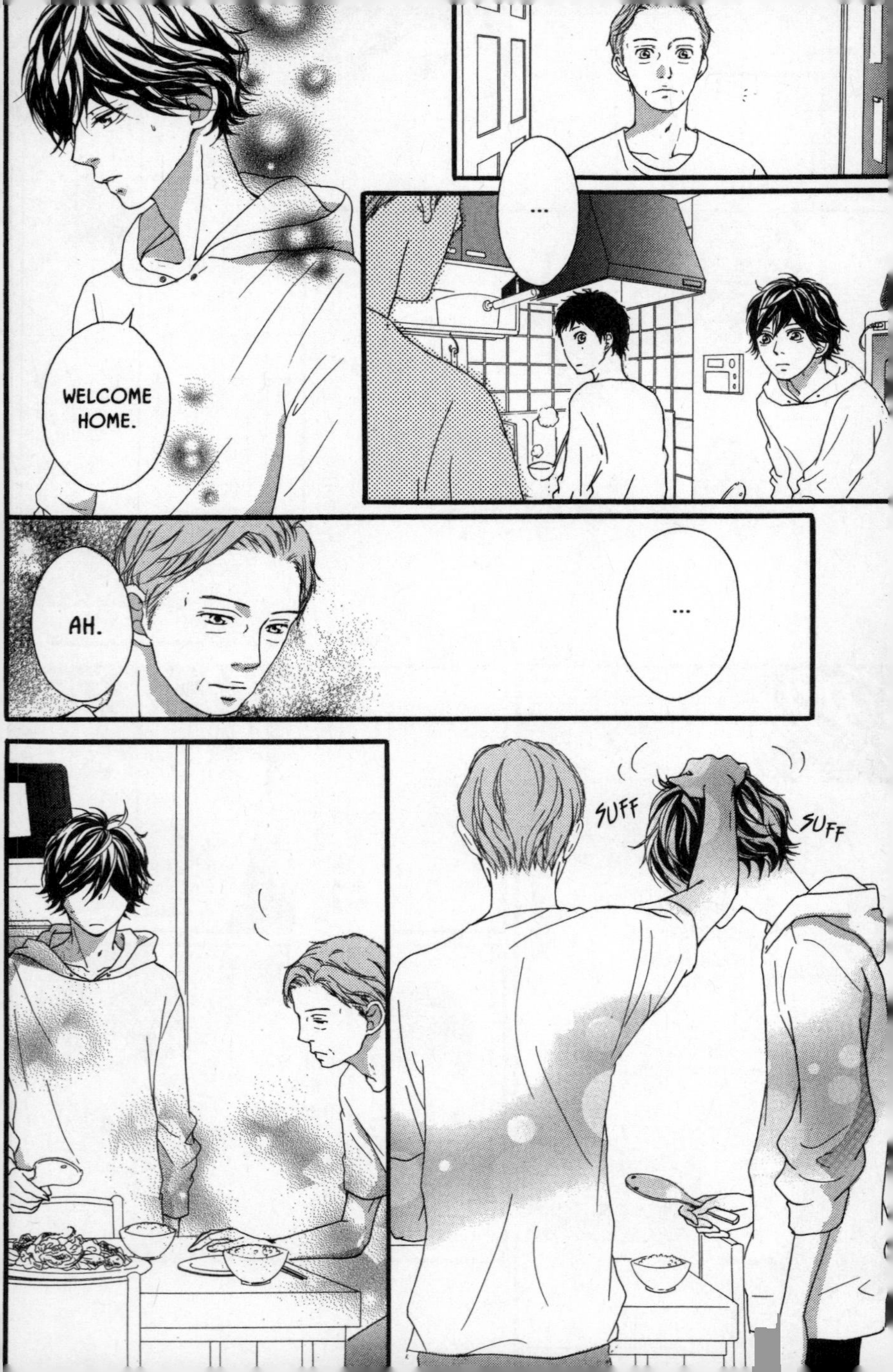
...
WELCOME HOME.
...
AH.
SUFF
SUFF

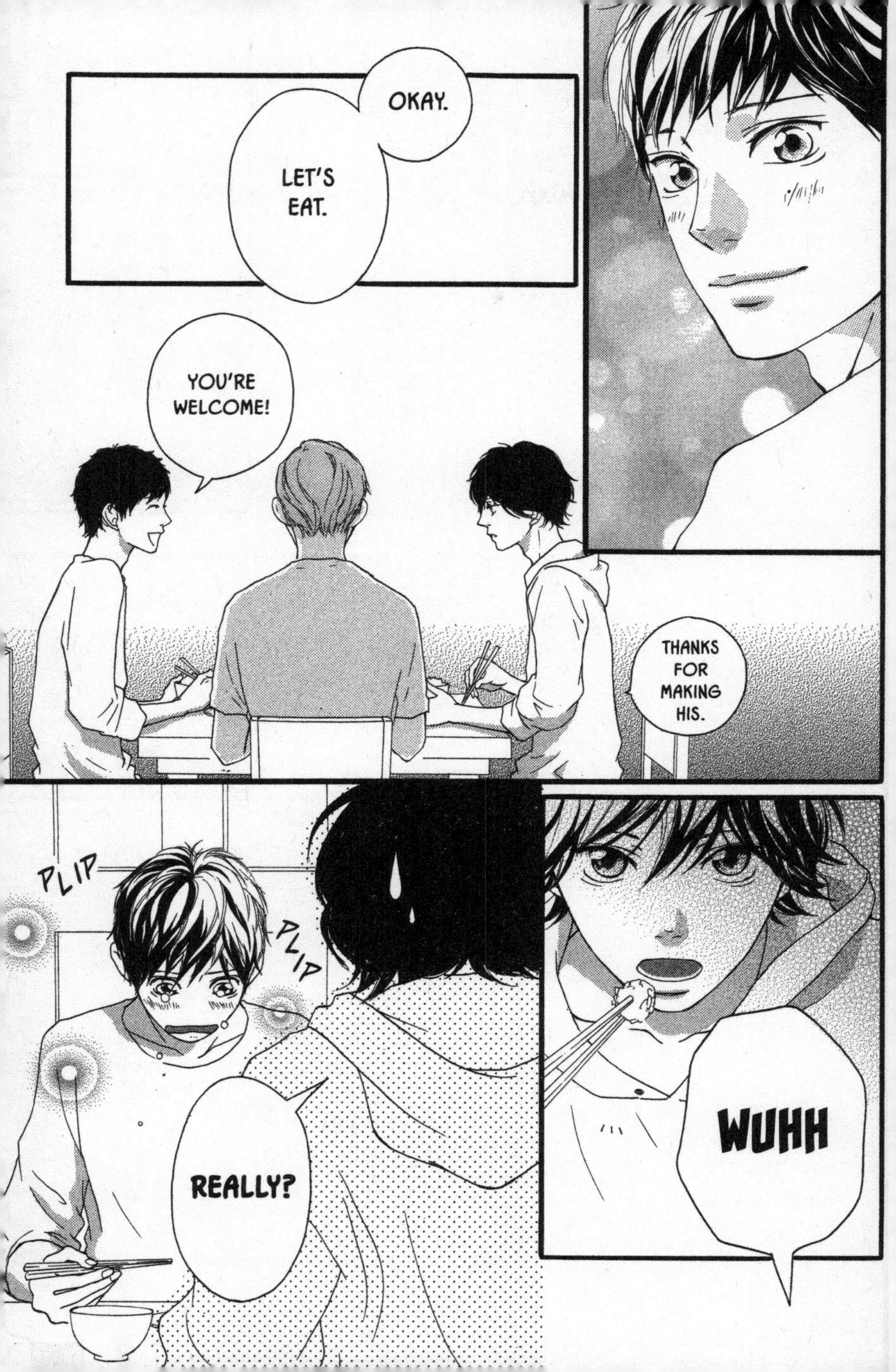
OKAY.
LET'S EAT.
THANKS FOR MAKING HIS.
YOU'RE WELCOME!
WUHH
PLIP
PLIP
REALLY?

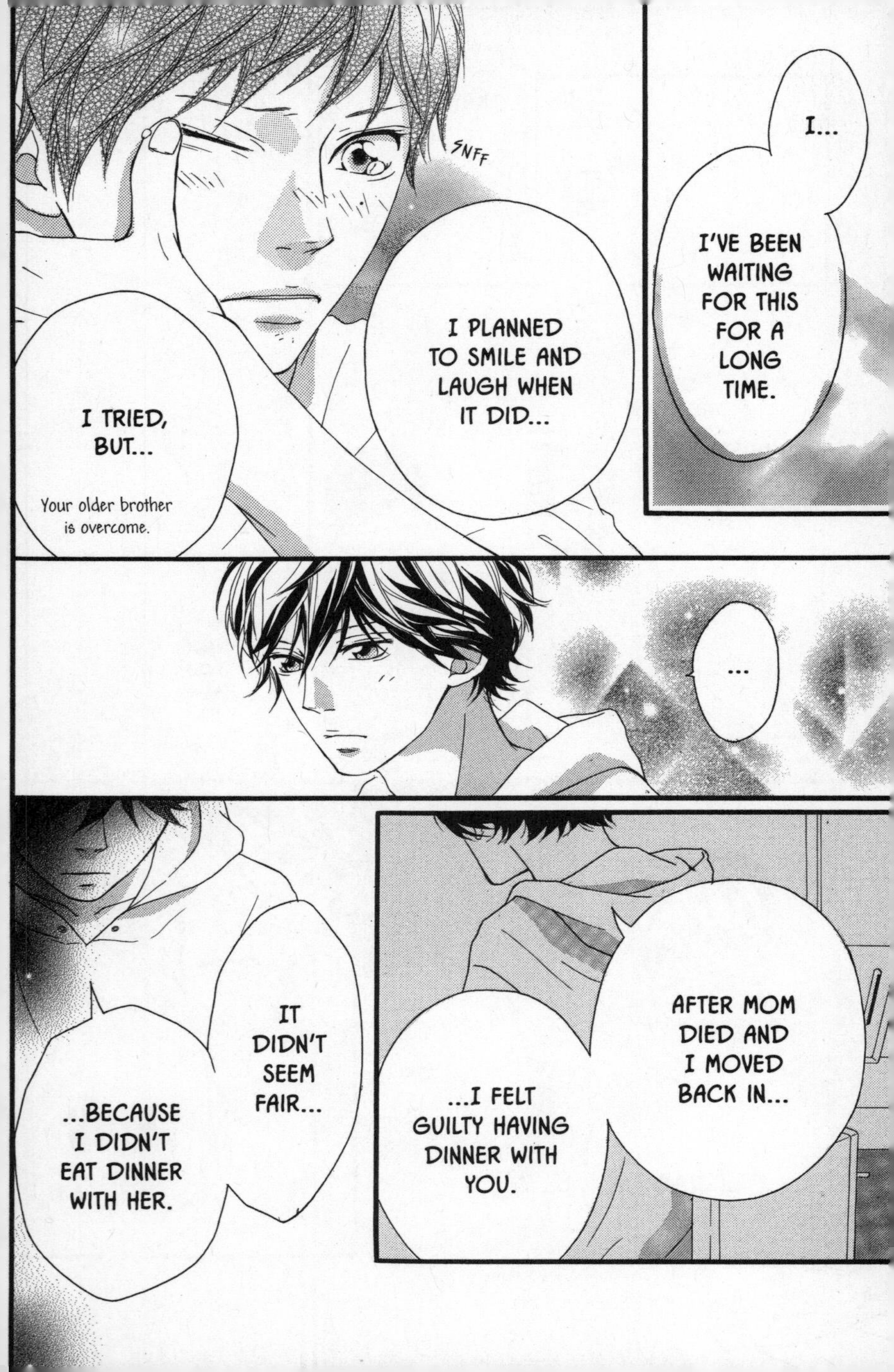
I...
I'VE BEEN WAITING FOR THIS FOR A LONG TIME.
SNFF
I PLANNED TO SMILE AND LAUGH WHEN IT DID...
I TRIED, BUT...
Your older brother is overcome.
...
AFTER MOM DIED AND I MOVED BACK IN...
...I FELT GUILTY HAVING DINNER WITH YOU.
IT DIDN'T SEEM FAIR...
...BECAUSE I DIDN'T EAT DINNER WITH HER.

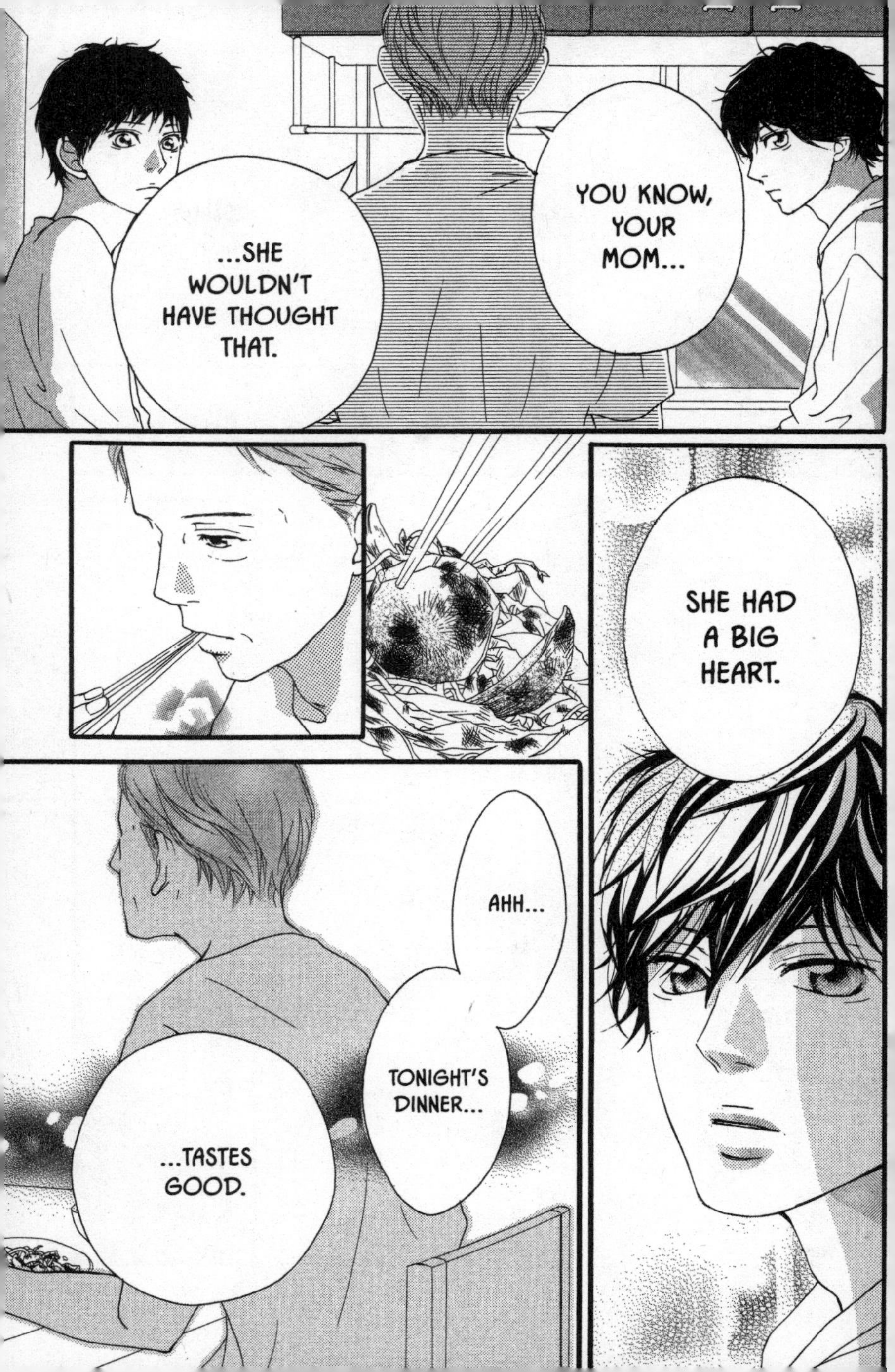
YOU KNOW, YOUR MOM...
...SHE WOULDN'T HAVE THOUGHT THAT.
SHE HAD A BIG HEART.
AHH...
TONIGHT'S DINNER...
...TASTES GOOD.

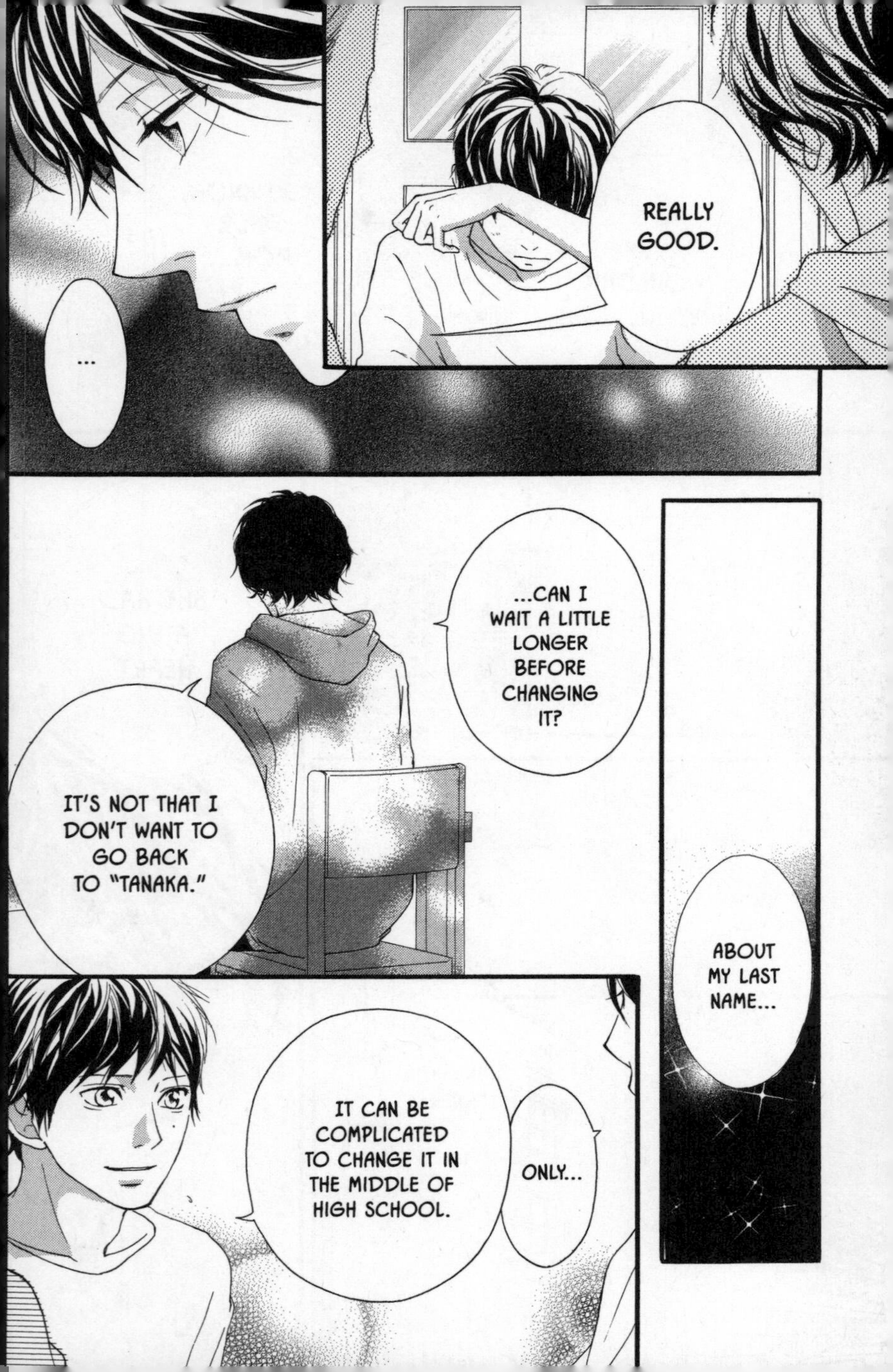
REALLY GOOD.
...
ABOUT MY LAST NAME...
...CAN I WAIT A LITTLE LONGER BEFORE CHANGING IT?
IT'S NOT THAT I DON'T WANT TO GO BACK TO "TANAKA."
ONLY...
IT CAN BE COMPLICATED TO CHANGE IT IN THE MIDDLE OF HIGH SCHOOL.

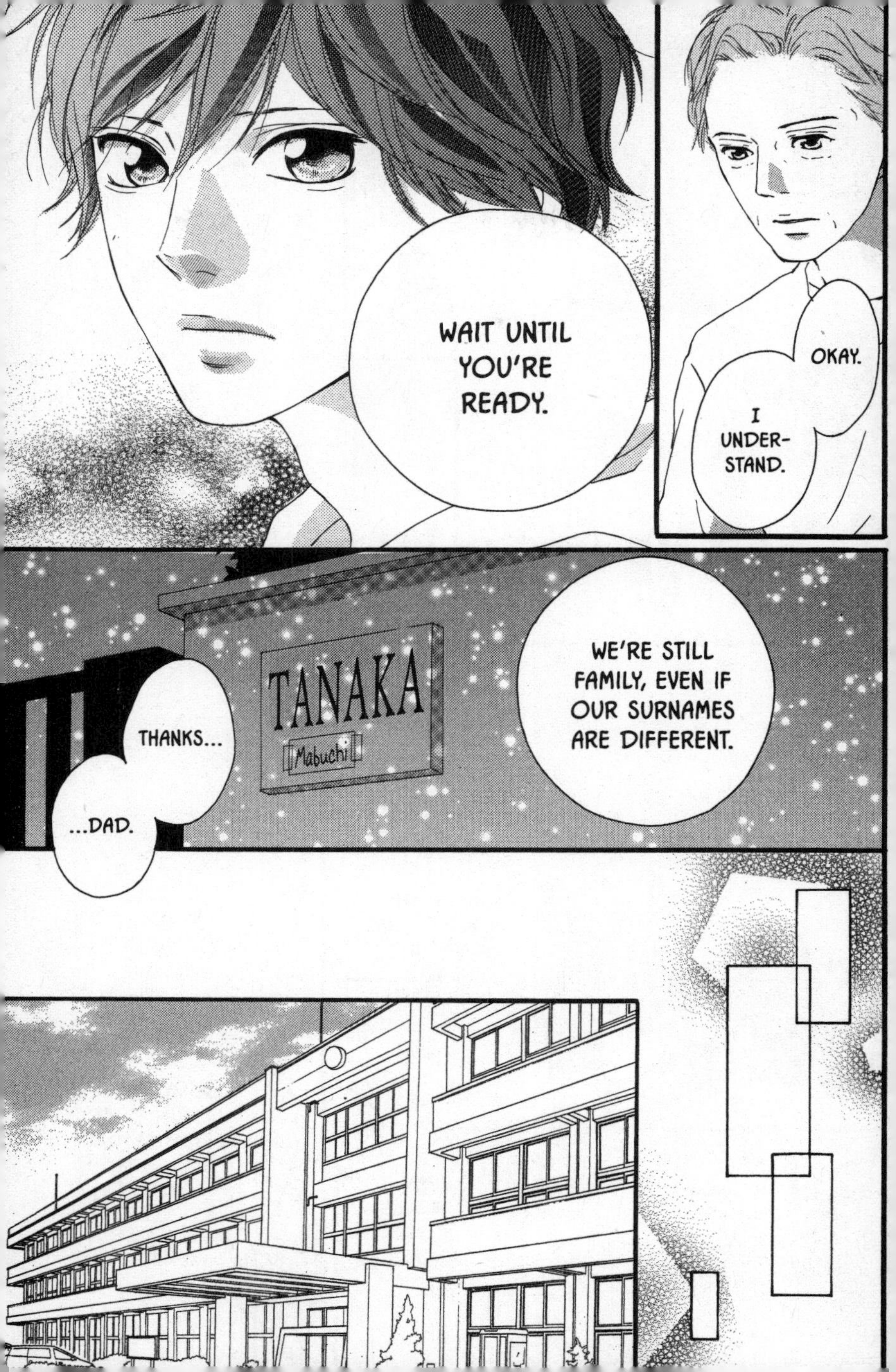
OKAY.
I UNDERSTAND.
WAIT UNTIL YOU'RE READY.
WE'RE STILL FAMILY, EVEN IF OUR SURNAMES ARE DIFFERENT.
TANAKA
Mabuchi
THANKS...
...DAD.

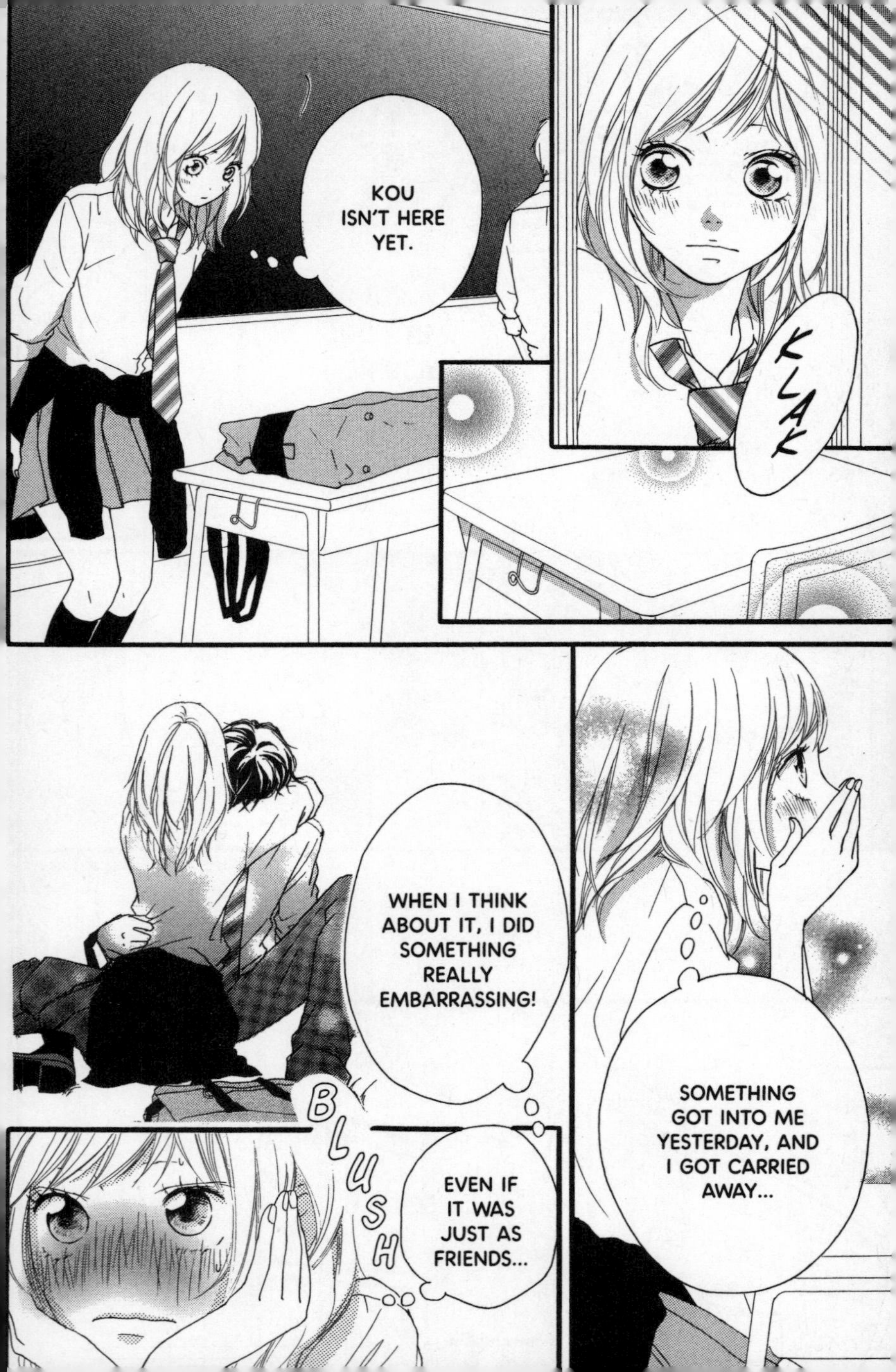
KLAK
KOU ISN'T HERE YET.
SOMETHING GOT INTO ME YESTERDAY, AND I GOT CARRIED AWAY...
WHEN I THINK ABOUT IT, I DID SOMETHING REALLY EMBARRASSING!
BLUSH
EVEN IF IT WAS JUST AS FRIENDS...

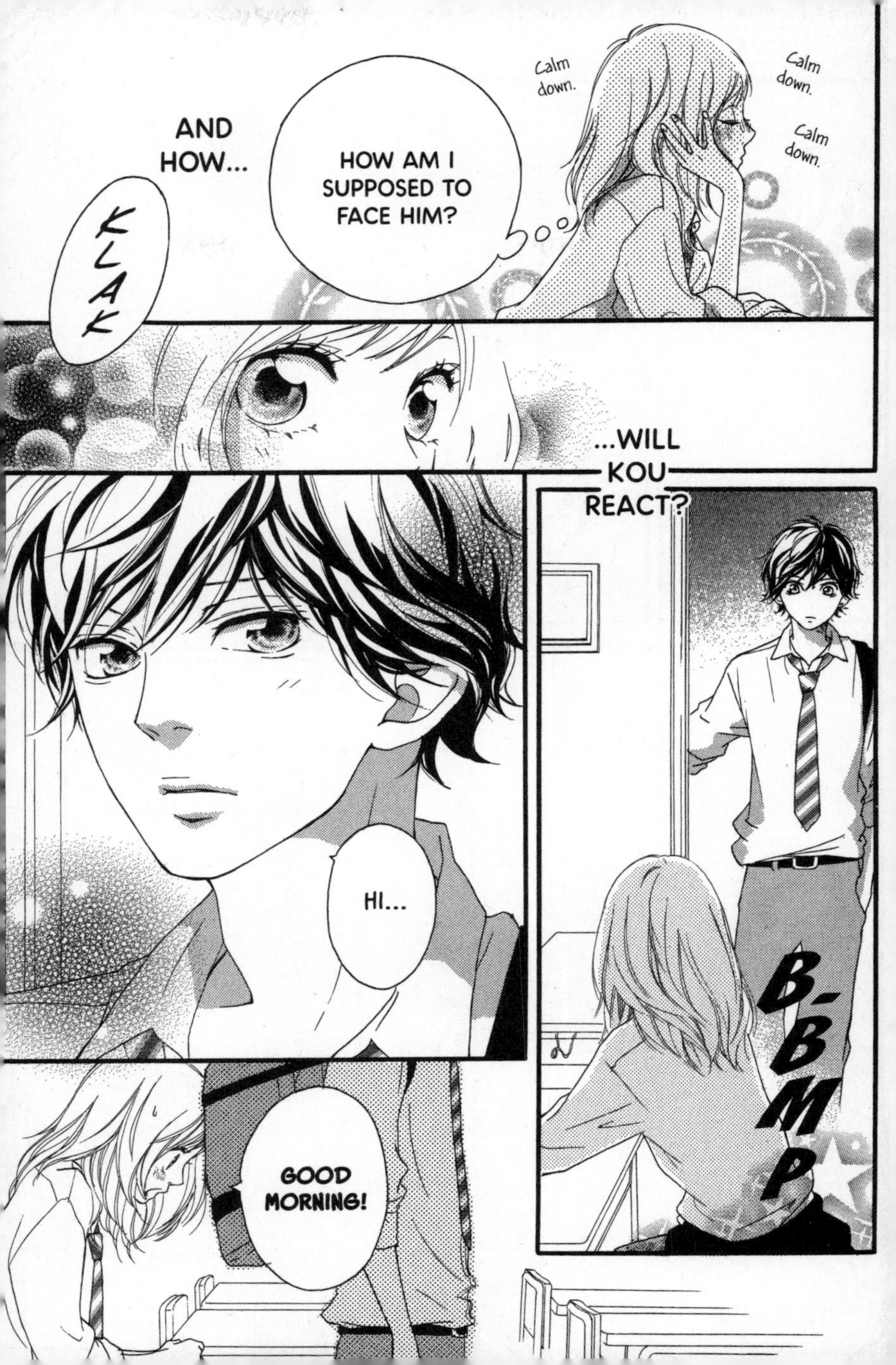

Calm down.
Calm down.
Calm down.
HOW AM I SUPPOSED TO FACE HIM?
AND HOW...
KLAK
...WILL KOU REACT?
B-BMP
HI...
GOOD MORNING!

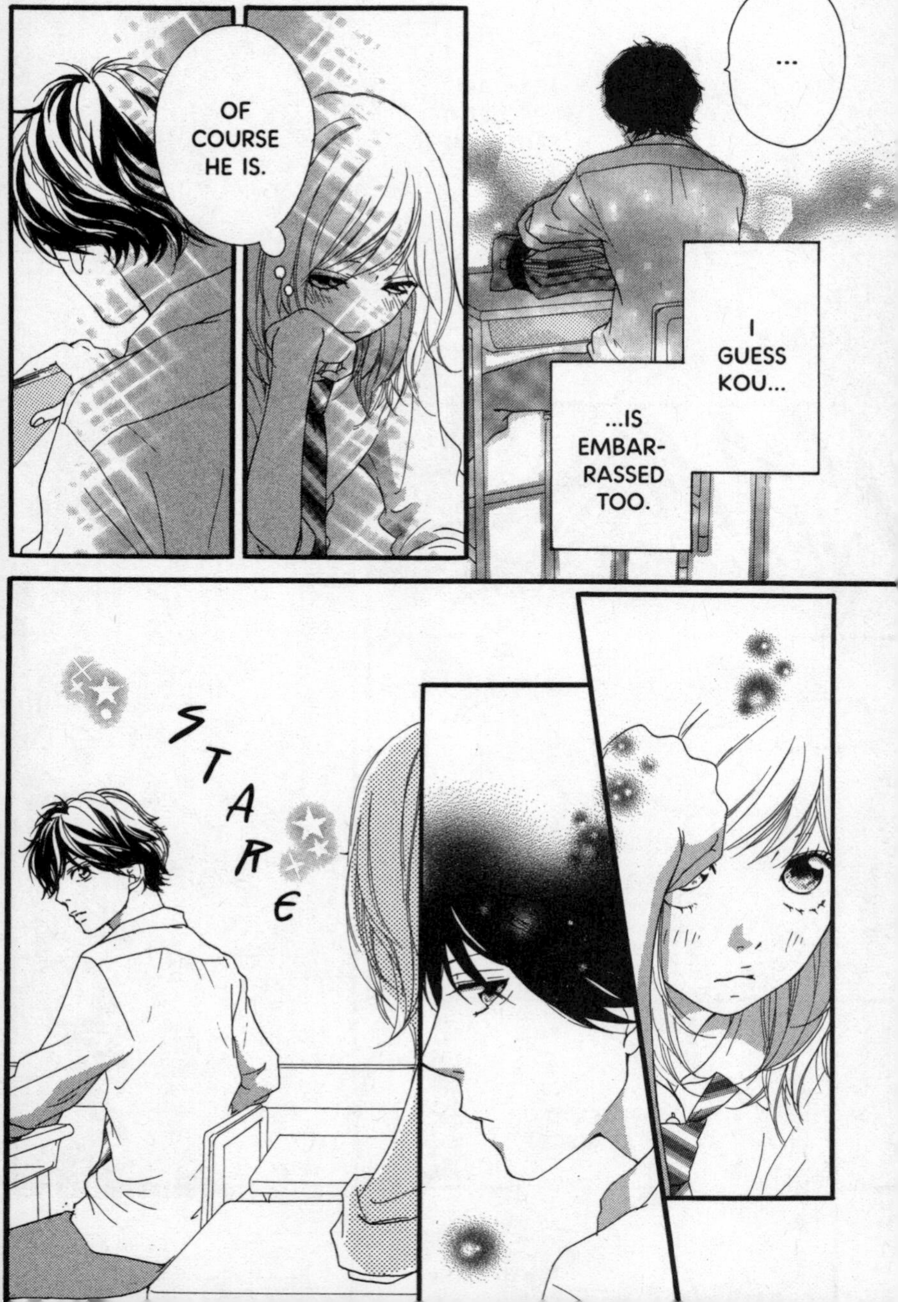
...
I GUESS KOU...
...IS EMBARRASSED TOO.
OF COURSE HE IS.
STARE

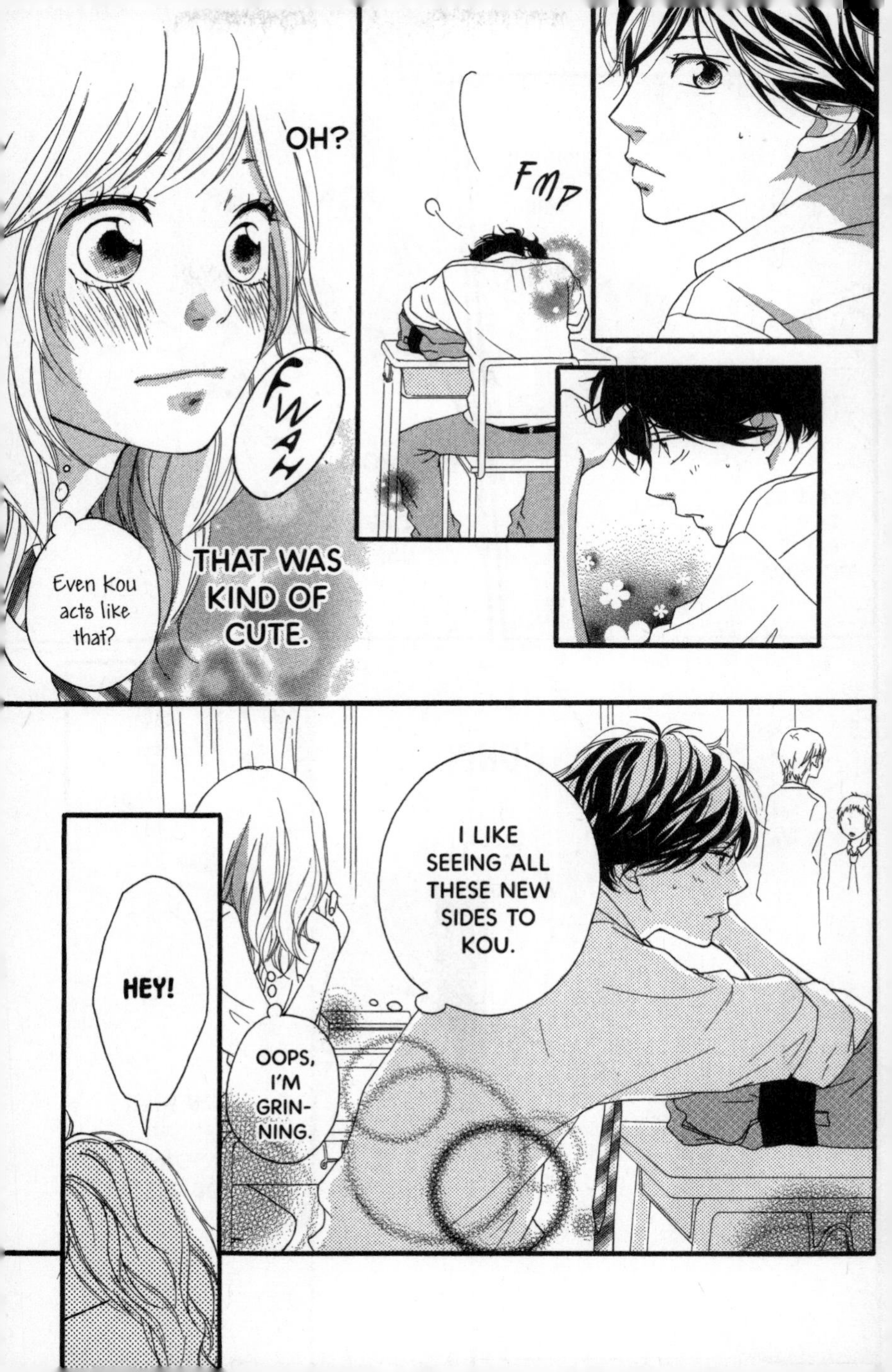

FMP
OH?
FWAH
THAT WAS KIND OF CUTE.
Even Kou acts like that?
I LIKE SEEING ALL THESE NEW SIDES TO KOU.
OOPS, I'M GRIN-NING.
HEY!

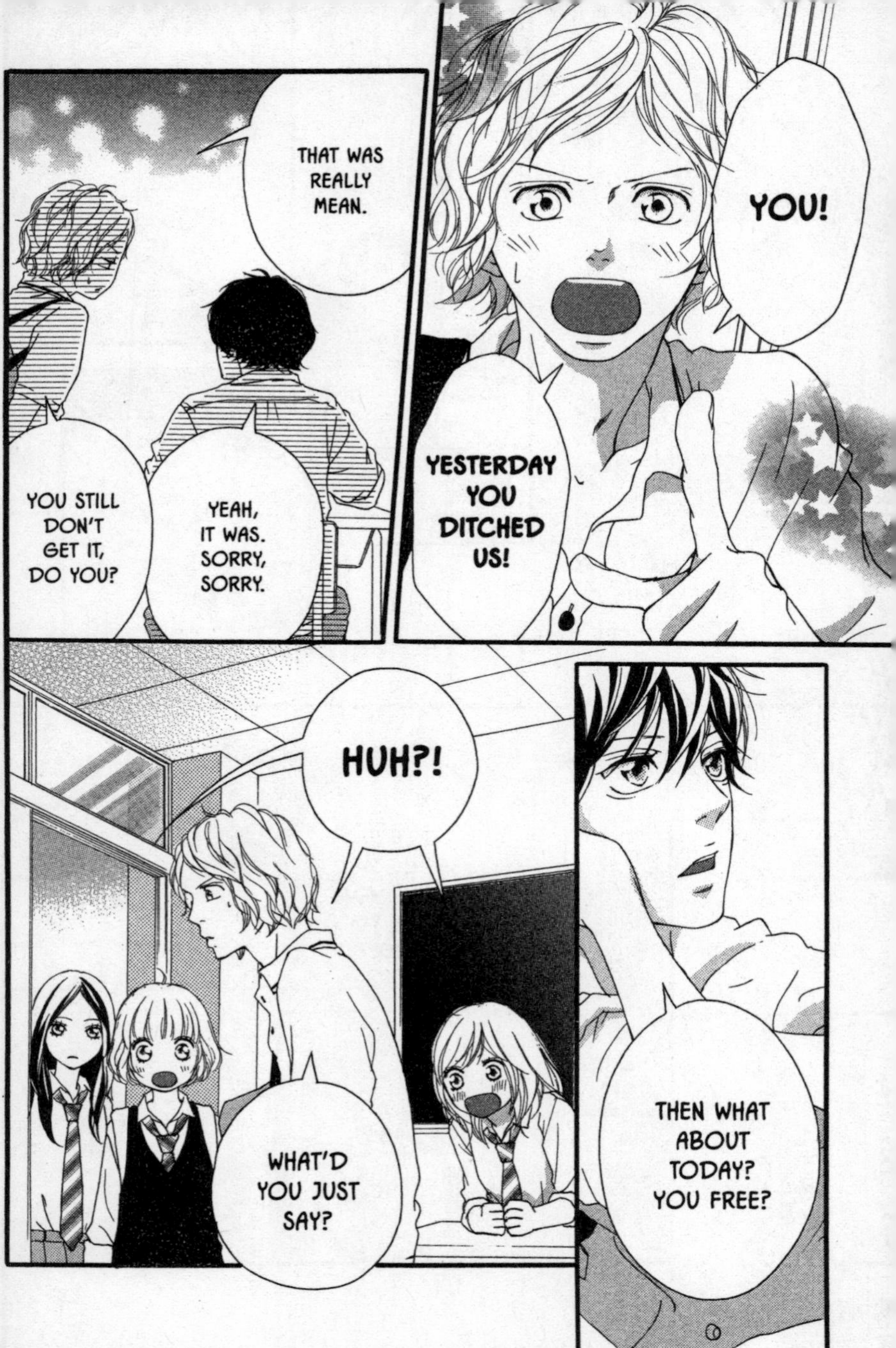
YOU!
YESTERDAY YOU DITCHED US!
THAT WAS REALLY MEAN.
YEAH, IT WAS. SORRY, SORRY.
YOU STILL DON'T GET IT, DO YOU?
THEN WHAT ABOUT TODAY? YOU FREE?
HUH?!
WHAT'D YOU JUST SAY?

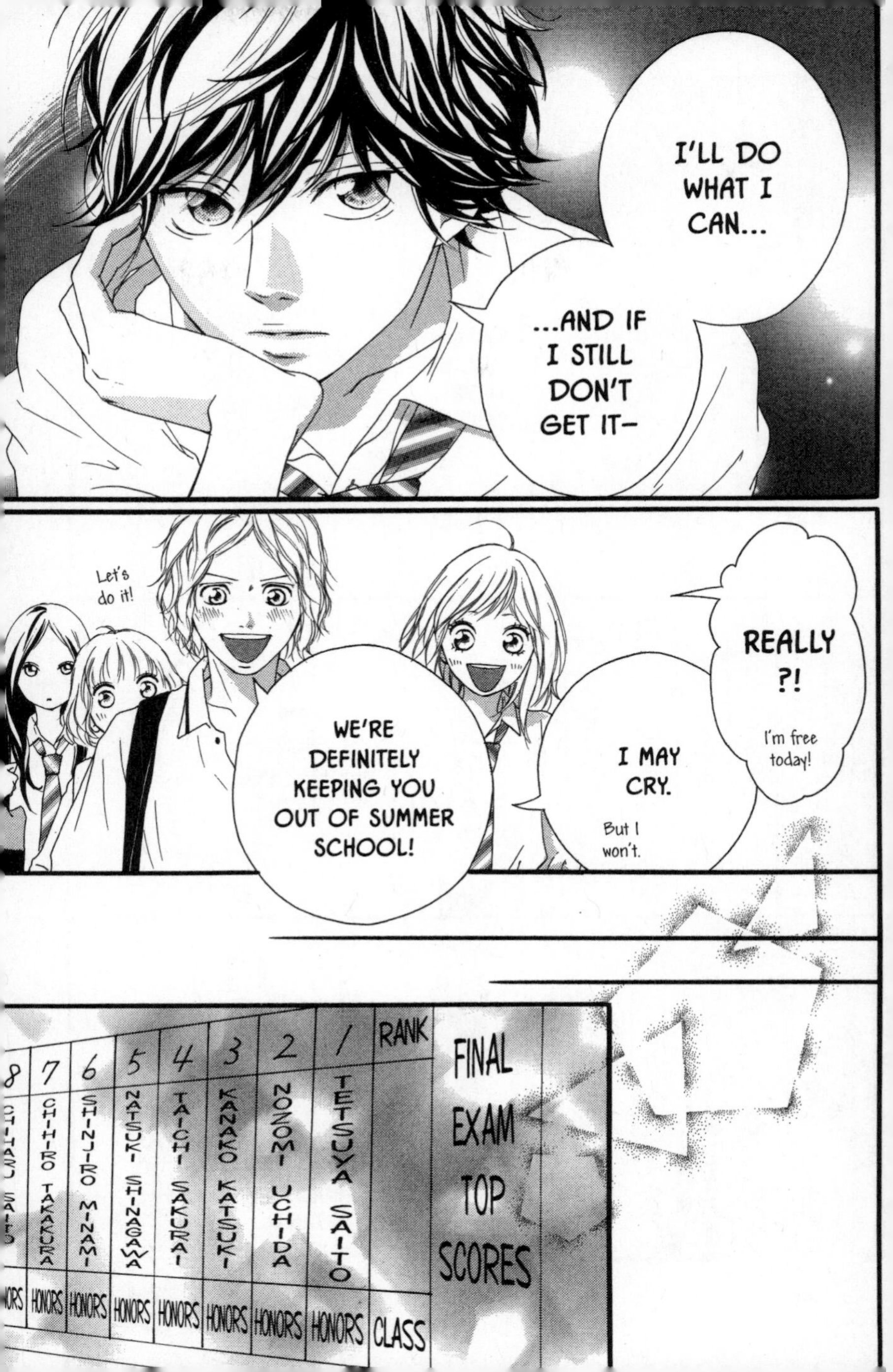
I'LL DO WHAT I CAN...
...AND IF I STILL DON'T GET IT–
REALLY ?!
I'm free today!
I MAY CRY.
But I won't.
WE'RE DEFINITELY KEEPING YOU OUT OF SUMMER SCHOOL!
Let's do it!
FINAL EXAM TOP SCORES
RANK | CLASS
1 TETSUYA SAITO HONORS
2 NOZOMI UCHIDA HONORS
3 KANAKO KATSUKI HONORS
4 TAICHI SAKURAI HONORS
5 NATSUKI SHINAGAWA HONORS
6 SHINJIRO MINAMI HONORS
7 CHIHIRO TAKAKURA HONORS
8

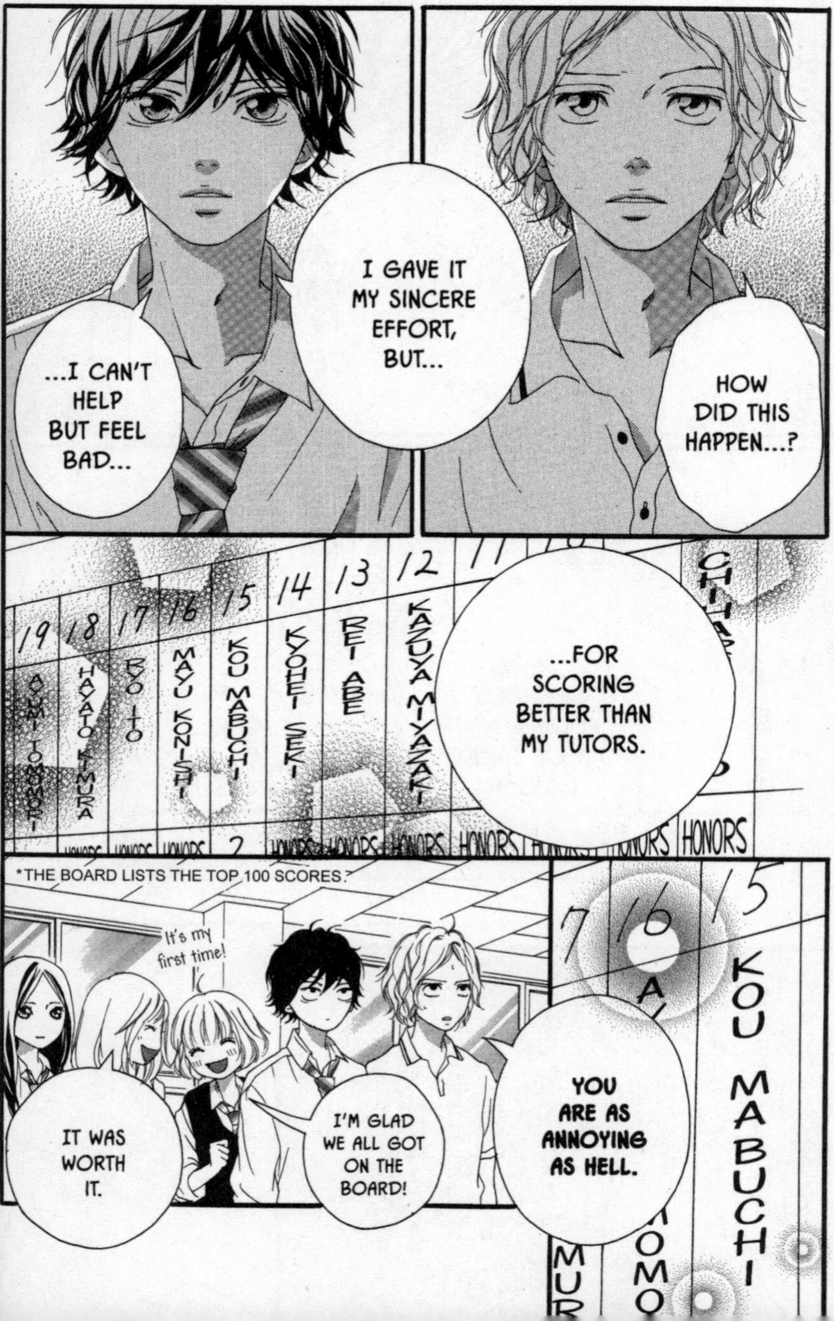
HOW DID THIS HAPPEN...?
I GAVE IT MY SINCERE EFFORT, BUT...
...I CAN'T HELP BUT FEEL BAD...
HONORS
12 KAZUYA MIYAZAKI
HONORS
13 REI ABE
HONORS
14 KYOHEI SEKI
HONORS
15 KOU MABUCHI
2
16 MAYU KONISHI
HONORS
17 RYO ITO
HONORS
18 HAYATO KIMURA
HONORS
19 AYUMI TOMOMORI
...FOR SCORING BETTER THAN MY TUTORS.
15 KOU MABUCHI
16
YOU ARE AS ANNOYING AS HELL.
*THE BOARD LISTS THE TOP 100 SCORES.
It's my first time!
I'M GLAD WE ALL GOT ON THE BOARD!
IT WAS WORTH IT.

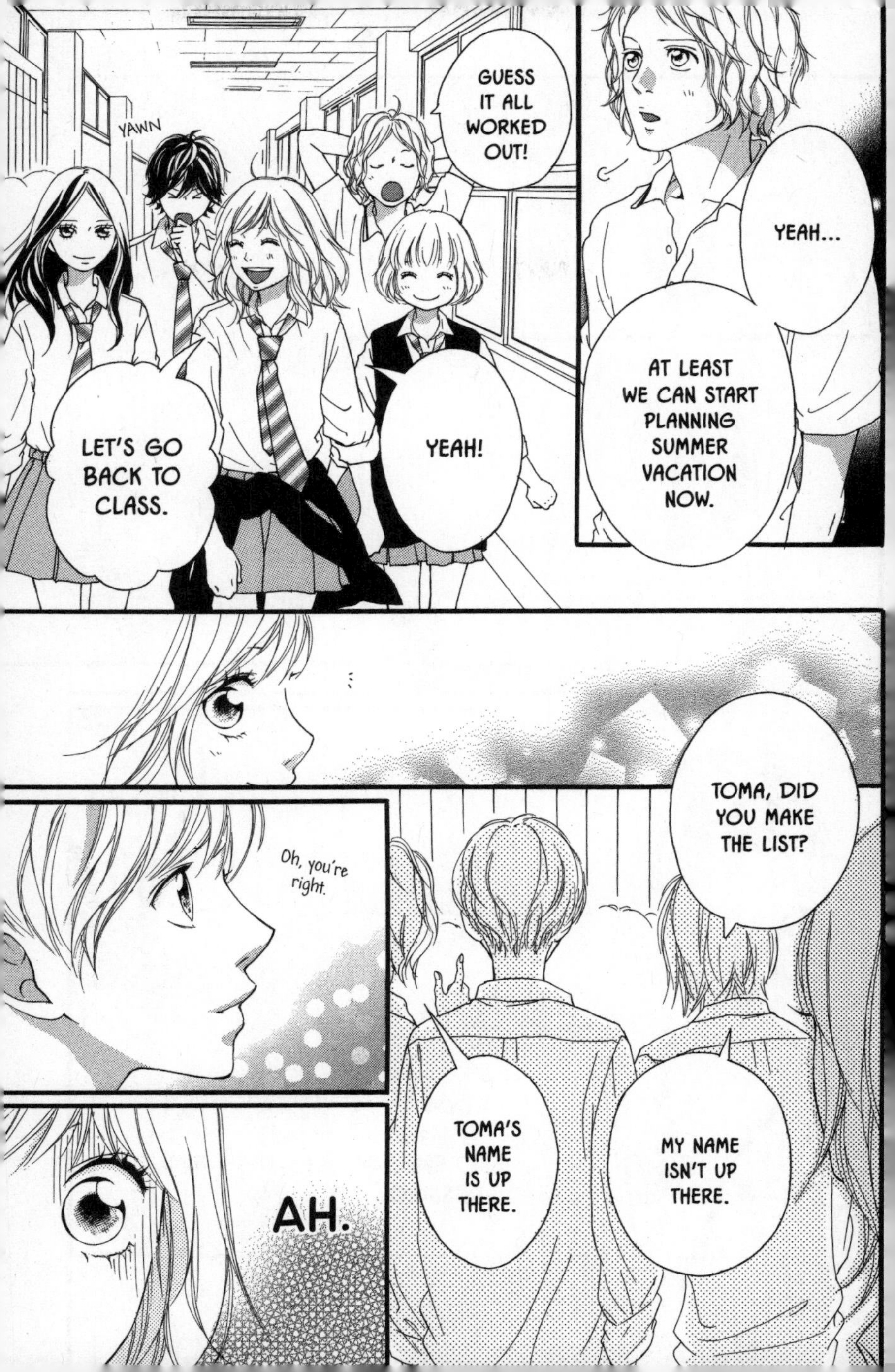
YEAH...
AT LEAST WE CAN START PLANNING SUMMER VACATION NOW.
GUESS IT ALL WORKED OUT!
YAWN
YEAH!
LET'S GO BACK TO CLASS.
TOMA, DID YOU MAKE THE LIST?
MY NAME ISN'T UP THERE.
TOMA'S NAME IS UP THERE.
Oh, you're right.
AH.

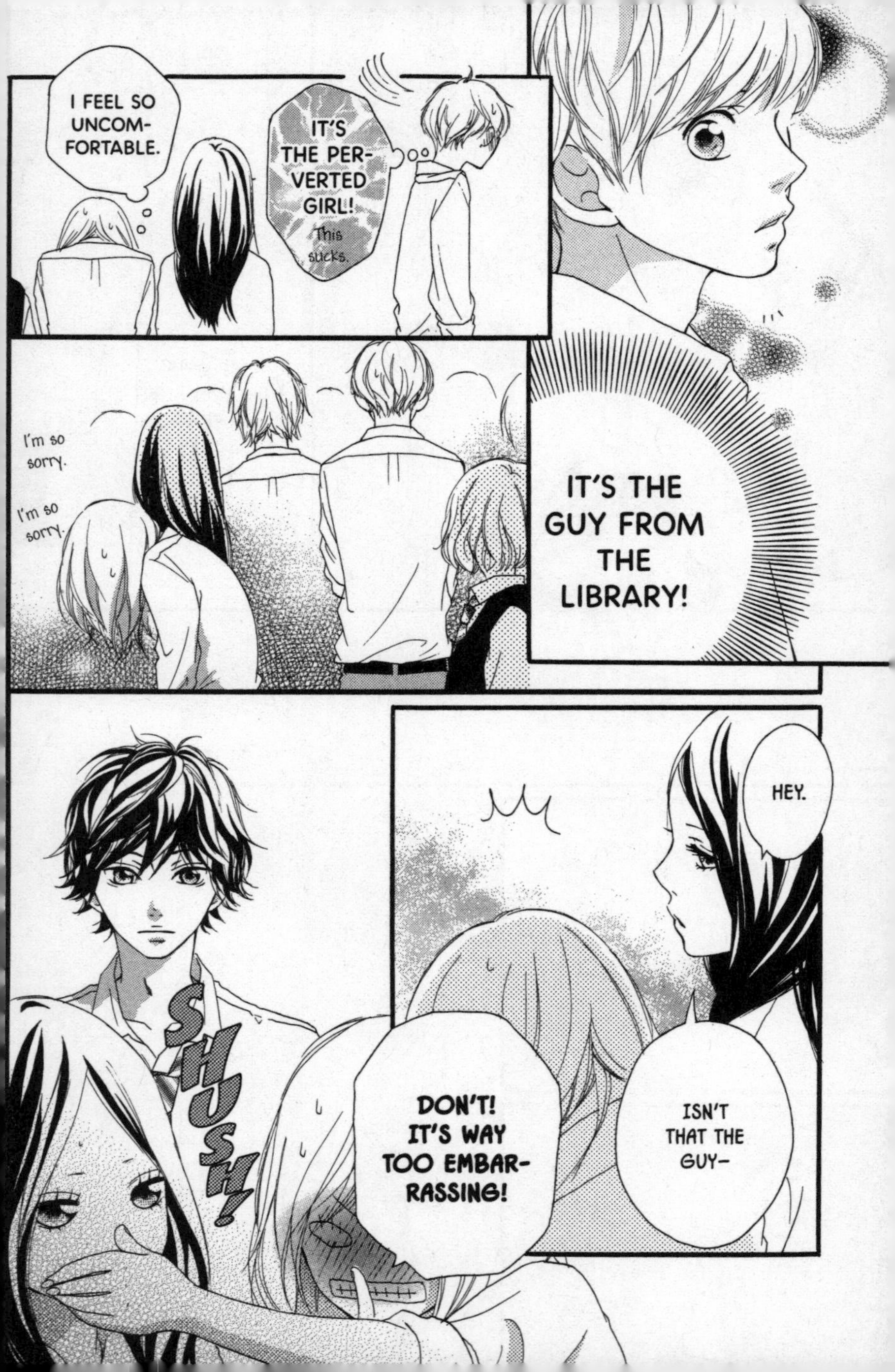
IT'S THE GUY FROM THE LIBRARY!
IT'S THE PER-VERTED GIRL!
This sucks.
I FEEL SO UNCOM-FORTABLE.
I'm so sorry.
I'm so sorry.
HEY.
ISN'T THAT THE GUY–
DON'T! IT'S WAY TOO EMBAR-RASSING!
SHUSH!

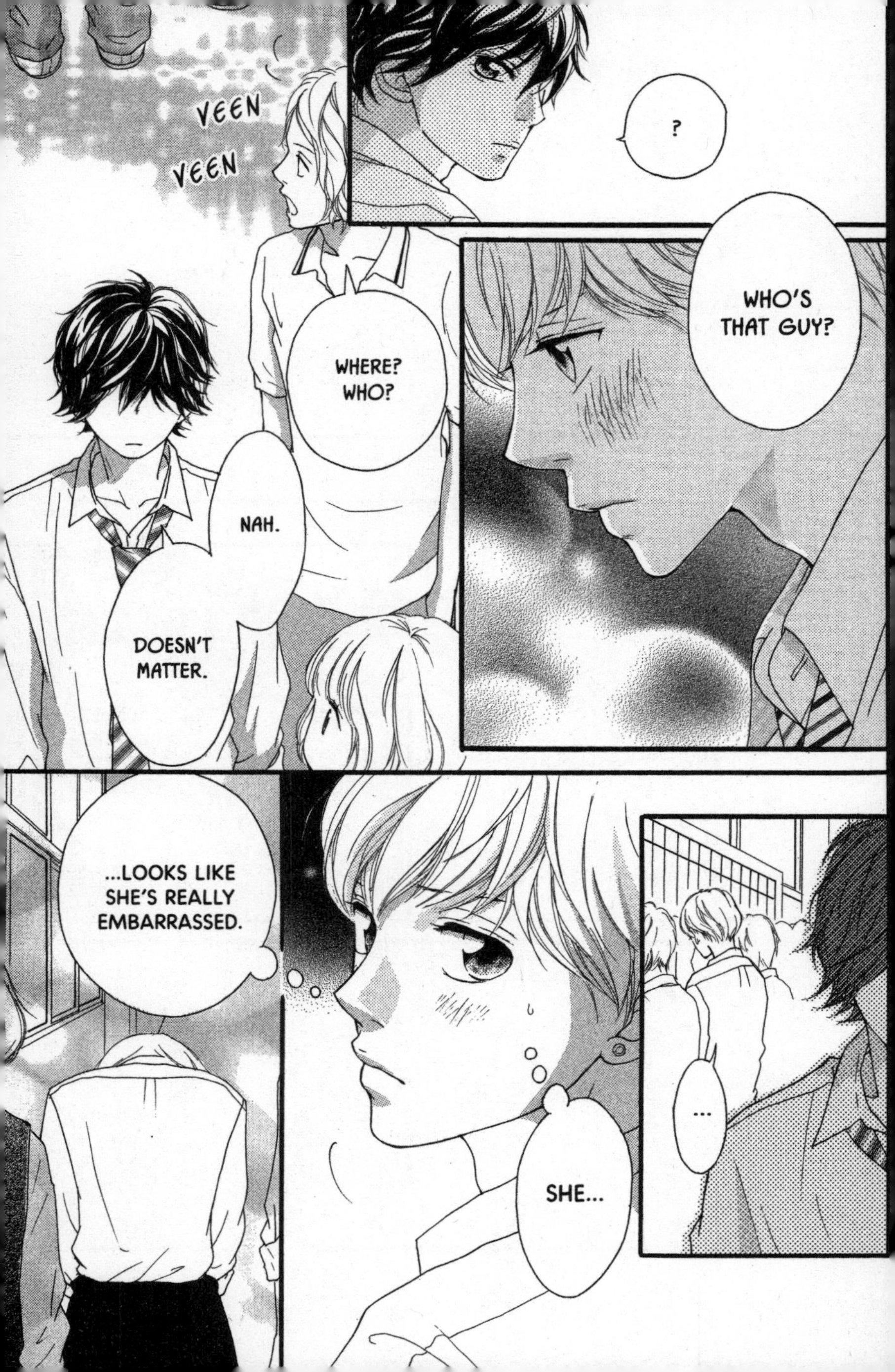
?
WHO'S THAT GUY?
VEEN
VEEN
WHERE? WHO?
NAH.
DOESN'T MATTER.
...
SHE...
...LOOKS LIKE SHE'S REALLY EMBARRASSED.

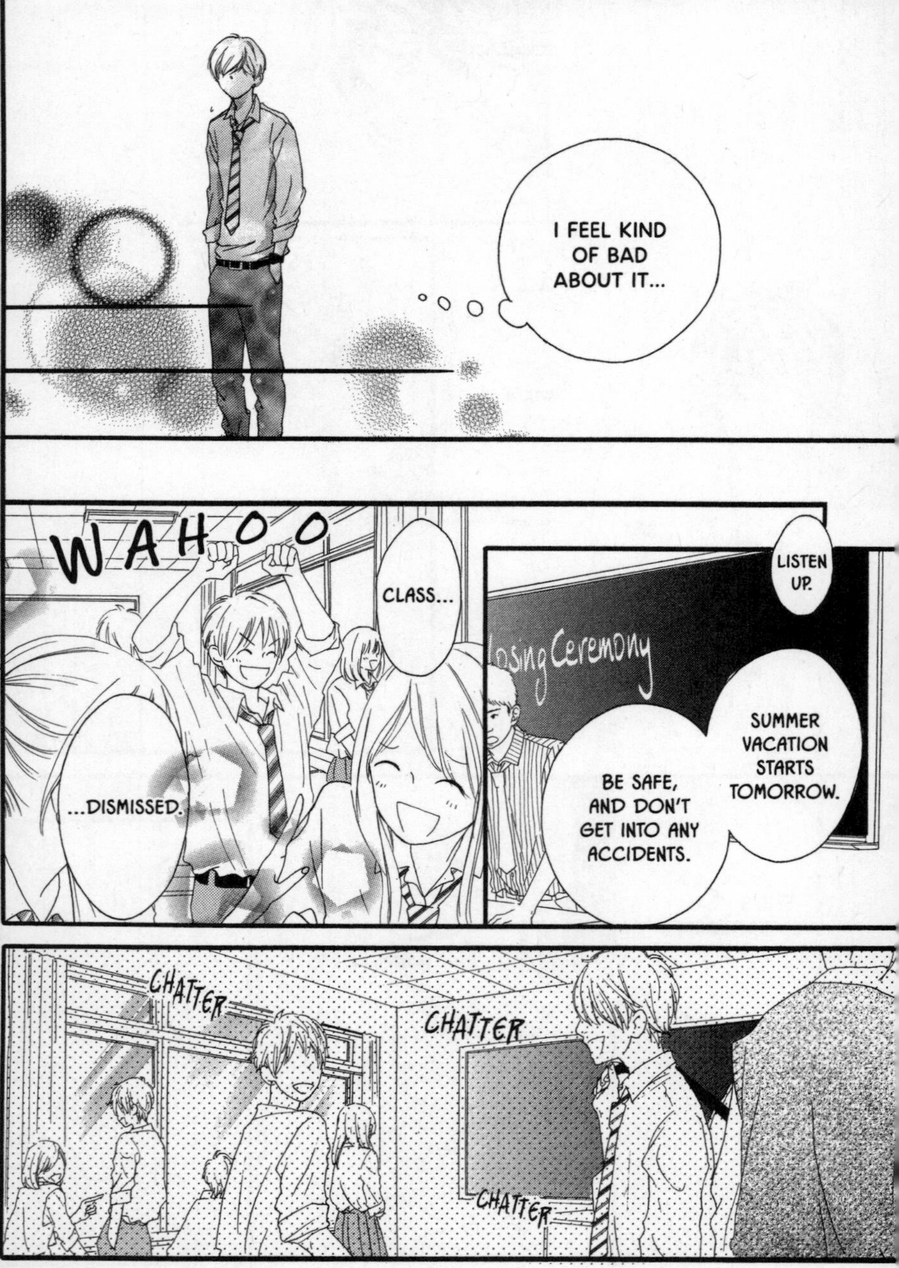
I FEEL KIND OF BAD ABOUT IT...
losing Ceremony
LISTEN UP.
SUMMER VACATION STARTS TOMORROW.
BE SAFE, AND DON'T GET INTO ANY ACCIDENTS.
CLASS...
...DISMISSED.
WAHOO
CHATTER
CHATTER
CHATTER

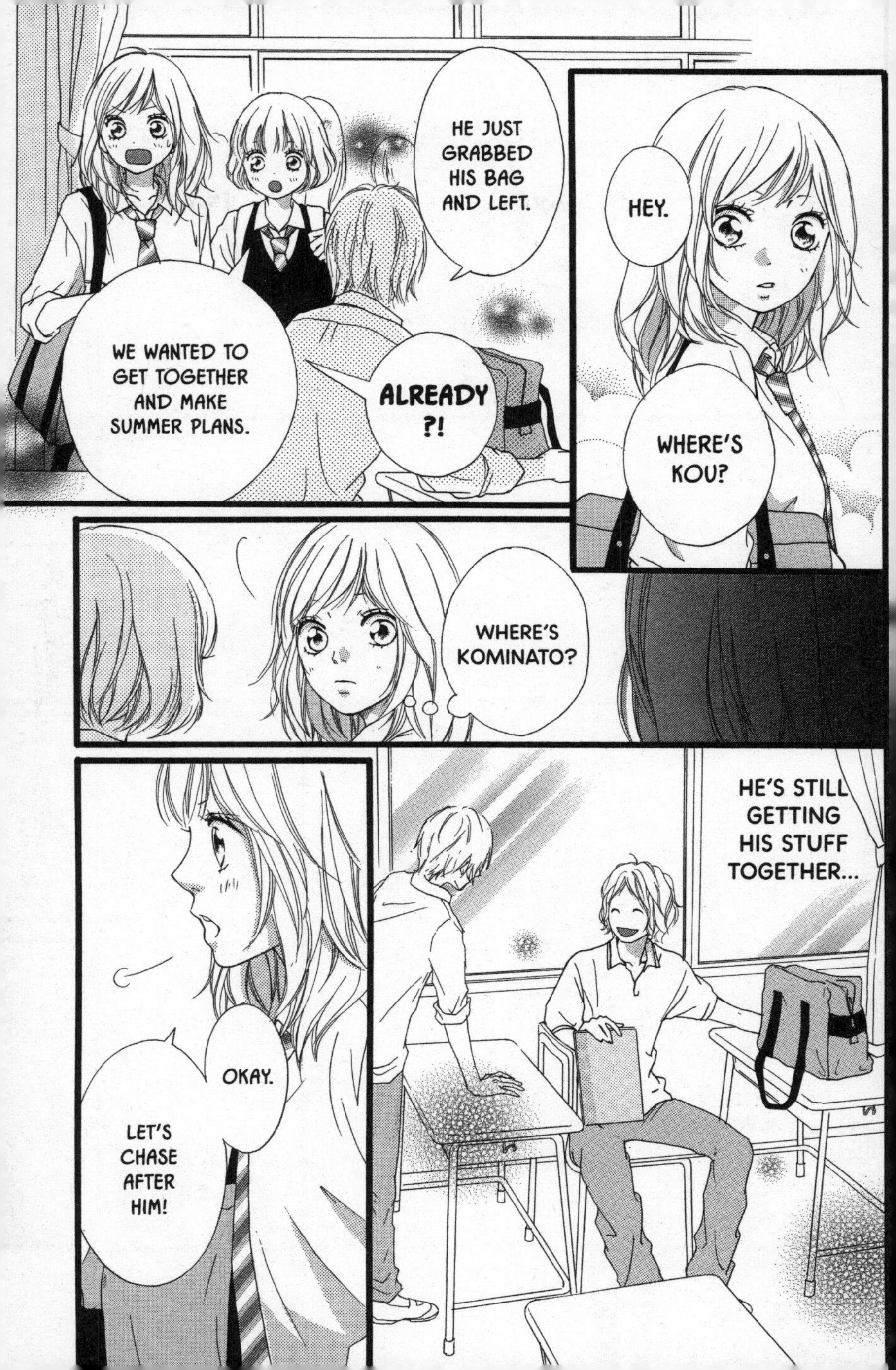
HEY.
WHERE'S KOU?
HE JUST GRABBED HIS BAG AND LEFT.
ALREADY?!
WE WANTED TO GET TOGETHER AND MAKE SUMMER PLANS.
WHERE'S KOMINATO?
HE'S STILL GETTING HIS STUFF TOGETHER...
OKAY.
LET'S CHASE AFTER HIM!

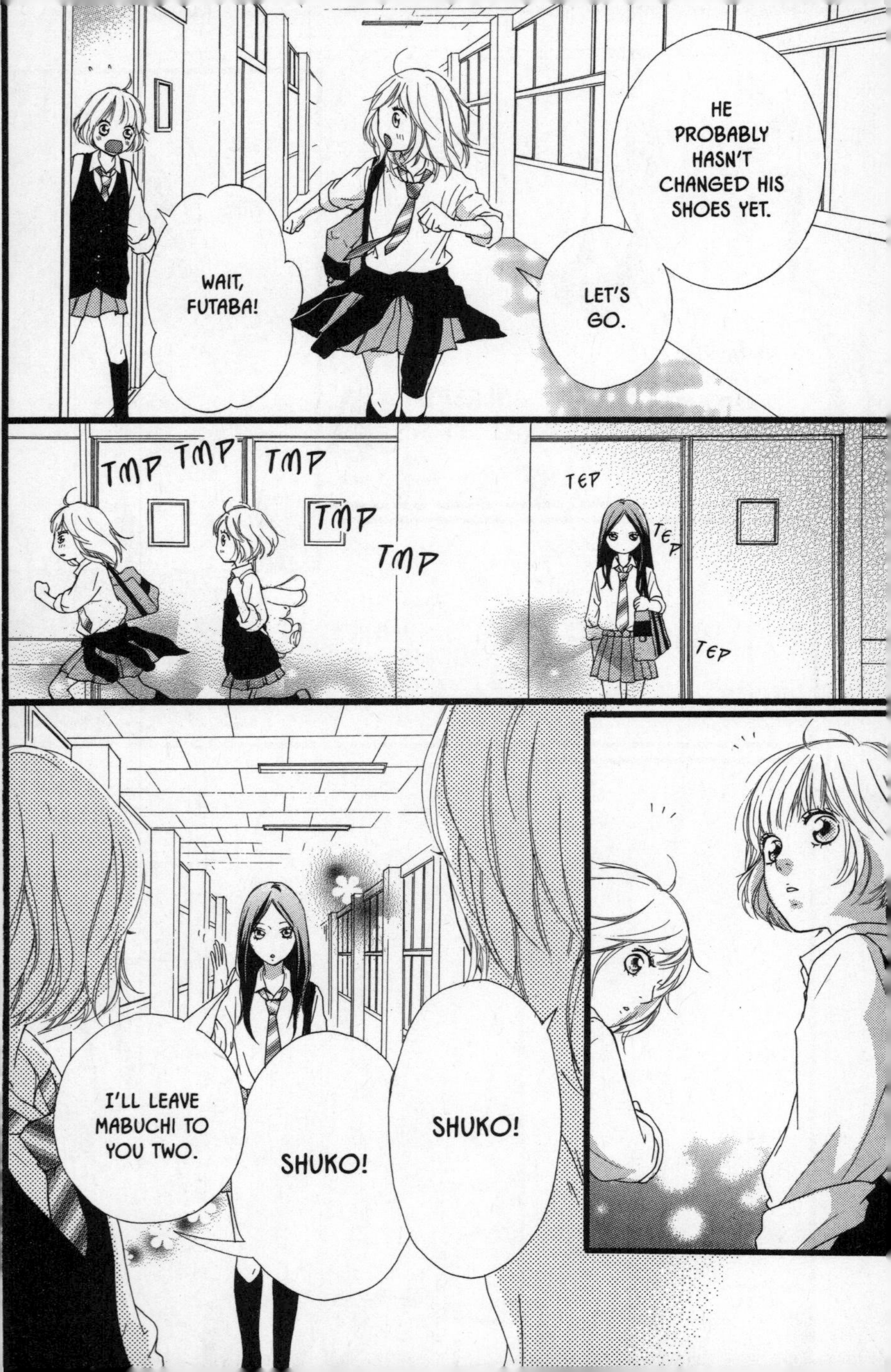
HE PROBABLY HASN'T CHANGED HIS SHOES YET.
LET'S GO.
WAIT, FUTABA!
TEP
TEP
TEP
TMP TMP
TMP
TMP
TMP
SHUKO!
SHUKO!
I'LL LEAVE MABUCHI TO YOU TWO.

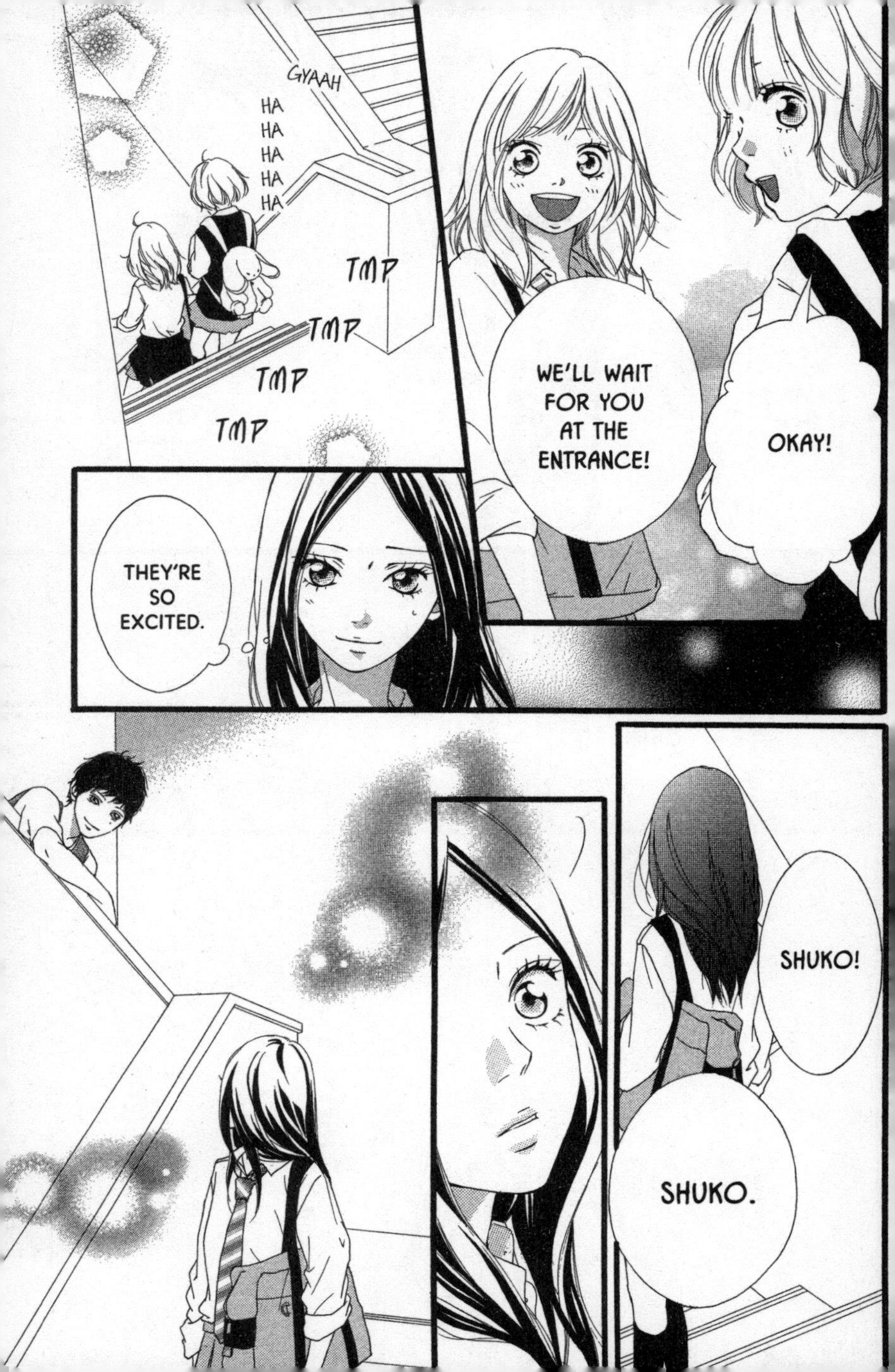
WE'LL WAIT FOR YOU AT THE ENTRANCE!
OKAY!
GYAAH
HA HA HA HA HA
TMP
TMP
TMP
TMP
THEY'RE SO EXCITED.
SHUKO!
SHUKO.

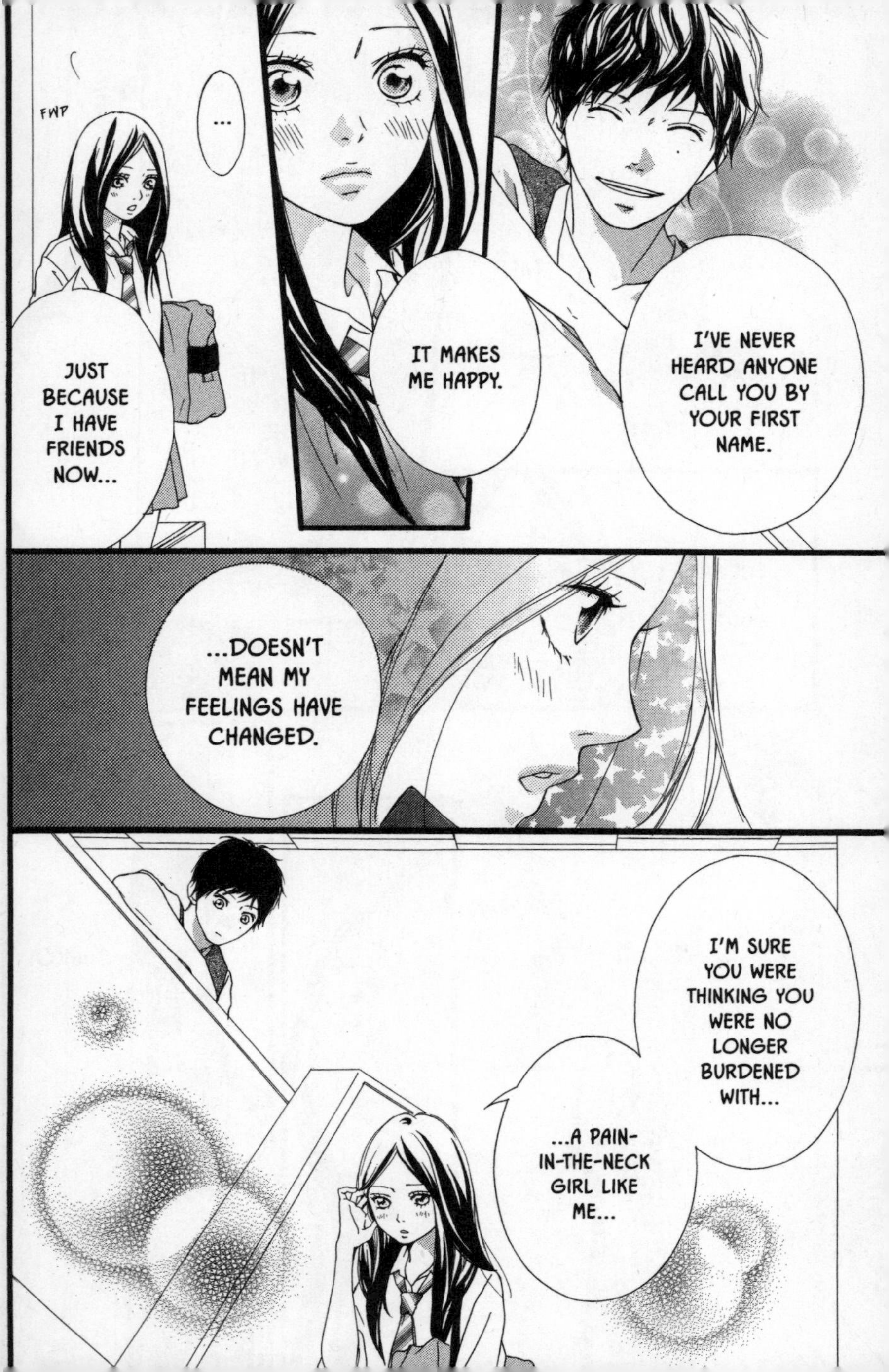
I'VE NEVER HEARD ANYONE CALL YOU BY YOUR FIRST NAME.
IT MAKES ME HAPPY.
...
FWP
JUST BECAUSE I HAVE FRIENDS NOW...
...DOESN'T MEAN MY FEELINGS HAVE CHANGED.
I'M SURE YOU WERE THINKING YOU WERE NO LONGER BURDENED WITH...
...A PAIN-IN-THE-NECK GIRL LIKE ME...

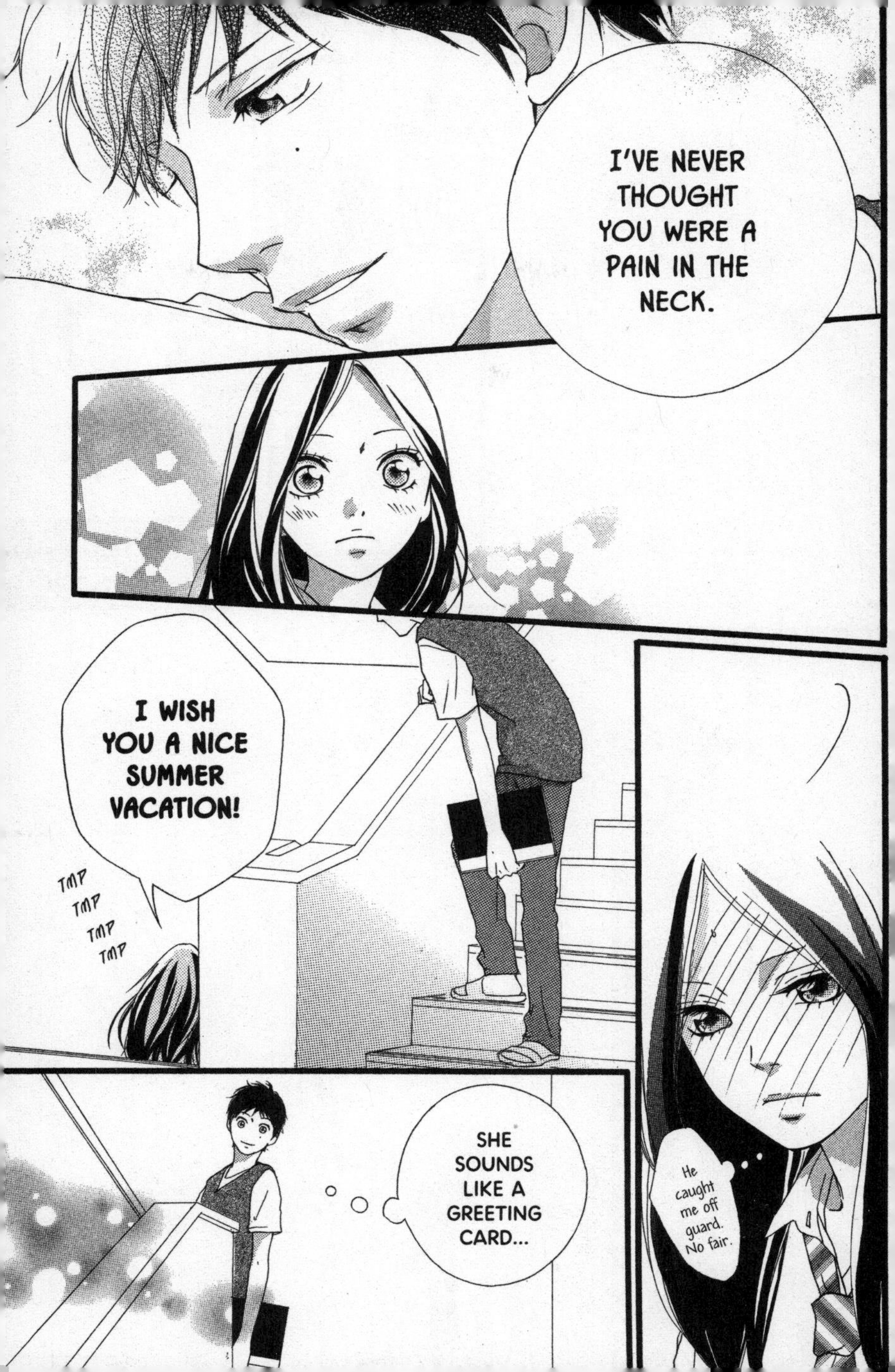
I'VE NEVER THOUGHT YOU WERE A PAIN IN THE NECK.
He caught me off guard. No fair.
I WISH YOU A NICE SUMMER VACATION!
TMP TMP TMP TMP
SHE SOUNDS LIKE A GREETING CARD...

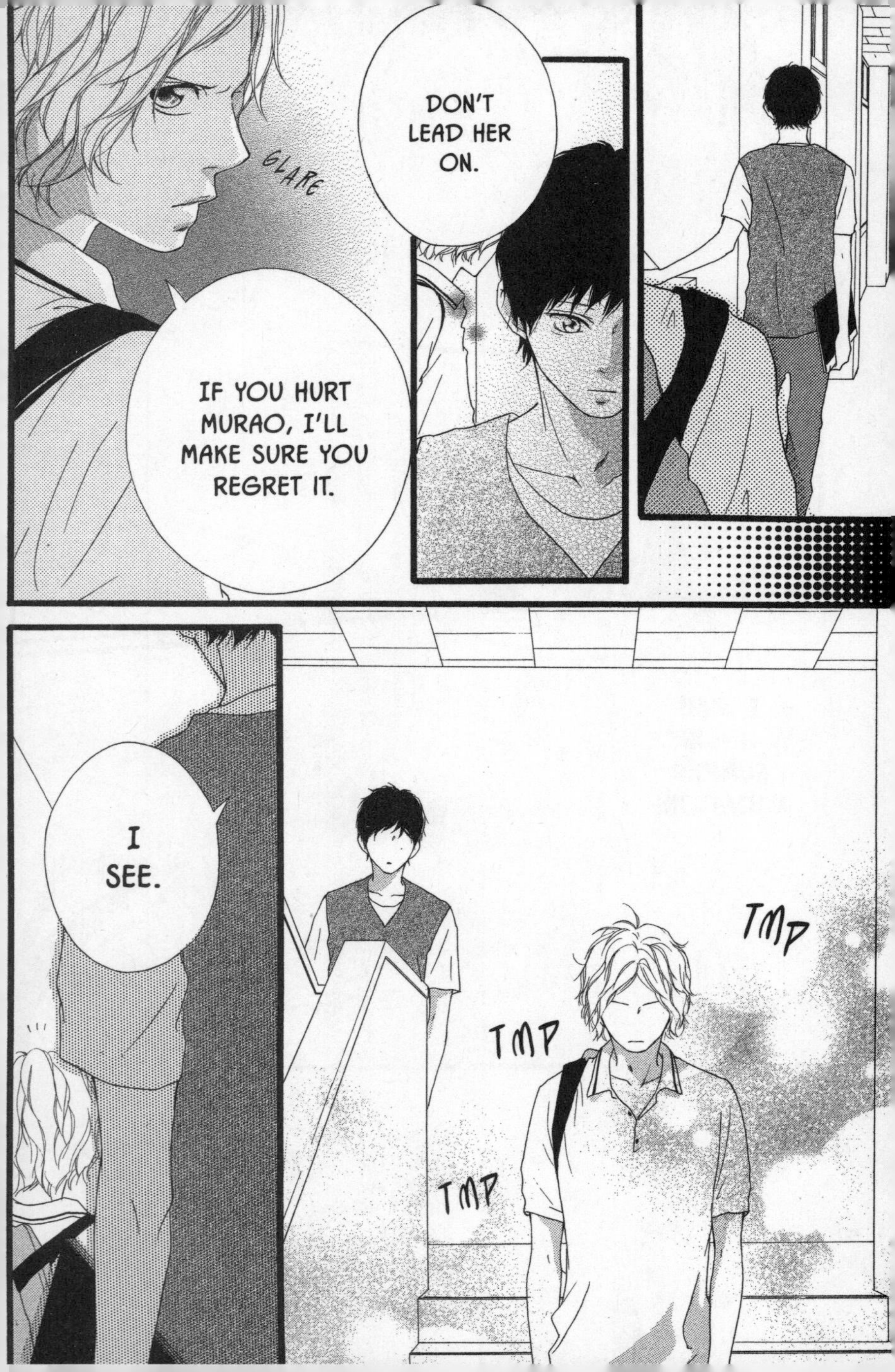
DON'T LEAD HER ON.
GLARE
IF YOU HURT MURAO, I'LL MAKE SURE YOU REGRET IT.
TMP
TMP
TMP
I SEE.

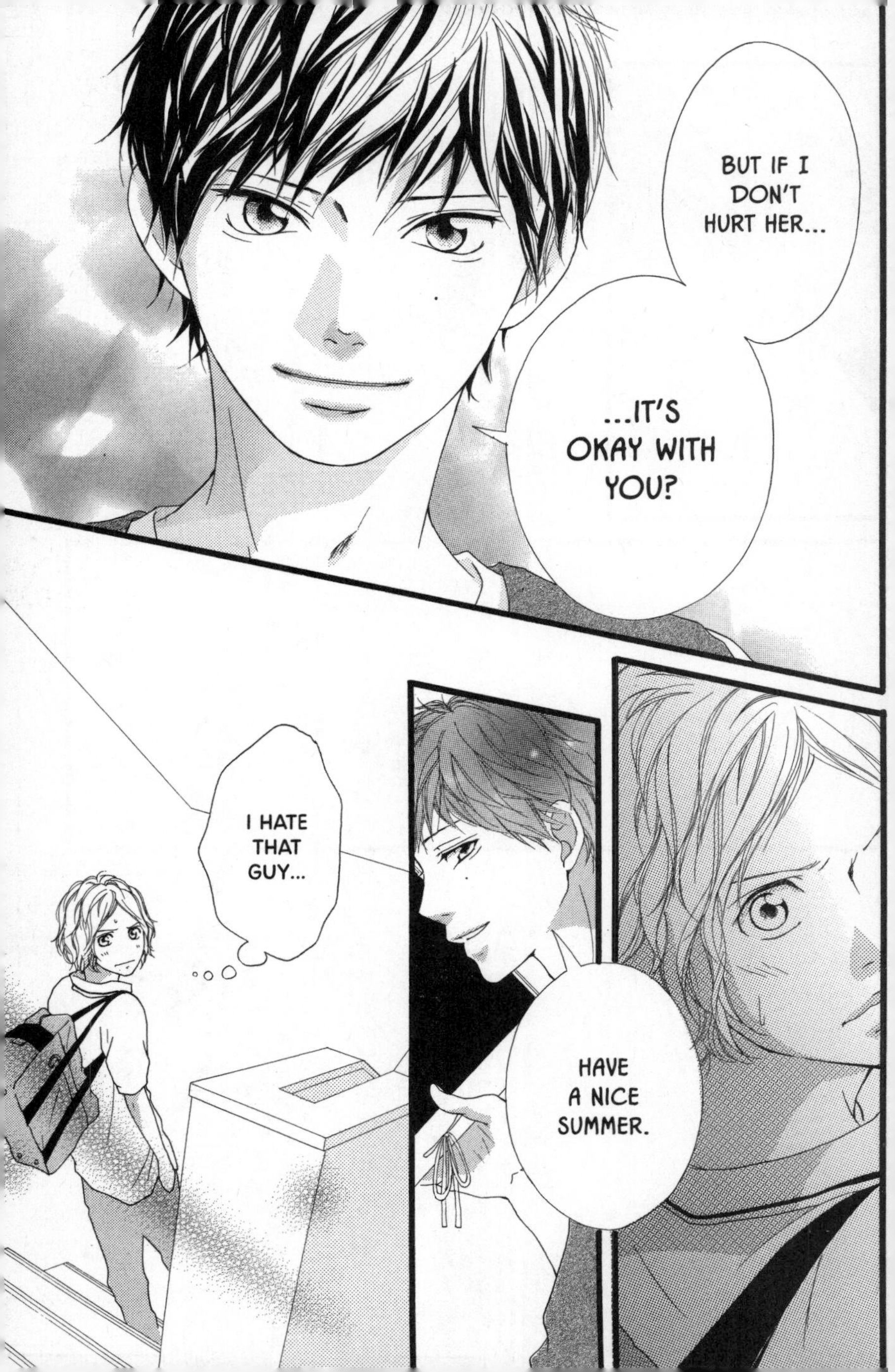
BUT IF I DON'T HURT HER...
...IT'S OKAY WITH YOU?
HAVE A NICE SUMMER.
I HATE THAT GUY...

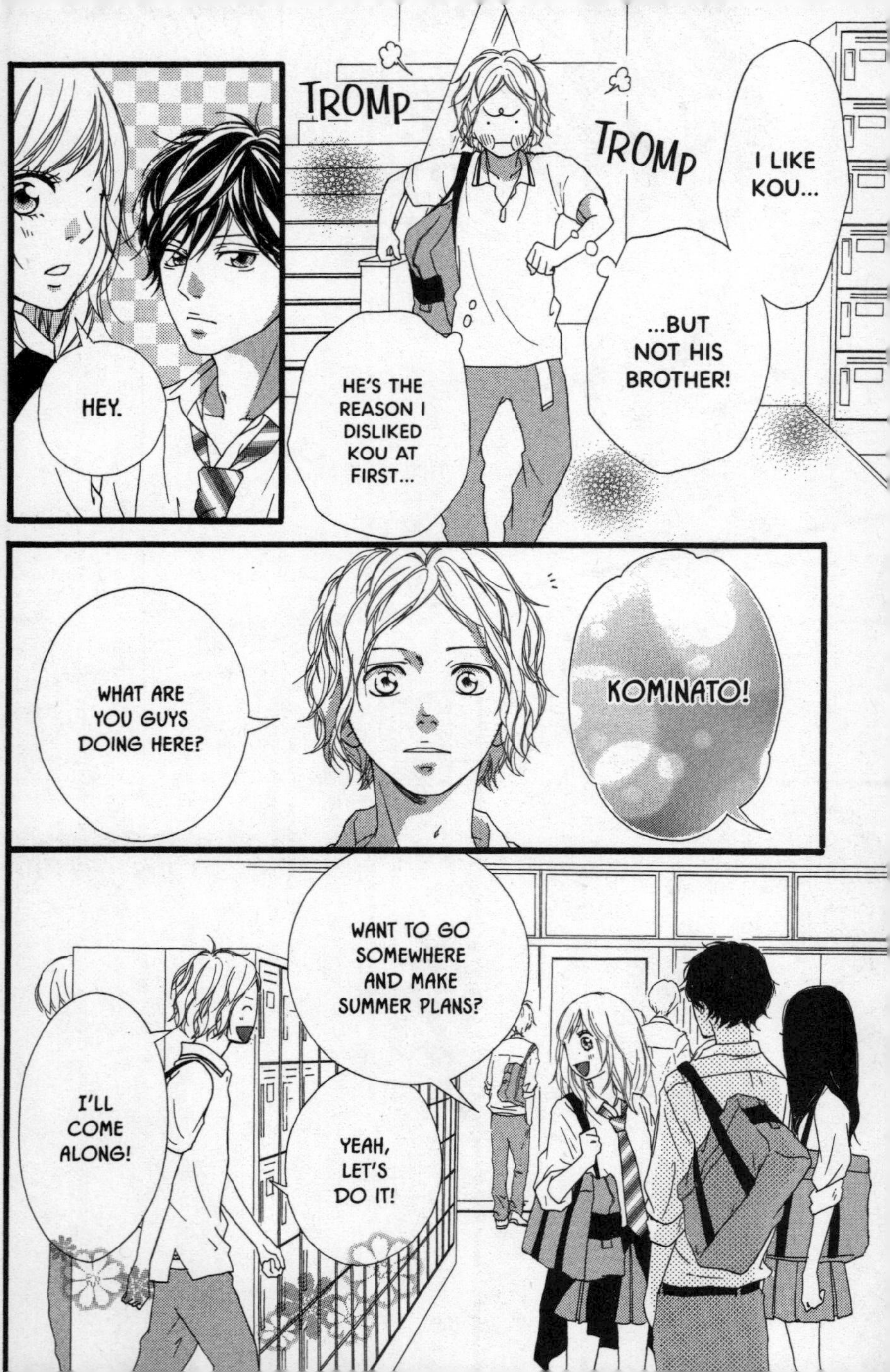
TROMP
TROMP
I LIKE KOU...
...BUT NOT HIS BROTHER!
HE'S THE REASON I DISLIKED KOU AT FIRST...
HEY.
KOMINATO!
WHAT ARE YOU GUYS DOING HERE?
WANT TO GO SOMEWHERE AND MAKE SUMMER PLANS?
YEAH, LET'S DO IT!
I'LL COME ALONG!

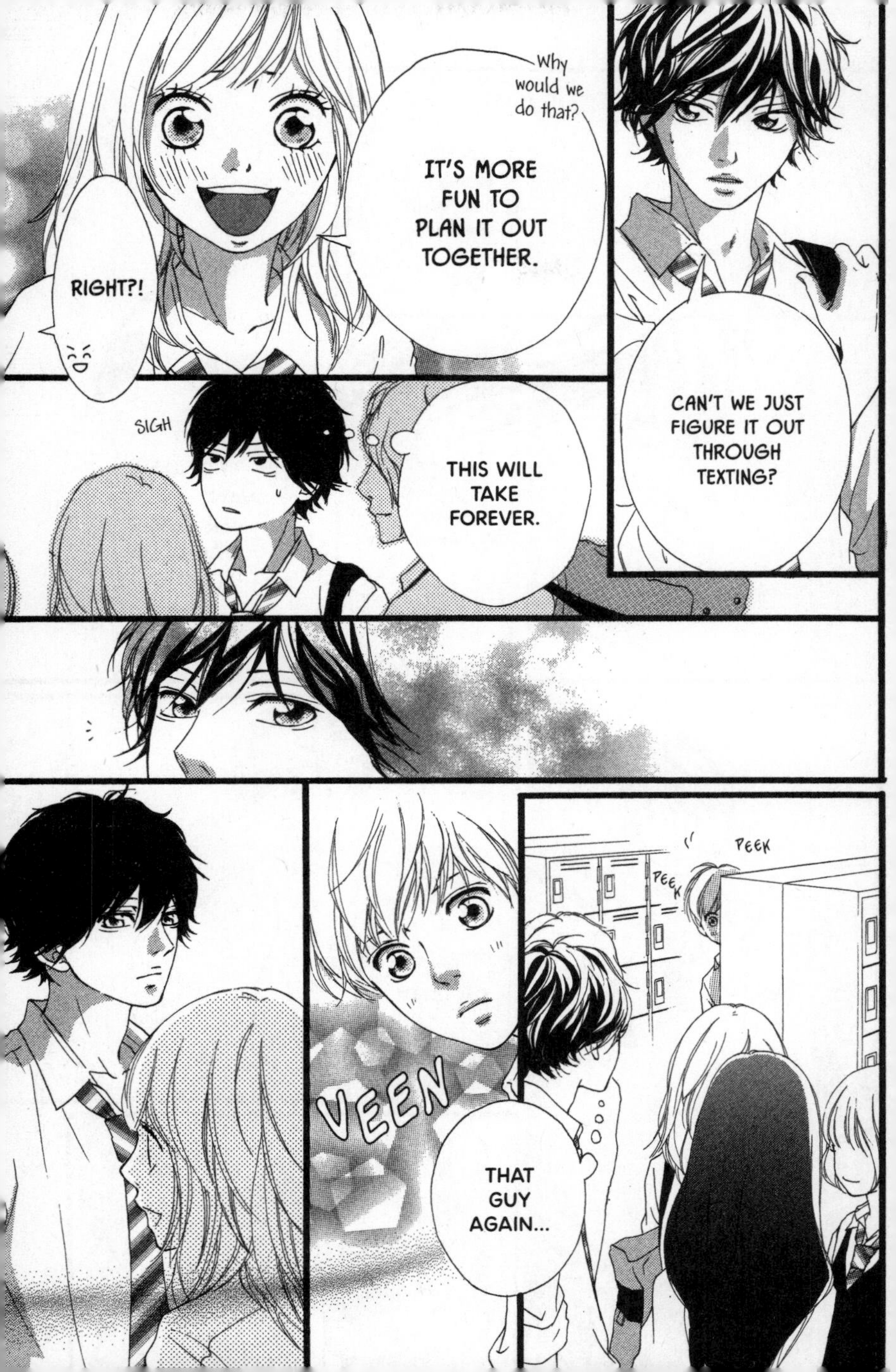
CAN'T WE JUST FIGURE IT OUT THROUGH TEXTING?
Why would we do that?
IT'S MORE FUN TO PLAN IT OUT TOGETHER.
RIGHT?!
SIGH
THIS WILL TAKE FOREVER.
PEEK
PEEK
VEEN
THAT GUY AGAIN...

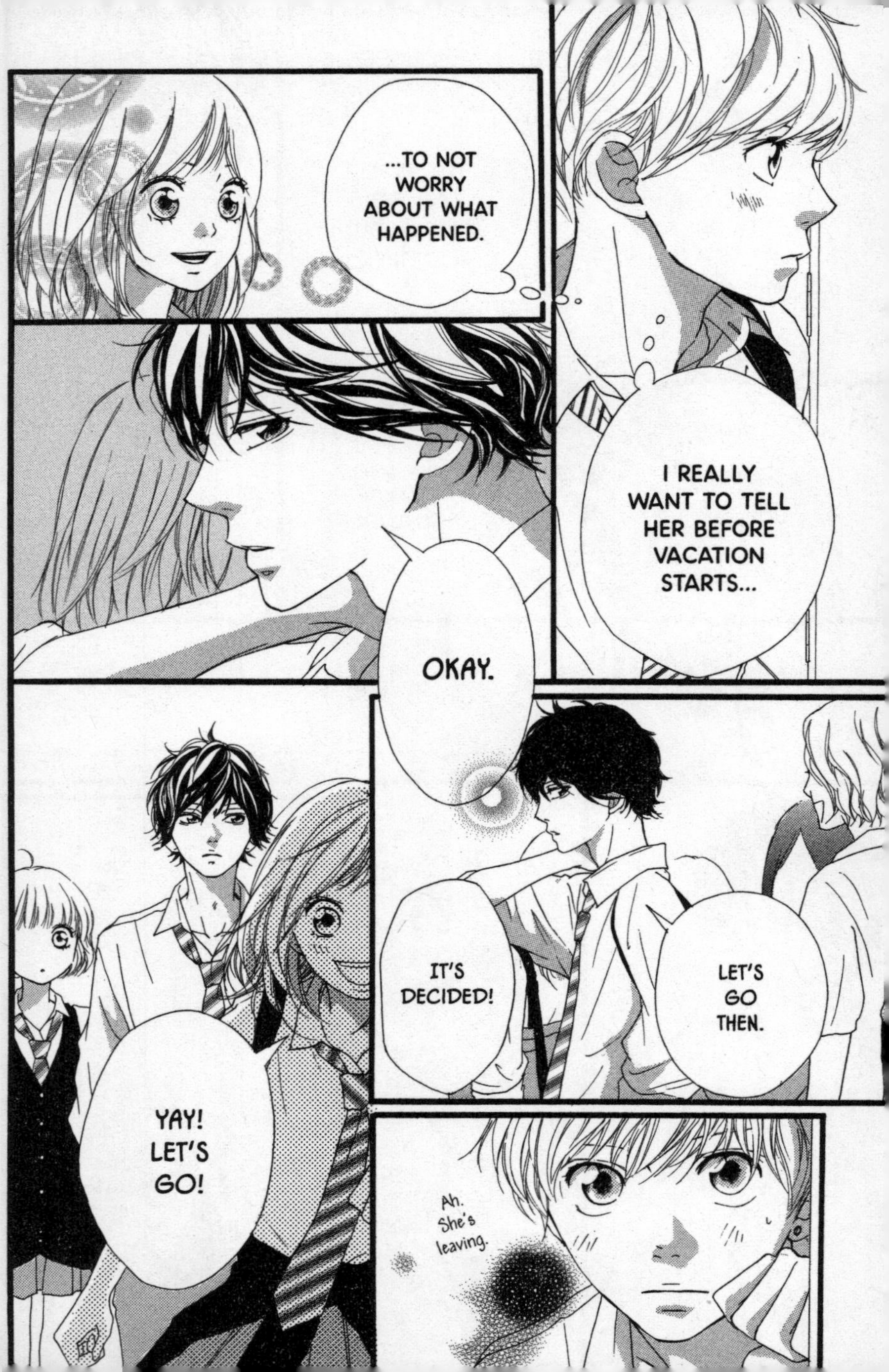
I REALLY WANT TO TELL HER BEFORE VACATION STARTS...
...TO NOT WORRY ABOUT WHAT HAPPENED.
OKAY.
LET'S GO THEN.
IT'S DECIDED!
Ah. She's leaving.
YAY! LET'S GO!

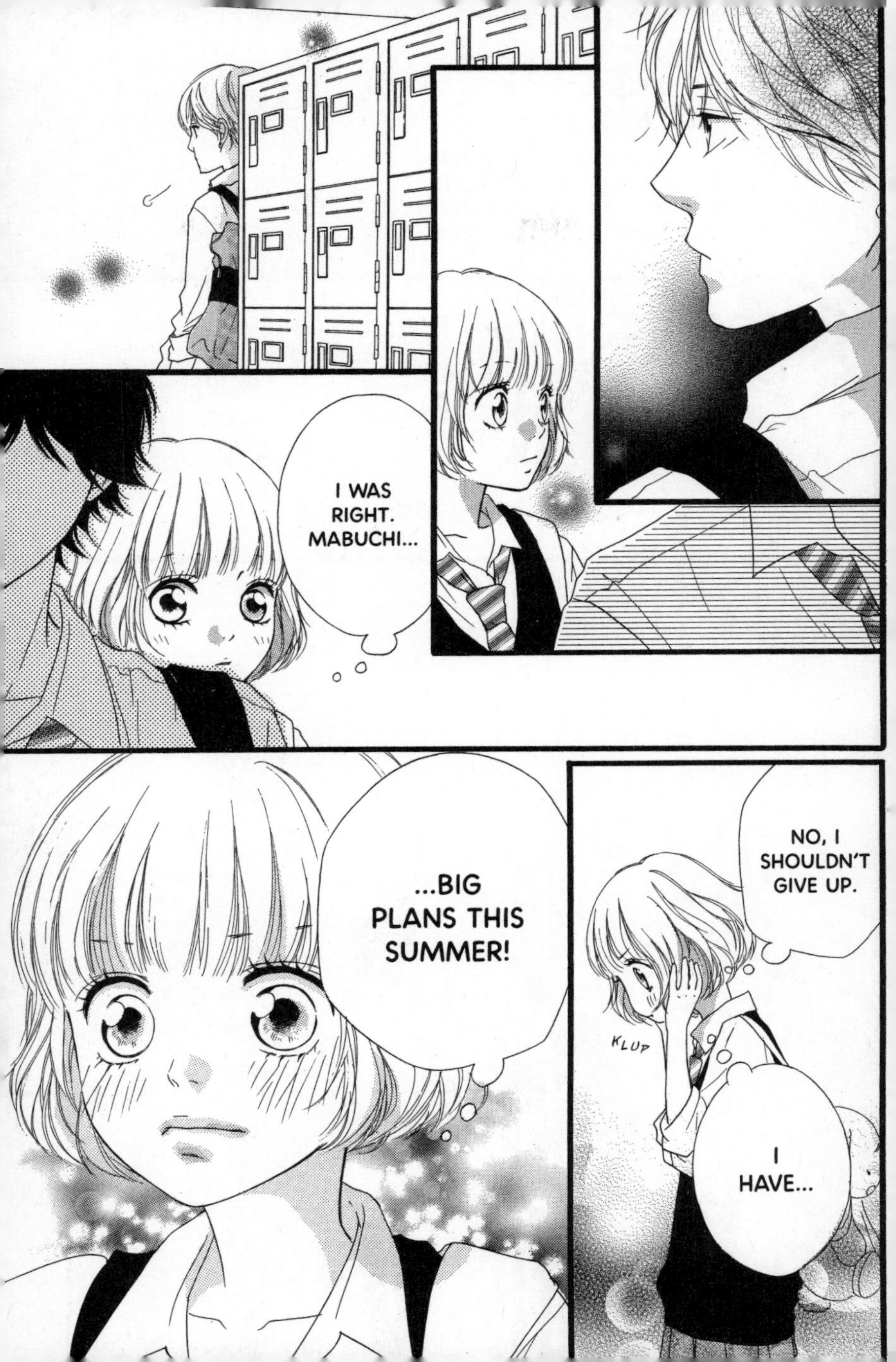
I WAS RIGHT. MABUCHI...
NO, I SHOULDN'T GIVE UP.
KLUP
I HAVE...
...BIG PLANS THIS SUMMER!

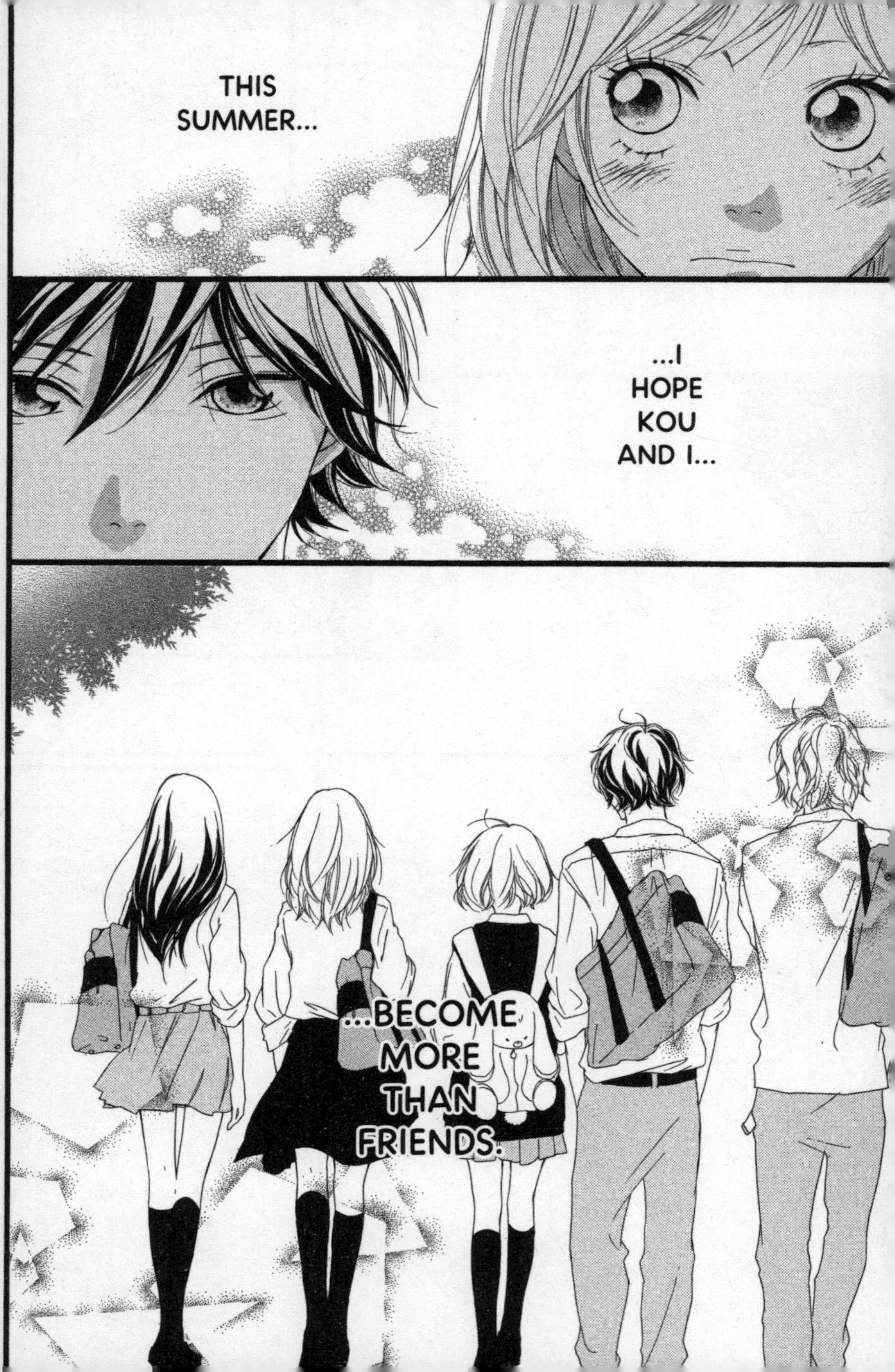
THIS SUMMER...
...I HOPE KOU AND I...
...BECOME MORE THAN FRIENDS.

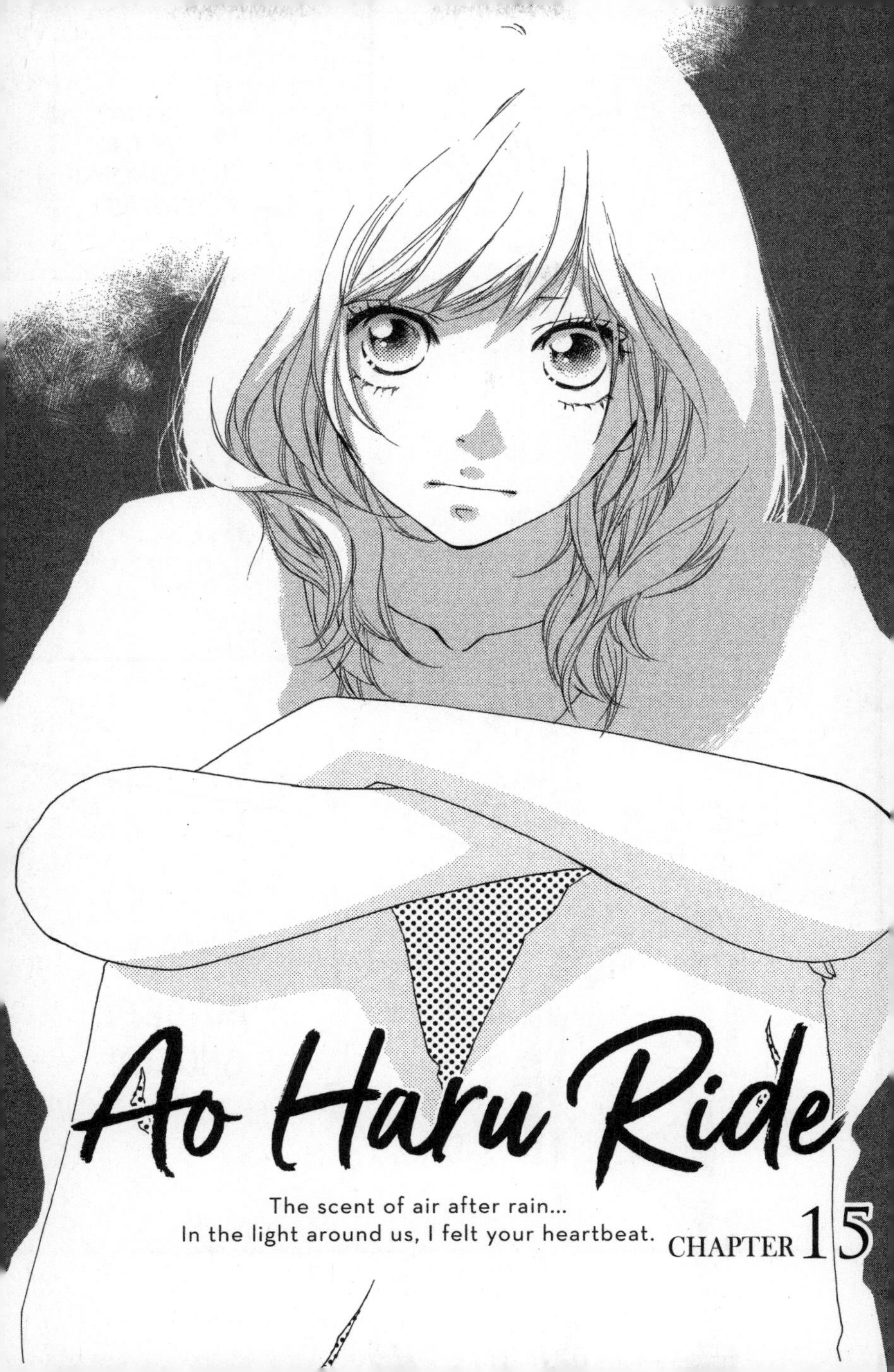
Ao Haru Ride
The scent of air after rain...
In the light around us, I felt your heartbeat.
CHAPTER 15

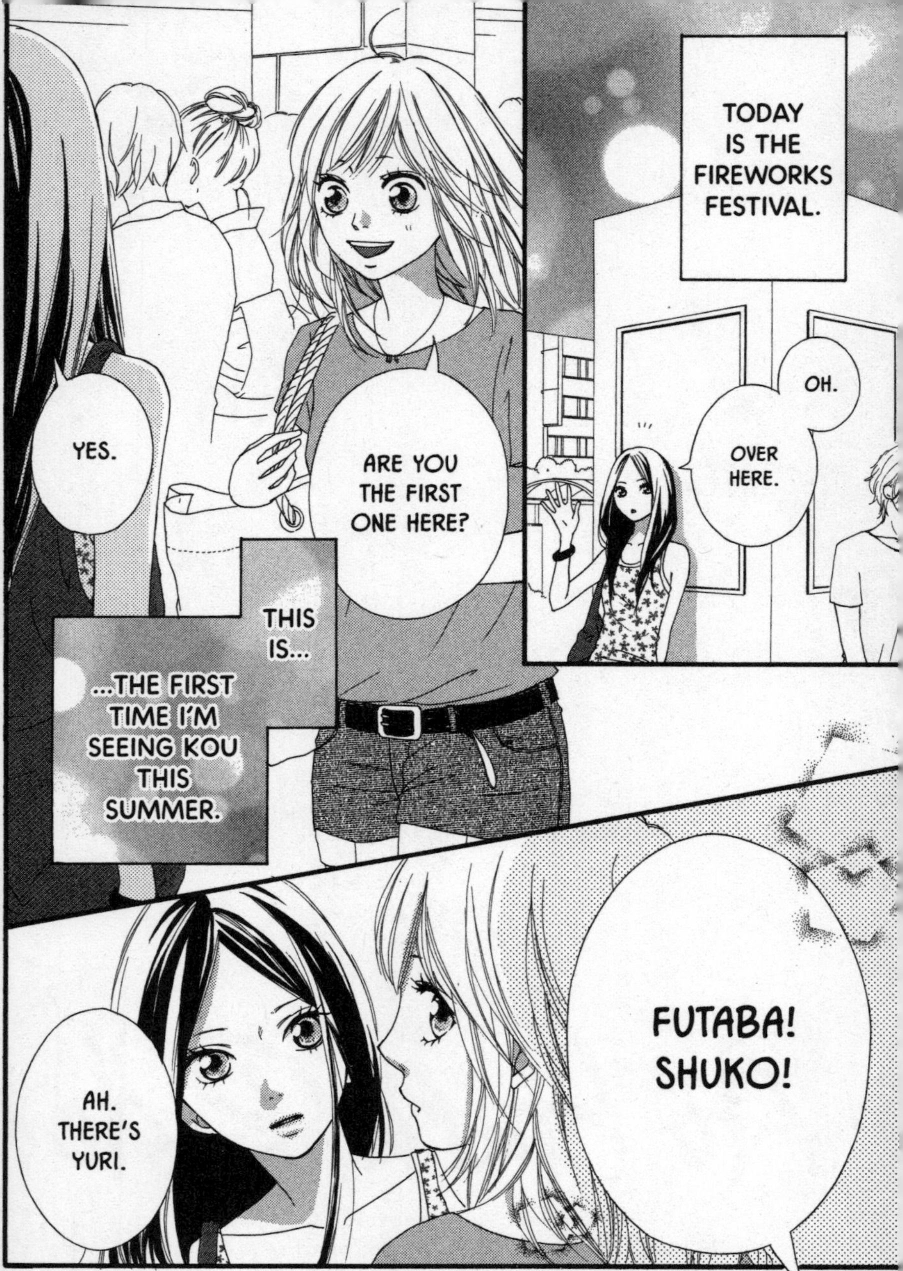
TODAY IS THE FIREWORKS FESTIVAL.
OH.
OVER HERE.
ARE YOU THE FIRST ONE HERE?
YES.
THIS IS...
...THE FIRST TIME I'M SEEING KOU THIS SUMMER.
FUTABA! SHUKO!
AH. THERE'S YURI.

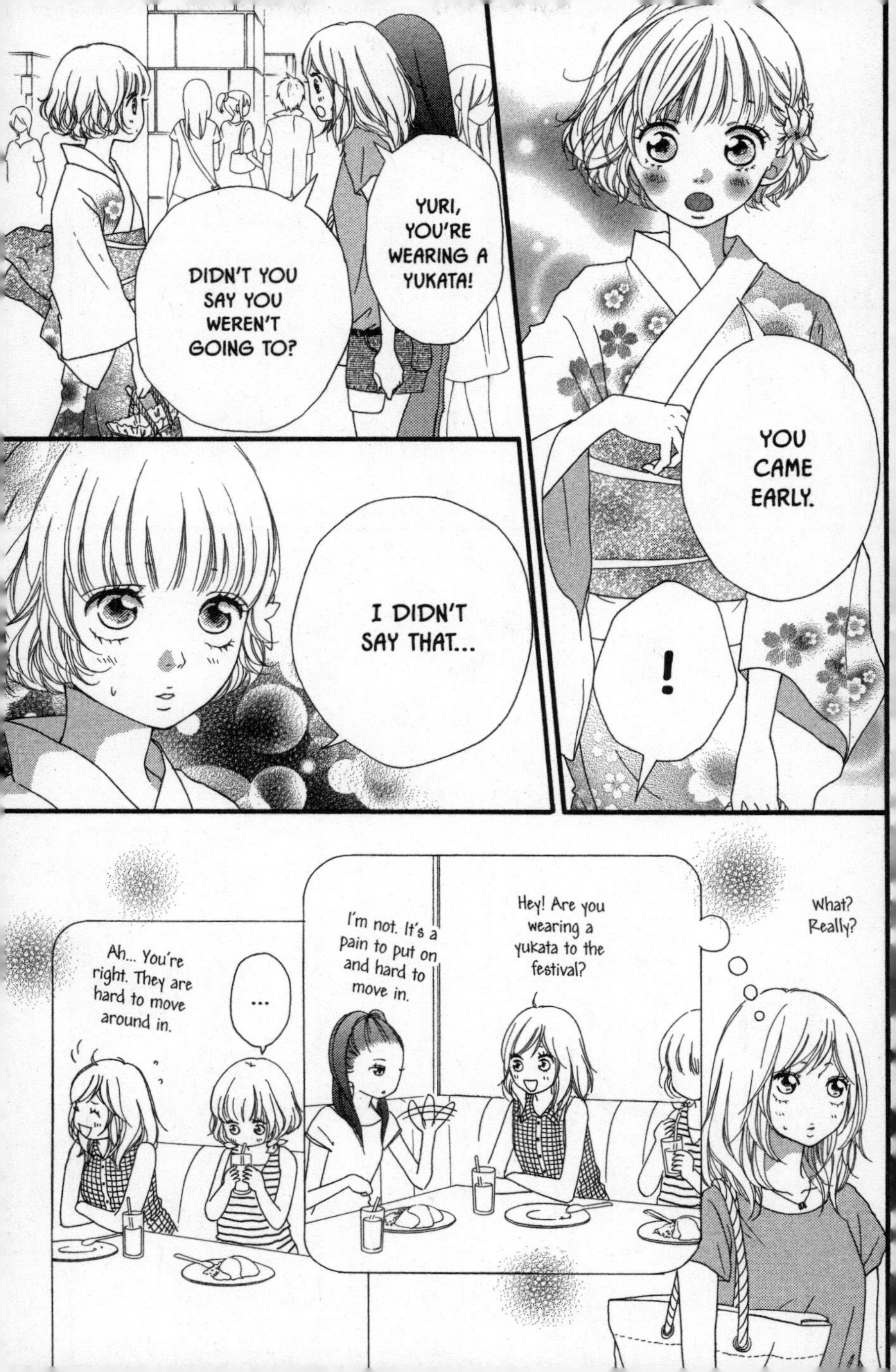
YOU CAME EARLY.
!
YURI, YOU'RE WEARING A YUKATA!
DIDN'T YOU SAY YOU WEREN'T GOING TO?
I DIDN'T SAY THAT...
What? Really?
Hey! Are you wearing a yukata to the festival?
I'm not. It's a pain to put on and hard to move in.
...
Ah... You're right. They are hard to move around in.

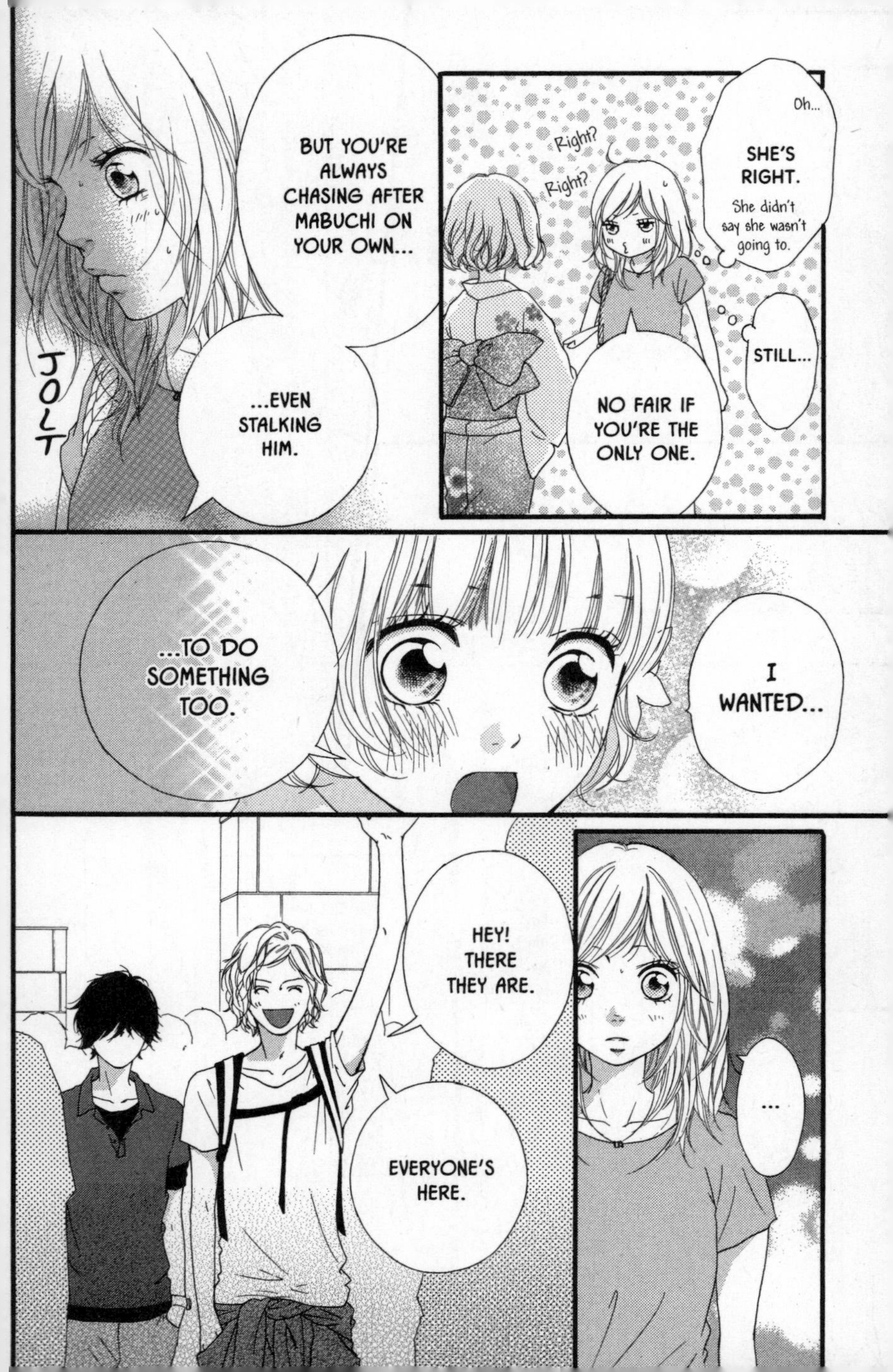
Oh...
SHE'S RIGHT.
She didn't say she wasn't going to.
Right?
Right?
STILL...
NO FAIR IF YOU'RE THE ONLY ONE.
BUT YOU'RE ALWAYS CHASING AFTER MABUCHI ON YOUR OWN...
...EVEN STALKING HIM.
JOLT
I WANTED...
...TO DO SOMETHING TOO.
...
HEY! THERE THEY ARE.
EVERYONE'S HERE.

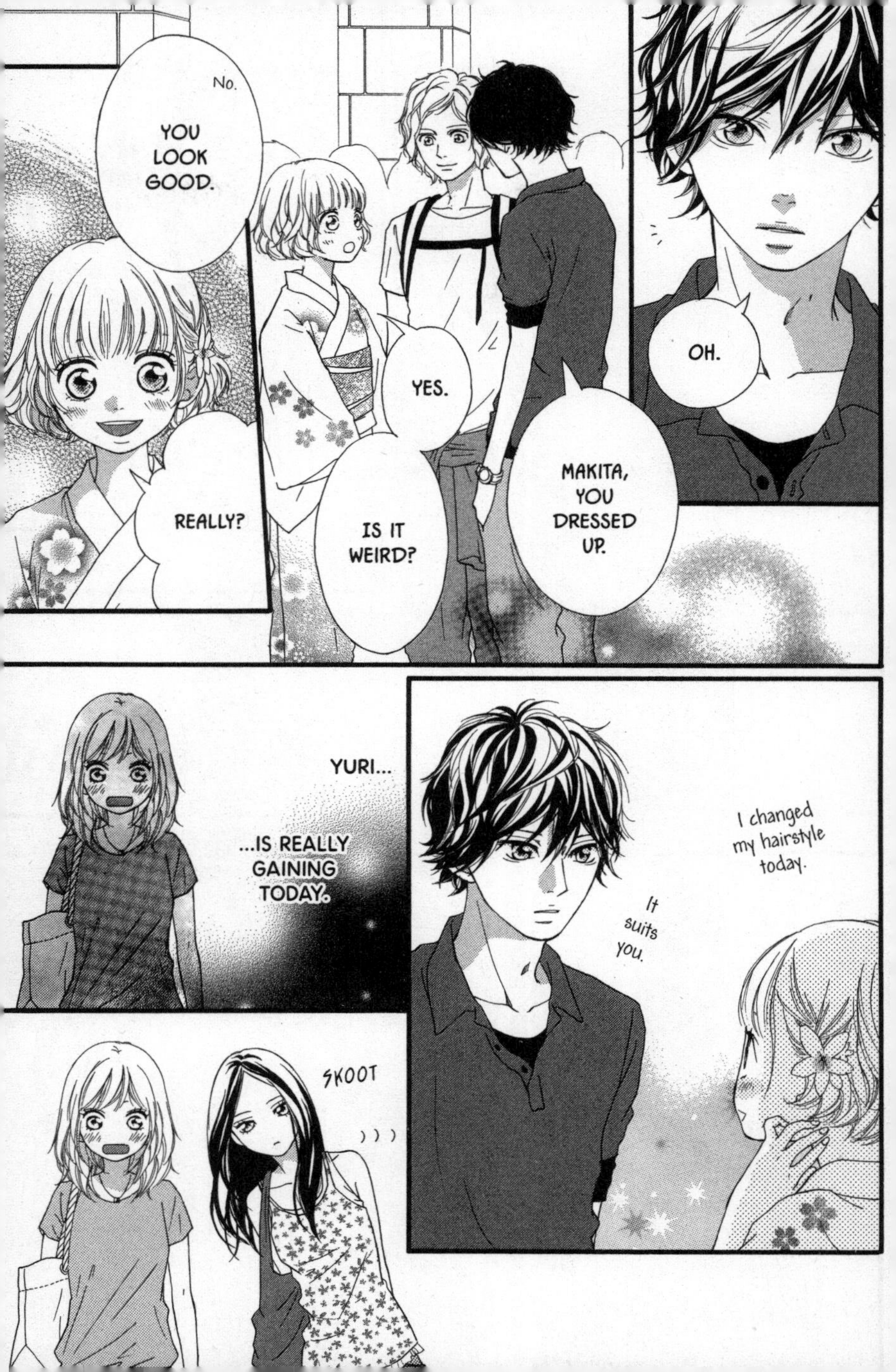
OH.
MAKITA, YOU DRESSED UP.
YES.
IS IT WEIRD?
No.
YOU LOOK GOOD.
REALLY?
I changed my hairstyle today.
It suits you.
YURI...
...IS REALLY GAINING TODAY.
SKOOT

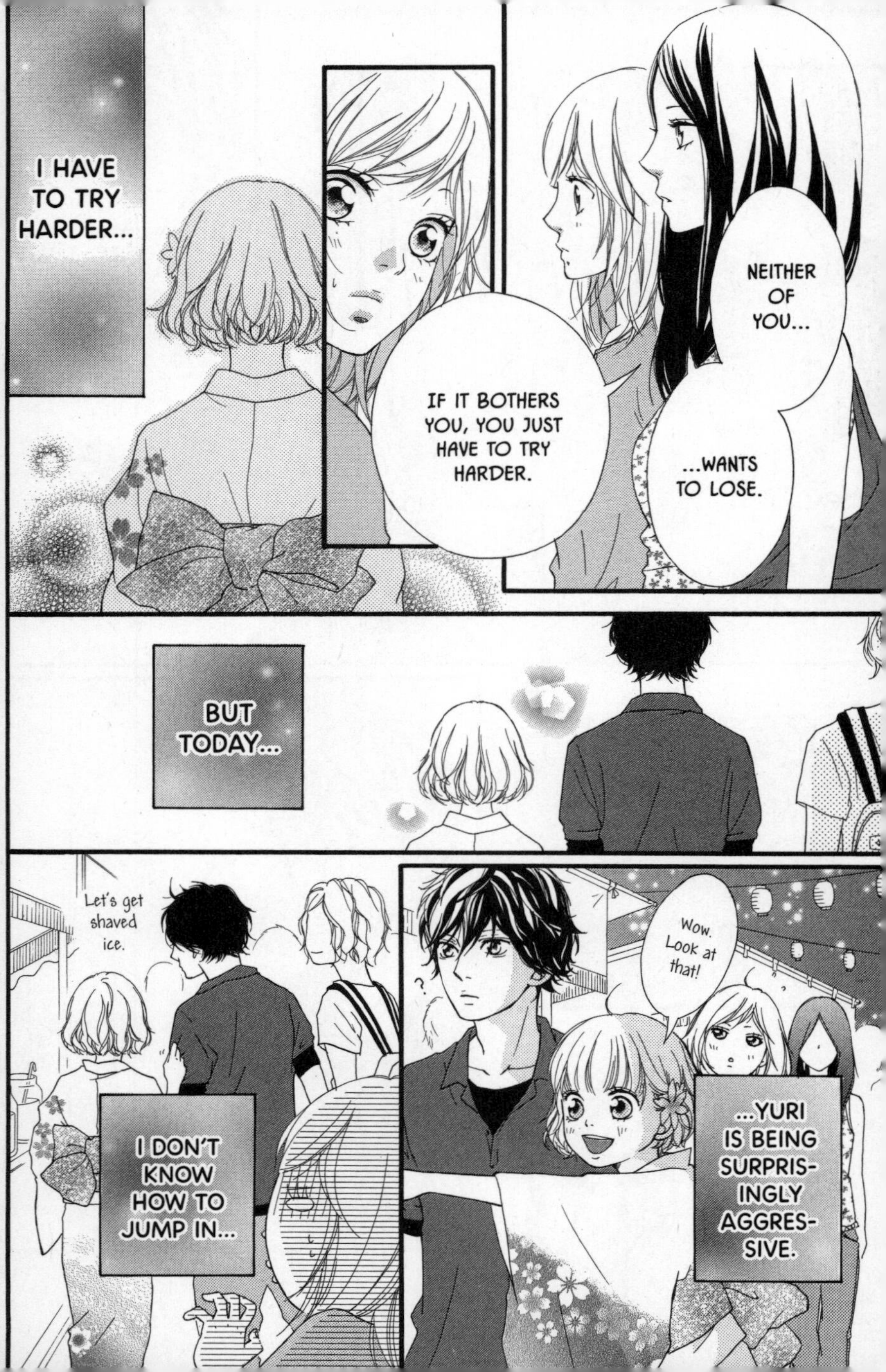
NEITHER OF YOU...
...WANTS TO LOSE.
IF IT BOTHERS YOU, YOU JUST HAVE TO TRY HARDER.
I HAVE TO TRY HARDER...
BUT TODAY...
Wow. Look at that!
...YURI IS BEING SURPRIS-INGLY AGGRES-SIVE.
Let's get shaved ice.
I DON'T KNOW HOW TO JUMP IN...

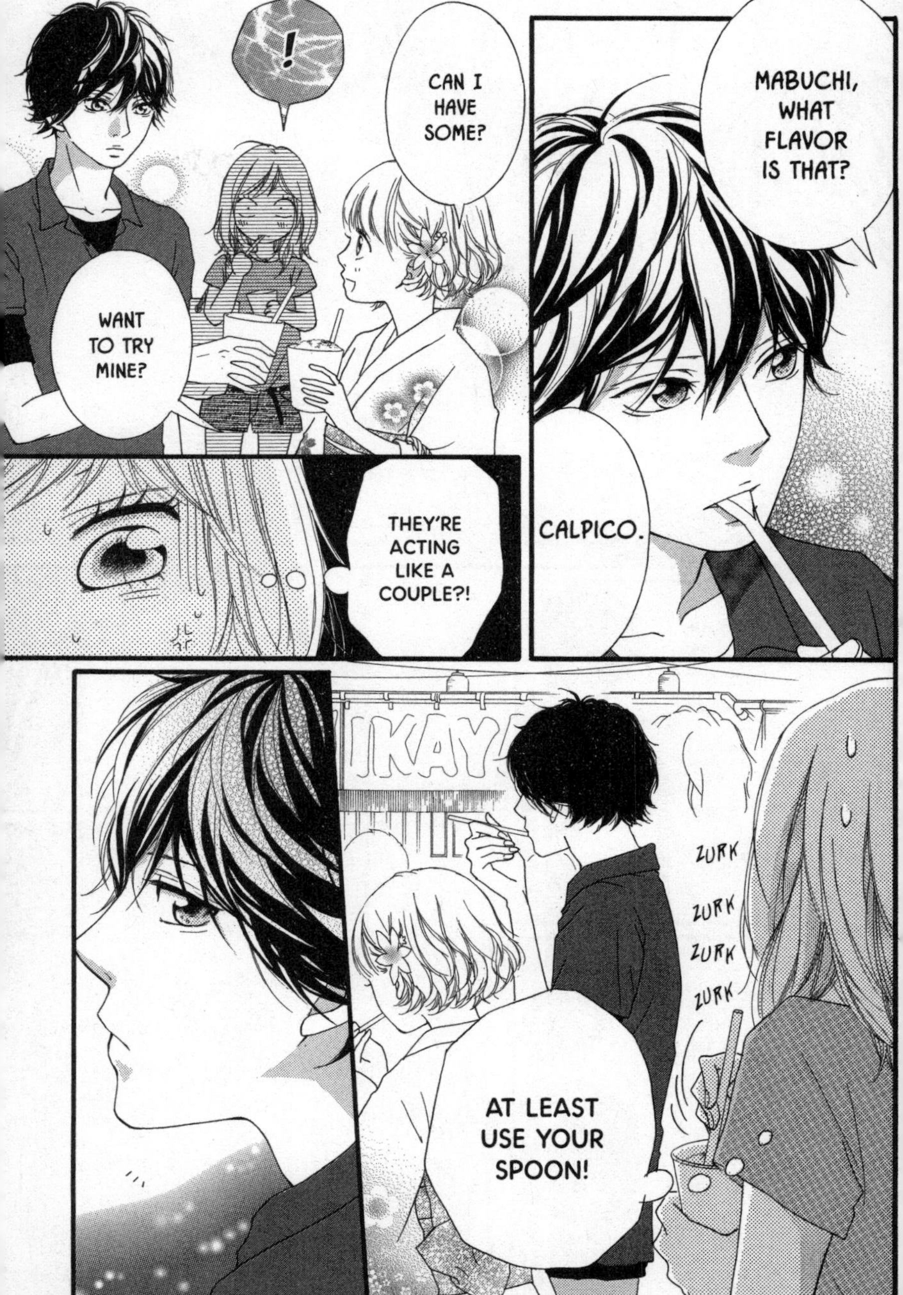
MABUCHI, WHAT FLAVOR IS THAT?
CALPICO.
CAN I HAVE SOME?
!
WANT TO TRY MINE?
THEY'RE ACTING LIKE A COUPLE?!
ZURK
ZURK
ZURK
ZURK
AT LEAST USE YOUR SPOON!

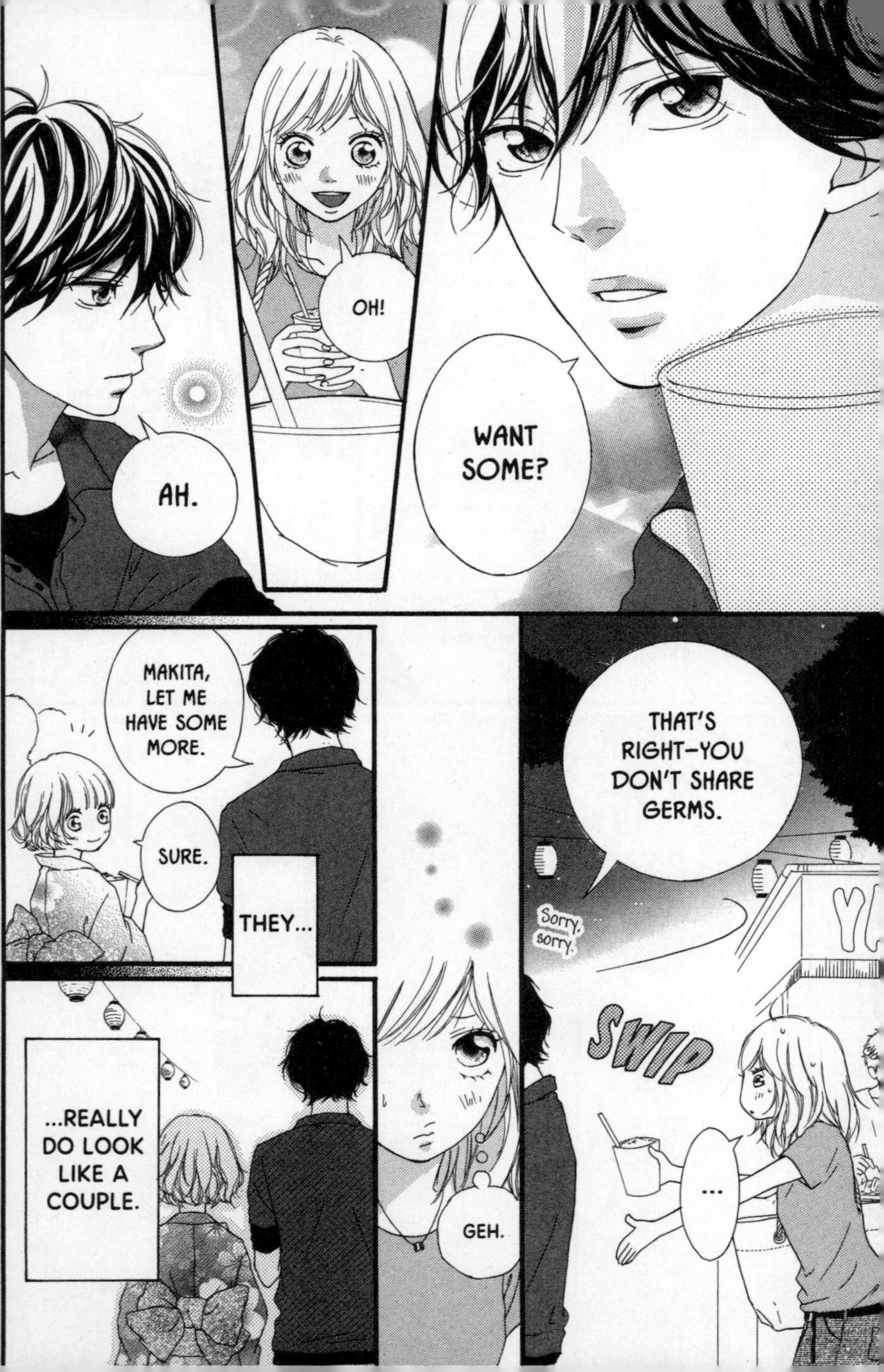
WANT SOME?
OH!
AH.
THAT'S RIGHT—YOU DON'T SHARE GERMS.
Sorry, sorry.
SWIP
...
MAKITA, LET ME HAVE SOME MORE.
SURE.
THEY...
GEH.
...REALLY DO LOOK LIKE A COUPLE.

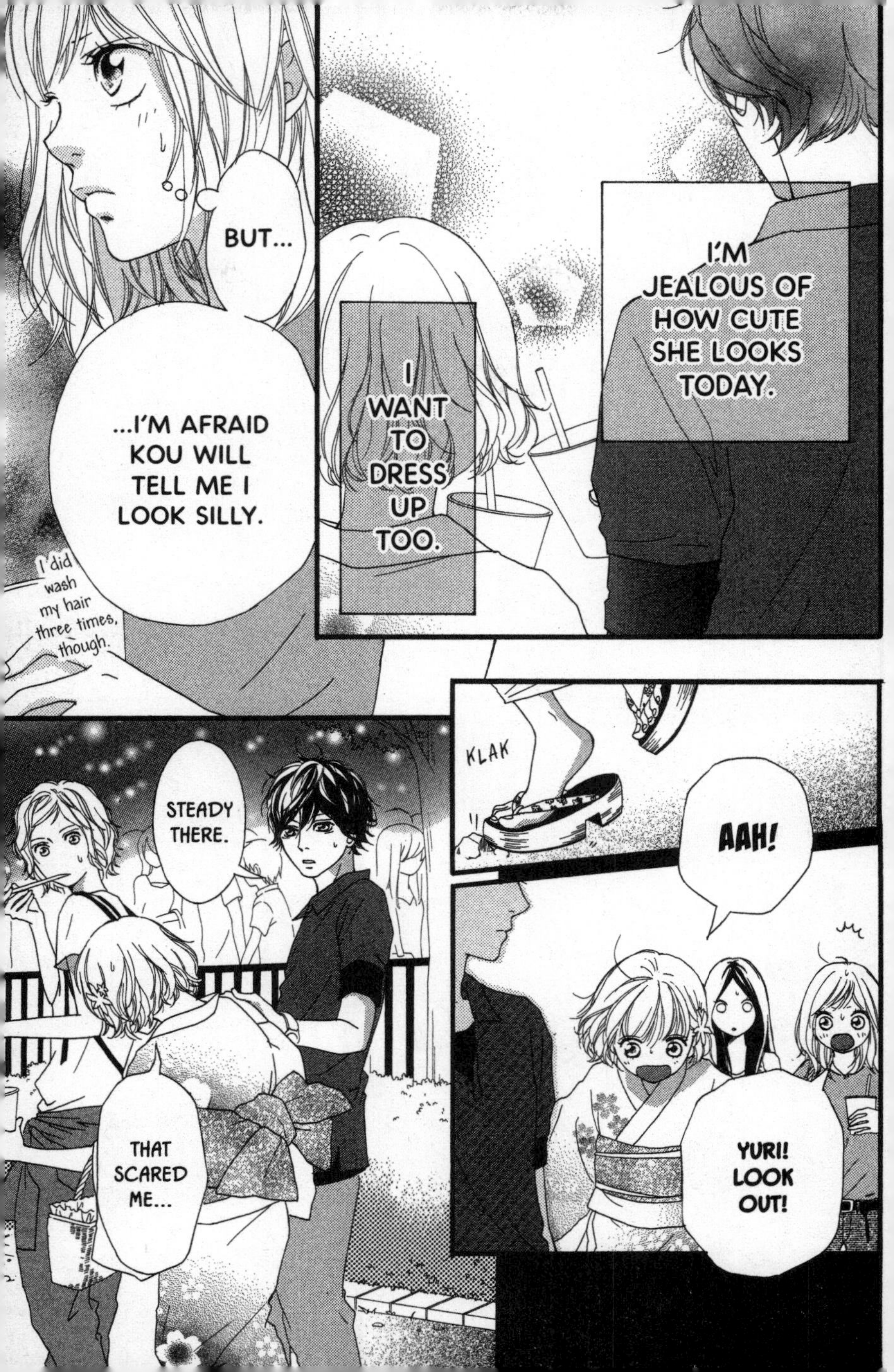
I'M JEALOUS OF HOW CUTE SHE LOOKS TODAY.
I WANT TO DRESS UP TOO.
BUT...
...I'M AFRAID KOU WILL TELL ME I LOOK SILLY.
I did wash my hair three times, though.
KLAK
AAH!
YURI! LOOK OUT!
STEADY THERE.
THAT SCARED ME...

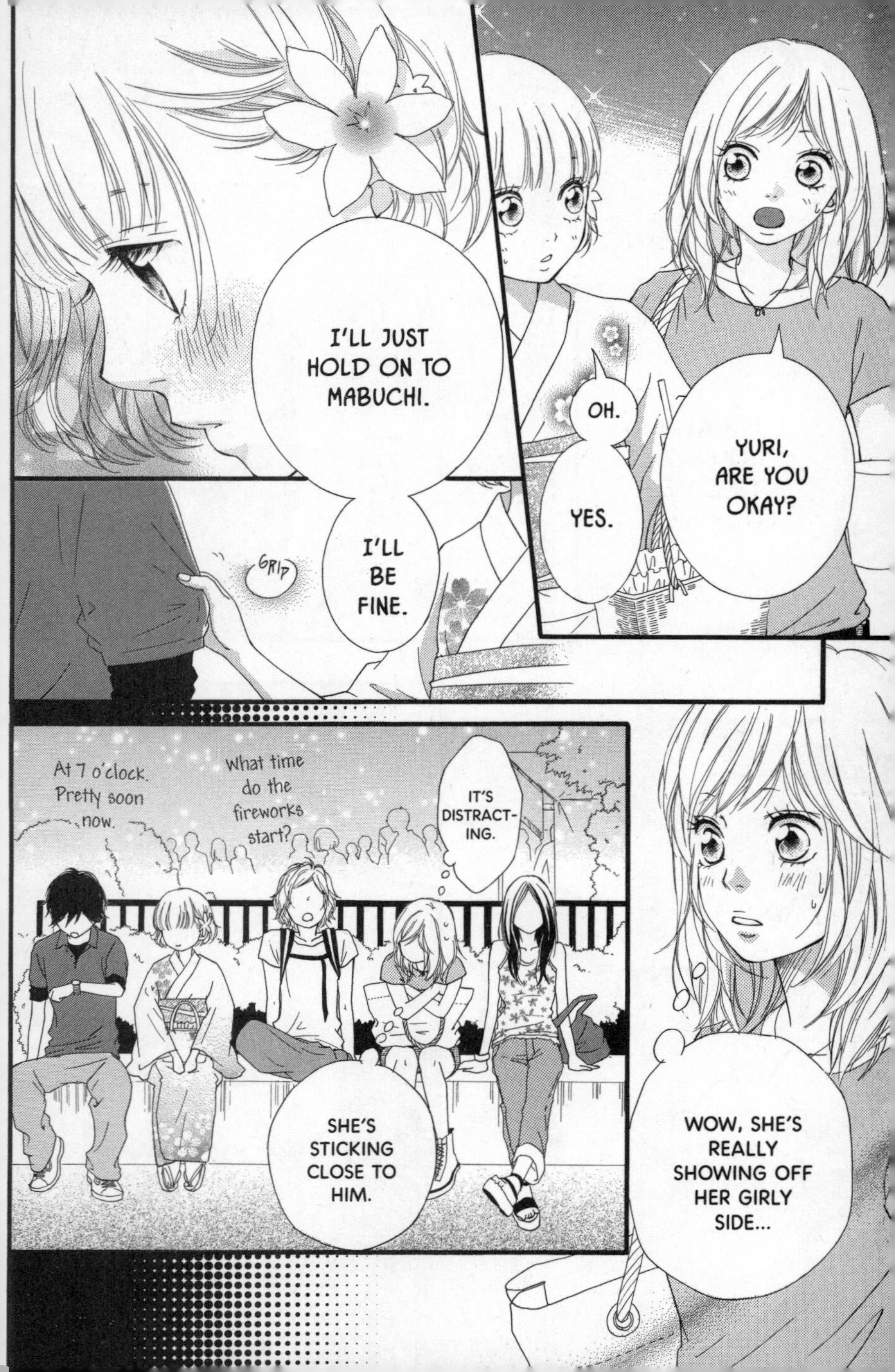
YURI, ARE YOU OKAY?
OH.
YES.
I'LL JUST HOLD ON TO MABUCHI.
I'LL BE FINE.
GRIP
WOW, SHE'S REALLY SHOWING OFF HER GIRLY SIDE...
IT'S DISTRACTING.
What time do the fireworks start?
At 7 o'clock. Pretty soon now.
SHE'S STICKING CLOSE TO HIM.

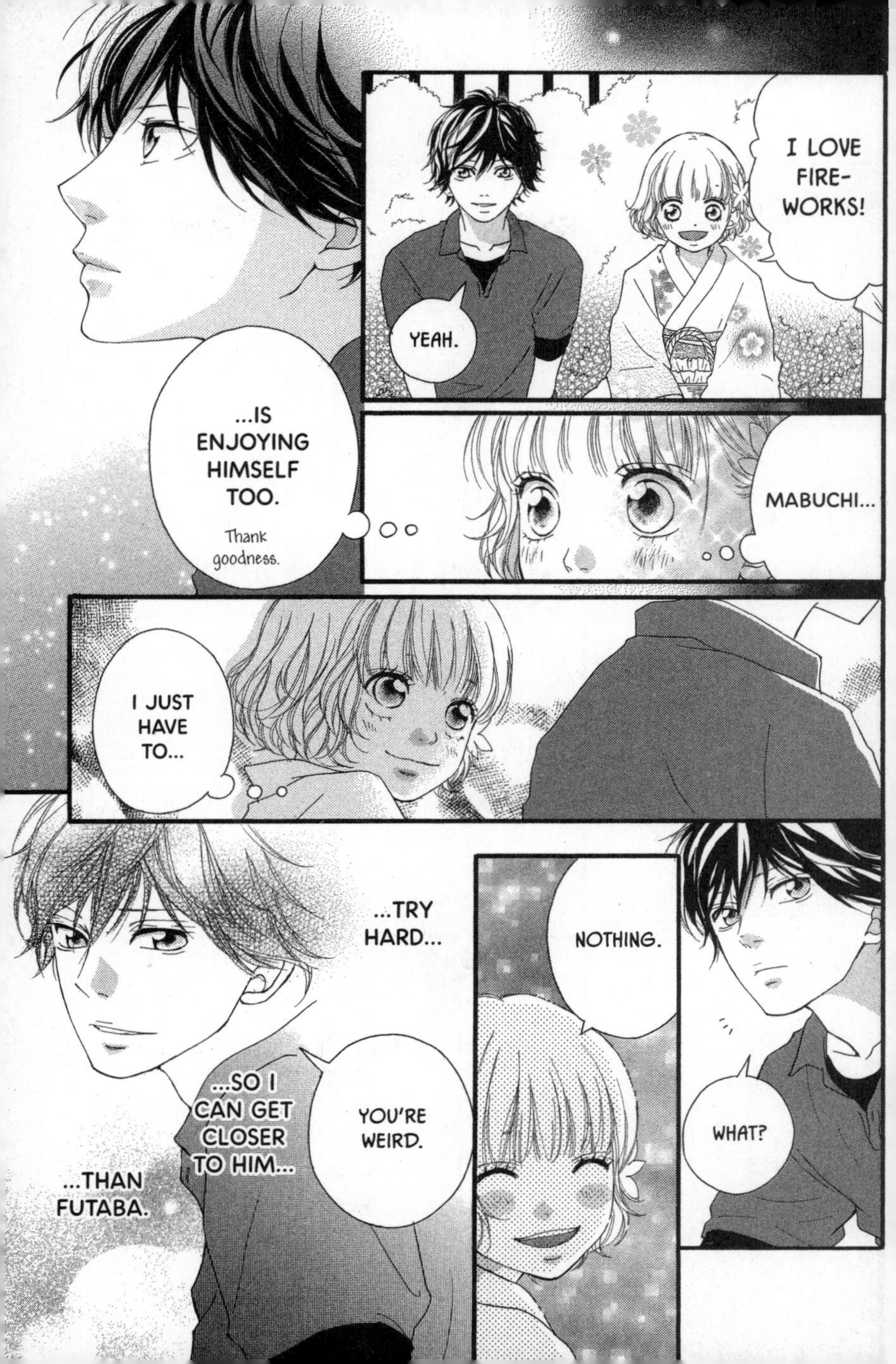
I LOVE FIRE-WORKS!
YEAH.
MABUCHI...
...IS ENJOYING HIMSELF TOO.
Thank goodness.
I JUST HAVE TO...
NOTHING.
WHAT?
...TRY HARD...
...SO I CAN GET CLOSER TO HIM...
YOU'RE WEIRD.
...THAN FUTABA.

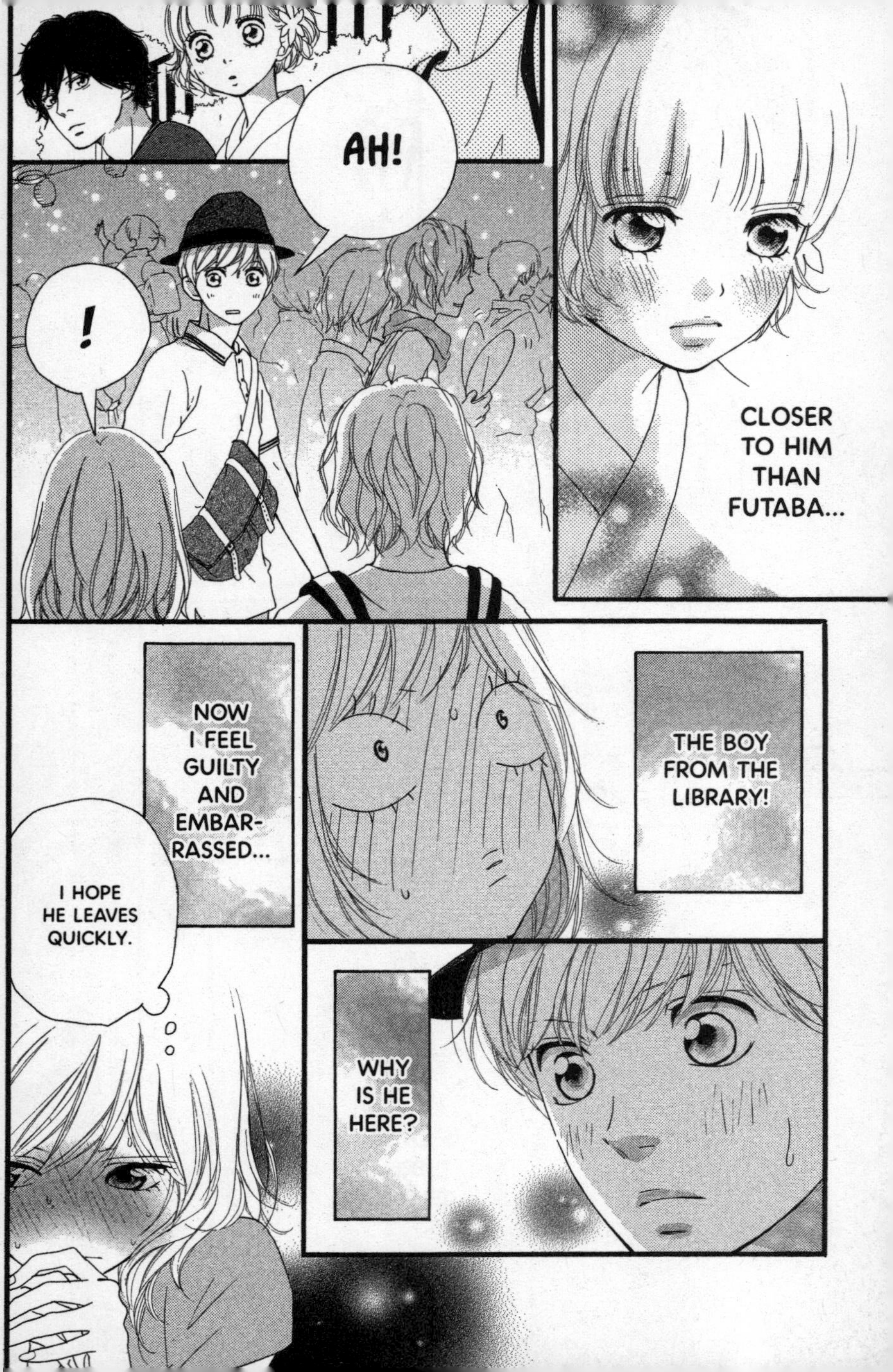
CLOSER TO HIM THAN FUTABA...
AH!
!
THE BOY FROM THE LIBRARY!
WHY IS HE HERE?
NOW I FEEL GUILTY AND EMBARRASSED...
I HOPE HE LEAVES QUICKLY.

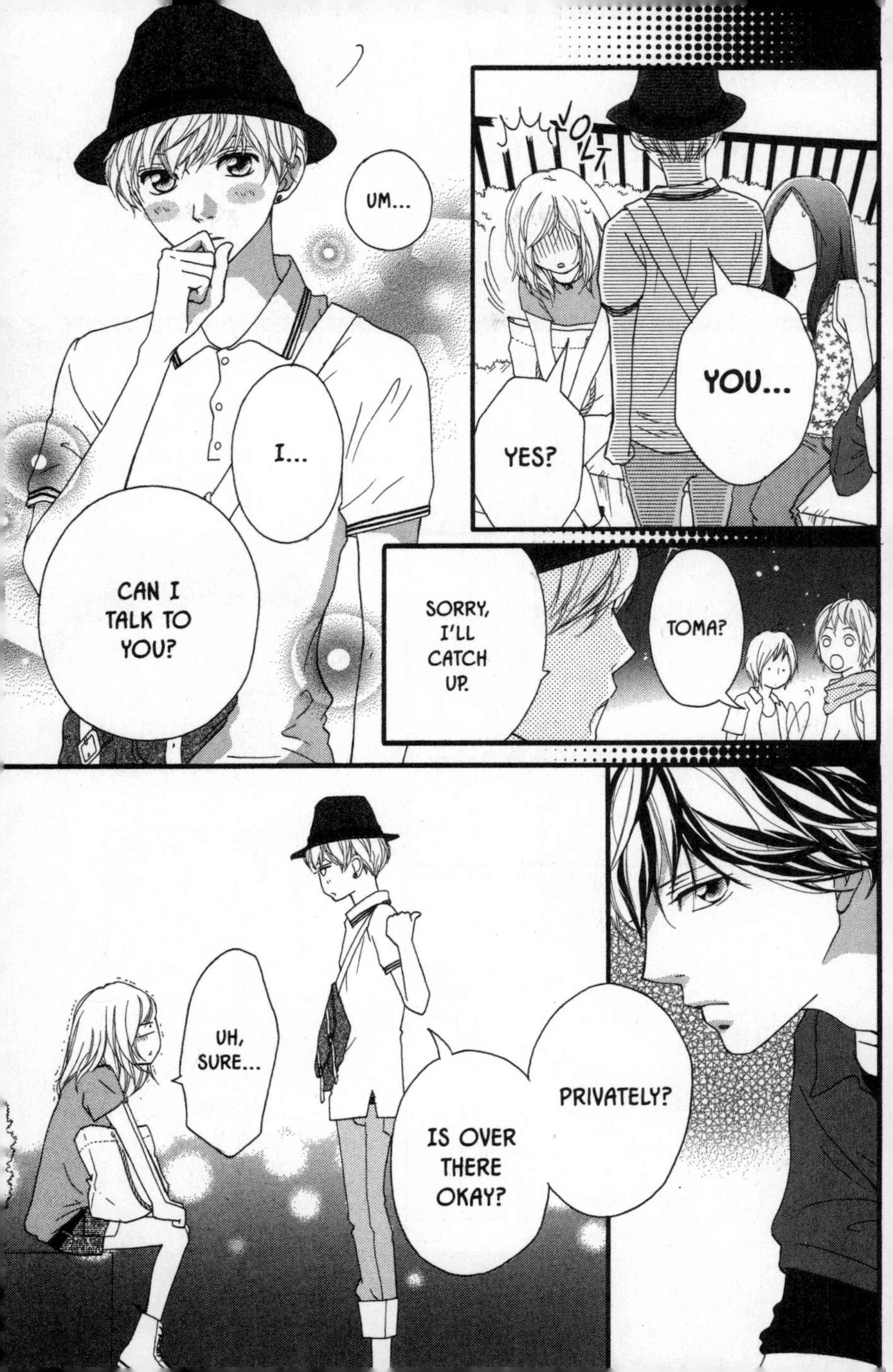
JOLT
YOU...
YES?
TOMA?
SORRY, I'LL CATCH UP.
UM...
I...
CAN I TALK TO YOU?
PRIVATELY?
IS OVER THERE OKAY?
UH, SURE...

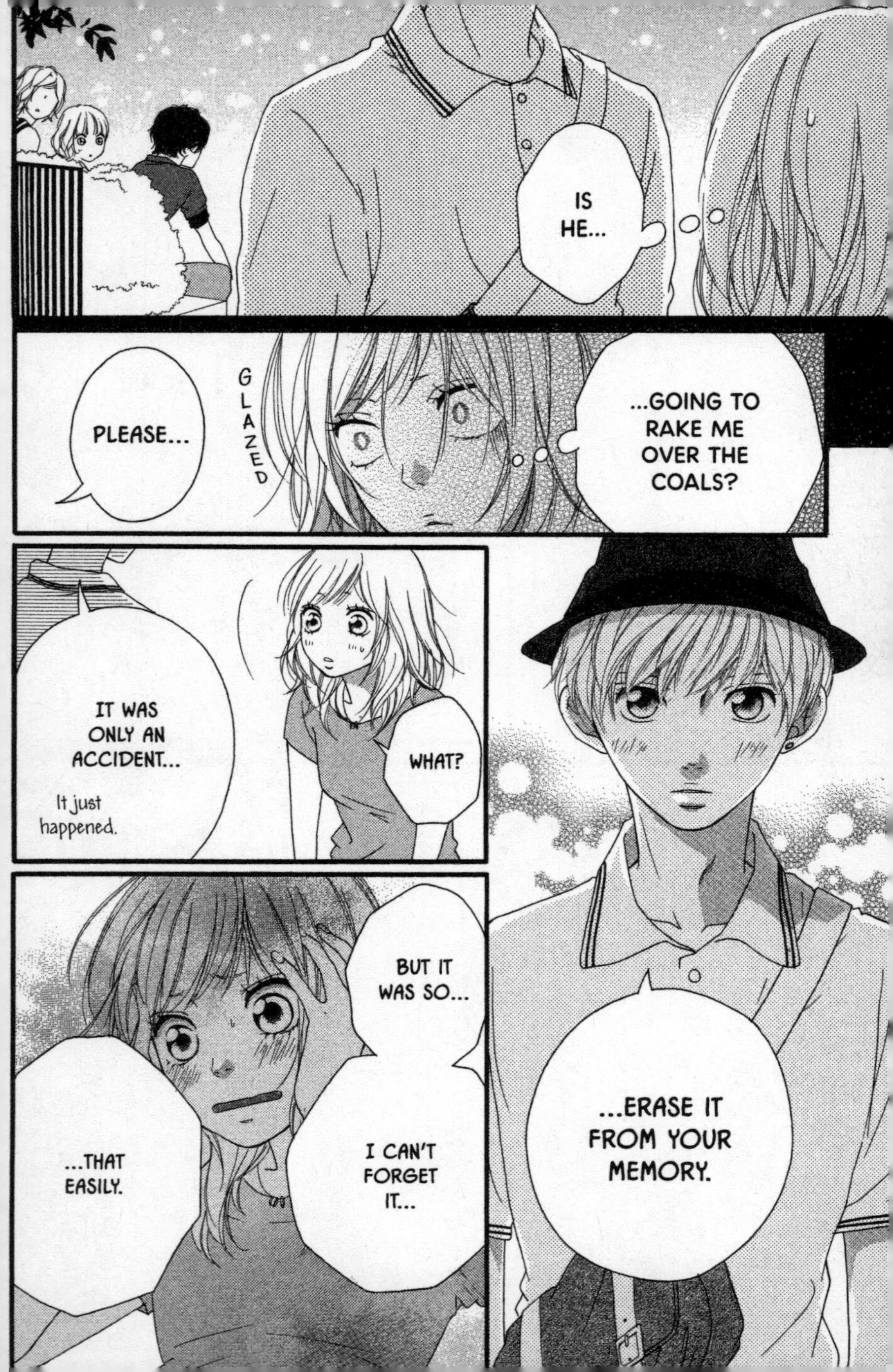
IS HE...
...GOING TO RAKE ME OVER THE COALS?
GLAZED
PLEASE...
...ERASE IT FROM YOUR MEMORY.
WHAT?
IT WAS ONLY AN ACCIDENT...
It just happened.
BUT IT WAS SO...
I CAN'T FORGET IT...
...THAT EASILY.

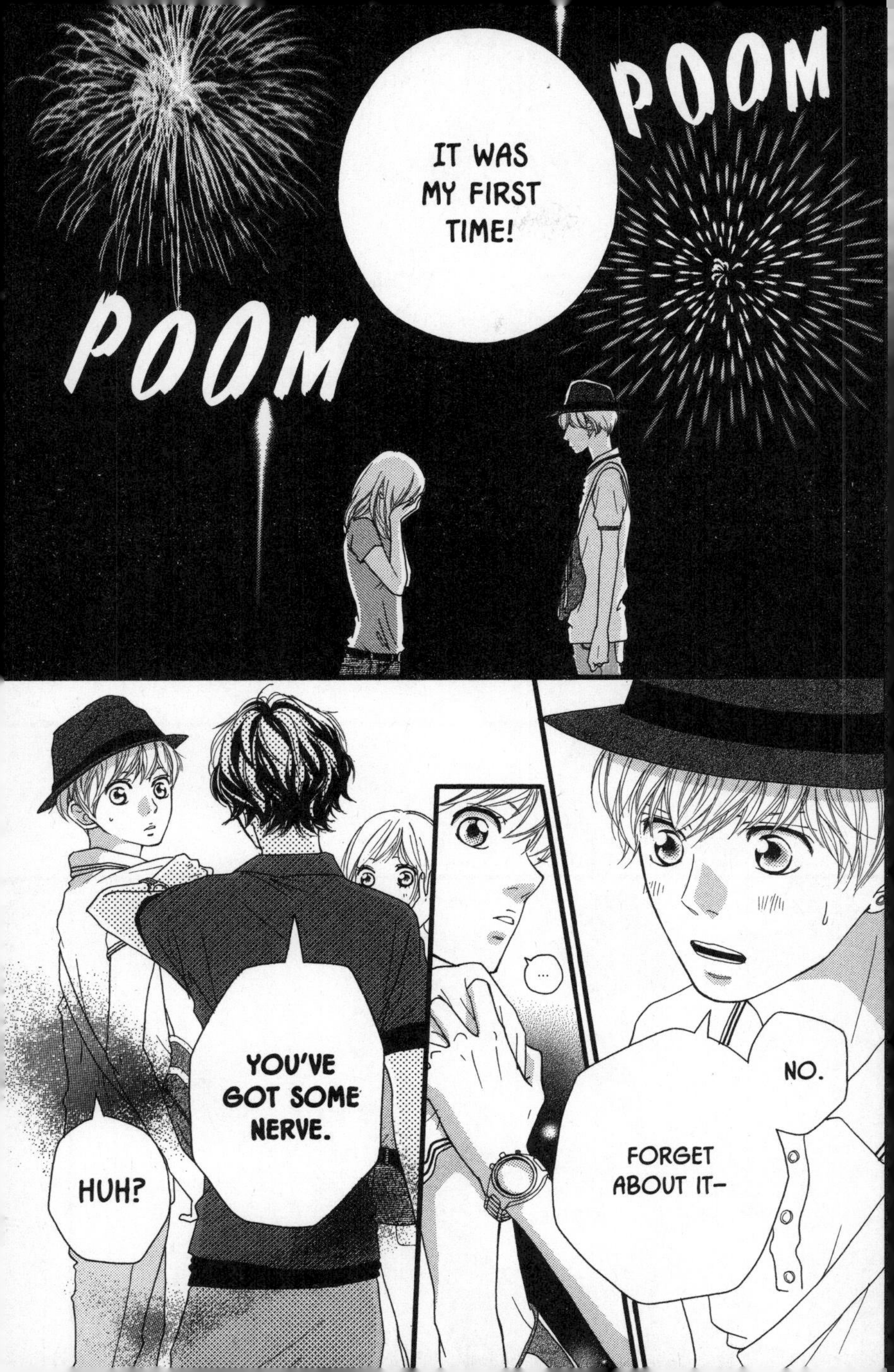
POOM
IT WAS MY FIRST TIME!
POOM
NO.
FORGET ABOUT IT—
...
YOU'VE GOT SOME NERVE.
HUH?

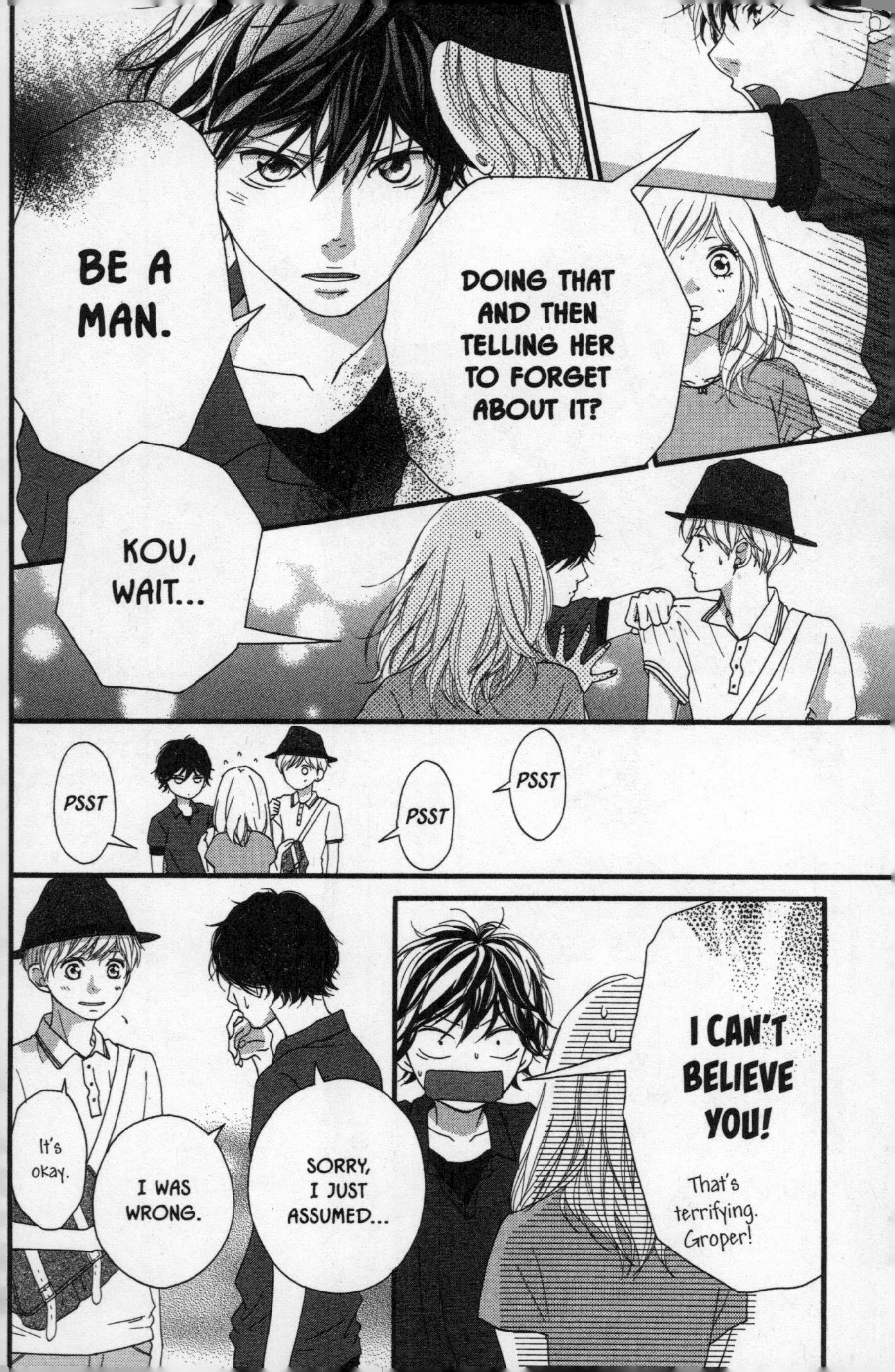
DOING THAT AND THEN TELLING HER TO FORGET ABOUT IT?
BE A MAN.
KOU, WAIT...
PSST
PSST
PSST
I CAN'T BELIEVE YOU!
That's terrifying. Groper!
SORRY, I JUST ASSUMED...
I WAS WRONG.
It's okay.

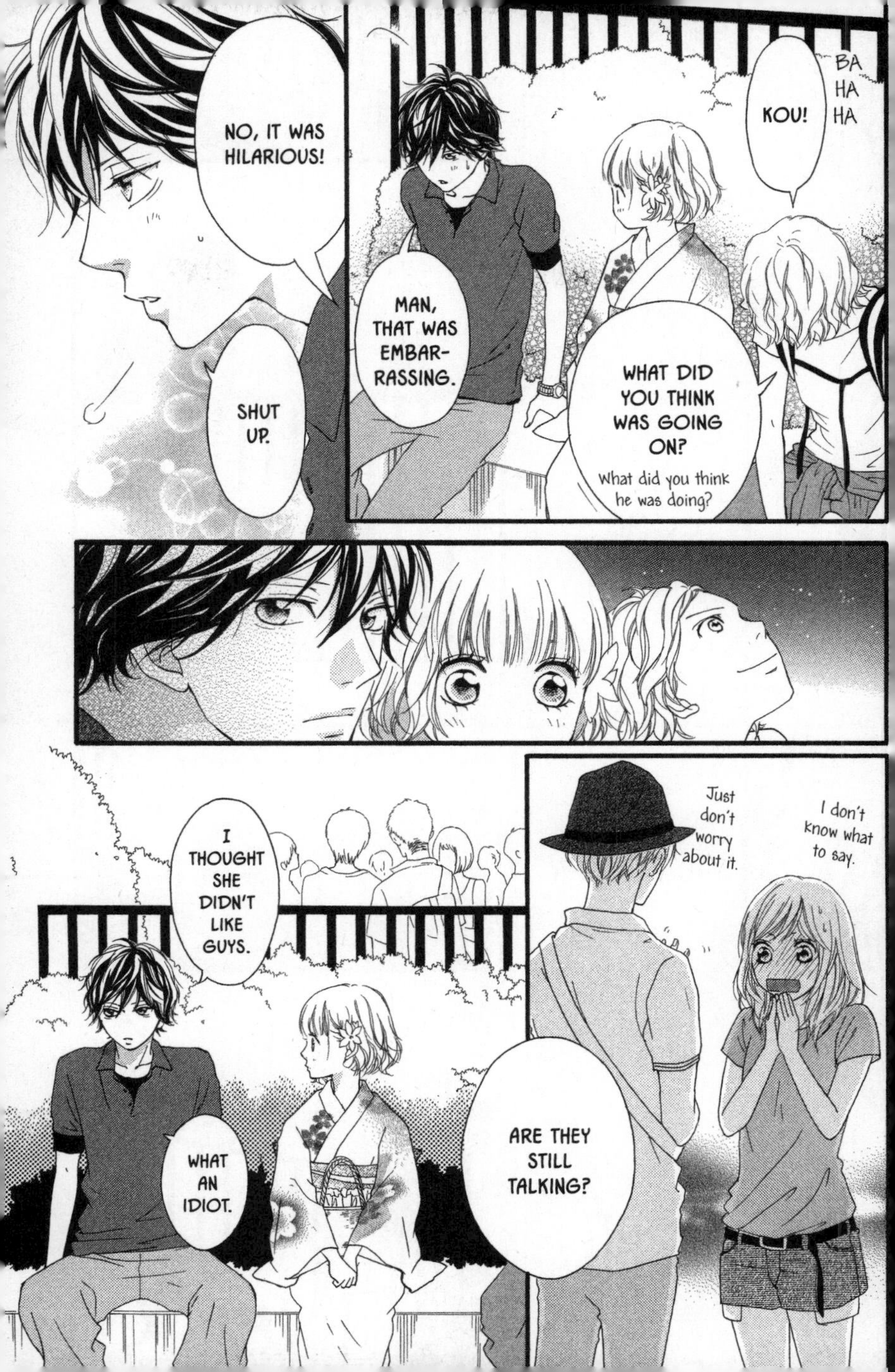
BA HA HA
KOU!
MAN, THAT WAS EMBARRASSING.
WHAT DID YOU THINK WAS GOING ON?
What did you think he was doing?
NO, IT WAS HILARIOUS!
SHUT UP.
I don't know what to say.
Just don't worry about it.
ARE THEY STILL TALKING?
I THOUGHT SHE DIDN'T LIKE GUYS.
WHAT AN IDIOT.

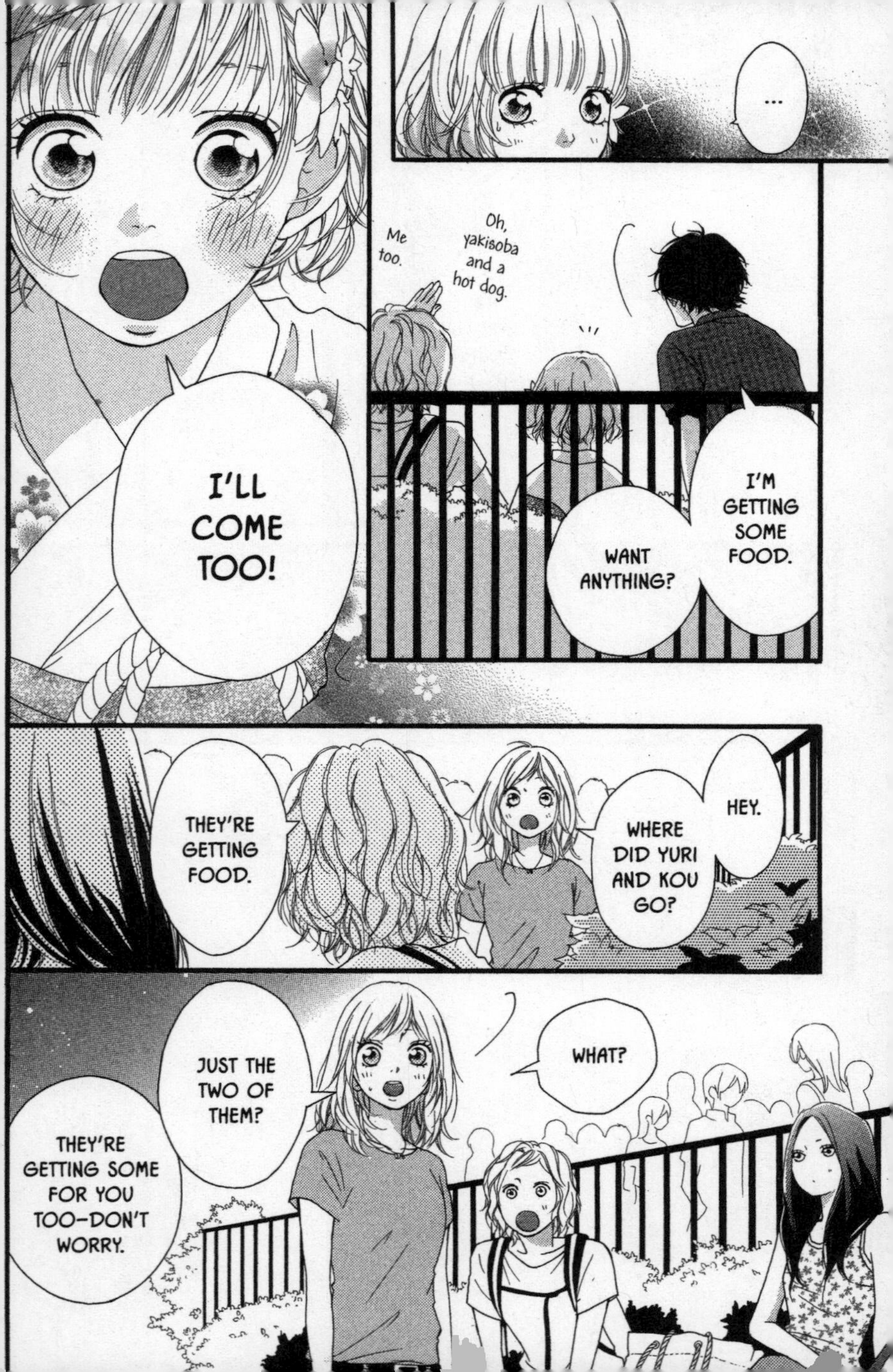
...
I'M GETTING SOME FOOD.
WANT ANYTHING?
Oh, yakisoba and a hot dog.
Me too.
I'LL COME TOO!
HEY.
WHERE DID YURI AND KOU GO?
THEY'RE GETTING FOOD.
WHAT?
JUST THE TWO OF THEM?
THEY'RE GETTING SOME FOR YOU TOO—DON'T WORRY.

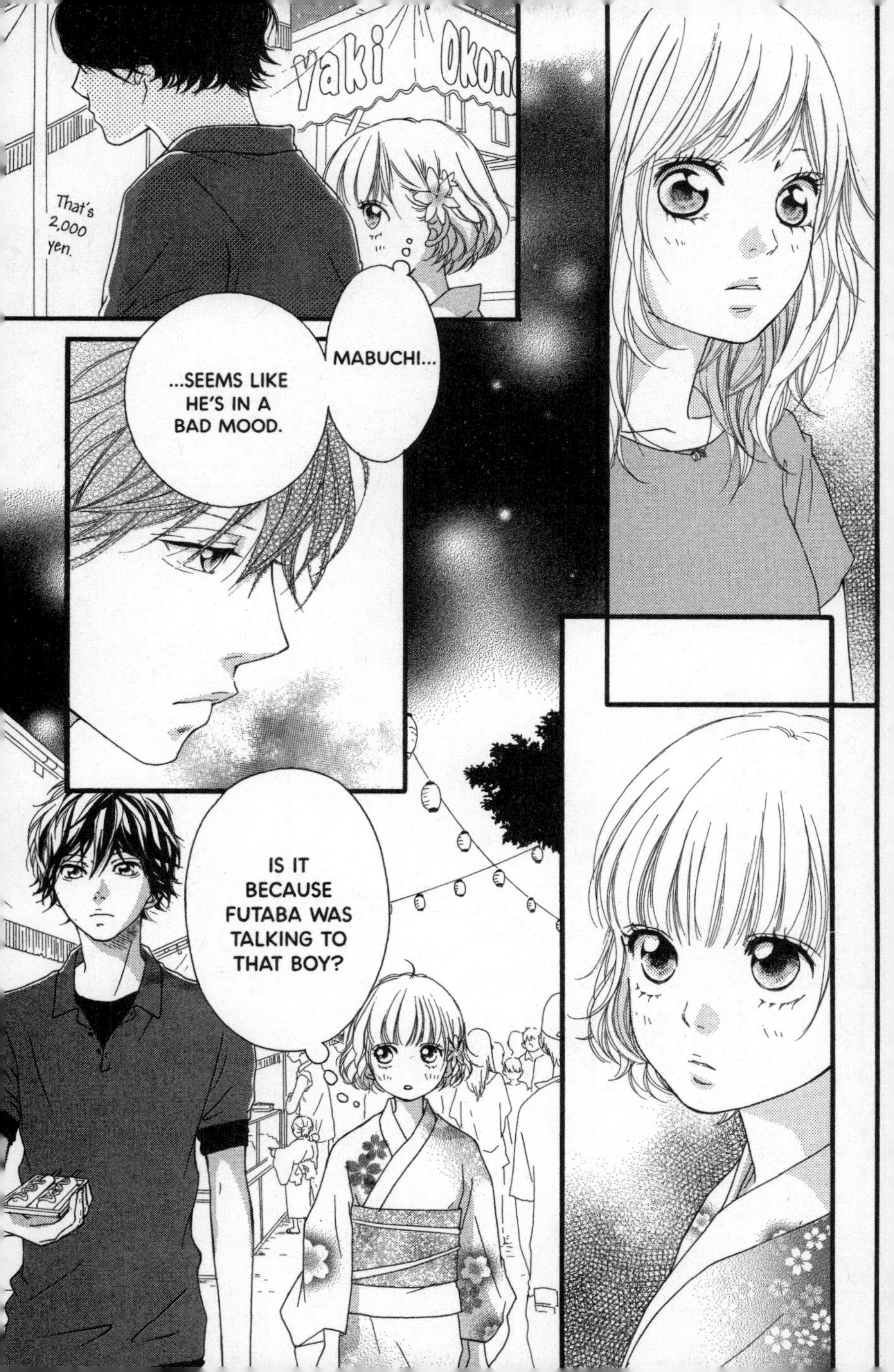
Yaki Okono
That's 2,000 yen.
MABUCHI...
...SEEMS LIKE HE'S IN A BAD MOOD.
IS IT BECAUSE FUTABA WAS TALKING TO THAT BOY?

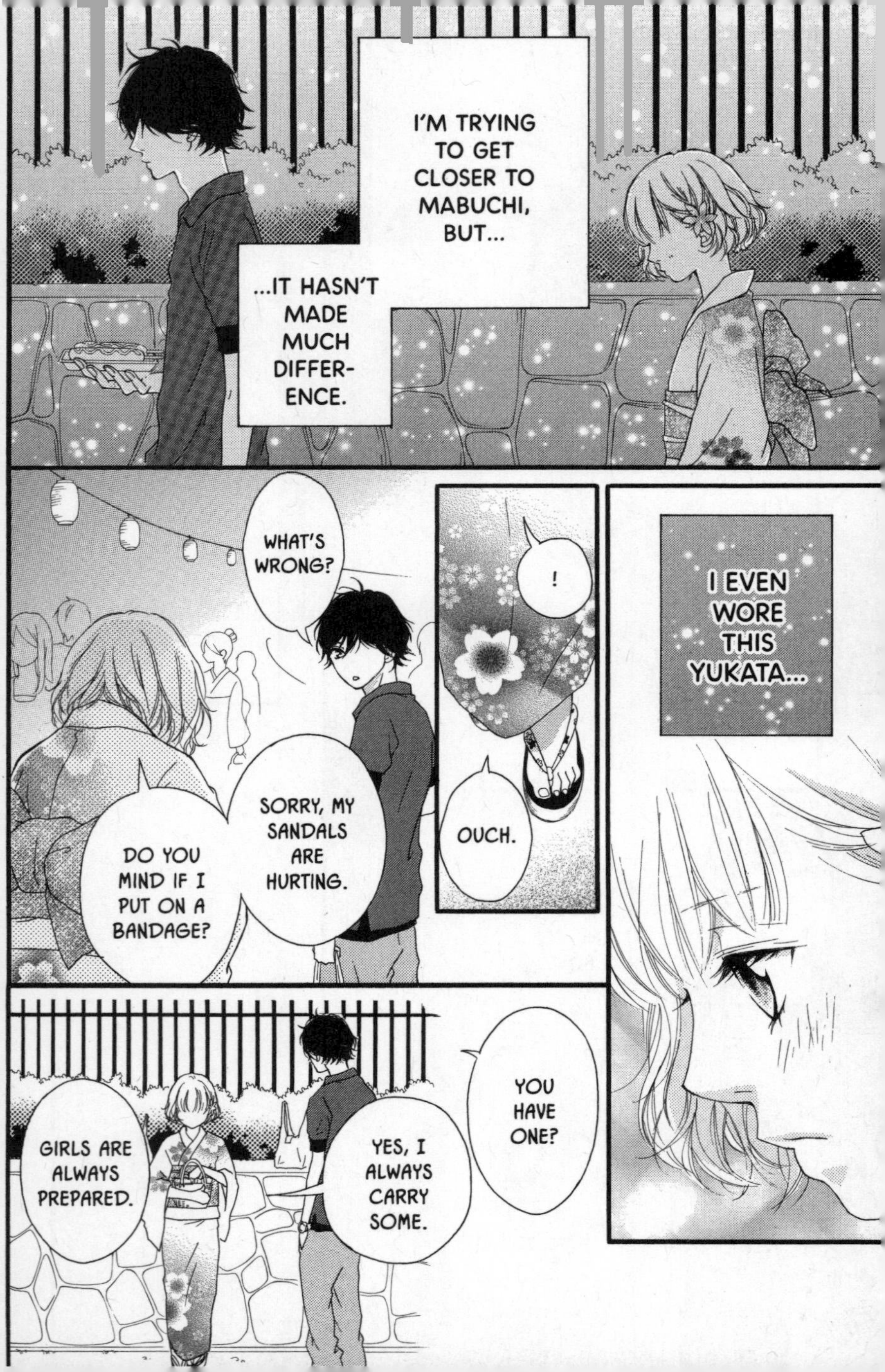
I'M TRYING TO GET CLOSER TO MABUCHI, BUT...
...IT HASN'T MADE MUCH DIFFER-ENCE.
I EVEN WORE THIS YUKATA...
!
OUCH.
WHAT'S WRONG?
SORRY, MY SANDALS ARE HURTING.
DO YOU MIND IF I PUT ON A BANDAGE?
YOU HAVE ONE?
YES, I ALWAYS CARRY SOME.
GIRLS ARE ALWAYS PREPARED.

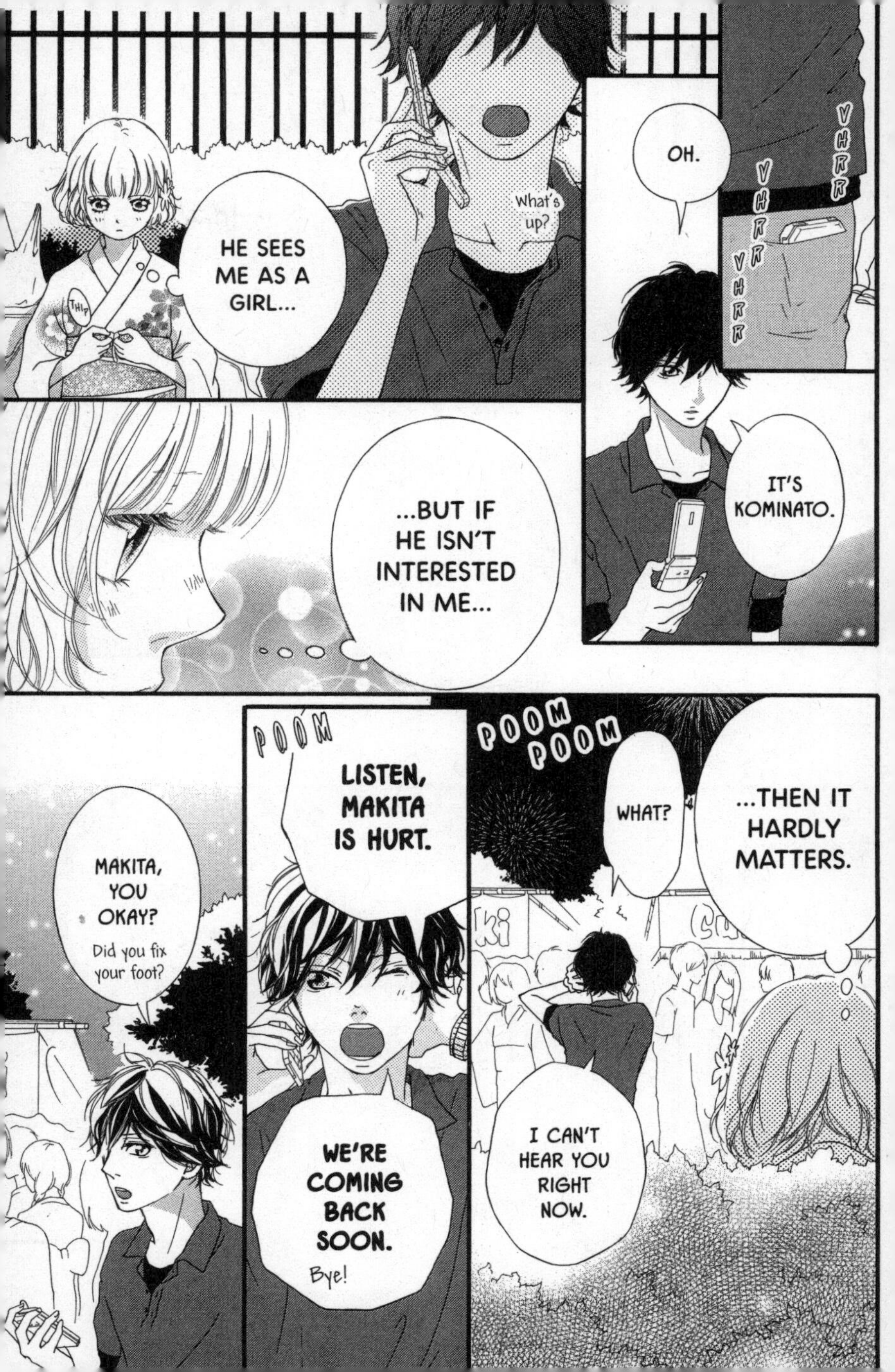

VHRR
VHRR
VHRR
OH.
IT'S KOMINATO.
What's up?
HE SEES ME AS A GIRL...
THIP
...BUT IF HE ISN'T INTERESTED IN ME...
...THEN IT HARDLY MATTERS.
POOM POOM
WHAT?
I CAN'T HEAR YOU RIGHT NOW.
POOM
LISTEN, MAKITA IS HURT.
WE'RE COMING BACK SOON.
Bye!
MAKITA, YOU OKAY?
Did you fix your foot?

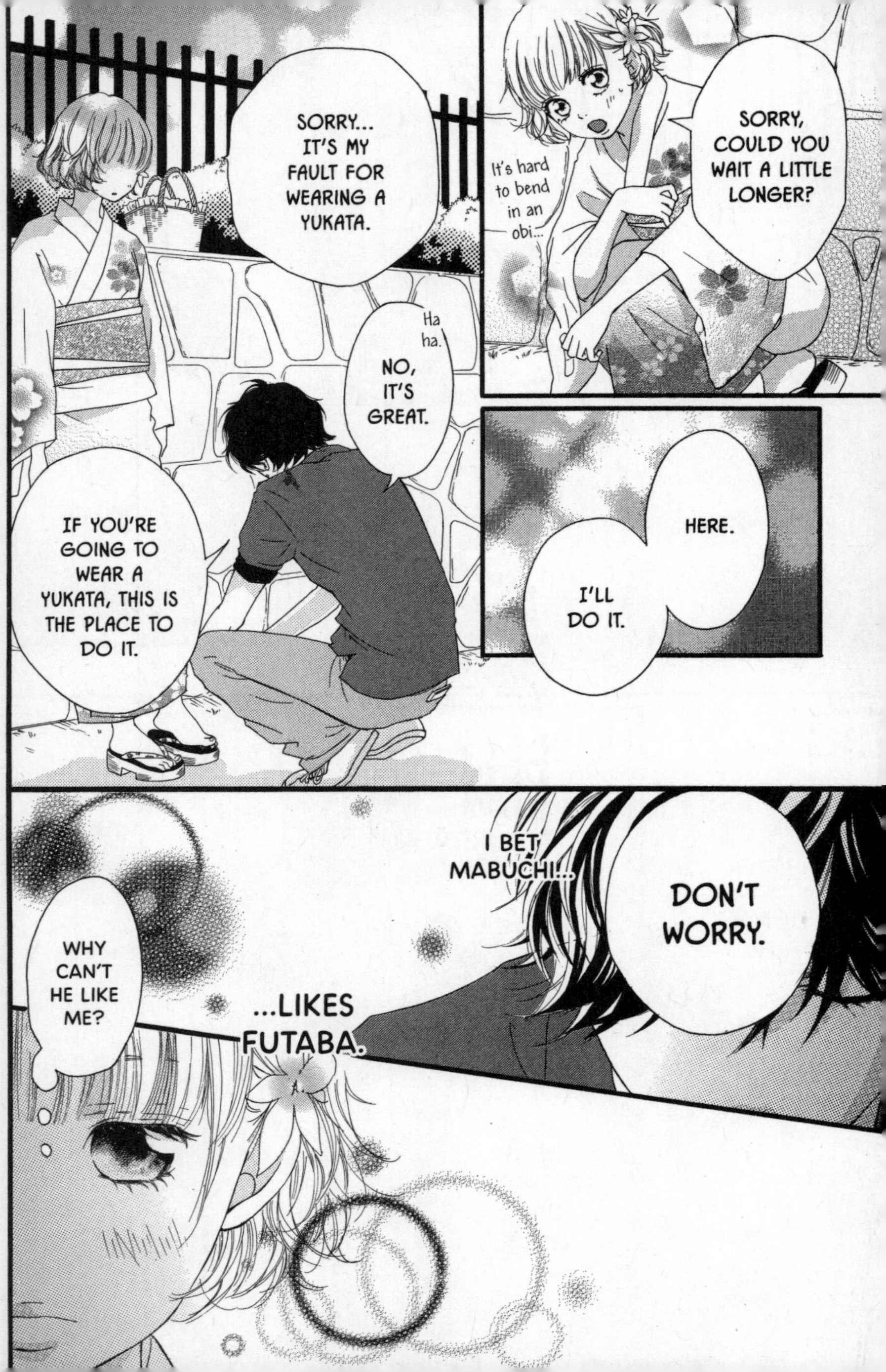
SORRY, COULD YOU WAIT A LITTLE LONGER?
It's hard to bend in an obi...
HERE.
I'LL DO IT.
SORRY... IT'S MY FAULT FOR WEARING A YUKATA.
Ha ha.
NO, IT'S GREAT.
IF YOU'RE GOING TO WEAR A YUKATA, THIS IS THE PLACE TO DO IT.
DON'T WORRY.
I BET MABUCHI...
...LIKES FUTABA.
WHY CAN'T HE LIKE ME?

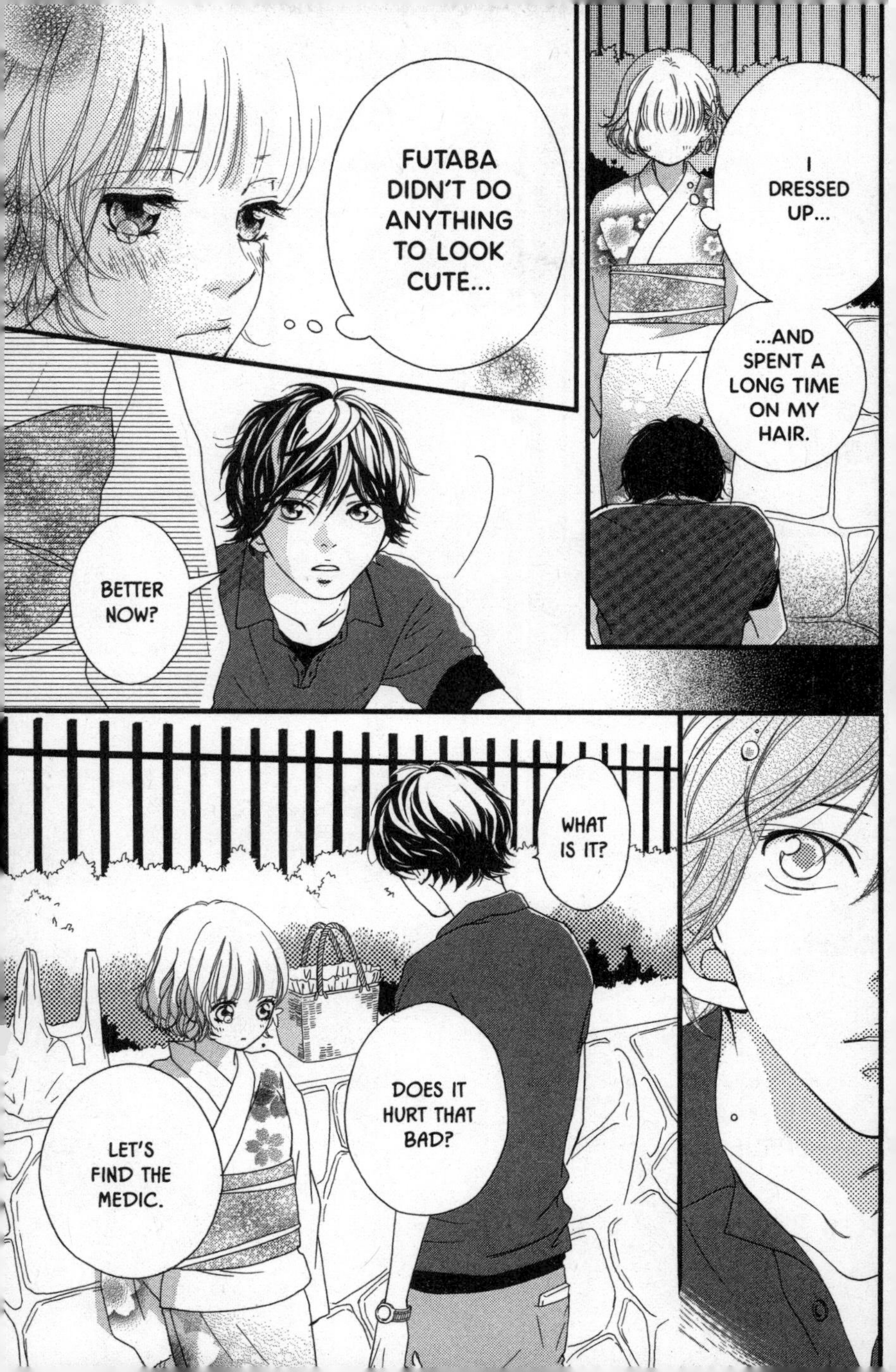
I DRESSED UP...
...AND SPENT A LONG TIME ON MY HAIR.
FUTABA DIDN'T DO ANYTHING TO LOOK CUTE...
BETTER NOW?
WHAT IS IT?
DOES IT HURT THAT BAD?
LET'S FIND THE MEDIC.

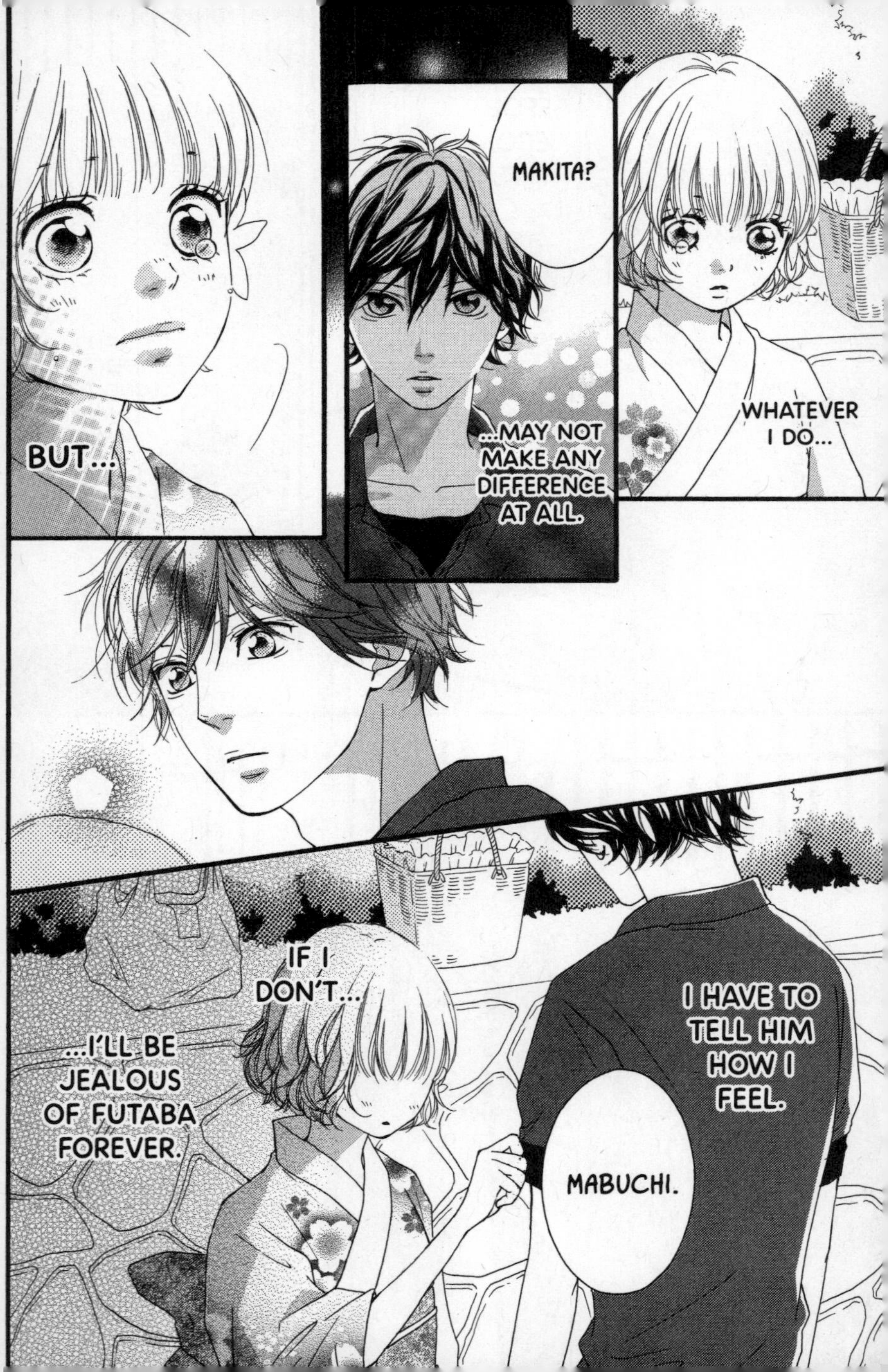
WHATEVER I DO...
MAKITA?
...MAY NOT MAKE ANY DIFFERENCE AT ALL.
BUT...
I HAVE TO TELL HIM HOW I FEEL.
MABUCHI.
IF I DON'T...
...I'LL BE JEALOUS OF FUTABA FOREVER.

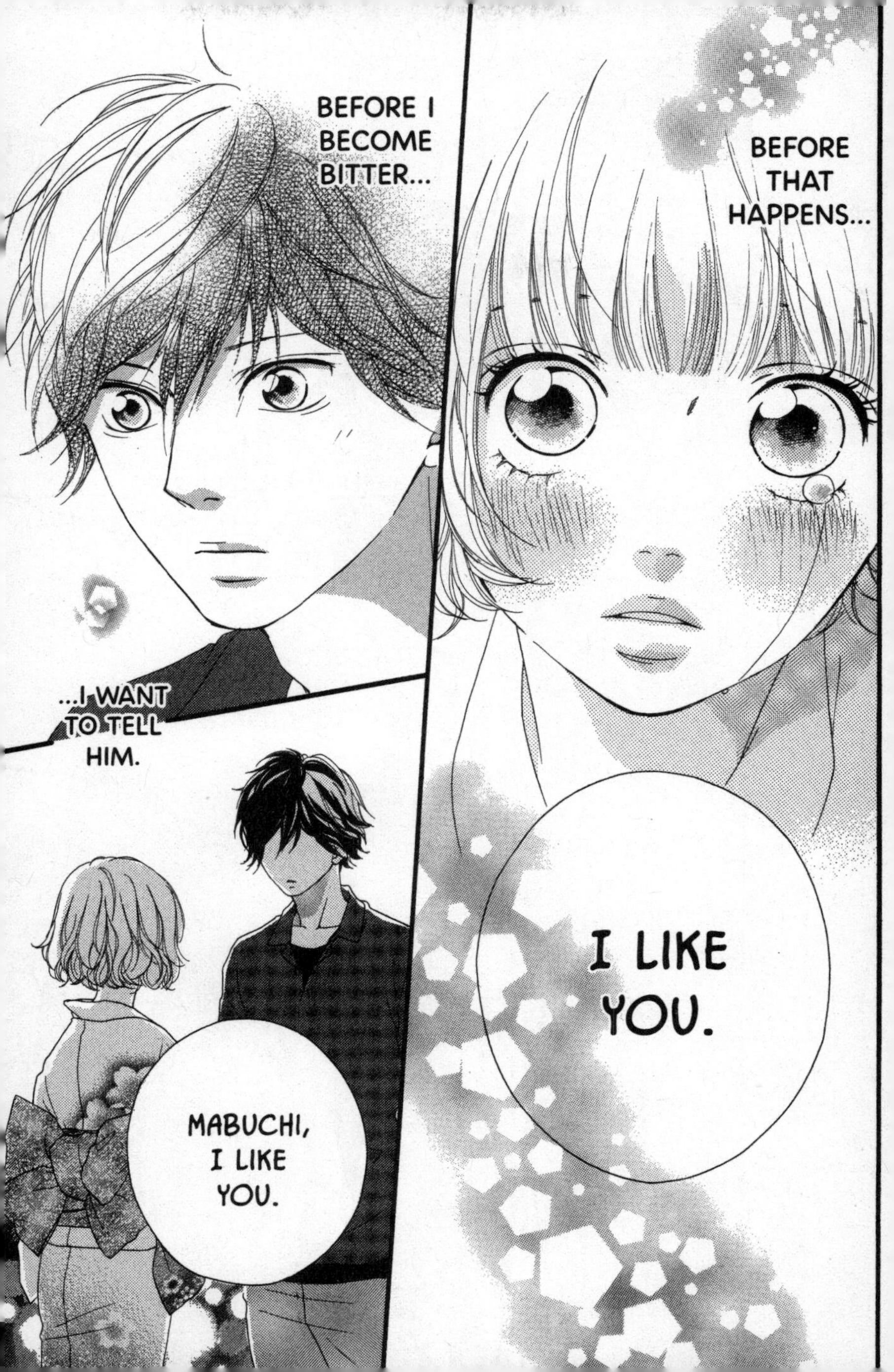
BEFORE THAT HAPPENS...
I LIKE YOU.
BEFORE I BECOME BITTER...
...I WANT TO TELL HIM.
MABUCHI, I LIKE YOU.

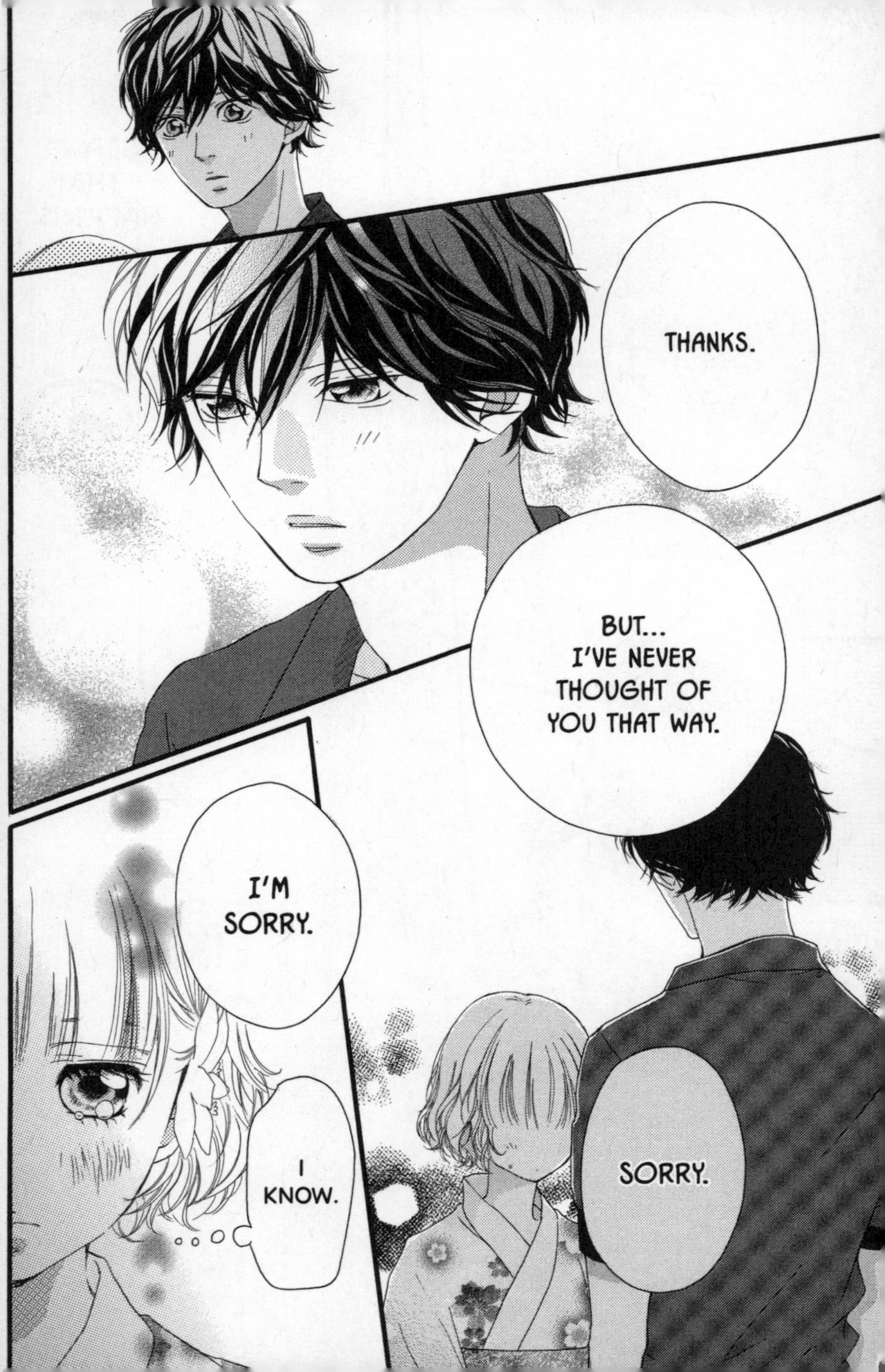
THANKS.
BUT... I'VE NEVER THOUGHT OF YOU THAT WAY.
I'M SORRY.
SORRY.
I KNOW.

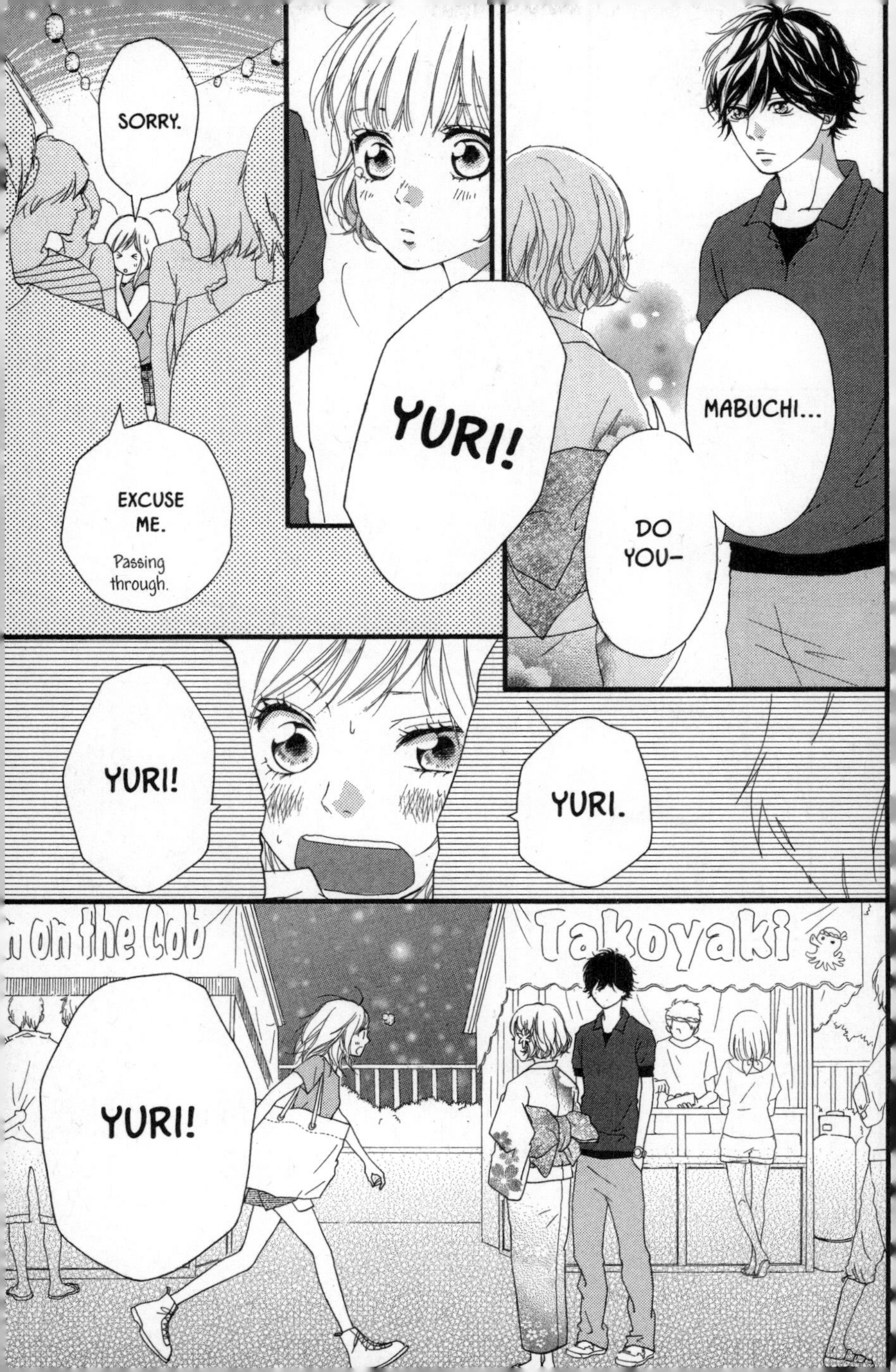
MABUCHI...
DO YOU-
YURI!
SORRY.
EXCUSE ME.
Passing through.
YURI.
YURI!
Takoyaki
n on the Cob
YURI!

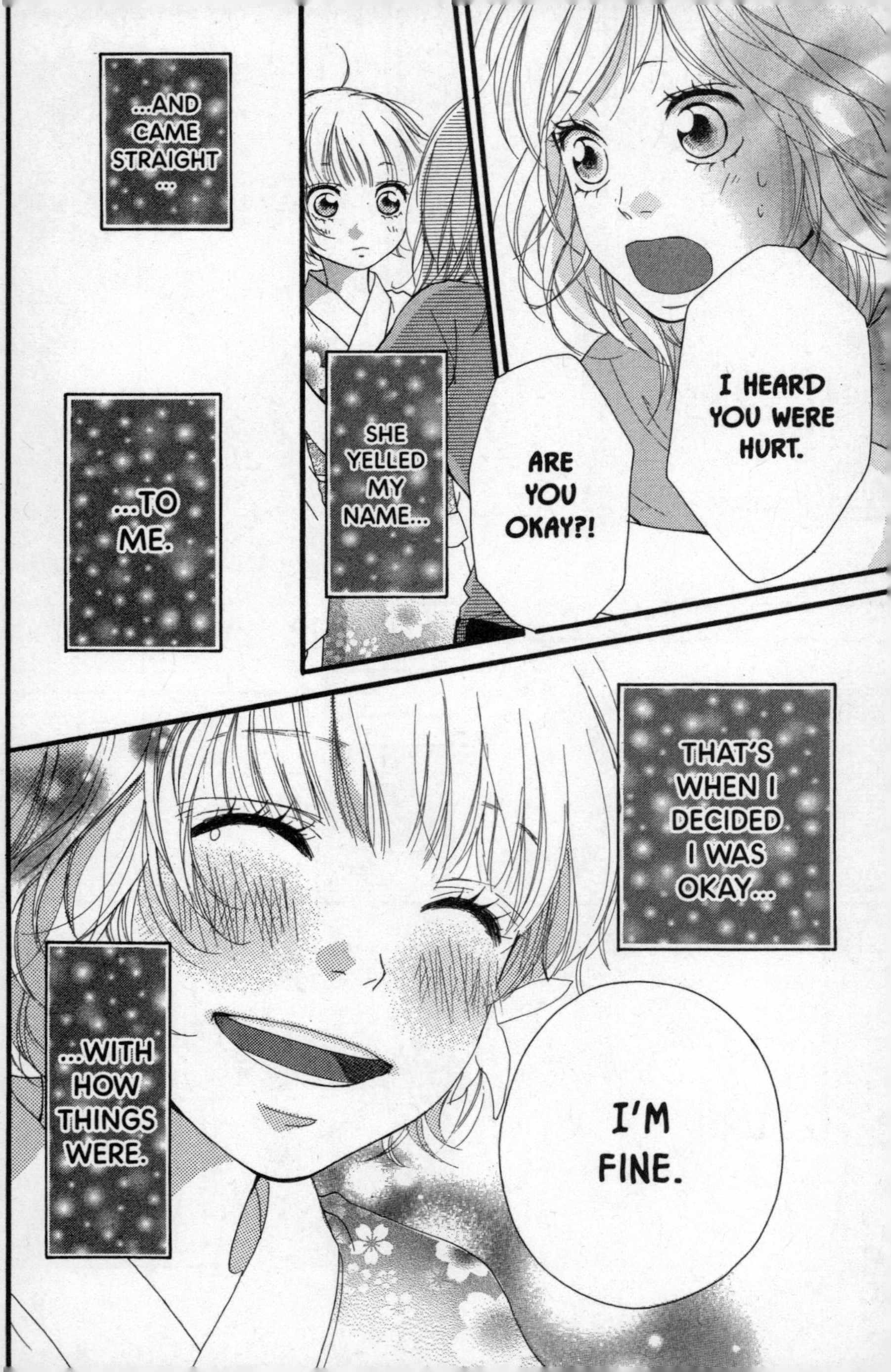
I HEARD YOU WERE HURT.
ARE YOU OKAY?!
SHE YELLED MY NAME...
...AND CAME STRAIGHT...
...TO ME.
THAT'S WHEN I DECIDED I WAS OKAY...
I'M FINE.
...WITH HOW THINGS WERE.

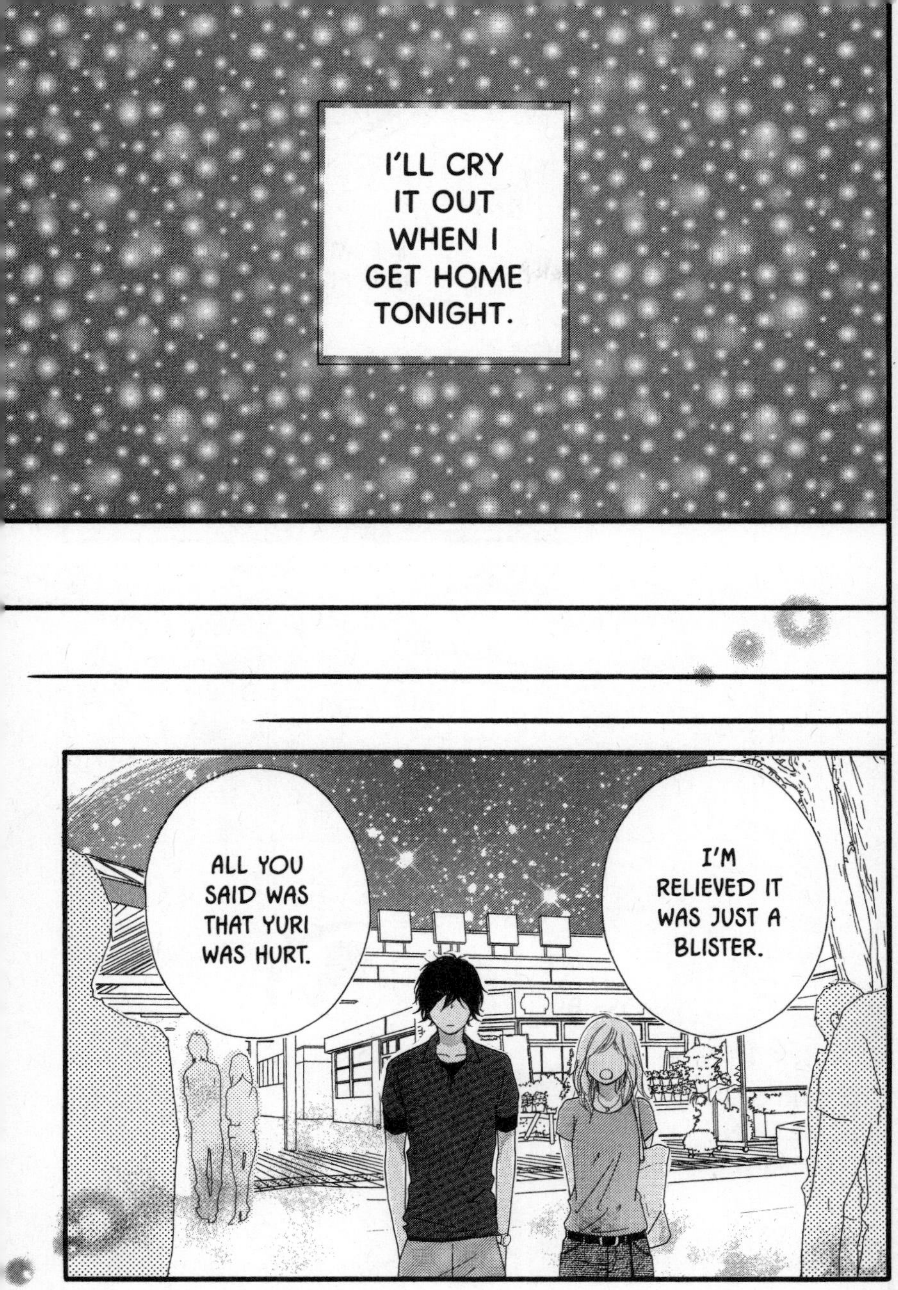
I'LL CRY IT OUT WHEN I GET HOME TONIGHT.
I'M RELIEVED IT WAS JUST A BLISTER.
ALL YOU SAID WAS THAT YURI WAS HURT.

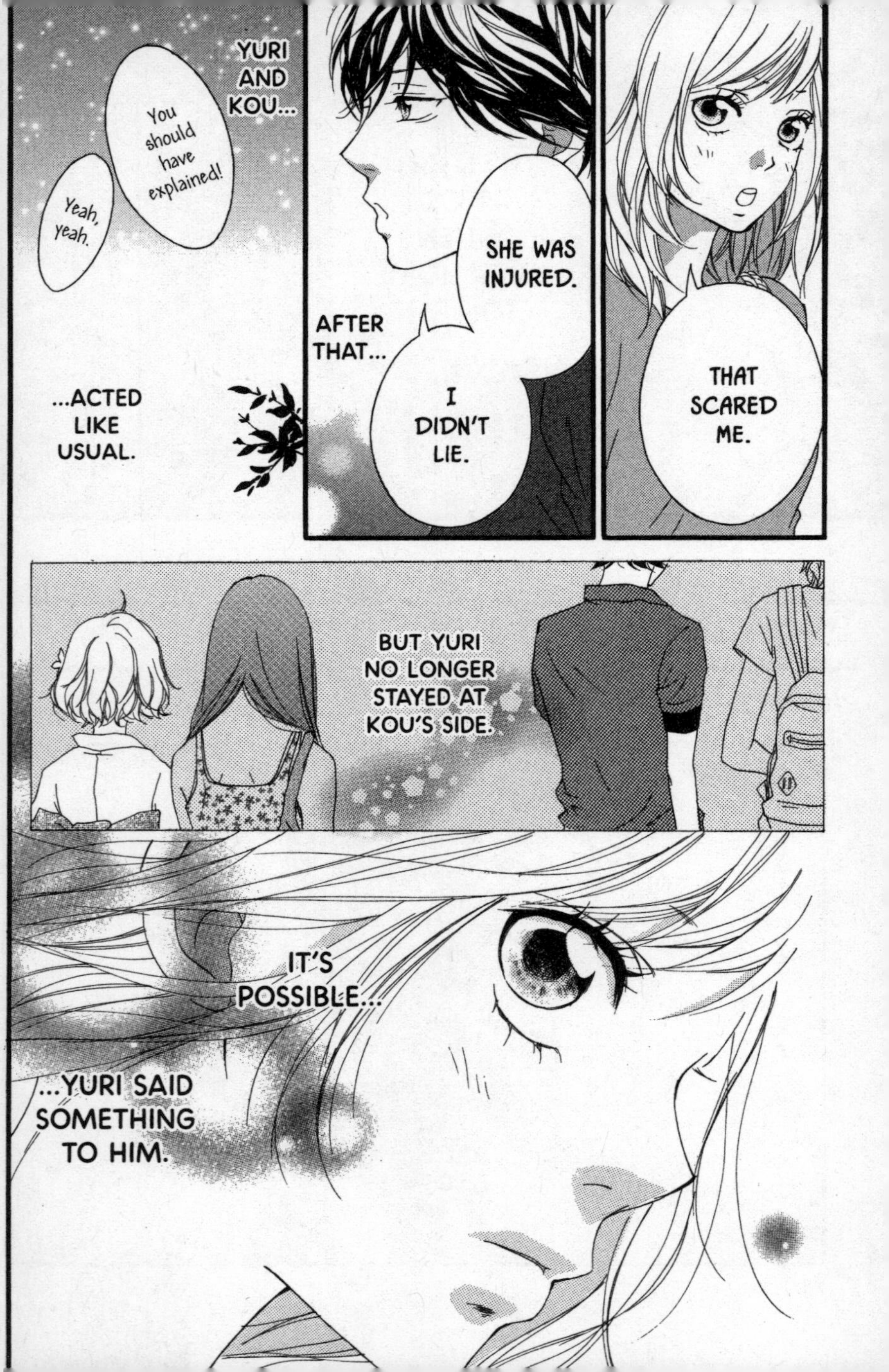
THAT SCARED ME.
SHE WAS INJURED.
I DIDN'T LIE.
AFTER THAT...
YURI AND KOU...
You should have explained!
Yeah, yeah.
...ACTED LIKE USUAL.
BUT YURI NO LONGER STAYED AT KOU'S SIDE.
IT'S POSSIBLE...
...YURI SAID SOMETHING TO HIM.

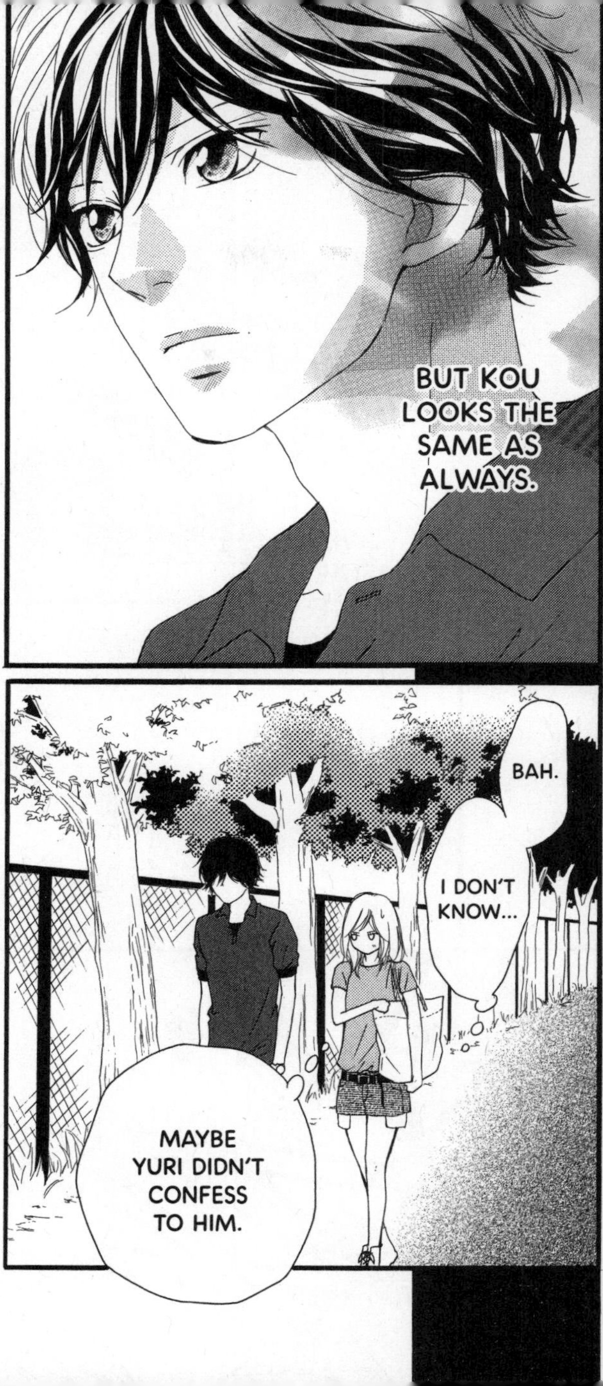
BUT KOU LOOKS THE SAME AS ALWAYS.
BAH.
I DON'T KNOW...
MAYBE YURI DIDN'T CONFESS TO HIM.

THANK YOU♡

Thank you for your letters and tweets! I wish I could reply to each and every one of them, but I promise that I do read everything! And they all make me so happy. ♡ Thank you very much. Sometimes people send me stories about their own love lives, and I always read them with my heart aflutter! To thank you for putting me in a good mood, I will do my best to make this story enjoyable for you!! I hope you'll continue to enjoy *Ao Haru Ride*. ☆

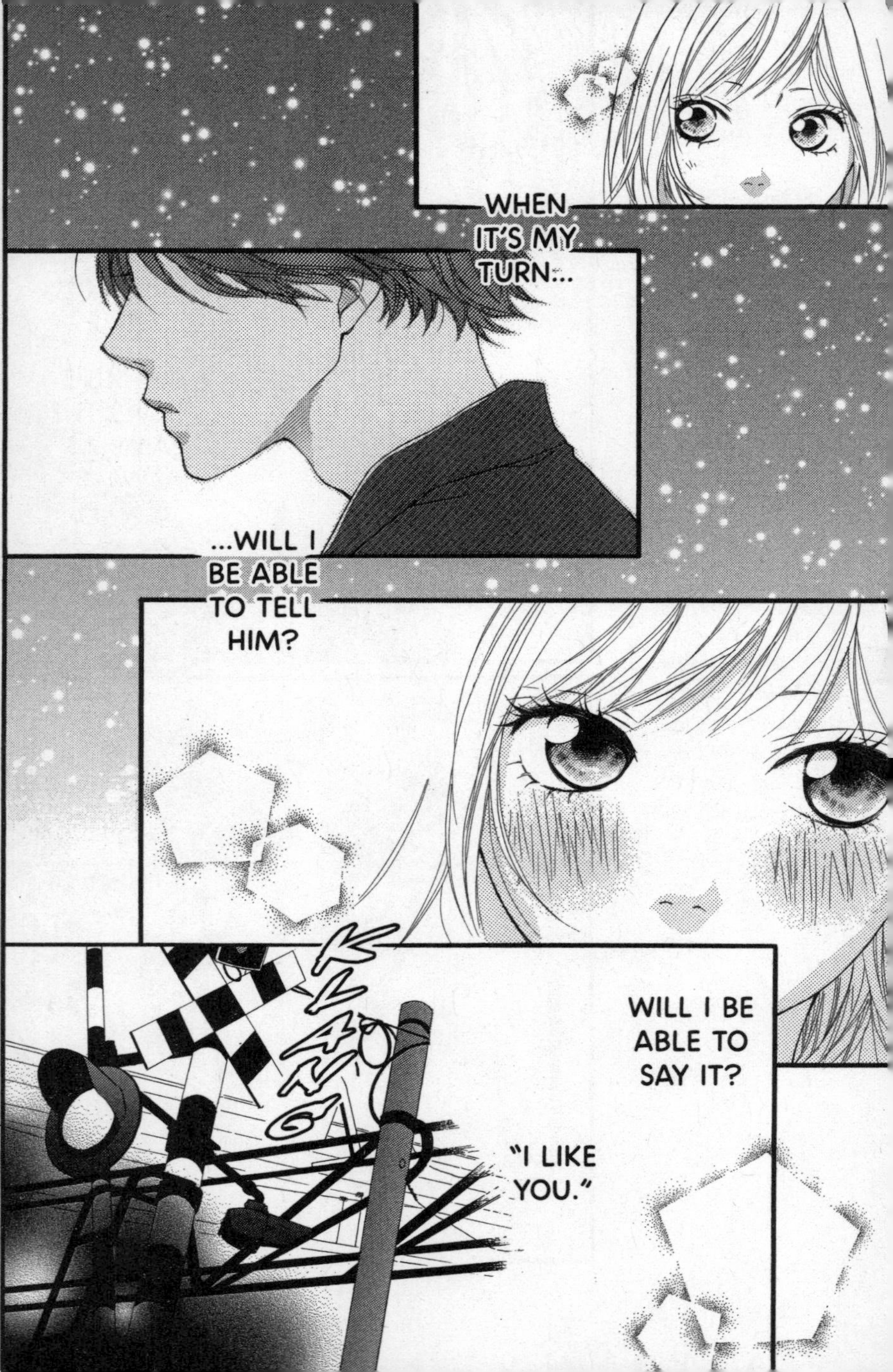
WHEN IT'S MY TURN...
...WILL I BE ABLE TO TELL HIM?
WILL I BE ABLE TO SAY IT?
"I LIKE YOU."

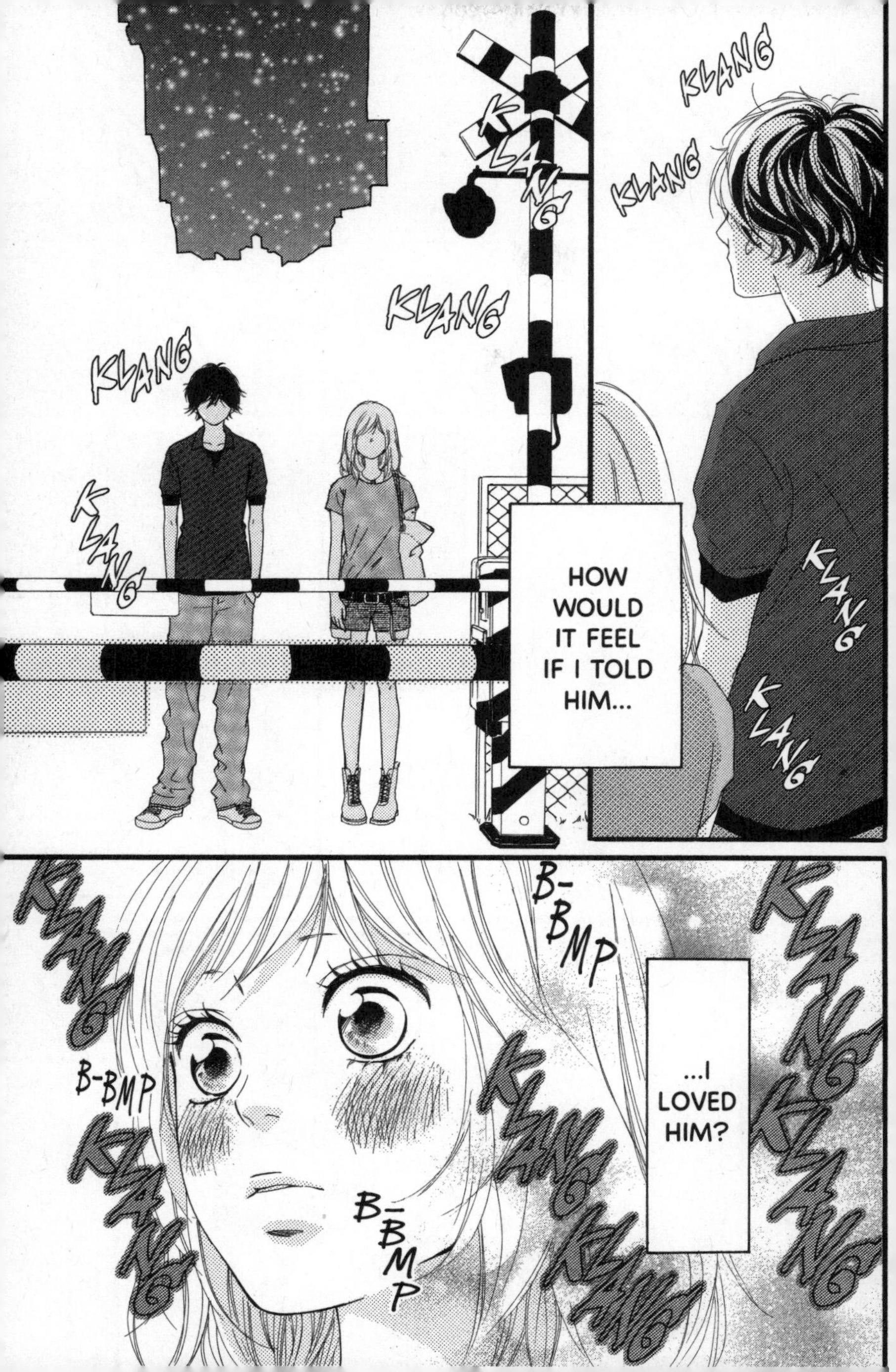
KLANG
KLANG
KLANG
KLANG
HOW WOULD IT FEEL IF I TOLD HIM...
KLANG
KLANG
KLANG
KLANG
B-BMP
...I LOVED HIM?
B-BMP
B-BMP

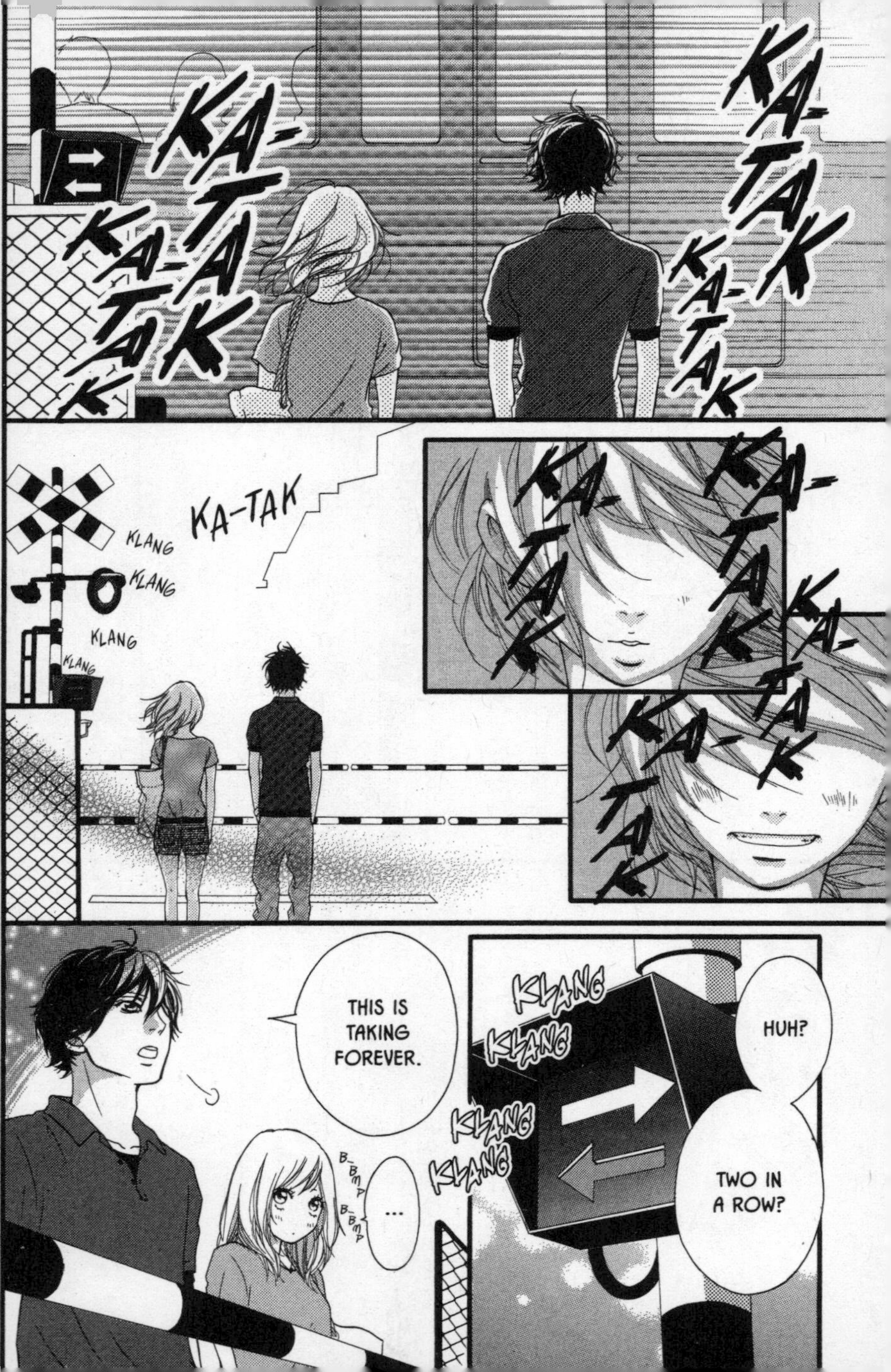
KA-TAK
KA-TAK
KA-TAK
KA-TAK
KA-TAK
KA-TAK
KA-TAK
KA-TAK
KA-TAK
KLANG
KLANG
KLANG
KLANG
HUH?
TWO IN A ROW?
KLANG
KLANG
KLANG
KLANG
THIS IS TAKING FOREVER.
B-BMP
B-BMP
...

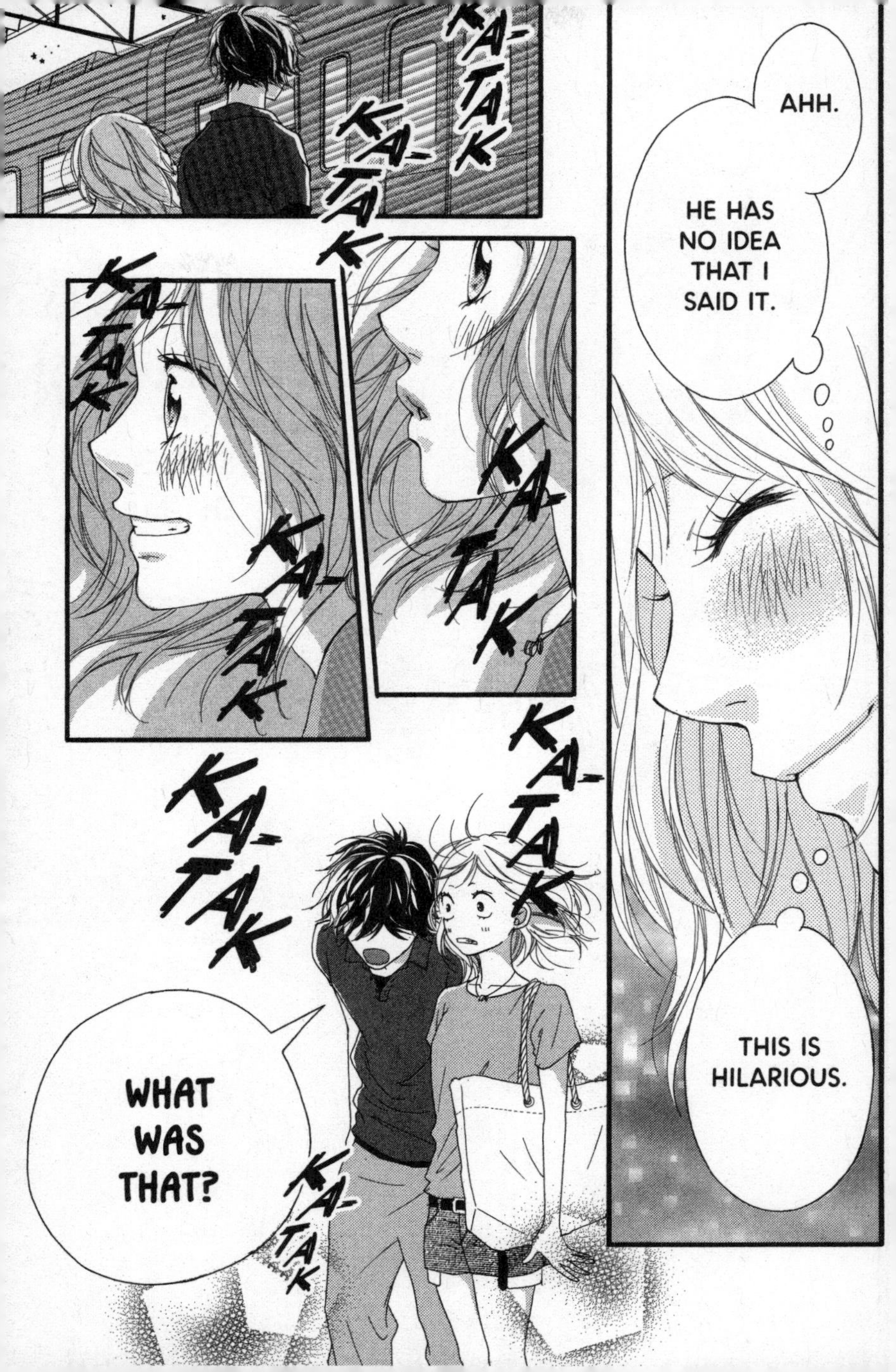
AHH.
HE HAS NO IDEA THAT I SAID IT.
THIS IS HILARIOUS.
KA-TAK
KA-TAK
KA-TAK
KA-TAK
KA-TAK
KA-TAK
KA-TAK
KA-TAK
WHAT WAS THAT?
KA-TAK

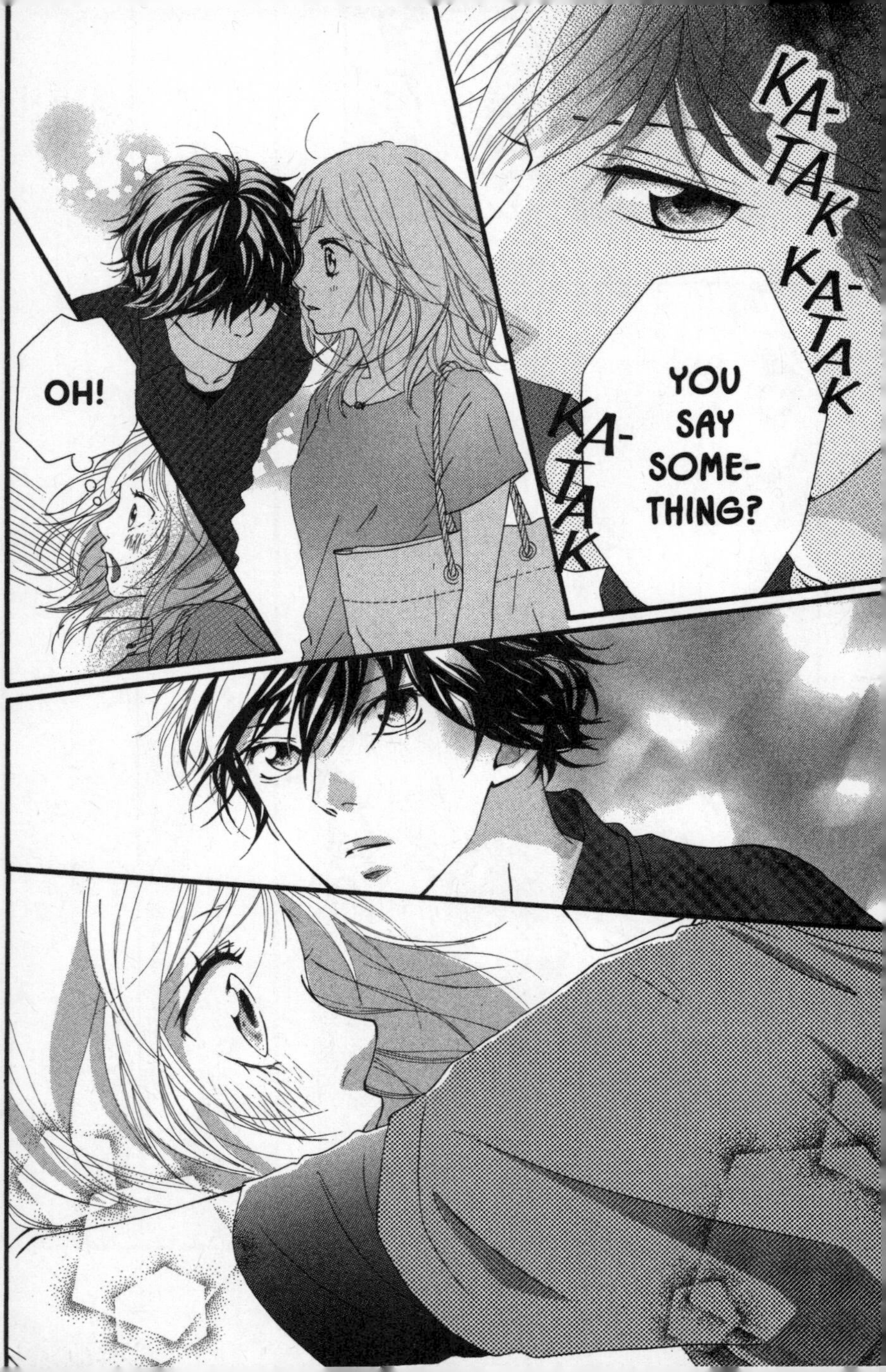
KA-TAK KA-TAK
YOU SAY SOME-THING?
KA-TAK
OH!

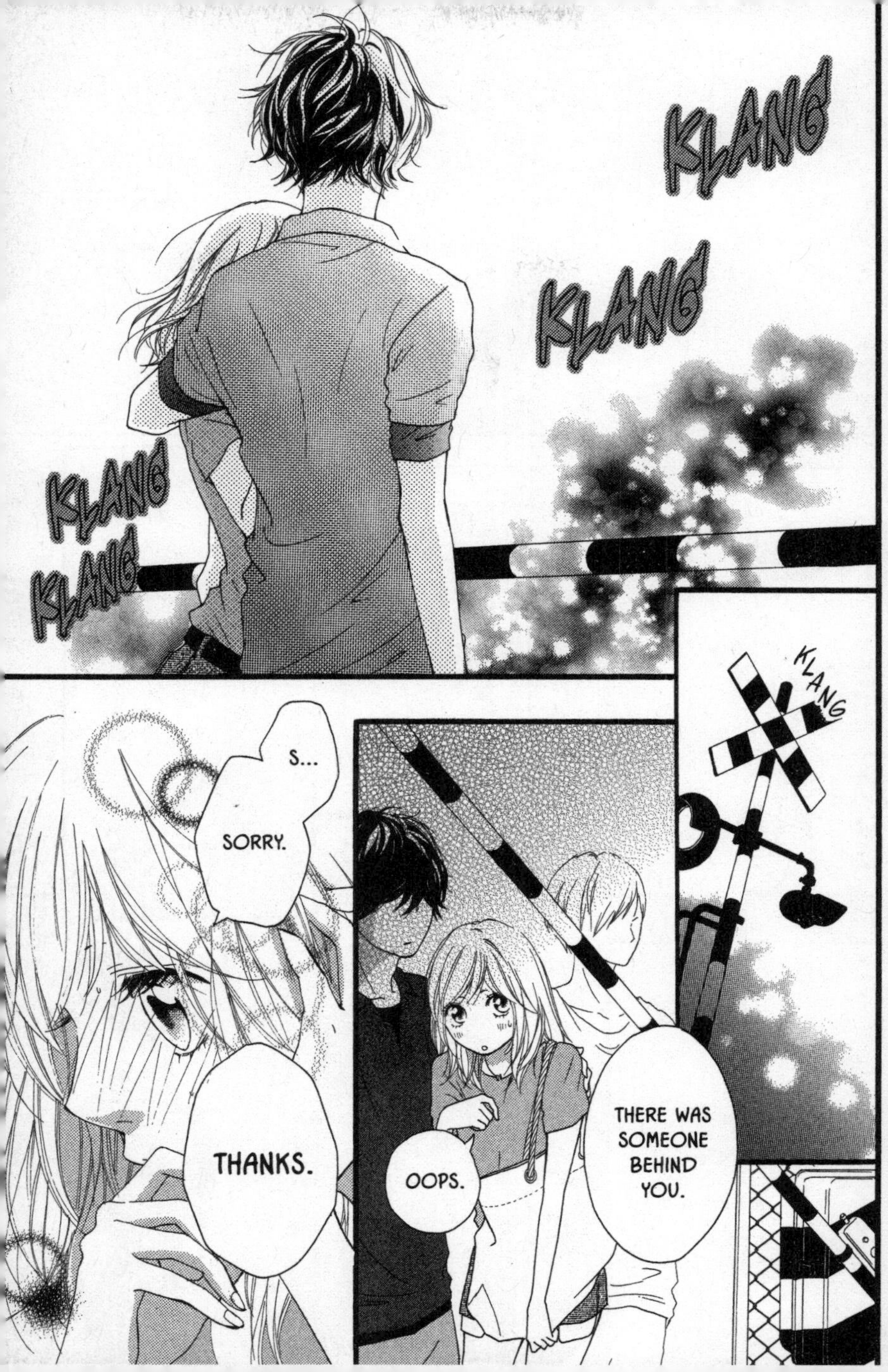
KLANG
KLANG
KLANG
KLANG
KLANG
THERE WAS SOMEONE BEHIND YOU.
OOPS.
S...
SORRY.
THANKS.

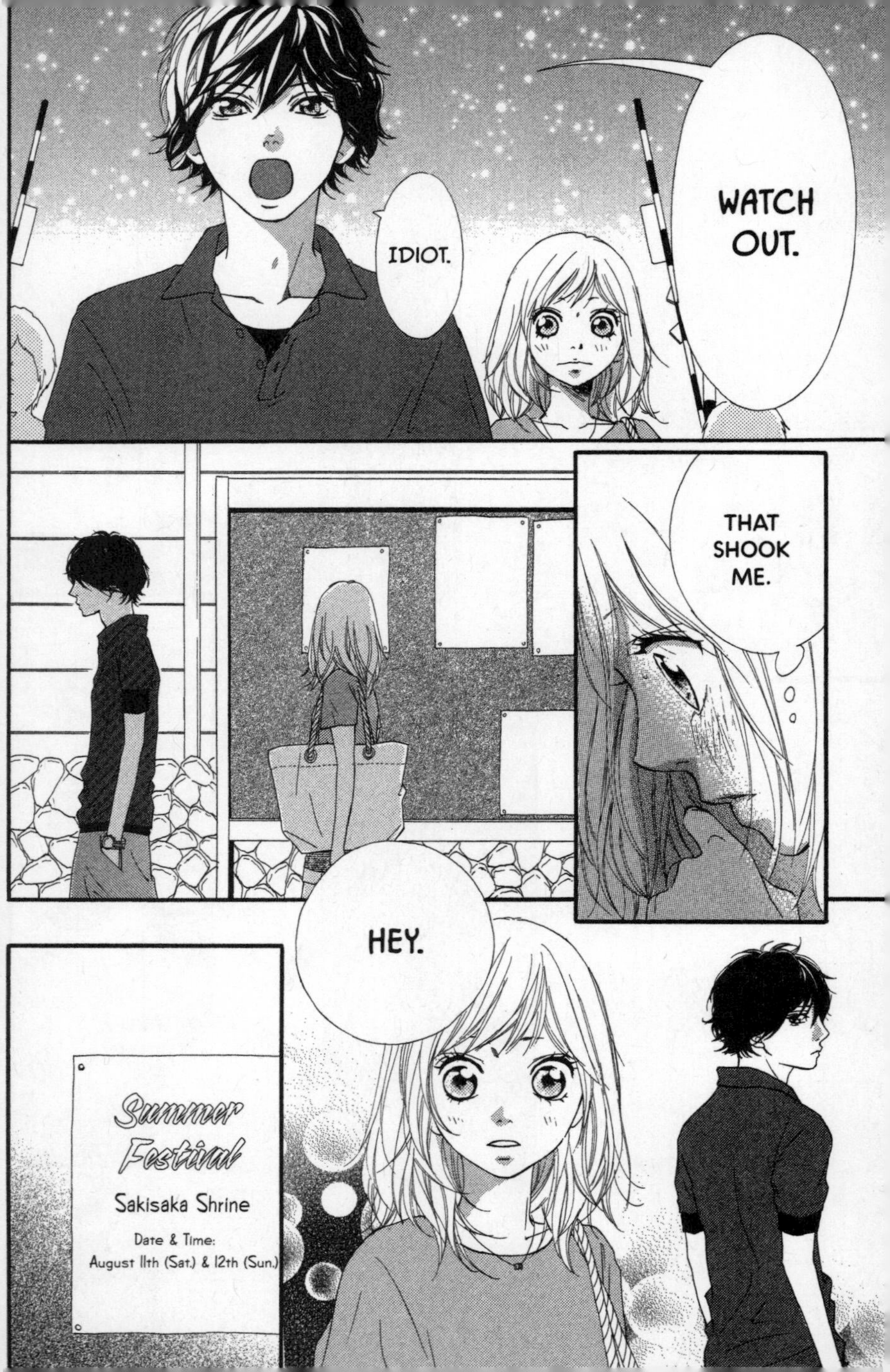
WATCH OUT.
IDIOT.
THAT SHOOK ME.
HEY.
Summer Festival
Sakisaka Shrine
Date & Time:
August 11th (Sat.) & 12th (Sun.)

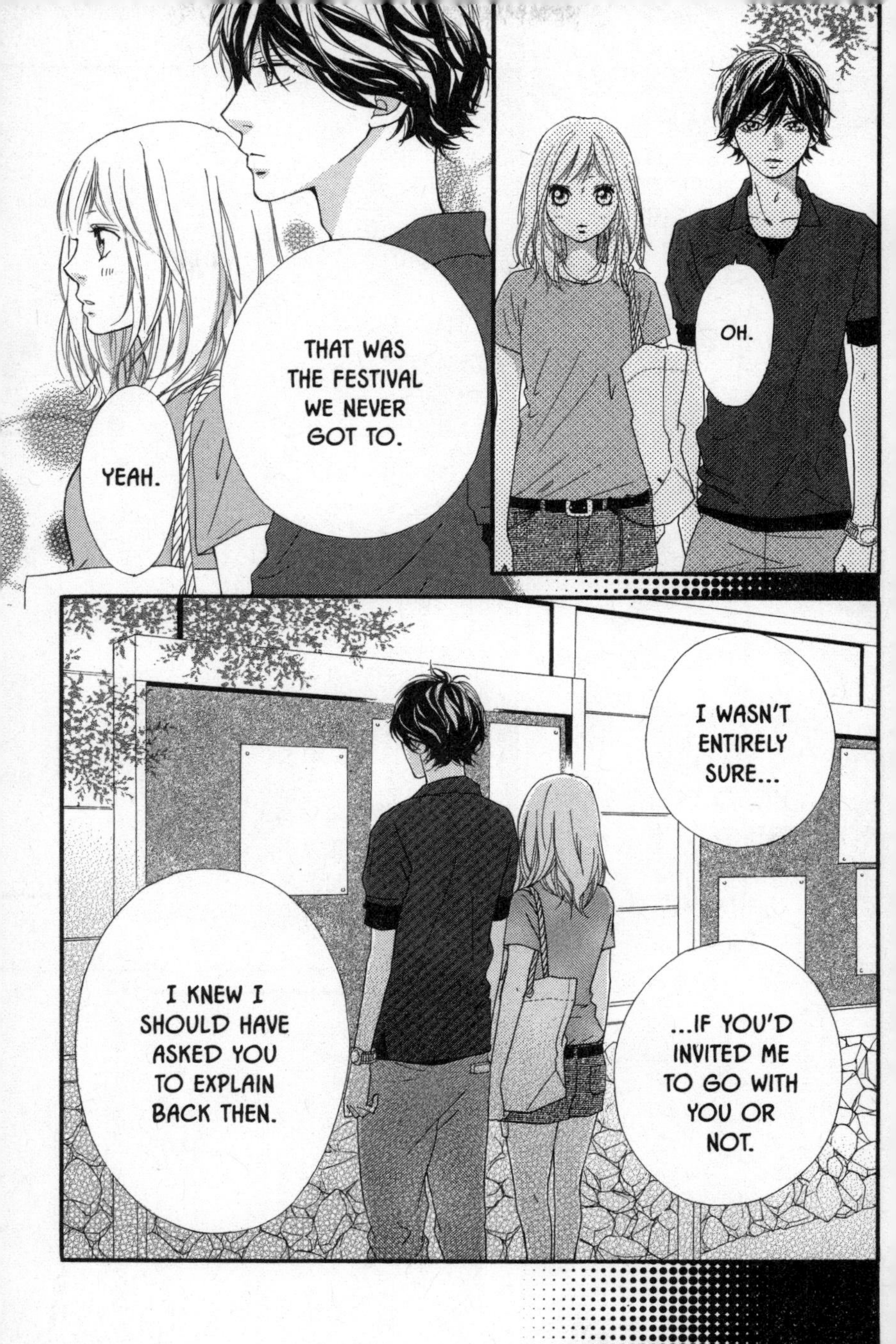
OH.
THAT WAS THE FESTIVAL WE NEVER GOT TO.
YEAH.
I WASN'T ENTIRELY SURE...
...IF YOU'D INVITED ME TO GO WITH YOU OR NOT.
I KNEW I SHOULD HAVE ASKED YOU TO EXPLAIN BACK THEN.

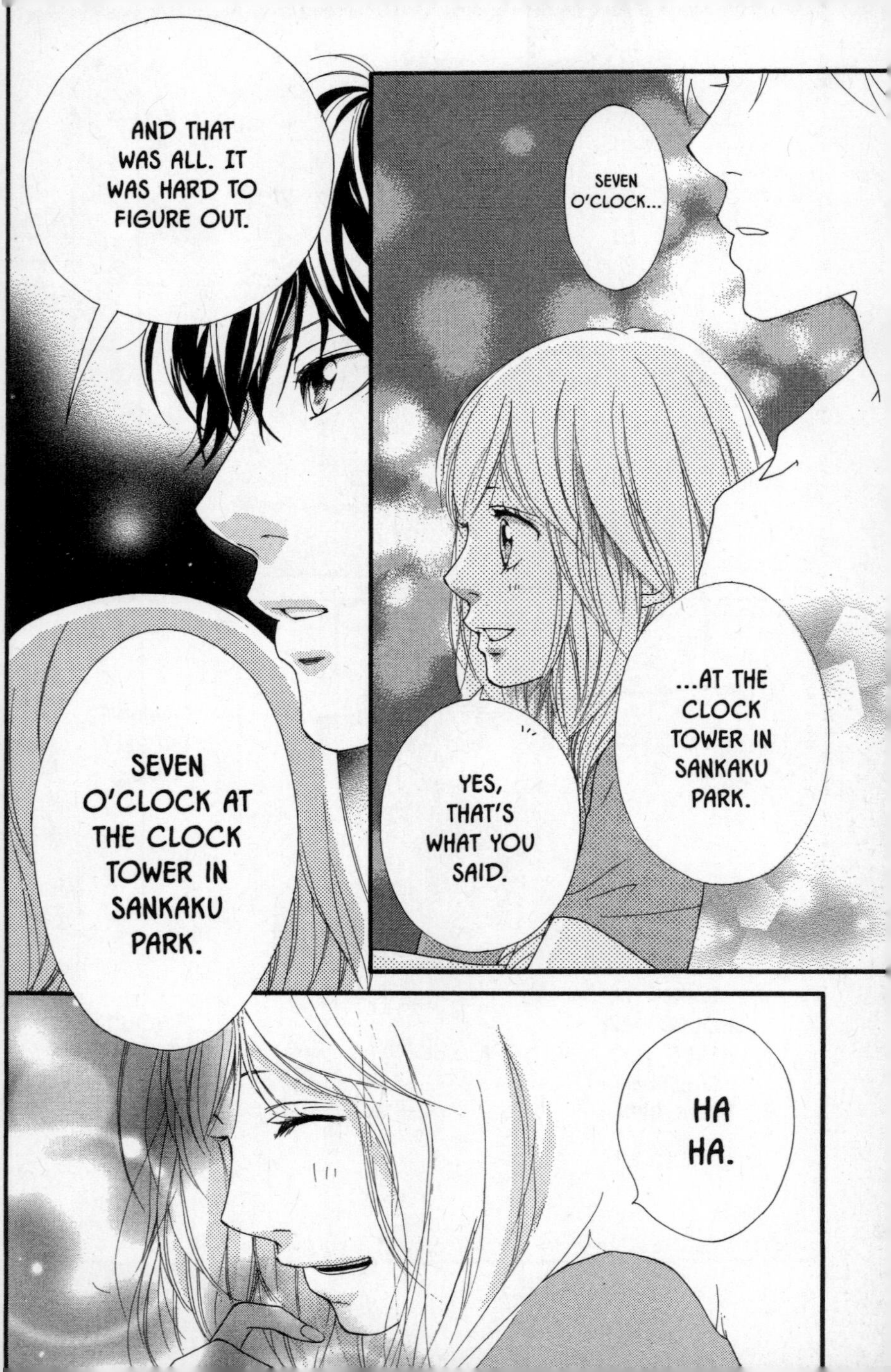
SEVEN O'CLOCK...
...AT THE CLOCK TOWER IN SANKAKU PARK.
YES, THAT'S WHAT YOU SAID.
AND THAT WAS ALL. IT WAS HARD TO FIGURE OUT.
SEVEN O'CLOCK AT THE CLOCK TOWER IN SANKAKU PARK.
HA HA.

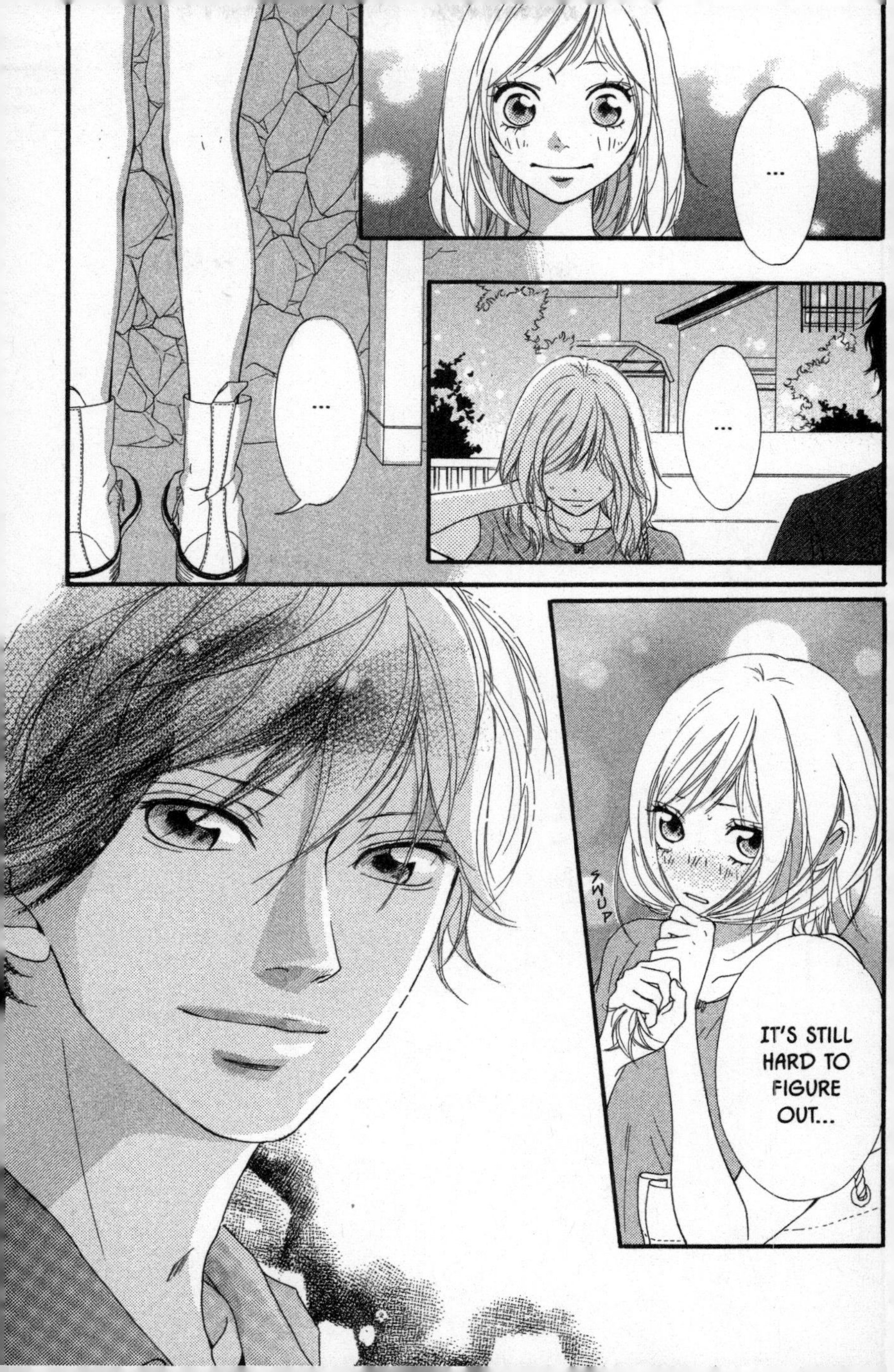
...
...
...
SWUP
IT'S STILL HARD TO FIGURE OUT...

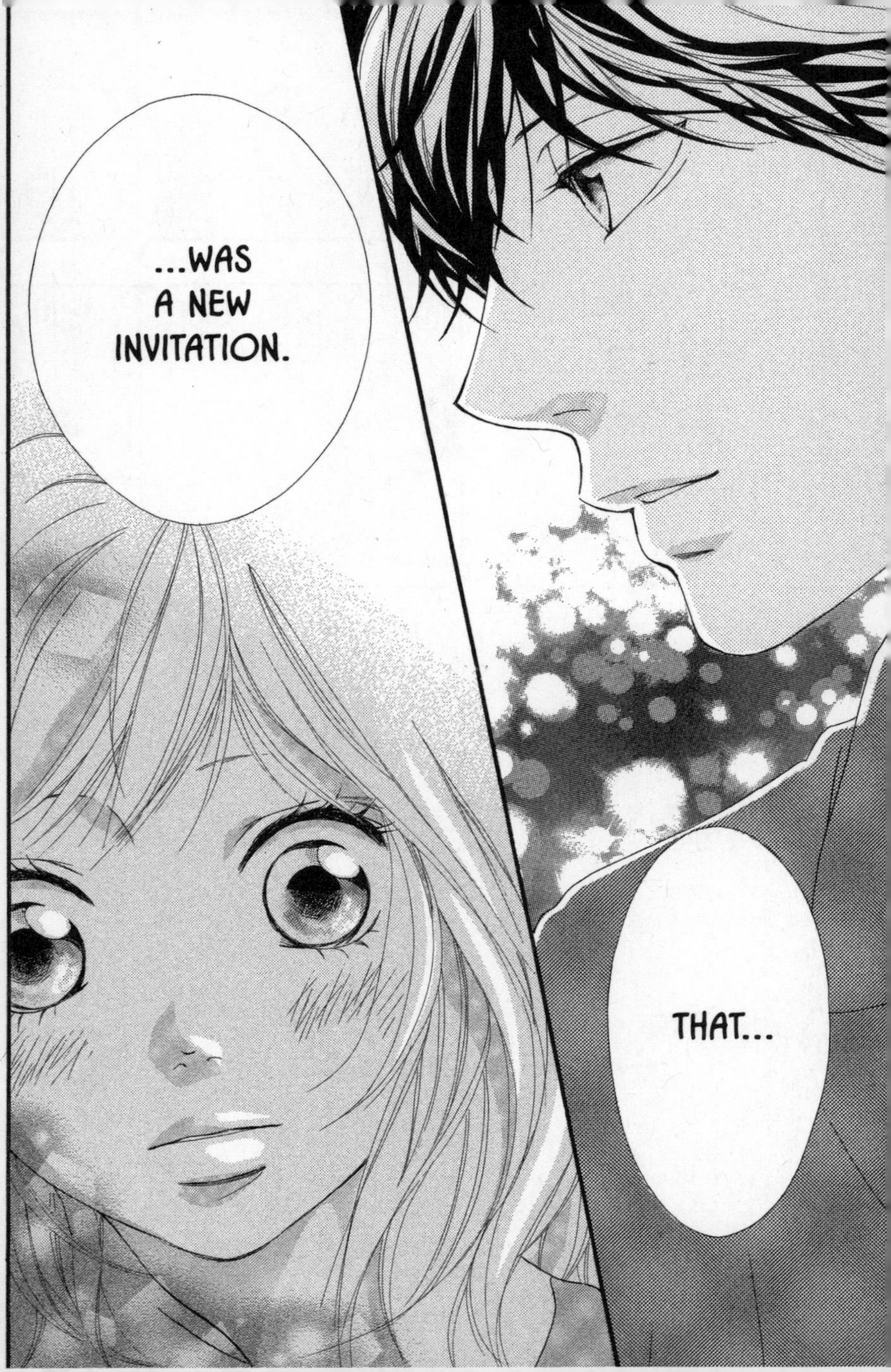
THAT...
...WAS A NEW INVITATION.

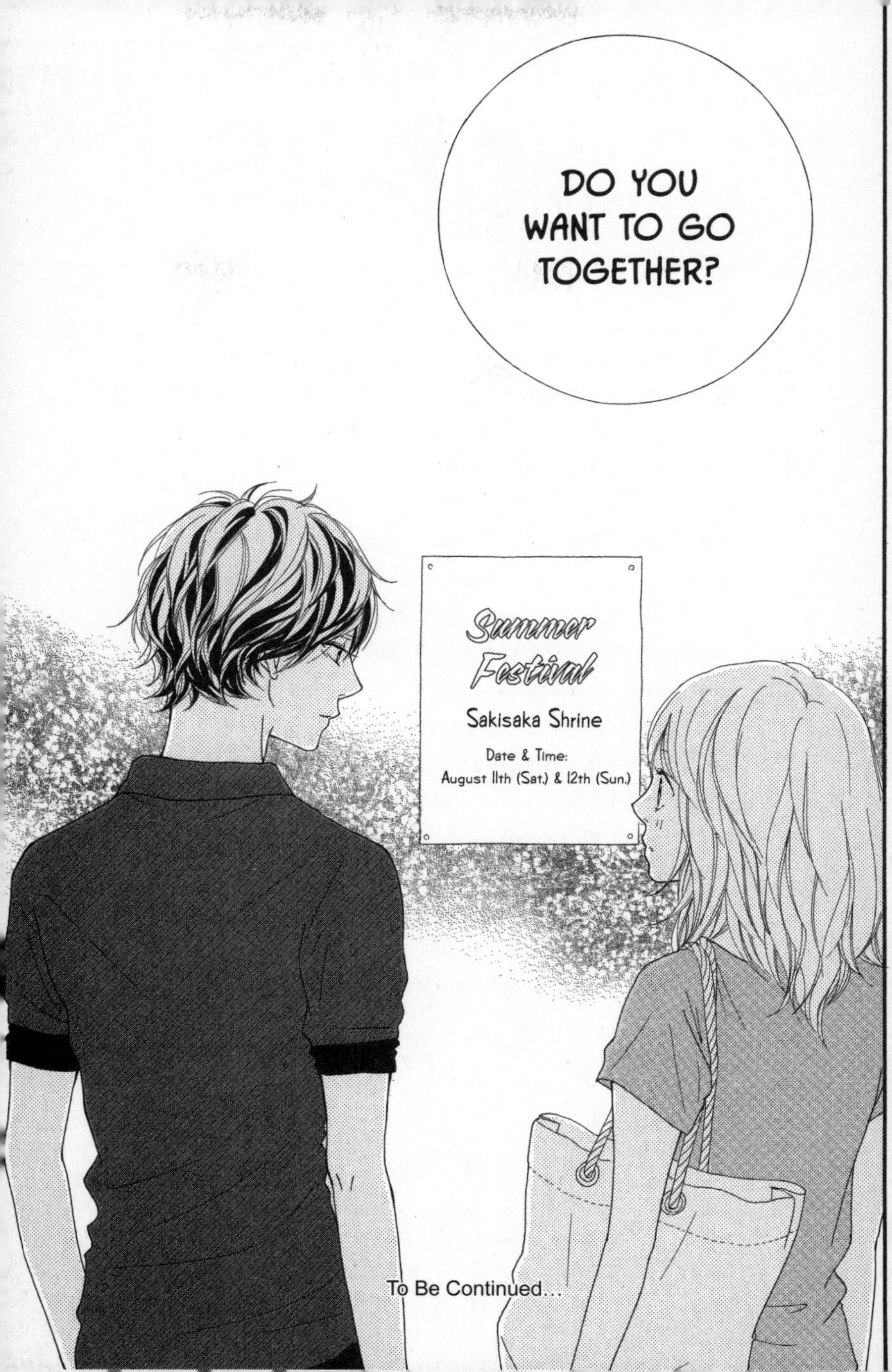
DO YOU WANT TO GO TOGETHER?
Summer Festival
Sakisaka Shrine
Date & Time:
August 11th (Sat.) & 12th (Sun.)
To Be Continued…

MUTTERINGS

I often use books showing people in different positions for work, and I wish that someone would please put out a book that is a collection of boys posing in school uniforms. A number of publishers have put out collections of girls in uniforms, but I can't find any with boys. Why is that? Is there no demand? I really want to study boys in well-worn uniforms from all sorts of angles. I almost want to go outside and get high school students to let me take photos of them, but I think that would cause a number of problems. I'm sure it would be difficult to get the angles that I'm looking for anyway, so I still want that book. If you know of a book like that, please do let me know. I also want one that shows kids on dates in their uniforms. That would be the ultimate. ♡ It would be so very cute... I mean, it would be a great resource! I'm sure other artists would agree. I basically have no chance of meeting high schoolers naturally.

In the same vein of the last note, I'd like to tell you about some of the tools and materials I use regularly...

🌸 Mechanical 🌸   0.5 mm and 0.3 mm. The 0.5 mm is for working on
     Pencil   the plot and storyboards. The 0.3 mm is for the
                      illustration drafts.

🌸 Blue Mechanical 🌸   I use blue lead that can be erased and doesn't
       Pencil   show up in copies. At least it's not supposed to...
                      In illustration drafts, I use it to draw people. Also
                      for noting the screentones.

🌸 Round Pen 🌸   Tachikawa. I use it for the "meat" of a person's face
                      (*laugh*), hair, crowd scenes and backgrounds.

🌸 G Pen 🌸   Zebra. Used for face shapes and bodies.

🌸 School Pen 🌸   Nikko or Zebra. Resistant to different pressures and
                      used for dialog bubbles.

🌸 Ink 🌸   Pilot brand drawing ink. Dries well and bleeds well.

🌸 Graphic Pens 🌸   PIGMA. I use the PIGMA 1 mm for drawing borders.
                      I like thick borders.

🌸 Paper 🌸   IC B4/135kg.

🌸 Brush Pens 🌸   Kuretake superfine. The one with the yellow-green
                      cap. I use it to ink shiny hair.

🌸 Tracing Table 🌸   I think the one I have is made by Sekaido. It's large
                      with two lights. I like having enough room to rest both
                      elbows on it.

If you've thought about becoming a mangaka but don't know which tools you'll need, you can use this as a starting place. One day I hope you'll find some favorite tools for yourself!

AFTERWORD

I like watching young people give everything they have in the midst of uncertainty. Over time they find their balance, gain control of their feelings and are able to do things without hesitation. Watching this progression is both a relief and somewhat sad, as it means they're growing up. As adults we're also faced with challenges to overcome, which is beautiful in itself, but it's just not the same. There is something about these youthful kids, striving to do what they can... It elicits an aching feeling that is difficult to describe. I really love it. And I love that this work lets me focus on just that.

The characters in *Ao Haru Ride* are right in the middle of this stage in their lives, and I look forward to illustrating much, much more. There will be trips and falls, but I hope you'll join me and root for them along the way. ♡

Until next time, I bid you adieu!

  Io Sakisaka

It's been several years since I've thought about upgrading my phone.

While I would like to experience swiping my finger across a smartphone, my current phone has barely any scratches and is in pretty good condition. It's a DoCoMo 901, and I'm long past being embarrassed about it being an older model.

Now I kind of want to keep using it to see how long it will last.

IO SAKISAKA

Born on June 8, Io Sakisaka made her debut as a manga creator with *Sakura, Chiru*. Her works include *Call My Name*, *Gate of Planet* and *Blue*. *Strobe Edge*, her previous work, is also published by VIZ Media's Shojo Beat imprint. *Ao Haru Ride* was adapted into an anime series in 2014. In her spare time, Sakisaka likes to paint things and sleep.

Ao Haru Ride

VOLUME 4
SHOJO BEAT EDITION

STORY AND ART BY **IO SAKISAKA**

TRANSLATION **Emi Louie-Nishikawa**
TOUCH-UP ART + LETTERING **Inori Fukuda Trant**
DESIGN **Shawn Carrico**
EDITOR **Nancy Thistlethwaite**

First published in Japan in 2011 by SHUEISHA Inc., Tokyo.
English translation rights arranged by SHUEISHA Inc.

Printed in the U.S.A.

Published by VIZ Media, LLC
P.O. Box 77010
San Francisco, CA 94107

10 9 8 7 6 5 4 3 2 1
First printing, April 2019

ratings.viz.com RATED T TEEN

PARENTAL ADVISORY
AO HARU RIDE is rated T for Teen and
is recommended for ages 13 and up.
This volume contains the redemption of youth.

VIZ MEDIA
viz.com

Shojo Beat
shojobeat.com

Written by the creator of **High School Debut!**

MY love STORY!!

KAZUNE KAWAHARA *Story*

ARUKO *Art*

Takeo Goda is a GIANT guy with a GIANT *heart*

Too bad the girls don't want him!
(They want his good-looking best friend, Sunakawa.)

Used to being on the sidelines, Takeo simply stands tall and accepts his fate. But one day when he saves a girl named Yamato from a harasser on the train, his (love!) life suddenly takes an incredible turn!

www.viz.com

www.shojobeat.com

RATED **T** TEEN
ratings.viz.com

ORE MONOGATARI!! © 2011 by Kazune Kawahara, Aruko/SHUEISHA I

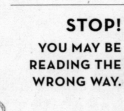

STOP!
YOU MAY BE READING THE WRONG WAY.

In keeping with the original Japanese comic format, this book reads from right to left—so action, sound effects and word balloons are completely reversed to preserve the orientation of the original artwork.